More praise for *Daughter of Moloka'i*

2019 LibraryReads Pick | Named a Best/Most Anticipated Book by: *USA Today* • BookRiot • BookBub • LibraryReads • *OC Register* • *Never Ending Voyage* | *Austin Woman* magazine "Nine Books on Our Summer Reading List"

"Stirring."
　　　　　　　　　　　　　　　　　　　　—*The Toronto Star*

"An intimate look at the experience of Japanese Americans growing up in California during WWII . . . beautifully written."
　　　　　　　　　　　　　　　—*Austin Woman* magazine

"A moving story of love, loss, and family bonds."
　　　　　　　　　　　　　—*The Orange County Register*

"Strikes all the right emotional notes. A historically solid, ultimately hopeful novel about injustice, survival, and unbreakable family bonds."
　　　　　　　　　　　　　　　　　　　　　—*Booklist*

"Compelling . . . will be welcomed by readers."　　　—*Library Journal*

"*Daughter of Moloka'i* brings to the reader the same heart-wrenching emotional engagement as its predecessor, but also adds another dimension as we witness the differences between the cultures of Hawaiians and Japanese."
　　　　—Andy Ross, former owner of Cody's Books in Berkeley

"If you enjoy *Moloka'i*, don't miss the new sequel, *Daughter of Moloka'i*, which follows Rachel's daughter. Although it's mostly set in California with a focus on the internment of Japanese Americans during WWII, it also features Honolulu and Maui."　　　　　　　—*Never Ending Voyage*

ALSO BY ALAN BRENNERT

Moloka'i

Honolulu

Palisades Park

Daughter of Moloka'i

ALAN BRENNERT

St. Martin's Griffin
New York

Published in the United States by St. Martin's Griffin, an imprint of St. Martin's Publishing Group

DAUGHTER OF MOLOKA'I. Copyright © 2019 by Alan Brennert. All rights reserved. Printed in the United States of America. For information, address St. Martin's Publishing Group, 120 Broadway, New York, NY 10271.

www.stmartins.com

The Library of Congress has cataloged the hardcover edition as follows:

Names: Brennert, Alan, author.
Title: Daughter of Moloka'i / Alan Brennert.
Description: First edition. | New York : St. Martin's Press, 2019.
Identifiers: LCCN 2018029158 | ISBN 9781250137661 (hardcover) | ISBN 9781250233097
    (International, sold outside the U.S., subject to rights availability) | ISBN 9781250137685
    (ebook)
Classification: LCC PS3552.R3865 D38 2019 | DDC 813/.54—dc23
LC record available at https://lccn.loc.gov/2018029158

ISBN 978-1-250-13767-8 (trade paperback)

Our books may be purchased in bulk for promotional, educational, or business use. Please contact your local bookseller or the Macmillan Corporate and Premium Sales Department at 1-800-221-7945, extension 5442, or by email at MacmillanSpecialMarkets@macmillan.com.

First St. Martin's Griffin Edition: January 2020

10 9 8 7 6 5 4 3 2 1

FOR CARTER SCHOLZ

An abiding friend

An inspiring writer

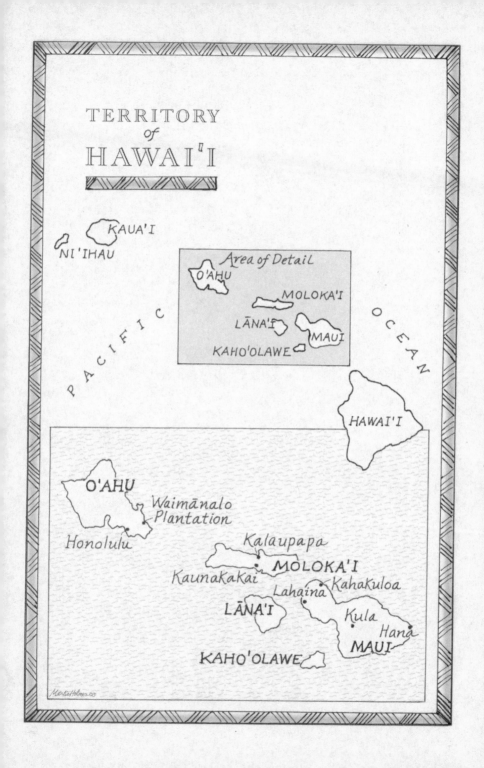

PART ONE

Hapa

Prologue

1917

A wave of Kona storm clouds rolled across the jagged peaks of the Wai'anae Range, arriving in Honolulu with a cannonade of thunder and the kind of wind and rain Hawaiians called *lani-pa'ina*, "crackling heavens." In the harbor even the largest ships seesawed in their berths; one little steamer, the *Claudine*, barely made it into port by sunset, before the sundered clouds began to weep and rage.

Sister Mary Louisa Hughes stood on the covered *lānai* of a house high atop a hill overlooking the Kalihi Valley, with a fine view of nature's wrath. Short and stocky, she didn't flinch at the trumpeting thunder or the spears of lightning in the distance—in fact, there was a smile on her broad, open face. Louisa had grown up on the South Side of Chicago, her family's cold-water flat wedged into the middle of a stack of sooty tenement apartments; she had never drifted to sleep to the soothing patter of rain on a rooftop, not until taking her novitiate at the Franciscan convent in Joliet. So what she was now witnessing—the majestic fury of a genuine tropical storm—this was glorious. God's glory, yes, but also Hawai'i's. She was more certain than ever that this was where she belonged—glad that she had answered the call for volunteers to make the long voyage to O'ahu to serve at the Kapi'olani Home for Girls.

But there was work to do: Kau'iokalani, the night nurse, was sick, and Louisa had taken her shift. There were fifty-eight girls—ranging in age from twenty months to twenty-one years—living at Kapi'olani Home, and as Louisa entered she could hear the youngest crying out in fright. She went to the nursery, going to each child in turn, lifting them from their cribs, holding and comforting them against the noise and the night. "Ssshh, ssshh," she told them, "it can't hurt you. I won't let it." Finally, when the storm had abated and the last child had fallen asleep, she went to check on the older girls; she suspected they were probably up long past their bedtime, telling each other blood-curdling tales of *obake*s—ghosts—in the dark.

But before she could reach the first dormitory, there was a furious knocking on the front door. At first she thought the wind was merely animating a tree branch, but when she recognized a human rhythm to the knocks she hurried to the foyer and swung open the door.

Standing on the porch was a tall, unfamiliar sister in a rain-soaked habit. She was holding a bundled child, its face tucked into her shoulder, shielded from the rain by a swath of blankets.

"Oh my heavens," Louisa cried out. "Sister, do come in!"

The nun—in her mid-forties, with a wet but pretty face—smiled gratefully and stepped inside. "Thank you, Sister," she said. She walked with a slight limp, but it didn't seem to slow her down much.

"My goodness, you're drenched. Did you walk all the way up the hill?"

"No, I took a cab from the harbor. Most of the moisture is from the steamer trip." She smiled. "I'm Sister Catherine Voorhies. And I've come bearing precious cargo."

She peeled back a layer of blanket, revealing the sweet round face of a frightened infant—no more than a year old—with the tawny skin of a Native Hawaiian and the slightly almond-shaped eyes of a Japanese.

She was an absolutely beautiful child, in the unexpected ways children could be in Hawai'i.

"Her name is Ruth Utagawa," Sister Catherine said, "and we've come from Kalaupapa."

"I thought as much. But let's get you both out of those wet clothes and in front of a warm fire."

*W*ithin five minutes Catherine had shed her waterlogged habit, toweled her short brown hair as dry as she could, and slipped into a freshly laundered bathrobe offered by the friendly and efficient Sister Louisa. Ruth's blankets were soaked almost all the way through but her corduroy frock was, thankfully, still dry. Louisa had brought them both into the kitchen, stoked a fire in the oven, heated up a bottle of milk for Ruth and a cup of coffee for Catherine. Ruth drank eagerly, and only when she was done did Catherine allow herself to take a sip of her coffee.

Louisa dragged a chair close to the fire and said, "Please, Sister, sit. You must be exhausted. Can I get you something to eat?"

"Not after that boat ride, thanks." Catherine sighed. It felt good to have her veil off and to feel the heat of the fire on her face. She reached up and touched her wet hair. "I must look a fright, Sister."

"Oh, nonsense." Louisa's gaze drifted to little Ruth and to those sweet brown eyes—so dark they almost looked black—glancing shyly away. "She's lovely. And I can tell she's special to you."

Catherine nodded. "Yes. Her parents are dear friends of mine. I promised them I would make sure she got here safely." She felt the first pang of loss, one she knew would only deepen as she drew closer to parting.

"The parents—they're lepers?"

"Yes. But Ruth is healthy. After a year of observation, she shows no sign of the disease."

"May I . . . hold her a moment?" Louisa asked.

"Of course."

Catherine hefted Ruth and handed her to Louisa—but as soon as the child was in Louisa's hands, she began to wail.

"Oh dear," Louisa said.

"Rock her. Bounce her. It took her a while to get used to me too."

After years of cradling orphans at Guardian Angel Home in Joliet, Louisa thought she knew how to soothe infants. She rocked Ruth gently back and forth, but the baby was not to be placated. Between sobs she repeated a single word: "Wih-wee," she cried, the word resonant with loss, "wih-wee, wih-wee!"

"You'd best take her back." Louisa handed her to Catherine, but Ruth continued her lament. "What is it she's trying to say?" Louisa asked.

"Lily."

"Is that her mother's name?"

Catherine shook her head. "Lillian Keamalu is the matron at the Kalaupapa nursery," she explained. "The babies are taken away from their mothers at birth. The parents are only allowed to see them from behind glass in the nursery. The only mother the children know—the only one who holds and comforts them—is Miss Keamalu."

Louisa ached to hear this. She was new to this world of children and leprosy; there were always, it seemed, fresh cruelties to discover.

They sat in silence a while, Ruth's cries gradually fading until the only sounds in the room were the drumming of the rain and the rattle of the windows as the wind shook the house like a tambourine.

Louisa noted, "Strange how a place as beautiful as Hawai'i can have such bursts of stark, sudden fury."

"Beneath that beauty," Catherine said, "the land has molten power. These islands have borne many wounds over the years—not the least of them leprosy. I think sometimes they wake and cry out in rage at the injustice."

Louisa hadn't the faintest inkling of what Catherine was talking about, and it sounded uncomfortably close to paganism, to boot, so she said nothing. Finally, Catherine spoke again.

"Sister," she said softly, "I would count it a great favor if you would do something for me."

"Yes, of course."

"Take care of her?"

Catherine's voice broke when she said it. It was clear to Louisa that this child meant a great deal to her.

"I will. I promise you. She will not want for affection."

"Thank you, Sister."

Not knowing what else she could say, Louisa stood. "Let me find you a fresh habit and a warm bed. We have an extra crib for Ruth in the nursery."

Catherine hesitated. "Would you mind if—if she sleeps with me to-night?"

"Of course."

Louisa led them outside, where they hurried through the downpour to the modest cottage that served as a convent. The other Sisters of St. Francis were all asleep but for the Home's matron, Sister Helena Haas; a sliver of light peeked out from under her door as she worked into the night. Louisa found Catherine a fresh habit, then brought her to a small, spartan room at the end of the corridor.

"Sleep well, Sister. Mass begins at six, if you care to join us."

"Thank you, I will."

Louisa left. Catherine sighed and walked to the room's single window. Out there, across the water, behind a wall of storm clouds, Ruth's parents on Moloka'i were mourning the loss of their daughter, hoping she would find a good home. Catherine felt something of the same emotions. She took off the girl's dress, slipped on her tiny pajamas, then climbed into bed beside her. She gave her a tender kiss on the head and said softly, "I love you, sweet baby. May God protect you." This was far from the first child Catherine had held and comforted in her twenty-four years at Kalaupapa—but Ruth was the one most dear to her. She was the daughter of a lonely child who had grown into a strong woman and a dear friend; she bore the same name Catherine had been christened with; and, most important, of all those girls Catherine had cared for, Ruth was the first one who would know what it was like to be free.

Chapter 1

1919

*T*he sky above Diamond Head was a spray of gold as the sun seemed to rise up out of the crater itself. From atop its windy hill in Kalihiuka—"inland Kalihi"—Kapi'olani Home took in the sweeping view, from the grassy caldera of Diamond Head to the concrete craters of the new dry docks at Pearl Harbor. On a clear day, even the neighbor islands of Lāna'i and Moloka'i could be seen straddling the horizon. The big, two-story plantation-style house on thirteen acres of trim lawn stood alongside the sisters' convent and chapel. The Kalihi Valley was largely agricultural, and the Home was surrounded by acres of sprawling cow pastures, hog breeders, and backyard poultry farms whose hens nested in old orange crates and whose roosters announced Morning Mass as well as any church bell. On the other side of Kamehameha IV Road there were groves of big-leafed banana plants, tall and thick as trees, prodigal with hanging clusters of green and yellow fruit; taro patches filled with heart-shaped leaves like fields of valentines; and terraced rice paddies glistening in the morning sun.

As in most Catholic orphanages and schools, the Sisters of St. Francis required that the corridors remain quiet, orderly—places of silent contemplation, not to be desecrated with idle conversation. Other than this, there were only three major rules at Kapi'olani Home:

1. After breakfast no standing around talking but do your work quickly and well.
2. Do not throw your clothes on the floor nor rubbish in the yard.
3. Line up and march orderly.

Morning call sent the girls springing out of bed, into washrooms to scrub faces and comb hair, then dress. Filing quietly down corridors and into the dining hall, they went to their tables—ten girls at each one—and stood behind their chairs, joining with Sister Bonaventure in reciting the blessing:

Thank you for the world so sweet,
Thank you for the food we eat.
Thank you for the birds that sing,
Thank you, God, for everything. Amen.

This was followed by the scraping of sixty chairs on the floor as the girls seated themselves and ate a breakfast of *poi*, rice, eggs, and sausages. It was near the end of breakfast that a three-year-old girl—standing on tiptoes and peering out the dining room windows—made an exciting announcement:

"Cow!"

As she ran delightedly out of the dining room, the other girls flocked to the windows. Yet another of Mr. Mendonca's cows, having decided that the grass was, in fact, greener on the other side the fence, was grazing contentedly on their front lawn.

"Wow, look at the size of its whatzit!" said one girl.

"I believe she needs to be milked," Sister Bonaventure noted calmly. "Now, girls, let's all get back to our—"

Too late. What moments before had been a docile group of girls eating breakfast became a stampede out of the dining hall.

On the second floor, Sister Louisa, hearing the drumbeat of footfalls below, raced down the staircase to find a raging river of girls surging past her.

And far ahead of them all was a three-year-old with amber skin and almond eyes, crying out, "Cow! Cow! Big brown cow!" at the top of her voice.

"Ruth!" Louisa immediately broke into a run herself. "Come back!"

Ruth burst out the front door, down the porch steps, and went straight to the grazing heifer, which was completely oblivious to the fuss it had stirred up.

"Hi, cow!" Ruth welcomed it. "Hi!"

Ruth stood about three feet tall; the cow, perhaps a foot taller. Ruth reached up and gently stroked the side of its neck as it chewed. "Good cow," she said, smiling. "You're a *good* cow."

As Sister Louisa rushed outside, she saw the child she had promised to protect petting an eight-hundred-pound Guernsey, whose right hoof, with one step, could have easily crushed the girl's small foot.

"Ruth! Please! Step back!"

But Ruth's attention was drawn to the cow's swollen udder. And what *were* those things sticking out of it like big fat fingers?

Intrigued, Ruth reached up and took one of the cow's teats in her hand—examining it, pulling it, squeezing it.

A stream of raw milk squirted out and into Ruth's face.

The other girls exploded into laughter. Sister Louisa pulled Ruth away from the animal. Either due to the warm, yellowish milk on her face or the mocking peal of the girls' laughter, Ruth began to cry.

"It's all right, little one," Louisa said, leading her away. "Let's go inside and wash that off your face."

The other girls clustered around the cow as the elderly Sister Helena arrived, frowning. "I do wish," she said, "that Mr. Mendonca would keep his livestock away from our live girls."

Eddie Kaohi, the Home's young groundskeeper, ran up, rope in hand. "I'll take her back where she belongs," he said, lassoing the cow's neck.

"*Mahalo*, Mr. Kaohi," said Sister Helena. Then, with a sigh: "Girls, really. You'd think none of you had ever seen a cow before."

"She's *cute*," said ten-year-old Addie as she swatted a fly away from the cow's face. "She has the prettiest eyes!"

Sister Helena gazed into the heifer's soulful brown eyes, her stern face softening. "Yes," she allowed, "I suppose she does."

In the bathroom Sister Louisa scrubbed Ruth's face with soap and water and asked her, "So what have you learned today, Ruth?"

"Cows shoot milk."

Louisa stifled a laugh. "That's why only dairy farmers should touch a cow's udder, not little girls who could get hurt."

"They laughed at me," Ruth said in a small voice. "Again."

"Again? When have the girls laughed at you before?"

"When I showed 'em my gecko."

Ah yes, the gecko. "Only because the gecko decided to run down the front of your dress."

"Ran *away*. I loved it and it ran away!"

"I know." Ruth loved every animal she had ever met. On a trip to the Honolulu Zoo, Ruth was enchanted by the monkeys, lions, swans, and Daisy, the African elephant. Sometimes Louisa thought the child would embrace a boa constrictor but for the welcome fact that there were no snakes in Hawai'i.

"An' they yelled at Ollie," Ruth lamented, "an' scared him away too!"

"Ollie was the mouse?"

Ruth nodded.

"Some of the younger girls were scared of Ollie," Louisa explained gently. "That's why they were yelling and—well, screaming."

"He was so cute!"

"I thought so too."

"They hate me," Ruth declared.

"No, they don't. They just don't love animals the way you do."

Ruth's face flushed with shame. "One girl called me a bad name."

Louisa straightened, concerned. "Who did?"

"Velma."

"What did she call you, Ruth?"

Ruth looked down and said quietly, "*Hapa*. She called me *hapa*."

Louisa laughed with relief. "Ruth, that isn't a bad word. It's just a Hawaiian word. It means half."

"Half?"

"Yes. Like if I gave you a cookie, then split it into two pieces and took away one piece, you'd have half of what I gave you."

Ruth's face wrinkled in confusion. "She called me a cookie?"

"Well, your papa was Japanese and your mama was Hawaiian, and so you're half Japanese and half Hawaiian. *Hapa*. There's absolutely nothing wrong with the word."

Ruth wasn't so sure. It still sounded like Velma was calling her half a cookie, which anyone knew wasn't as a good as a whole cookie.

"Sister Lu?"

"Yes, Ruth?"

"Can I meet my papa? And my mama?"

Louisa said softly, "I don't know, Ruth. Maybe someday."

Ruth considered that. "Sister Lu?"

"Yes, child?"

"Can I have a pet worm?"

Louisa did her best to reply with the same gravity as Ruth's question. "Well, you see, worms live underground. So if you wanted to have a pet worm, you'd have to live underground too. It's dark and cold and wet down there. I really don't think you'd like it."

"Oh."

The sister tenderly straightened Ruth's hair and said, "Let's go to the playroom, all right?"

ue to public fear and prejudice, children of leprous parents were banned from attending public or private schools. But the Board of Education did, at least, provide the sisters with schoolroom equipment, and the Free Kindergarten and Children's Aid Association had years ago established a kindergarten at Kapi'olani Home and assisted the order in its operation. Girls from six to fifteen were taught by Sister Valeria Gerdes, who gave lessons in arithmetic and English.

After classes, the older girls sewed shirts and dresses for inmates at Kalaupapa—some of them, perhaps unwittingly, for their own parents.

Saturdays were housekeeping days and Sundays were for Mass and Benediction, but they were holy in another way: they were visiting days for friends and family—'ohana, a word Ruth knew, even if she had no use for it.

Ruth would listen as a brass bell rang, announcing the arrival of a visitor, and young Sister Praxedes would enter the dormitory to inform Maile that her uncle had come to see her, or Freda that her cousins from Wai'anae had arrived, or Addie that her friends from Kaimukī were here. The girls would jump off their beds, thrilled, and rush out of the room.

No bell ever rang for Ruth.

Until, one day, it did.

Sister Praxedes came in unexpectedly that afternoon and told her, "Ruth, there's a nice gentleman and lady here who want to meet you!"

Ruth, who knew no one outside the Home, could only think of one thing. She asked hopefully, "Are they my mama and papa?"

"They might be. They're looking for a little girl to adopt. To make part of their family."

"Really?" Ruth said excitedly.

Most of the time, when a resident girl was adopted, she was taken by relatives or friends in what was called a *hānai* adoption. But occasionally a couple with no relation to anyone in the Home would come seeking a girl to adopt. Usually these were Native Hawaiians, who were less afraid of leprosy and less mindful of the stigma that attached itself to children of lepers.

Ruth had watched as other girls were chosen to meet potential parents, but now, for the first time, she was taken to the Home's library where she was introduced to a man and woman, both Hawaiian. Ruth's heart raced with a new feeling—hope—as the man smiled warmly at her.

"Such a pretty little *wahine*. What's your name, *keiki*?" he asked, using the Hawaiian word for "child."

"Ruth," she answered, seeing kindness in his eyes.

"How old are you, Ruth?" the lady asked.

Ruth counted off three fingers on her hand. "T'ree?" she said uncertainly.

"Very good, Ruth," Sister Praxedes said, then, to the couple: "Ruth is a very bright little girl."

"Do you want a real home, Ruth, with a mama and a papa?" he asked.

"Oh yes!" Ruth cried out. "I do!"

The nice couple laughed and smiled, asked her a few more questions, then told her she was very sweet and thanked her for seeing them. Sister

Praxedes escorted Ruth back to her dormitory and Ruth excitedly began wondering what her new home would be like, would she have brothers and sisters, would they have pets? She started planning which of her scant belongings she would pack first, until Sister Praxedes returned to tell her regretfully, "I'm so sorry, Ruth. They chose another girl."

Crushed by the weight of her hopes, Ruth asked, "Din't they like me?"

"They liked you fine, Ruth, it's just—"

"'Cause I'm *hapa*?" she asked, forlorn.

"No no, not at all. These things are hard to understand, Ruth."

She left, and Freda, a world-wise nine-year-old, said, "Same t'ing wen happen to me too. Sometimes they don't choose nobody at all. Don't let it get you down, yeah?"

Ruth nodded gratefully but felt no better.

Later, before lights out, Sister Lu came into the dorm, gave Ruth a hug, and assured her she would be chosen by someone, someday. "And meanwhile you have a home here and someone who loves you very much."

The warmth of Sister's embrace cast out the chill of rejection . . . for now.

Over the course of the next year, three more couples would ask to see Ruth. With each request her heart soared like a kite and after each rejection she was dashed to earth, convinced there was something lacking in her. She was *hapa*, half, incomplete. Half a cookie; who would want that? And eventually she learned a valuable lesson: she learned not to hope.

On Sunday evenings the parish priest would preside over the Benediction of the Blessed Sacrament, and as the older girls sang prayers and devotions in the chapel, the youngest sat in a classroom, supervised by an older girl whose job was to read Bible stories to them. On the last Sunday night of October 1920—which also happened to be All Hallow's Eve—that girl was Maile, who extinguished all the lights in the room save for a lone candle and regaled the little girls with a less devout tale about an *obake* that resided inside a *koa* tree. When the tree was cut down for lumber, the things made from it—a spear, a calabash, the handle of a knife—all contained a piece of the ghost, which was not at all happy at being dismembered and set about doing the same thing to everyone who owned a piece of that *koa* wood.

Ruth—now four years old—grew bored and quietly left the room. At first she intended to return to bed, but as she stood in the corridor she heard something that sounded like . . . whimpering? But not a *human* whimpering.

Curious, Ruth went into an empty classroom, stood on tiptoe at a window, and looked out.

It was dark and cloudy and the only light on the grounds came from the flicker of candles in the chapel. Ruth managed to push open the window an inch or two. Now she could tell that the whimpering was clearly coming from the side of the road—Meyers Street—bordering the convent.

Then she saw a shadow detach itself from the dark contours of a *noni*, mulberry, bush. It shuffled on four legs, low to the ground, until its hindquarters dropped and it sat there in the dimness.

It was a dog!

Ruth had seen dogs before—some of the local farmers owned them, and she even got to pet one once. Thrilled, she raced out of the classroom and out the back door. As she rounded the Home, she saw the dog sitting on the side of the road, whining plaintively.

She slowed down and approached it.

"Hi, dog," she said softly. "Hi."

It turned its head to her and its black eyes, ringed in amber, shone in the darkness.

Ruth got close enough to gently, cautiously, stroke its back. It didn't object. "Good dog," she said happily.

It was a scruffy, medium-sized mutt with matted, light brown fur—but to Ruth it was the most beautiful dog she had ever seen. As she petted it, it stopped whimpering, rubbing its wet nose against her arm. She scratched under its chin, its head tipped up and its mouth opened in a smile.

As she stroked its side she could feel its bony ribs.

"You hungry?" she asked. "I'll get some food. You stay here, okay?" When she got up and moved away the dog started to follow, but she put up a hand and said, as loudly as she dared, "No! Stay here. I'll be back."

The dog stopped, sat. "Good doggie!" she whispered, then ran back into the Home, down the corridor, and into the kitchen.

Maria Nunes, the Home's Portuguese cook, was washing the last of the supper dishes when Ruth burst in and announced, "I'm hungry!"

Maria had to smile at the urgency in the little girl's voice. "Didn't you finish your supper tonight?"

"I did. But I'm still hungry."

"Well . . ." Maria went to the big icebox and opened it. "We got a little Sunday ham left over . . . I can make you a sandwich, you like?"

"Oh yes. Thank you!" Ruth said.

A minute later, Ruth accepted the fat sandwich, thanked Maria again, and rushed out of the kitchen. She worried that the dog might have left, but when she emerged from the Home, he—he *seemed* like a "he"—was still sitting patiently where she had left him.

"Good dog!" She tore off a chunk of sandwich and offered it on the palm of her hand. His tongue ladled it up and into his mouth, and Ruth giggled at the pleasant tickle of it on her skin. She tore off another chunk and he wolfed that down too, then another, until the sandwich was gone and he was licking the last crumbs of bread from her palm.

She was petting him when she suddenly heard the sound of a door opening, followed by footsteps. She turned quickly. Benediction was over, and the sisters and older girls were leaving the chapel.

Skittish, the dog sprang to his feet and ran away down the road.

Ruth watched, disappointed, as he seemed to melt away into the darkness; but her palm was still wet from his tongue, a nice feeling.

Before anyone could see her, she hurried back into the Home. She went to bed thinking happily of her new friend.

All day she stole glances out the windows, but there was no sign of the dog. At dinner she was careful not to eat all of her chicken and mashed potatoes, but squirreled away the remainder into her napkin and stuffed it into the pocket of her dress.

At bedtime Ruth hid the napkin under her blanket as she changed into her pajamas, then slid under the covers. When the air became heavy with the rhythmic breathing of sleeping girls, Ruth took the napkin filled with food and went into the washroom. Above a toilet stall was a single window, lit faintly by moonlight. Ruth climbed onto the toilet seat, then up onto the back of the toilet, and quietly pushed up the window as high as she could.

She heard a familiar whimper. Eagerly she climbed up onto the windowsill, swung her legs over the edge, and jumped out, landing in the garden below. She hurried around the building to find her new friend waiting patiently for her on the side of the road.

As soon as he saw her, his tail began happily thumping the ground.

He gulped down the chicken and potatoes while Ruth stroked his back: "Good doggie." When his slobbery tongue darted out to lick her face, she giggled. Finally he rolled over on his side and closed his eyes. Ruth nestled beside him, face to face, draping an arm across his torso. Their chests touched and she felt the comforting warmth of his body. She felt his heart beating, and for a moment it felt as though their heartbeats were one and the same. Because they *were* the same. He was alone. She was alone. They needed each other.

And he needed a name. She'd been thinking of one and now whispered it into his ear, which twitched noncommittally at the suggestion. Ruth closed her eyes, enjoying the softness of his fur, their shared contentment. She wanted to stay like this, warm and loved, forever.

In minutes she was asleep.

"Ruth."

Suddenly an earthquake threw her dreams into disarray. She woke to find that the upheaval was the dog bolting upright beside her. She looked up and saw Sister Lu gazing worriedly down at her. "Ruth, what—"

The dog fled into the night. She told herself that was all right—he came back before, didn't he?

Sister Lu squatted down beside her. "Are you all right, Ruth? Are you cold?"

Ruth just shook her head.

"No," she said. "He kept me warm."

Louisa stood before Sister Helena, summoning every ounce of persuasion as she pled Ruth's case: "Mr. Kaohi rounded the dog up; it appears to be a stray. We've checked with all the neighbors and no one knows him. He's malnourished, mangy—"

"But retains all his working parts," Sister Helena noted wryly.

"That can always be fixed." Louisa always felt intimidated by Sister Helena, even though the sister wore her authority gently. "He *is* a sweet dog, and looks like he could use a home. And Ruth—Ruth needs something like this. Something she can care for. And you must admit, she was very resourceful in finding something for Only to eat."

"'He has a name?" Sister Helena asked. Then, realizing what she had just heard: "'Only'?"

"That's what Ruth calls him."

Sister Helena could not help but be moved. "Is that how she sees herself too?"

"In a way, they're all onlies here," Louisa said quietly.

Sister Helena sighed. "Sister, I simply can't establish the precedent of an individual child owning a dog. What if another stray shows up? What if a cat has kittens on our doorstep?"

"He could be the Home's mascot," Louisa suggested, "belonging to all the girls, not any one. I'm told that even at Kalaupapa, there was a kind of mascot at Bishop Home. I believe he was called 'Denis the pig' and he used to sun himself in the front yard."

Sister Helena rolled her eyes. "'Denis' was actually a huge boar—so huge, according to Mother Marianne, God rest her soul, that he sunned himself wherever he pleased.

"Sister, we don't know anything about this animal. He could have rabies. He could bite one of the girls. I can't risk that. I'm sorry. Truly I am."

"This will be . . . very hard on Ruth," Louisa said.

"She's only four. She won't even remember this dog in two years."

Louisa had run out of arguments. "Thank you, Sister. May I—allow Ruth to say goodbye to him?"

"I think that would only make things worse, don't you?"

Louisa nodded her obeisance without actually agreeing, then went to crush Ruth's fondest desire.

uth didn't understand why Only had to leave. But she knew he would be back—as indeed he was the very next evening. Ruth had hidden half of her fish and rice from supper in a handkerchief and lay in bed expectantly until she heard the familiar whimper outside. She jumped out of bed, hurried into the corridor and toward the back door—

When she heard Sister Lu say "Ruth," she froze on the spot.

The sister squatted in front of her. She held out her hand. "Give me the food," she said gently.

"But he's hungry!"

"He'll find someone else to feed him. Dogs usually do."

"But he's *my* dog!"

"No he's not. I'm sorry, Ruth. Give me the food."

Ruth slowly handed her the soggy bundle.

"Thank you. Now go back to bed."

"Can't I go look at him?"

"It's better you didn't."

Louisa escorted Ruth back to her bed, where Ruth immediately buried her head in a pillow and refused to acknowledge the sister's "good night."

Ruth listened for an hour to the dog's whines, all the while sobbing to herself. Finally it stopped, and Ruth fell into a troubled sleep.

Supper the next day was Portuguese bean soup, and the only thing Ruth could abscond with was a piece of cornbread. She stuffed it into her pocket, not caring that it began to crumble almost immediately. No matter: Sister Bonaventure, alert to the situation, confiscated the bread at the door.

Later that evening, the dog's cries returned. Not caring whether she woke anyone up, Ruth ran out of the dorm and into the classroom from which she had first seen her friend. She looked out the window.

Only sat on the side of the road, whimpering. She gazed at him—his light brown fur painted black by the night, the amber circles in his eyes flashing briefly as he turned his head. Ruth listened helplessly to his cries, feeling a grief and sorrow and anger unlike anything she had ever known. But she cherished every second she could still see him, until finally his cries stopped, his silhouette merged with that of the *noni* bush, and he was gone.

The next night there was only silence outside, and that—that was so much worse. Ruth cried into her pillow until she found another use for it and began punching it furiously, *bam bam bam*, then holding it by the ends and smashing it against the wall again and again.

Suddenly Sister Louisa was there, taking the pillow away from her. "Ruth, stop, please," she said. "I'm sorry. I'm so sorry."

"I hate you!" Ruth screamed at her. *"Go away!"*

There was such hurt and venom in her voice that it brought tears to Louisa's eyes. She dropped the pillow on the bed. Ruth snapped it up, threw it at the head of the bed, then dove into it, sobbing.

Louisa left, a dagger in her heart—no worse, she knew, than the one in Ruth's—and desecrated the silence of the corridors with her own sobs.

Chapter 2

1920–1921

The following evening after supper, Ruth slipped like a *pō makani*, a night breeze, through a back window. As dusk fell she began walking purposefully down Meyers Street, intent on finding her friend. She didn't dare call his name at first, afraid the sisters might hear, so she poked her head through the wood post fences surrounding Mr. Mendonca's pastures, looking for anything that did not seem cow-shaped. "Only?" she whispered. "Only, it's me." All she heard in reply was the lowing of cattle. She continued downhill.

The sky deepened to a dark blue, a thin moon rising above Diamond Head. The quickening darkness turned benign sights into fearsome shadows: a banyan tree's dense cluster of aerial roots looked like a forest of bone, a thicket of skeletons. The thick gray trunk and branches of an earpod tree loomed over Ruth like some headless beast with scores of arms. She brushed against a spiky protea plant whose leaves cut her like a bundle of knives.

Occasionally a dog barked from afar, but the bark was either too high-pitched or too low.

"*On-ly!*" she called, raising her voice the farther she wandered from the Home.

She had thought he'd be here, waiting for her. "*Only!*" The steeply sloping hill plunged down and down. Barely able to see where she was putting her feet, she tripped on something in the road. She fell tumbling down the hill, rocks and pebbles raking her skin.

She came to an abrupt stop, slamming into a fence post, and cried out. On the other side of the fence, pigs were gorging themselves at a feed trough. She reached down to feel the cut on her leg and her fingers came back sticky with blood—more blood than she had ever seen before. She started crying, crying and calling, "Please, Only, I love you, please come *back*!"

Suddenly she heard a bark, muffled as if from a distance. Hopefully, she kept calling his name. The barking drew closer and closer, a four-footed shape separating itself from the shadows.

But it was a big black German shepherd and he was barking combatively at her. Moments later came the crunch of feet on gravel, a golden halo of light from a kerosene lantern, and a man's voice saying, "Well, now. Who's this you've found, Hugo?"

In the lantern light she saw a man in overalls who stooped down and smiled at her. "'Ey, little *wahine*, it's okay. I'll help you."

But as grateful as she was to see the man, it was not the help she wanted, from the one she wanted. Only was gone. She knew that now.

She had traveled more than a mile downhill to Mr. Silva's hog farm on Rose Street, a feat that grudgingly impressed the sisters even as they scolded her for running away. Sister Lu cleaned and bandaged her wound—minor, if messy—but when she tried to engage Ruth, the little girl refused to answer.

Her anger was like the tough, leathery skin of the lychee fruit, which only grew harder with time. She woke up angry and went to bed angry. When a sister asked her to do something, she did the opposite. Whenever a girl tried to comfort her, she turned her back on her. She refused to eat Thanksgiving dinner because she had nothing to be thankful for. Christmas

Day she spent in bed, feigning illness, stubbornly refusing to enjoy the gifts and treats the sisters had gone to great lengths to provide.

In January, when she turned five—a slice of birthday cake thrown against the wall—Ruth was advanced to kindergarten in the hope the change in routine might improve her mood. Young Sister Augusta was the teacher, and she introduced Ruth to a stack of square wooden blocks—colored yellow, blue, green, orange, red—with funny markings on their sides that the sister said were "numbers" and "letters." But what piqued Ruth's interest despite herself were the shapes printed on the other sides, shapes that Ruth immediately identified as animals: a cow, a horse, a fish, even . . .

"Is this a dog?" It was a blue shape with four legs, fur, and a muzzle.

"No, that's a wolf," Sister Augusta said. "But there may be a dog in there somewhere. Why don't you find out?"

Ruth picked up the blocks one at a time, able to make no sense of the ones with marks like "M," "8," "Q," "2," or "G"—but whenever she turned a cube over and found an animal, she set it aside with the animal facing up. Soon she had a cow, turtle, duck, eagle, lamb, fish, hen, goose, wolf, and . . . yes, a dog! She smiled as she admired her wooden menagerie.

"That's very good, Ruth," the sister said. "You've sorted out all the animals. Now can you put all the *kinds* of animals together? The ones with fur, the ones with feathers, the ones that live in the sea?"

Ruth shuffled the blocks around, grouping the dog, cow, wolf, horse, and lamb together; then the duck, goose, hen, and eagle; and, finally, the fish and the . . . She frowned. Turtles walked on land, they had four feet like a cow or a horse—but she remembered on a visit to the beach seeing a turtle swimming in the water, so hesitantly she put the turtle alongside the fish.

"Very good, Ruth!"

Ruth was indifferent to the sister's praise. But she liked the blocks.

She learned quickly that she could stack them too and began building towers of animals, arranging them by color. Halfway through, another girl, Opal, came up and sighed, "Oooh, pretty. Is that a cow? I like cows."

"Me too."

"Can I have him? My blocks don't have a cow."

Opal snatched the orange cow off the top of its stack.

"That's *mine*. Give it back!" Ruth said.

"No!"

Opal jealously gripped the block in her hand and began to walk away.

Shrieking with fury, Ruth jumped Opal from behind, the two of them toppling like a stack of falling blocks. "Give me my cow, give me my *cow*!" Ruth yelled, trying to grab it out of Opal's hand.

Opal wouldn't give an inch: "No! It's mine now!"

Sister Augusta rushed over, separated the combatants, and said in her loudest, harshest tone, "That's *enough*! Both of you. Right now!"

The sister hoisted them both to their feet. "Now you young ladies are going to have to learn how to *share*," she scolded. A long speech followed about how Jesus would want them to share and share alike.

The sister took the cow block away from Opal, handed it back to Ruth. "Now, Ruth," she said, "I want you to give the cow to Opal."

"Why? You just gave it to me!"

"You're going to give it back like a good Christian."

"No! It was mine first!"

"*Give* it to her, Ruth," the sister said, rapidly losing her patience.

Ruth thought for a moment then said angrily, "Here!"

She lobbed the block directly at Opal. The wooden cube caromed off the side of her head like a foul ball. Opal wailed.

Ruth was yanked away by Sister Augusta, who then swatted her repeatedly in her backside, hard: "This—will teach you—not to *hit* people!"

The swats stung, but Ruth stubbornly refused to show her pain.

She was sent to her room for the rest of the day, where she proceeded to energetically punch the pillows on her bed, imagining them to be Opal's head. Or Sister Augusta's.

Not long after, Sister Lu entered the room. Ruth stopped punching and rolled over onto her stomach on the bed. The sister sat down beside her.

"How are you feeling, Ruth?" she asked quietly.

"I hate kindergarten! I hate it here!"

"Sister Augusta told me what happened," Louisa continued calmly. "I wish I'd been there. I could have explained to her why you did what you did."

Ruth rolled over on her back, looking at Sister Lu with confusion and anger. "Everything I want gets taken *away*!"

"I know it seems unfair. I know you loved Only."

Hearing the dog's name, Ruth burst into tears. Louisa wrapped her arms around her, rocked and comforted her as she had when Ruth was barely more than a baby. "It's all right, Ruth. Someday you'll have everything you want. I promise." An empty promise, Louisa knew. Ruth kept sobbing.

Louisa suddenly recalled the words of a Jesuit priest who, years before, had counseled the young nursing sister: *"While administering to these little ones, your charges, under God's care, your hands are His hands; your eyes, His eyes; and your heart, His Sacred Heart, working by, in, and through your very being . . ."*

Louisa prayed for God's love and succor to travel from her body, her arms, into Ruth's. The sobs finally ceased and, mercifully, Ruth fell asleep. Louisa looked at her and remembered other children, in Joliet, who had borne even worse pain—the violent abuse of parents—and whom to this day Louisa regretted not being able to save from their own rage and bitterness. But Ruth was different. She *had* to be different, Louisa told herself. *I am God's instrument, and I will not fail this child.*

The following week, Louisa and three other sisters assembled every girl old enough to walk and marched them two miles down the hill to King Street, where the *keiki* awaited the arrival of the eastbound streetcar from Fort Shafter. Within fifteen minutes Car No. 55 rattled into view, its exterior painted fire-engine red, its destination sign identifying it as traveling between KALIHI AND WAIKIKI. The girls (all but Ruth) cheered as it braked to a stop. It was empty this early in the morning, which was provident since the fifty girls and four nuns filled the entire car.

Ruth's anger had cooled to indifference; even the prospect of a trip to Waikīkī Beach could not arouse her interest. Glumly she followed the older girls onto the car and down the aisle. On either side were wooden benches that each sat two—three, if they were small—girls. Ruth started to seat herself up front—until she felt Sister Lu's hand on her shoulder. "We can find you a better seat than that, Ruth," the sister said. "Here, why don't you sit with Mara." Louisa gently steered Ruth into a seat next to a twelve-year-old Hawaiian girl. "Mara, this is Ruth." Mara said "Hi," but Ruth just sat in sullen silence.

The trip to Waikīkī was long and rough at times—the car's wheels clattering over the track-joints, the bumps and jolts when it hit uneven terrain, the clanging of the bell at every cross street. But the girls loved every minute of it.

"Some fancy ride, 'ey?" Mara said to Ruth over the clangor.

Ruth shrugged.

"Oh, you seen it all, huh?" Mara smiled. "You one cool cucumber."

"I'm not a cucumber." Ruth had yet to embrace metaphor.

"You like Waikīkī?"

"Yeah, sure."

"What place you like best?"

"The zoo."

Mara smiled again. "I like that too. My mama used to take me an' my brothers there. I liked the *pikake*—the peacocks. Struttin' around with their tail feathers stickin' outta their *'ōkole*."

She laughed, but Ruth was focused on something else Mara had said: "Your mama took you there?"

"Uh huh."

"What happened to her?"

"Nothin' happened. She lives in Kaimukī."

Ruth didn't understand this at all. "Then why don't you live with her?"

Mara shrugged casually, but her smile had faded. "My papa, he got leprosy. Got sent Kalaupapa. Mama, she couldn't afford to keep us anymore, so—I come here, and my brothers go to St. Anthony's orphanage."

"She . . . couldn't keep you?" Ruth said, not quite grasping it.

"Papa made alla money. Mama took a job in a factory, but it still wasn't enough, not with four mouths to feed. She told me, 'You be better off with the sisters, they feed you an' take care of you.'" Seeing the sadness in Ruth's eyes, Mara added brightly, "It's not so bad. Mama comes visit me when she can. The sisters even let her take me to St. Anthony's to see my brothers."

Mara told her about Kaimukī—playing in the red volcanic dirt, beneath a ceiling of sheltering *kiawe* trees—and about her brothers, how they all used to take the trolley to Waikīkī to go body-surfing. Ruth could tell how much she loved them and missed them. She talked about her papa, how the bounty hunter had arrested him and sent him to Moloka'i just before Mara's birthday. And as she listened, Ruth began to understand that maybe there were even worse things in the world than not being able to keep a dog you loved.

Soon the streetcar was rattling across the McCully Street Bridge, as the girls all groaned at the rotten-egg stink floating up from the duck ponds and hog farms that still made up a large part of Waikīkī. A bulldozer roared nearby, dredging one of the three streams that emptied into Waikīkī, working to build a new canal that would one day drain all the duck ponds and rice paddies. Then Car No. 55 headed down Kalākaua Avenue, driving past the stands of tall coconut palms that lined the street, and excitement bubbled among the girls as the car approached the end of the line at Kapi'olani Park.

Sister Louisa and the other nuns led the girls out of the car, but instead of turning toward Waikīkī Beach, Louisa stepped off the curb as if to cross the street. "Before we go swimming, what do you say to a visit to the zoo?"

A chorus of cheers greeted this suggestion. At the entrance to the Honolulu Zoo, Sister Louisa paused to take a head count. Ruth had already entered at record speed, but Louisa saw Mara standing a few feet away and gave her a small smile of thanks—a smile that faded once she saw the girl's face.

Mara stood gazing up at the entrance to the zoo, tears in her eyes.

Louisa was helping Sister Bonaventure clear away the Sunday breakfast dishes when Sister Praxedes breathlessly appeared in the doorway to the dining hall. "Sister Louisa, I thought you should know. There's a couple here—a *Japanese* couple. They're Issei—first-generation Japanese nationals, born in Japan—and they're looking for a Japanese girl to adopt."

Sister Bonaventure raised an eyebrow at this.

"And unless I'm mistaken," Sister Praxedes went on, "the only girl here with any Japanese blood is—"

"Ruth Utagawa," Louisa finished for her.

"Perhaps you might like to join me in taking Ruth to meet them?"

Louisa looked to Sister Bonaventure, who nodded her assent. "Go ahead, Sister. I'll be . . . interested to hear what comes of it."

Louisa thanked her and, with Sister Praxedes, hurried to find Ruth.

Ruth had quieted down enormously after her chat with Mara, but when Louisa and Praxedes told her about the couple who wished to see her, a shadow of her old anger eclipsed her sunny mood. "No," she declared defiantly. "I won't go!"

"This time it's different, Ruth," Praxedes insisted.

"No!"

Louisa could hardly blame her; she had been disappointed often enough. "It *is* different, Ruth. This couple—they asked especially for *you*."

God forgive me. But it was, in a sense, the truth.

Ruth said, "Me?"

"Yes. They don't want to see any other girl in the Home. Only you."

Ruth didn't know what to make of that. "Why?"

"Why don't you come with us and find out?"

Ruth grudgingly agreed and even allowed Sister Lu to scrub the dirt from her hands and knees. But she was determined not to show the slightest bit of interest in these people. She knew better than that.

The Japanese couple was waiting in the library. They were in their late thirties, the husband thin and dressed in a dark Western business suit; the wife petite, smiling, wearing a black cotton kimono.

But Ruth only noticed one thing about them.

Their eyes. Their eyes were just like *hers*.

She forgot her indifference and stared at them in absolute fascination.

"Ruth," Sister Praxedes said, "this is Mr. and Mrs. Watanabe."

"Hello," Ruth said, still staring.

The couple bowed in greeting. The wife said, "*Konnichiwa*. Hello, Ruth."

"Sit down, Ruth." Louisa gave her a little nudge. Ruth went to the small chair reserved for children.

The couple sat opposite her, the man studying Ruth closely.

"She is—part *kanaka*?" he asked in halting English.

"Yes. Her mother is Hawaiian. Her father is a Nisei," Sister Praxedes explained, using the term for second-generation, American-born Japanese.

"She is very pretty, don't you think, *Otōsan*?" the wife said with a smile. Her English was a bit smoother, more assured.

Mr. Watanabe nodded, both in agreement and, it seemed, giving license to his wife to continue speaking. "How old are you, little one?" she asked.

"Five," Ruth answered. Now *this* was starting to feel familiar. Even the woman's smile, as friendly as it was. All the smiles were friendly, weren't they? But it always ended in tears.

"Such a serious face," Mrs. Watanabe said. "Why do you keep looking at us like that, Ruth?"

"'Cause of your eyes," Ruth said bluntly.

"Ah, I see. We have eyes like yours, yes?"

Ruth nodded.

"That is because we come from Japan. Do you know where Japan is?"

Ruth shook her head.

"It is an island like this, but far, far across the sea. We came a long way to get here."

"Why?"

"We came to Hawai'i to work."

"I'm told you were both contract laborers at Waimānalo Plantation," said Sister Praxedes.

The husband nodded. "Three years. I grew up on a small farm—in Hōfuna, Okayama Prefecture. I wished to buy my own farm here, but . . . too difficult."

"So much of the land in Hawai'i," Mrs. Watanabe noted, "is in the hands of a very few."

"Very few *haole*s," Mr. Watanabe added, then, realizing his tactlessness: "*Sumimasen*. Beg pardon. I mean no offense."

"None taken," Sister Praxedes said with a smile. "So you moved to Honolulu and became a contractor?"

He nodded. "On a farm you are always building, fixing things. I like farming numbah one, but I like building too."

Mrs. Watanabe turned to Ruth. "And what do *you* like to do, Ruth?"

Ruth had never been asked this before. "I like animals," she blurted out.

"You do?"

"We went to the zoo and I saw a bear and a monkey and an elephant and a lion and a bear," Ruth exhaled all in one breath.

The woman smiled. "Do you like cats? We have a cat."

Ruth's eyes widened. "You *do*?"

"Oh yes. In Japan, cats are very popular. They are said to bring good luck."

Ruth's indifference forgotten, she asked, "What *color* is your cat?"

"She is black," Mr. Watanabe declared. Ruth's eyes went to him. "Americans think black cats bad luck. No cat is bad luck."

"Mr. Watanabe found her in an alley," his wife explained. "And she has brought us nothing but good fortune."

"What's her name?" Ruth asked.

"Mayonaka," the wife replied. "It means 'midnight.'"

"Mayo . . . na . . . ka?" Ruth repeated.

"Yes, very good," Mrs. Watanabe said.

"I wish I could meet her," Ruth said wistfully.

Mrs. Watanabe glanced at her husband. He gazed at Ruth a long moment, then looked back to his wife and nodded.

Mrs. Watanabe told Ruth, "You will meet her—and your three brothers—when you come home with us, if you choose. Would you like to be part of our family?"

Ruth's heart fluttered. Joy, hope, longing, and fear washed over her in waves. She began to cry.

Mrs. Watanabe blinked. "Did I say some wrong thing?"

"No, no," Sister Louisa said quickly. She bent down to meet Ruth's eyes. "It's all right, Ruth. It's not like before. Do you *want* to go with them?"

Afraid to put the thought into words, Ruth merely nodded. But the longing in her eyes was unambiguous.

Mrs. Watanabe smiled. "Good. That makes us very happy."

Her husband stood, businesslike, and said to Sister Praxedes, "We will fill out necessary papers now?"

"Yes. Yes, of course," Praxedes said. "I'll take you to see Sister Helena. She'll have you fill out a petition for adoption, which will then be submitted to the family court here in Honolulu. If all goes smoothly, you should be able to take Ruth home with you within the week."

Louisa accompanied a jubilant Ruth back to her dormitory, which was empty this time of day. "I told you, didn't I," Louisa said, "that someday you'd have a home and a mama and a papa all your own?"

"And a *cat*," Ruth added wonderingly.

"Yes, mustn't forget the cat." Louisa looked at Ruth, seeing the memory of the year-old infant being carried in Sister Catherine's arms, and smiled. "I'm going to miss you, Ruth. But I'm very, very happy for you."

Ruth hugged her legs. "I'll miss you too, Sister Lu. Every day."

"Oh, you'll be much too happy and busy to miss me," Louisa said, even as she blinked back tears.

ouisa returned to the dining hall to share the good news with Sister Bonaventure—but the older sister's response was troubling, a look of concern wrinkling her usually impassive face.

"This is . . . odd," she said gravely.

"What do you mean? What's odd about it?"

"You've only been in Hawai'i a few years, Sister, but . . . to the Japanese, there is nothing more important than the family name. There is nothing worse than to dishonor it. There's a book called the *Yakuba*, a sort of neighborhood family history . . . a black mark in this book shames the family, disgraces their ancestors. They would do anything to avoid that."

"But what on earth does this have to do with Ruth?" Louisa asked.

"Leprosy," the older sister said, "is considered the blackest of black marks on a family's lineage—one that can never be expunged. The stigma is so great, the family is shunned; no one will marry into it. I've known lepers at Kalaupapa whose families had completely disowned them."

Louisa was at a loss to comprehend this. "But Ruth isn't a leper! She's as healthy as you or I."

"Even so. To the Japanese, a family adopting her would be stigmatized for all time. Why would any Japanese couple knowingly risk that?"

Louisa considered a moment, then suggested, "Do you . . . suppose they just don't *know*?"

"Everyone in Hawai'i knows that our girls are the children of lepers." She frowned. "But if by some chance they *don't* know, they should be made aware of the implications of their actions. The possibility that they could be ostracized—forced to move away, as so many families of lepers have had to—"

"Sister, no!" Louisa was startled by her own vehemence. Sister Bonaventure, taken aback by the outburst, broke off in midsentence.

"Forgive me for shouting, Sister," Louisa said. "But you know as well as I do . . . there are girls at this Home who have been here all their lives.

Girls who will never be adopted. Who may never *leave* here. Would you deny Ruth a chance at a normal, happy life and a family who loves her?"

Sister Bonaventure nodded slowly.

"Yes. Of course, you're right, Sister," she said. "It's not for us to judge. The Lord sent these people here; we should leave this matter to Him." Then, soberly: "But you must prepare yourself, Sister, for the possibility that all may not turn out as you hope. And if so, this may not be the last we see of Ruth."

Louisa nodded as calmly as she could. But her hands were trembling.

hree days later the Watanabes' petition was presented to Judge John DeBolt of the First Circuit Court of Honolulu, a Texas-born *haole* in his early sixties who seemed at ease with Japanese people and asked some routine questions—about their financial status, religious background, and family health history—before granting their petition. Ruth was then issued a new birth certificate, legally rechristening her "Ruth Dai Watanabe."

On the following Monday—when the Watanabes arrived in a taxicab to take Ruth home with them—Louisa squatted down and hugged Ruth, feeling as if she were losing a piece of herself. Fighting back tears she told her, "You are a lucky little girl, Ruth. And I've been very lucky to have known you."

"I love you, Sister Lu," Ruth said, holding her friend tight.

"I love you too, Ruth. But you have such an exciting life ahead of you! A new home, three brothers—and a *cat*."

"Yeah!" Ruth was happier than Louisa had ever seen her. "Will you come visit and see my cat?"

Louisa glanced at Etsuko Watanabe, who smiled and said, "You are always welcome in our house, Sister."

Louisa forced herself to let go of Ruth. "I will, then. So this isn't goodbye, it's just . . . be seeing you."

Ruth smiled and, as her new mother helped her into the car, she waved at Louisa. Even as the cab wound its way downhill, Ruth continued to wave. Louisa prayed that the road ahead of her would be a happy one.

Chapter 3

𝒞 hinatown in 1921 was a microcosm of what Hawai'i was becoming and a reflection of the multiethnic culture that the plantation owners had unwittingly fostered. As sugar boomed and the Native Hawaiian population declined due to Western diseases, the plantations began importing immigrant labor—first Chinese *kuli*s, then Portuguese and Japanese laborers. But when after a decade the Japanese became the largest minority population in the islands, the sugar barons—determined not to let any one ethnic group dominate and wield too much bargaining power—turned to Koreans, Puerto Ricans, Spaniards, and Filipinos. Hawaiian "pidgin," the lingua franca that allowed the different ethnicities to communicate on the plantation, united the tens of thousands of immigrants who left the plantations when their contracts expired and then opened up shops or found better-paying jobs in Honolulu. And most of them lived in Chinatown—an island within an island. These were working-class people—carpenters, plumbers, stevedores, bartenders, fishermen, salesmen, butchers, shoe-makers, teachers—living and working in a motley bramble of wooden tenements, pool rooms, restaurants, tailor shops, bakeries, and general stores.

Kukui Street was the beating heart of Chinatown, and as the Watanabes' taxicab made its way down this main artery, Ruth sat with her face pressed up against the side window, taking in the life's blood of the street: old men peddling steaming *saimin* from pushcarts; Chinese and Japanese housewives culling the best eggplant, bitter melon, *bok choy*, and lotus root from gro-cers' bins; laughing *keiki* wielding softballs and bats, headed for a game in the grassy triangle of A'ala Park. Commingled with the traffic noise was the babble of multiple languages—the higher-pitched tones of Asian tongues and the raucous baritone of Western voices.

But rather than being frightened by it all, Etsuko observed, Ruth seemed to be enjoying it . . . even as Etsuko herself enjoyed it. After fourteen years in Chinatown, she had come to appreciate the boisterous vitality of these streets, where commerce and congress transcended race and poverty. De-spite its chaotic surface, it embodied to her the Japanese principle of *wa*—harmony—in a most American way. For all their many differences, the people of Chinatown lived and worked together in an unlikely sort of *wa*.

"You have never been here before?" Etsuko asked Ruth.

Ruth shook her head.

"So many people . . ." she said wonderingly. "Is this where you live?"

"This is where *we* live," Etsuko corrected her.

Ruth smiled, her face glowing with pleasure.

Finally the cab stopped in front of a two-story business whose front win-dow announced: T. WATANABE—GENERAL CONTRACTOR & BUILDER—CARPENTRY & CONTRUCTION SERVICE OF ALL KIND.

"Here we are. We're home," Etsuko said.

She helped Ruth out of the cab as Taizo paid the fare, then unlocked the store. Inside was a wooden counter like the ones Ruth had seen in candy and ice cream shops, but there were no packets of crackseed or funnels of shave ice here, just big pieces of lumber—planks, posts, beams—and instead of sweet sugary smells, the scent of freshly cut pine pleasantly tickled her nose. Behind the counter she recognized hammers, saws, and screwdrivers but only later would she learn to name tools like the lathe, drill press, and planer.

One thing began to alarm her, however.

"We live in *here*?" she asked, searching in vain for something like a bed.

Etsuko laughed. "No no, this is your father's workshop. We live upstairs." They rounded a tall room divider; in the rear of the shop there was a staircase against one wall, and along the other, a stove, icebox, sink, and countertop. "This is our kitchen, Dai. Perhaps you can help me make—"

"*Otōsan?*" "*Okāsan?*" Boyish voices erupted from the top of the staircase, followed quickly by actual boys galloping down the steps in their bare feet, eager to meet this mysterious new thing called a "sister." The two youngest—Satoshi, twelve, and Ryuu, seven—collided at the bottom of the stairs. The oldest boy, Haruo—a strapping and worldly fourteen—paused a few steps up, watching his two younger brothers with amusement.

Etsuko said, "Dai, these are your brothers—Haruo, Satoshi, and Ryuu. Boys, this is your new sister, Dai. She speaks no Japanese, so you have our permission to speak English at home until she learns."

Satoshi, thin and gangly, stepped forward, gave a small, formal bow of greeting to Ruth, and said, "*Konnichiwa*, Dai."

"English, Satoshi," Etsuko reminded him.

Haruo bowed and said warmly, "Hello, Dai. Welcome to our family."

Ruth felt a surge of joy at that word: *family*.

Ryuu, small but brash, stepped up, bowed, then shook her hand. "Hi, Sis. Don't worry, I'll show you the ropes around here."

"Upstairs now," Taizo said in a tone that indicated he was used to being obeyed. "Dai, please remove shoes. Leave here at foot of stairs."

"We Japanese don't wear shoes inside our homes," Etsuko explained.

Ruth was delighted. "The sisters made us wear shoes everywhere!"

"Here. Put these on when you reach the top of the stairs." Ruth was handed a pair of blue slippers. They felt as soft as a cow's tummy.

Etsuko watched as Ruth entered her new home. As with most apartments above storefronts, it was essentially one large room—not unlike the average home back in Japan. But because this was Hawai'i, the home reflected a mix of two cultures. In one corner stood a *kyodai*, a Japanese bureau, and in another, a Western-style dresser made of *koa* wood. Red, yellow, and green *tatami* mats covered the floor of the main living area. The walls were adorned with Buddhist icons as well as athletic awards Haruo had won at school. Japanese folding screens discreetly partitioned off sleeping areas.

The front windows afforded a glimpse of the green hills behind Honolulu and the extinct cinder cone of Mount Tantalus.

Ruth was fascinated by the wooden dining table, which was far lower than she was used to—and, strangely, had no chairs around it, only bright green pillows decorated with a cascading waterfall design. She pointed to them with her index finger. "Ooh, those are pretty, what are they?"

"Don't point with that finger, Dai, it's considered impolite," Etsuko said. "And those are *zabuton*. We sit on them when dining."

"We do? Can I sit on one?"

"That *is* what they are for."

Ruth ran over and sank into one of the plush green cushions. "It's like sitting on a marshmallow! And we get to eat on the floor? Really?"

The boys laughed, and Etsuko showed Ruth the proper way for a girl to sit on a *zabuton*, folding her legs under her body.

"Come, let me show you where you will be sleeping," Etsuko said, leading Ruth behind a folding screen, where a big green-and-white mat lay directly on the floor. "This is where your *otōsan*—your father—and I sleep. This thick mattress is called a *futon*, but you have your choice of sleeping on a *futon* or a bed, which the boys use."

Ruth lowered herself onto the *futon*. It was as comfortable as a bed—but it was on the floor! *Everything* here was on the floor. This was fun!

"I like this!"

"We will take one out tonight and you can sleep here with us."

Another voice unexpectedly entered the conversation with a querulous *"Miaow?"*

Ruth quickly sat up. A beautiful cat, black as a starless night, sat by the folding screen, its slitted green gaze on this new, alien presence in its home.

"And here is the last member of the family," Etsuko said. "Mayonaka."

"Can I pet her?" Ruth asked excitedly.

"That is up to her, not me," Etsuko said with a smile.

Ruth crawled on her knees toward the cat, moving slowly so as not to frighten her. "Mayonaka, Mayonaka, you're so *pretty*," she cooed.

"Miaow," Mayonaka agreed.

Ruth held out her hand to the cat, who sniffed it judiciously. Ruth slowly raised her hand and gently stroked the top of the animal's head.

Mayonaka abruptly hissed, hackles raised, then jumped away.

Ruth looked so dejected that Etsuko patted her on the arm. "She just needs to get used to you, that's all. Give her time."

Once Ruth's belongings were put away in the sleeping area and she had seen all there was to see of her new home, Father and Haruo went downstairs to the woodshop to work, Etsuko left for the kitchen to prepare supper, and Ryuu offered to teach Ruth how to play Sun-and-Moon ball. This toy consisted of a wooden spike with two round cups on both sides and a red ball attached to it by a string. "The whole idea," he explained, "is to get the Sun into one of the half-moons, or cups. Here, watch." With a flick of his wrist the ball went swinging upward, and then he deftly caught it in one of the cups.

"Ohhh!" Ruth said, watching him do it again before he handed it to her and said, "Here, now you try." She took it eagerly, but her first try missed by a foot and her second nearly clobbered her brother in the nose. "Uh, maybe a little less spin on the ball, okay?" he suggested. Ruth continued to go at it, giggling and laughing, until she finally caught the Sun in the Moon.

From downstairs came the grinding of saws and the pounding of hammers, as well as unfamiliar but delicious aromas wafting up from the kitchen. Soon Etsuko was setting soup bowls, rice bowls, and plates of sizzling beef *sukiyaki* in a pleasing arrangement on the dining table. As the family gathered for dinner, Ruth realized how hungry she was. With everyone settled, all but Ruth said in unison, *"Itadakimasu."*

Etsuko told her, "That means 'I humbly receive.' Can you say that? *Itadakimasu.*"

"Ita . . . da . . . ki . . . masu?" Ruth repeated slowly, all her emphases wrong.

"Close enough for your first meal," Etsuko said.

She filled Taizo's rice bowl with rice and his soup bowl with *miso* soup, then offered the plate of *sukiyaki* to him. Ruth was puzzled that he had no dinner plate, and even more so when he picked up a pair of wooden sticks and began eating pieces of beef, mushroom, and bamboo shoots directly from the serving plate. When he was done, Etsuko served Haruo, then Satoshi, Ryuu, Ruth, and finally Etsuko herself. Ruth couldn't help but notice that Father received the largest and choicest cut of meat, and the most rice and vegetables as well. Her brothers got the next largest portions, then Ruth, with Mama serving the smallest and poorest portions to herself. Ruth almost asked why, but she was too preoccupied trying to figure out how to use the chopsticks she had been given.

"Here," Ryuu offered, "watch me."

Ruth did her best to imitate what she saw, but it took five tries before she was able to pick up anything—and then it slipped, like a noodle off a knife, before it was halfway to her mouth. The combination of frustration and hunger on her face would have elicited laughter back at Kapi'olani Home, but though her brothers smiled in amusement, no one laughed at her.

Instead, Etsuko merely unfolded a napkin to reveal a metal fork, which she now handed to Ruth. "If you starve to death," she said wryly, "you will never learn how to use chopsticks."

Gratefully Ruth took the fork and attacked her dinner.

Later, when they each took turns bathing in the *very* hot waters of a wooden tub in the alleyway out back—the *furo*—Ruth noticed it was in the same order: her father, her brothers, Ruth, her mother. Etsuko dried Ruth off next to a fragrant plumeria plant growing by the rear entrance. By the time her mother stepped into the bath, its waters were only tepid.

Later, Ruth asked Ryuu quietly why this should be so.

"It's like a train," he answered cheerfully. "The engineer—*Otōsan*—is up front. He drives the train, makes all the big decisions. Behind him, in the next car, is the oldest son, who takes over if anything happens to the engineer. Behind him is second oldest, then me, you, and *Okāsan* is kind of the caboose."

"Mama is the caboose?" Ruth repeated.

"Aw, not really. It's just tradition. Like when we're inside the house and I say something to my brothers, I can't call them by their first names but only as *niisan*—'older brother.' That's what you have to call me too, when you're at home. But outside you can call me Ryuu or Ralph."

Ruth was thoroughly confused. "Why do we have two first names?"

"We have Japanese names and we have English names that the *haole* teachers gave us because they can't pronounce Japanese: Haruo is Horace, Satoshi is Stanley. At home you're Dai, but at school you'll still be Ruth."

Ruth was feeling a little overwhelmed by so many new things to learn, but Ryuu assured her, "You'll get the hang of it." And she was pleased to hear that she would get to keep her old name, at least for part of the time.

At bedtime Taizo brought out a smaller *futon* from a closet and laid it at the foot of the one he and Etsuko shared. Ruth climbed on and Etsuko covered her with a blue-and-white fleece blanket, brightly embroidered with a Japanese wave design, and tucked her in. "There. Now you are—what do they say?—'snug as a bug in a rug.'"

Ruth giggled. It was so good, Etsuko thought, to see the happiness in those sparkling brown eyes.

She said, "There is a saying in Japanese: 'To love a child as if it were a butterfly or a flower.' Will you be my flower, little one?"

Ruth considered that. "I'd rather be a butterfly."

"Then so you are. Good night, butterfly." She leaned over and kissed her on the forehead, then went to join Taizo, who was already asleep.

Ruth lay there in the dark for a minute, listening to her father's soft snoring and the rustle of blankets as her mother settled into bed.

Her father. Her mother. She had a father and a mother! It was a source of wonder and delight to her. She would have to work extra hard at mastering the chopsticks and pronouncing the Japanese words, so they had no reason to send her back to Kapi'olani Home.

That was her last waking thought before, exhausted, she drifted asleep.

Etsuko woke in the dark hours of the morning to find Mayonaka, as was her wont, curled up on her hip. Etsuko lifted the cat up, gently and quietly so as not to wake her, then carried her over to Ruth. She lay the cat down beside her daughter—*my daughter; how strange and wonderful that sounds!*—with Mayonaka's back brushing Dai's arm. The cat stirred, eyes opening to take in her new surroundings; then, deciding it wasn't worth the effort to move, she closed her eyes and drifted back into cat dreams.

Etsuko smiled and returned to Taizo's side.

Later—when Mayonaka decided, for reasons only a cat knows, to turn 360 degrees around and then curl up again in precisely the same position—Ruth woke. When she saw the cat dozing contentedly on her arm—felt the soft warmth of its fur on her skin—her eyes filled with tears of joy. She smiled, then closed her eyes, doing her best not to move, and was lulled back to sleep by the soothing trill of Mayonaka's soft purr.

*I*n September Ruth entered the first grade at Kauluwela Grammar School, where she was part of a class of about thirty students—Japanese, Chinese, Filipino, and Hawaiian. Even her teacher, Miss Fukuda, was a Nisei born twenty-two years ago in Honolulu. Ruth liked Miss Fukuda; she was smart and nice and made learning the alphabet fun.

But after the Kauluwela school day ended at three P.M., classes were far from over. Each afternoon she and her brothers had to attend Japanese school in the basement of the Buddhist church. There they learned about Japanese culture—etiquette, piety toward ancestors, patience, courtesy, obligation, and the Japanese language itself. At her first class the teacher began by declaring *"Kiritsu!"*—"Attention," as Ralph whispered to her—and all the students stood and recited the *kōkun*, the school motto. To Ruth, at first, the Japanese words were unintelligible, like one of the sinister magic spells, spoken in Hawaiian, in the ghost stories Maile used to tell. But over the next four months, Ruth's six-year-old brain soaked up both the English alphabet and the Chinese *kanji* characters as a sea sponge absorbs water, and within four months she was able to join in reciting the *kōkun* and understood it to mean:

Let us become worthy individuals.
Let us study together in a friendly atmosphere.
Let us take care of our health by eating properly.
Let us be good to our parents.

This was a far cry from a *kahuna* sorcerer's spell and, frankly, a bit of a disappointment.

But Japanese school was valuable in explaining the unspoken, often mystifying rules that Ruth found herself unknowingly breaking at home: Lift your rice bowl politely with both hands to ask for more, but it is acceptable to lift it with your left hand when eating from it. Never, ever cross your chopsticks when putting them down. Always remove socks or stockings before walking on a *tatami* mat, as their finely woven fibers are very delicate. When being taught by an elder, always be attentive, deferential, respectful, and display a willingness to learn.

The hardest thing for Ruth to learn was to speak more softly, avoiding loudness, confrontation, and physical displays of affection in public.

It was also at Japanese school that Ruth heard something that would soon become a disturbing refrain. On her first day she overheard a boy ask Stanley in pidgin, "Why your parents *hānai* a girl? Dey *pupule* or somethin'?"

Hānai, Ruth knew, meant "adopt"; *pupule* meant "crazy."

"I dunno why," Stanley shot back, "but dey ain't *pupule* so no talk stink about 'em!"

The other boy shrugged and let it go. Ruth tried to do the same.

But she overheard variations on this from other boys and each time her brothers defended their parents with a very un-Japanese belligerence.

She shrugged it off as silly boy-talk until, one day, she and Ralph were walking home and they passed Mr. Komenaka's general store. They saw him watching them from the doorway, then laugh and say to a coworker:

"Shinji rareru? Ano bakana Watanabe ga on'nanoko wo morrate kitanda!"

Ruth was surprised to find that she understood both the laugh *and* the words: "Can you believe it? That fool Watanabe adopted a girl!"

She turned and glared at the man, who saw the hurt and confusion in her eyes and quickly retreated to the safety of his store.

"Hey," Ralph said, "it's okay, Ruth, he's just a—"

Ruth burst into tears and ran. She raced down Kukui Street, jostling pedestrians, nearly colliding with rickety food carts, Ralph in hot pursuit but half a length behind. At the back door of the store, Ruth rushed past a startled Etsuko in the downstairs kitchen, kicked off her sandals, then ran upstairs and into the apartment's sleeping area, where she flung herself, sobbing, onto her *futon*.

A few minutes later—having been told what transpired by a still-huffing-and-puffing Ralph—Etsuko appeared and said softly, "Butterfly?" When Ruth didn't respond, Etsuko sat down next to her, put a hand on her back consolingly, and said, "I'm sorry, little one. Komenaka-*san* was very rude. I will never enter his store again."

"It's not just him!" Ruth said between sobs. "I hear it at school too!"

Etsuko sighed. "I had hoped you would not. Dai, come here." She gathered Ruth up in her arms and held her close. "Do not take this personally. It's just that . . .

"In Japan, the birth of sons is favored over that of daughters because boys carry the family name, and the family name is very, very important. A girl marries into someone else's family, you see, and takes their name. So Komenaka-*san* could not understand why we would choose to adopt a girl."

Ruth sniffed back her tears and said, "Why did you?"

Etsuko said quietly, "I had always secretly hoped to have a girl, so I might have someone to make a pretty kimono for, to teach how to sew and cook and pass on all I've learned in life. But after Ralph was born, the doctor said I could not have any more children. Your father is not like other men. He knows what sorrow is. He knew my sorrow and was willing to brave the smirks and ridicule of foolish men." She smiled. "But the reason I wanted *you*, butterfly, was because I fell in love with you the instant I saw you."

Ruth said meekly, "So—you're not going to give me back? To the sisters?"

"Oh, dearest one, no, never, never. We will love you forever."

Ruth held tight to her mother, more tightly than she had ever held anyone. For the first time in her life, she felt she truly belonged somewhere.

Etsuko held on just as tightly. What she told Ruth was only half the truth—but it was Etsuko's truth.

Ruth celebrated the New Year, 1922, in Japanese fashion, enjoying a feast of special foods including New Year's soup, mashed sweet potatoes with chestnuts, fish cake, sweetened black beans, and—Ruth's favorite—*mochi*, sticky white rice cakes (she helped her mother prepare them by gleefully mashing the grains of rice with a wooden mallet). She was thrilled to learn that by tradition, the birthdays of everyone in the family were all celebrated on New Year's, with even more gifts and sweets. Being Japanese was fun!

Sister Lu visited on Ruth's actual birthday, February 8. After she hugged her, Ruth ran over to Mayonaka, snapped her up, and brought the startled cat to Louisa. "This is Mayonaka," Ruth said as if introducing a queen.

Louisa scratched the cat's head and smiled. "Oh, she's quite beautiful. You *are* a lucky girl, Ruth."

Later, after drinking hot tea and sampling *mochi* prepared by Etsuko, Louisa gave Ruth a small stuffed cow as a birthday present: "This is to make sure you don't forget all the people who loved you at Kapi'olani Home."

But of course she would, eventually. And soon even Honolulu itself would recede like a dream into memory.

Late in the year, as the red fruit of the Christmasberry tree could be seen gracing the slopes of Mount Tantalus, Etsuko was mopping the floors when she heard Taizo ascending the stairs. Usually he only came up once a day, for lunch. Now he stood in the doorway looking like a scarecrow that's had the straw knocked out of it, holding a letter in his callused hands.

"I just received this," he told her in Japanese. "From Jiro."

Jiro—"second son"—was Taizo's brother, older by three years. He had been the first in the family to immigrate to Hawai'i when, according to tradition, their eldest brother, Ichirō, inherited the family farm in Hōfuna. Taizo, who had always idolized the brash, boastful Jiro, followed him, seven years later, to Hawai'i—only to discover that Jiro, after years of work as an itinerant laborer, had saved enough money to move to faraway California, where he was eventually able to purchase his own farm.

Etsuko had never cared much for Jiro but was still alarmed by her husband's demeanor. "Taizo, what is it? Is Jiro all right?"

"He has a rich man's problem. Says the farm has grown too large for him to manage on his own."

"How large *is* it?"

"A hundred acres. A huge estate by any measure." He read: "'All of my daughters have married and I have only my son Akira to help me. The farm is not producing as abundantly as it once did, and I have need of someone with your experience. You always were the better farmer, little brother.'"

Etsuko could see the pride in Taizo's eyes as he looked up, but she couldn't help frowning. "A braggart's flattery is not worth filling a thimble."

Taizo ignored this, finished reading: "'And so I humbly ask you, Taizo, to give due consideration to becoming my partner in the farm.'"

Etsuko was genuinely astonished. *"What?"*

"He is serious. He says he will give me half ownership in the farm if I—if we—move to California."

Etsuko, as stunned as if Jiro had reached across the Pacific to swat her on the head, sank slowly onto a *zabuton* at the dining table.

Taizo had expected this response and said dryly, "Such fervid displays of enthusiasm are most unseemly, *Okāsan*."

She looked up at him, in no mood for jokes. "You cannot be serious."

"Land, Etsuko! We can own our own *land*, as we always dreamed of."

"Land in Hawai'i, yes," she countered. "We have built a life *here*, fifteen years' worth. You would toss all that aside?"

"I would exchange it for a better life, in California."

"And what of the *keiki*?" She had been here so long she used the Hawaiian word as a matter of course.

"Children can adapt to any circumstance."

Etsuko shook her head. "I don't understand any of this. Why doesn't he just hire someone to help him?"

"Because he wants *me*, his brother. Is that so unusual?"

"It is for Jiro."

"Etsuko, believe me. I would not consider moving you and the children across another ocean just because Jiro's words please me."

"Then why?"

Taizo sat down beside her. "You know why. I love farming. Not laboring on a plantation, but our own farm, growing the food my family eats and the crops we sell—as my ancestors did. And if this is not my ancestors' land, it would be ours to bequeath, in part, to Haruo and his children. You knew me in Hōfuna—have you ever seen me as happy doing anything else?"

Etsuko saw the light in his eyes and knew she could not deny him. In Japan, a husband would not even have bothered to discuss this with his wife. But this was America, and it had worked its alchemy on Taizo as it did on all who settled there.

She softened, trying to put aside her trepidation. "You say he offers— half ownership?"

"It would have to be done in Haruo's name once he comes of age, since noncitizens cannot own land in California. The other half is in Akira's name, since he is an American citizen. There is more than enough land for us all."

She had to admit to herself, it was a substantial offer.

"It *would* be a blessing," she allowed, "to be able to pass on land to our children. Would it not?"

He nodded.

She considered a long moment—then forced a smile, feigning an excitement she hoped someday to feel.

Here, in the privacy of their home, she tenderly put a hand on his.

"Then when the children come home from school," she said, "we shall tell them they are about to go on an exciting new adventure—in California."

The joy in his face made her heart sing.

"We will have a better life. Trust me."

She smiled. "I always have."

Their children would have been quite shocked, then, to see their decorous, undemonstrative parents seal that trust—with a long, ardent kiss.

Chapter 4

*I*t was early in April of 1895—just before the start of the school year in Okayama-ken—when Jiro, then fifteen, invited Taizo, twelve, on a fishing trip to the Asahi River. The sky was overcast with a light wind combing the water's surface, which Jiro preferred: *"The fish don't move as much on a cloudy, windy day."* His theory seemed to be borne out. At first they caught only tiny tanago, *but soon they were pulling in some of the larger, rainbow-hued* kyusen, *a few smaller* shiro-gisu, *and finally, one or two big* suzuki, *Japanese bass. The flopping, twitching fish soon filled the big metal bucket they had brought along. But before they turned to the long trek back to Hōfuna, Jiro spontaneously began stripping off his work jacket.*

"What are you doing, Niisan?" *Taizo asked.*

"Going for a swim." Jiro slipped his shoes and trousers off and stood there in his undergarments. "Race you across!"

"The water seems a little cold," Taizo noted warily.

"If you are afraid of a little cold water," Jiro taunted, "then stay here with your tail between your legs until I return." He dove into the crystalline waters.

The taunt stung, as usual, and Taizo began peeling off his clothes. He really didn't want to go swimming, but he would not let Jiro think he was afraid. He jumped in, and the frigid slap of the water chilled him to his marrow.

But Jiro was happily swimming across the river and Taizo was damned if he would get out now. Stroke for stroke, he followed his elder brother.

At this point, the Asahi was fairly narrow—barely a hundred-odd yards wide—so swimming across it was hardly difficult. And Taizo had to admit that it was lovely looking up at the mountains, like towering green pagodas on either side of the river.

They swam to the other shore and back again. Jiro won, of course. When Taizo emerged from the water the wind gave him goose pimples, but he followed Jiro's example of toweling off with his jacket, then dressed quickly and picked up his fishing pole and the bucket of fish they had caught.

Soon the wind raking his wet jacket set Taizo's teeth to chattering, and though at first Jiro joked about this, he quickly realized his brother's discomfort. "Here, let me take those," he said, grabbing Taizo's fishing pole and the bucket of fish. Taizo nodded his thanks, then crossed his arms and tried in vain to warm himself with his hands, like a wet match that could not be lit.

When they got home Taizo barely ate his supper, was allowed to take a hot bath in the furo even before his father, and then went straight to bed.

By morning he was running a high fever. The doctor arrived and grimly diagnosed Taizo as having "winter fever," pneumonia. He prescribed a treatment regimen that would only increase Taizo's discomfort: hot mustard plaster on his chest, back, and soles of his feet, to bring the fever down; yaito, the application of burning herbs; and the drinking of fluids Taizo preferred not to think about, such as the blood of a carp and an extract of boiled earthworms.

And bed rest. Complete bed rest for—how long? No one could know.

Privately, Jiro apologized to Taizo for goading him into swimming but asked that Taizo not tell their parents it was his idea. As usual, Taizo complied.

Taizo would remain bedridden for the next six months, getting worse before he got better, coming close to losing his battle with the winter fever. In fact, he would *have* lost it, if not for . . .

* * *

Taizo sighed, reminded again—as if it were ever in question—that Mayonaka was not happy. Her miseries had begun with her being unceremoniously forced into a small cage and then obliged to share quarters with assorted dogs, cats, parrots, and cockatoos on the lower deck of the Oriental Steamship Company's *America Maru*. The Watanabes had booked second-class passage bound for San Francisco—the whole family sharing a single cabin with six bunks and a communal bathroom in the passageway—but pets traveled steerage. Ruth had spent as much time as she could belowdecks, stroking Mayonaka's head through the wire mesh of her cage for as long as *Okāsan* allowed her to stay—or until they both grew seasick in the rocking bowels of the ship.

The cat was relatively sedate up to the boarding of the train, but from the first blast of the steam whistle she had made her disapproval known with her aria of *miaow*s. Even now Ruth was gently stroking the cat's neck through the cage as she whispered consoling words to her. Taizo smiled with affection at his daughter's compassion; she had indeed been a worthy choice.

Outside the train window a landscape grander than he had expected was rolling past. The Southern Pacific Railroad cut through the plains south of Sacramento like stitches through a floral quilt; on either side of the train were fields embroidered with pink, yellow, blue, and violet wildflowers, fertile vineyards bursting with fruit, and acre upon acre of strawberry plants, their green bouquets extending in long rows to the horizon. Standing astride the fields were lofty towers crowned by windmills that spun like a child's pinwheel, pumping water to the thirsty plants.

So much sky, so much land—everything was on a much grander scale than in Hōfuna. But farmland was farmland, and it always made Taizo feel at home.

The train slowed as it approached the tiny Florin depot. As soon as it stopped, the ice-packed freight cars began taking on hundreds of crates of strawberries for delivery to Sacramento. As Taizo's family got off the train, Jiro's only son—twenty-four, tanned, broad-shouldered—stood waiting for them, wearing a dark Western business suit for the occasion. He gave a deep, respectful bow.

"*Konnichiwa, Ojisan,*" he greeted Taizo. "I am Akira. My father has asked me to bring you to our farm. We are honored by your presence."

Taizo returned the bow. "The honor is ours, nephew," he replied in Japanese. He allowed the young man to pick up some of their luggage, while he signaled his own sons to carry the rest of the bags and steamer trunks.

"It may be a bumpy ride in back for some of you. My apologies for the shortcomings of our vehicle," Akira said with typical Japanese self-deprecation.

But the "vehicle" turned out to be a handsome, nearly new Ford Model TT truck, its wooden stake bed painted a glossy green, the cab and chassis a shiny black. Taizo had seen rich *haoles* driving this kind of truck in Honolulu; he was amazed and impressed that Jiro owned one.

"Nonsense," Taizo said. "We shall be honored to ride in such fine style. *Okāsan*, you and Dai sit up front with Akira. The boys and I will ride in back."

With one hand on the steering wheel and the other on the hand throttle, Akira backed the truck—making its signature, deep-throated *chugga-chugga*—out of the train station. Florin's business district in 1923 was a dusty collection of wooden storefronts that seemed plucked from a Tom Mix movie, but for one difference: the majority of the stores boasted Japanese names. Hayashi Fish Shop, Kawamura Tofu Company, T. Tanikawa General Merchandise . . . Taizo had not seen so many *nihonjin*, Japanese, names in one neighborhood since leaving Japan! He felt even more at home now.

But as the truck passed the Florin Supply Company, Taizo caught a brief glimpse of a chipped and faded poster nailed to its wall, flapping defiantly in the breeze, reading:

KEEP CALIFORNIA WHITE

RE-ELECT

JAMES D. PHELAN

UNITED STATES SENATOR

And then they were past it, Taizo not quite putting together the jumble of English words and quickly forgetting it amid the excitement.

They drove up a dirt road, past flourishing fields of strawberries and grapes. Each plot of land seemed enormous to Taizo, as did the American-style homes: clapboard walls painted white, green, or blue, mostly one-story, with adjacent barns or laborers' barracks. Farmhands—largely Japanese, men and women, adults and youngsters—were out picking grapes.

Finally, Akira turned, heading for a two-story home in the distance. The land surrounding it was as expansive as Taizo had been told. The house, painted white with green trim, was much larger than its nearest neighbors; its front porch was decorated with *bonsai* trees in pots, their saucer-shaped branches meticulously trimmed. Akira parked the truck and helped Etsuko, Ruth, and the caged Mayonaka out of the cab. Taizo and his sons folded down the back of the stake bed and jumped out.

Ruth took in the adjoining barn and pasture with delight. "Cow! You have a cow! And horses!" A lone dairy cow grazed in the pasture, while two horses—one tan, the other black—chewed hay in the barn.

"Ah! You must be Dai!" came a deep, booming voice speaking excellent English.

A tall, strapping man wearing the same kind of dark business suit as Akira, his broad face split by a big grin, strode over, bent down, and lifted Ruth as easily as he might a bowl of rice. She giggled to find her legs dangling in the air like the strings of a kite. "Such a pretty little girl! And you like animals? Well, we have plenty of them here for you. Get yourself unpacked and Akira will introduce you to our cow, Mamie. Have you ever milked a cow, Dai?"

"Only by accident."

"You will have to tell me about that sometime."

He lowered her to the ground, as Taizo—intimidated, as usual, by his brother's outsized personality—approached, bowed, and said in Japanese, "It is good to see you again, *Niisan*. You remember my wife, Etsuko?"

Jiro bowed to her. "Of course. It has been too long since I have seen my beautiful sister-in-law."

"Indeed, too long," Etsuko answered with apparent, if not sincere, warmth.

Taizo introduced his sons to Jiro's wife, Nishi—as shrinking a presence as her husband was gregarious—and Akira's wife, Tamiko. After everyone removed their shoes, they were led by Jiro into the house. It was a traditional American structure, and in many ways it reflected that culture, notably a tall Western-style dining table made of oak, with matching chairs. A piano stood near the window, its pearl-white keys reminding Etsuko uneasily of Jiro's broad smile. But there were Japanese accents as well, stylish ones: the polished wood floors were decorated by elegantly woven *tatami* mats, a Japanese scroll hung in a *tokonoma* alcove, and tables and cabinets were ornamented with blue and white ceramic vases, bowls, teacups, and plates, their faces adorned with delicate designs of mountains, sea, and sky.

"Welcome, my family," Jiro said expansively, "to your new home."

"And a grand home it is, *Niisan*," Taizo complimented him.

"Taizo, this is America. We need not stand on tradition. I am not *Niisan*, just Jiro. We are equals in this farm and in my heart."

Taizo was quite touched by this, nodding in response. "As you wish."

As Jiro showed them about, Taizo's astonishment only multiplied. The living room boasted both a wood console phonograph *and* a radio receiver. The kitchen was also a fount of technological wonders, equipped with a wall telephone and an electric washing machine with a steel tub—two marvels Taizo had only ever glimpsed in the pages of the Sears, Roebuck catalog.

Jiro escorted them to their bedrooms on the second floor. He and Nishi shared one, Akira and Tamiko another. The others—once occupied by Jiro's three daughters—were quickly assigned to Ruth's brothers, with one, as in Honolulu, to be occupied by Taizo, Etsuko, and Ruth. All the rooms were furnished not with *futon*s but with beds, but Taizo made no complaint.

"Are we going to live *here*?" Ruth asked her mother wonderingly.

"Yes, it is quite a palace, is it not, butterfly?"

"Can we let Mayonaka out now?"

"Yes, I think so."

Ruth eagerly opened the cage and swung the door open wide. But Mayonaka no longer seemed so eager to get out. "Come on, it's all right," Ruth cooed, finally giving her a little nudge. Mayonaka padded out very slowly indeed, hissed once, then darted under the bed.

Etsuko smiled. "Let her be, Dai. She just needs to adjust to this new place. We will bring her up some supper later."

"There are days I feel like that myself," Jiro said with a laugh. "Do not worry, Dai. She will emerge in her own time." He turned to his brother. "While the women settle in, Taizo, may I show you some of my— *our* land?"

* * *

hey walked at least a mile into the fields, Jiro proudly showing off the farm, Taizo enjoying the warmth of the sun and a cooling breeze. The hundred acres were covered with green, leafy strawberry plants—marching in rows east to west, to reduce shading—interspersed with trellises bearing flame-red Tokay grapes ripening on vines. It made their little vineyard in Hōfuna seem like a window garden.

"Grapes, as you know," Jiro said in Japanese, "take five years to mature. So the strawberries produce a marketable crop in the meantime. We dig our irrigation ditches two feet deep, every other row, to conserve moisture, thus allowing the plants to yield two, sometimes three harvests a year."

"Remarkable," Taizo said.

"Florin's soil is ideal for growing strawberries. It's shallow and it rests on a bed of hardpan, which helps the soil retain water."

"From the train I saw the windmills irrigating the fields. So water is easily obtainable?"

"Plentiful. Sink a well anywhere, you find water."

"These grapes are ripe," Taizo noted, puzzled. "Why isn't anyone out here picking them? I saw other farms harvesting their vineyards."

Jiro winced, as if he had hoped the question might never be raised.

"Ah, well," Jiro sighed, "as they say, 'God dwells in the details.'"

"You said in your letter that you needed my help because the farm was no longer producing as well as it once did, but from what I can see, the opposite is true. You underestimate your skill as a farmer, Jiro."

But instead of the familiar gleam of pleasure in his eyes at a compliment, Jiro actually looked dejected.

"I am not worthy of such praise, Taizo."

These were sentiments never before uttered by Jiro Watanabe, at least not in Taizo's presence.

"There is no one harvesting the grapes," Jiro admitted, "because I lack the funds to hire enough skilled laborers."

Taizo did not know what to make of this. "Is this a joke?"

"I wish that it were. This, you see, is why I need your assistance."

"To . . . harvest your crop?"

"Yes."

The implications of this began to sink in. "*My* assistance," Taizo asked sharply, "or my *family's* assistance?"

Jiro sighed again.

"Both," he admitted, eyes downcast.

Taizo said in disbelief, "You expect me and my sons to harvest a hundred acres by ourselves? That is why you called me here?"

"Not just you and your sons," Jiro said quickly. "Of course Akira, Tamiko, and Nishi and I will all help."

"And what of my sons' schooling?"

"We have a few weeks before school begins in September. We won't be able to harvest *all* the grapes, of course, since some mature late in the season, but we should be able to pick enough to make a profit."

"Surely you have *some* money to pay laborers—" Taizo began, but Jiro interrupted:

"You do not understand how things work here, Taizo. At the start of the season, we owners receive an advance from the fruit distributors against the strawberry harvest. We live on that, use it to pay our expenses, until the crop is harvested, and the cycle is repeated with the next crop."

"Then you must have received an advance against the grape harvest."

"Similarly, we buy food from the grocer and provisions from the supply store against the harvest—"

Taizo abruptly cut him off: "What happened to the advance for the grape harvest?"

Jiro looked deflated, defeated. "Gone. All the money is all gone."

"Where did it go?"

"To pay interest on debt, among other things."

Taizo's mind was reeling. "Debt?"

Jiro revealed, shame-faced, "I owe money to everyone—the distributors, the supply store, the grocer, and the Sumitomo Bank in Sacramento, where Akira took on a second mortgage against the property."

Taizo's incredulity was giving way to anger. "And you wish *my* eldest son to someday take on half that debt? How much is it?"

Jiro could not look him in the eye as he said, "Five thousand dollars."

Taizo could not have been more stunned had five thousand gold bars just fallen on his head.

"*Five thousand dollars?*"

"Agriculture runs in cycles, Taizo, you know this. Before the war, times were hard; we eked out a living. Afterward, the economy improved, and—"

"You bought a six-hundred-dollar truck!" Taizo shouted, surprising even himself. "You own a phonograph, a radio, an electric dishwasher—"

"I only wished my family to be comfortable after years of struggle!"

"No, you wished to brag to your neighbors about how wealthy you were and have them envy your fine possessions," Taizo shot back. "So you spend and spend, letting your debt grow and grow—and *then*—"

Truly, Taizo had never been angrier in his life. He took a step toward his brother, his hands clenched into fists. "*Then* you offer me half of your great estate, without mentioning its great *debt* as well—and believing in you, as always, I uproot my family and close my business! And for what? To be your *chattel* and to take on half your—"

His words ended in a cry of inchoate fury. Barely aware he was doing it, Taizo took a wild swing at his brother. His fist connected with Jiro's mouth, splitting his lip, and Jiro toppled like a felled tree onto a row of strawberries.

Taizo stood above him, breathing hard, but Jiro made no move to get up. He wiped blood from his lip, his face filled not with anger but with shame.

"I believe I had that coming," he said softly.

"That? *That* was for giving me pneumonia when I was twelve!" Taizo yelled. "I have not even begun to address *this* situation!"

"I apologize for deceiving you," Jiro said. "But would you have come had I told you the truth?"

"No! I would have been a fool to come. I *am* a fool to have come!"

Taizo's dreams came crashing down like a fallen star. He had no money left to return to Honolulu. He and his family were marooned here, shipwrecked on an island of debt and deceit. The sky, which minutes ago had appeared so infinite and welcoming, now seemed to press down on him. He felt caught in a vise of guilt and shame.

As he struggled to breathe, he heard sobs, and thought: My shame is complete, I am weeping.

But it was not Taizo weeping. It was Jiro.

"I am sorry," Jiro gasped out between sobs. "I have dishonored my family's name. I have dishonored you, my brother. I am sorry."

Only once had Taizo seen a grown man cry—his father, on the day Taizo's youngest brother, born prematurely, died within hours of birth.

Seeing Jiro brought so low quelled the fury in Taizo's heart and allowed him to think rationally again. He had no other prospects in California. What else could he do but to make the best of a bad situation? He drew a long breath to calm himself.

Taizo stepped forward and extended a hand to Jiro.

"Get up, *Niisan*," he said, and the implied respect in that word so startled Jiro that he stopped weeping.

Taizo helped him to his feet.

"I would be dishonored if I allowed my own brother to lose face," he told him. "My family and I will help you with the grape harvest. And I will look at your accounting and see if there is any way to reduce your financial burden. Once Haruo comes of age, we will see. I will not burden my eldest son with your debt, at least not unless I can find a way to expunge it.

"And I insist on one thing: from this point on *I* will manage your business, since you are obviously incapable of doing so."

"Yes. Yes, whatever you say, Taizo. Thank you."

"And the first thing we are going to do is sell that damned Ford truck. Even if we only get thirty cents on the dollar, that will help pay for laborers to finish picking the grapes and perhaps the next strawberry crop too."

"What! But how will I transport my crop to market?"

"You have two horses. Do you still have a wagon?"

"Yes, but . . ."

"Today we use your expensive telephone to look for a buyer for the truck. Tomorrow we hitch horses to the wagon and work begins in earnest."

That evening, Taizo got up the nerve to tell Etsuko what their true circumstances were, bracing himself for a justifiably furious response. But after the initial shock, Etsuko could plainly see the shame in her husband's eyes—and chose not to worsen it. She said only, "Well. We had best get to bed, then. It will be an early morning tomorrow."

They rose before dawn, Etsuko and Nishi putting large pots of coffee and tea on the stove and preparing a breakfast of rice, dried fish, *natto*—fermented soybeans—*miso* soup, and eggs.

By six A.M. they were in the fields. Etsuko had worked long hours with Taizo at Waimānalo but had never picked grapes before; she and the boys had to be shown what to do. Jiro and Taizo handed out "picking knives" with sharp, scythelike blades, as Taizo demonstrated their proper use.

Ruth was too young to be put to work, so she was free to play in the fields, running between rows of strawberry plants, chasing fleecy clouds propelled by swift winds, and digging holes to lovingly examine the insects, worms, and garden snakes that made their home in the earth. When she tired of this, Jiro took her to the pasture and showed her how to milk a cow.

"Very good!" he said as Ruth's small hands produced a dribble of milk from the cow's udder. "From now on you are the official family cow milker!"

"I like it here, Uncle Jiro," Ruth said, beaming.

"I am glad someone does," he replied, his meaning lost on her.

The rest of the Watanabe clan was having considerably less fun as, stooped over, they cut and picked the grapes, swatting away predatory wasps and occasionally nicking themselves with their knives. As the picking baskets filled up with fruit, Nishi and Etsuko took them to the cool interior of the barn, where they trimmed and cleaned them, then gently placed them into wooden boxes that were to be delivered daily to the Florin Fruit Growers Association—which then transferred them to train cars, packed with ice, to be shipped east.

At noon they paused to eat lunch—rice, dried fish, pickled radish—from their *bentō* boxes and later sang Japanese songs as they worked to keep their spirits up. By the end of a long, backbreaking day they were all aching and weary, but no one complained. Tonight all anyone wanted was a hearty dinner, a hot bath, and a good night's sleep—knowing full well they would wake the next morning before dawn and start all over again.

As Nishi began to serve supper to Taizo and Jiro first, Taizo saw the hunger in his family's eyes and suggested, "Inasmuch as we have all worked equally hard today, perhaps from now on everyone should be served at the same time." Jiro made no objection, and another tradition toppled that day.

Late that night—after Ruth had fallen asleep and Taizo and Etsuko lay uncomfortably in bed, struggling to fall asleep on a mattress much softer than their familiar *futon*—Taizo said, quietly, into the darkness: "I am sorry, *Okāsan*. I should have listened to you. You were right about him."

After a moment she replied, "What does the proverb say? 'Let the things of long ago drift away on the water.'"

She reached out, took his hand in hers, and they lay like that until exhaustion claimed them.

On Sunday, after Taizo and Jiro had returned from Sacramento—where they sold the truck for enough money to hire itinerant laborers to help pick the remainder of the crop—the family was just sitting down to dinner when there was a knock on the front door. Jiro opened it. Standing on his doorstep was the local sheriff, a white man in his fifties with a rugged, tanned face and a sturdy build. He was wearing work denims and boots and chewing something that might have been tobacco.

"Evening, Watanabe-*san*," he said, his emphasis making it sound less like an honorific than a pejorative. He peered inside. "Sorry. Didn't mean to interrupt your supper."

Even from where he sat, Taizo could see that Jiro was startled.

"Perfectly all right. What can I do for you, Sheriff Dreesen?"

"I understand you got some family who've moved in with you."

"Yes. My brother and his family have come from Hawai'i to help me with the farm."

"I'd like to meet your brother. And see his passport. If you don't mind."

The tone in his voice indicated this was not merely a request.

Jiro turned and said, "Taizo—"

"Yes, I heard. I shall get it." Taizo went upstairs, retrieved his Japanese passport from his luggage, and came back to find his brother and Dreesen still standing on opposite sides of the doorway.

"I don't much like takin' off my shoes," Dreesen said. "Mind if we talk outside?"

Taizo and Jiro put on their shoes, closing the door behind them. Jiro said, "Taizo, this is Joseph Dreesen. He is a local farmer and also serves as sheriff for the town of Florin. Mr. Dreesen, my brother Taizo."

Dreesen just nodded and chewed. Taizo gave him his passport.

"It's my understanding of immigration law," Dreesen said, opening the passport, "that Japanese nationals in Hawai'i are prohibited from emigrating to California, or anywhere else in the mainland United States."

"That is true," Jiro said. "But exceptions are made for close family and for those coming to work on established farms in which they have a financial interest, as my brother does."

Dreesen flipped through the passport with evident disdain, then laughed shortly.

"You wily Japs always have all the angles figured, don't you?" he said, dropping any pretense of civility.

He handed the document back to Taizo. "Let's take a walk."

He started out into the fields; all Jiro and Taizo could do was follow. "Looks like you got a good crop of Tokays this year," Dreesen noted.

"Thank you."

"Twenty-five years ago, white men owned all this land," Dreesen said, squinting into the distance. "Like they owned all the shops in Florin. You Japs couldn't be satisfied sharecropping or leasing our land, you had to go buy it all out from under us."

Dreesen turned and spat tobacco juice onto a strawberry plant.

Jiro's face hardened. "We bought low-quality land that white men did not want and with hard work turned it into productive farmland."

"You put native-born Californians out of work, then set about breedin' like rats till you outnumbered real Americans."

Taizo could only listen in disbelief.

"There are still many white farmers here in Florin," Jiro pointed out, "and most of them have no problem with us. They only go to your Anti-Japanese League meetings because you intimidate them into coming. They fear the league will do damage to their ranches and farms."

Anti-Japanese League? Taizo tried not to show his alarm.

"You got a smart mouth, Watanabe," Dreesen snapped. "Just like those fifty-eight Jap bastards who got rode out of Turlock on a rail."

"Is that why you are here, Sheriff?" Jiro asked. "To 'ride' us out of town? Because you will not find us so easily ridden."

Dreesen spat out more tobacco juice and smiled. "Actually, I came here to help you, Watanabe-*san*."

Jiro laughed. "We do not need your help."

"Mr. Ochida says otherwise. Good man. I lease forty acres to his son— they make money, I make money, I keep the land. The way things used to be. Anyways, Mr. Ochida says you're in debt to the tune of five thousand dollars."

Jiro said nothing. Dreesen took a step closer. "I'm willing to buy your whole spread, including the house, for six thousand dollars. Hell, that'll give you enough of a grubstake to go back to Japan if you want."

"I do not wish to return to Japan. Why are you making this offer?"

"So's I can get another hundred acres outta the hands of Japs like you and back into the hands of white Christian men, where it belongs."

Barely concealing his contempt, Jiro said, "I am not interested."

"Then you're a goddamn fool. You Japs are damn good farmers, I give you that—but even the best of you couldn't get out from under that kind of debt. And you ain't the best Jap farmer 'round here by a long shot. Sixty-five hundred, top dollar."

"How do you put it? 'No deal.'"

Dreesen looked at him stonily for a moment, then just shrugged.

"No skin off my nose if the bank forecloses on this place," he said. "Least then it'll be goin' back to the white man. But if you change your mind, I'd prefer to *be* that white man." He turned to Taizo, nodded, and said with fine-tuned sarcasm, "Welcome to California, Taizo-*san*."

As Dreesen walked away, Taizo saw that Jiro's hands were trembling with rage and—fear?

"'Anti-Japanese League'?" Taizo said.

"Yes. They meet in Redmen's Hall. But they are hardly the only ones who hate us. There is the Oriental Exclusion League, the Native Sons and Daughters of the Golden West, the Anti-Asiatic League . . ."

"Have they ever done what you said? Damage someone's property?"

"Not here, not yet. But in Turlock a mob of several hundred white men—with the help of the local police—did round up fifty-eight *nihonjin* workers, forced them onto a train, and told them never to return."

"They hate us because we buy farms? And make a success of it?"

"Yes. And because they hate and fear the country we come from. They lust for a war between Japan and America. So Dreesen tells *Collier's Weekly* and the *Sacramento Bee* that we have 'taken over' Florin and Walnut Grove and we will take over all the farmland in all of California unless we are stopped. And these articles keep stoked the fires of war."

Taizo felt as frightened as he did incredulous.

"I encountered little prejudice against Japanese in Hawai'i," he said. "We were a part of the community."

"You are no longer in Hawai'i, Taizo. For which I must apologize again." He started back to the house. "No need to tell the family about this."

Taizo nodded dully. He felt unmoored, and afraid. He had dragged his family across an ocean to a failing farm in a land of race hatreds. He only prayed that he could keep his children protected from men such as Dreesen and from the bigotry and malice that made their cold hearts beat.

In September Horace enrolled at Elk Grove Union High School—Elk Grove being the next nearest town to Florin. Ruth, Stanley, and Ralph were to attend Florin Grammar School. On the first day of class the three of them—guided by several neighbor children, white and Japanese—traipsed through vineyards to Pritchett and McNie Roads, cutting behind Redmen's Hall on Florin Road, then crossed the Southern Pacific Railroad tracks. They passed the Florin Basket Factory, Morita's Barber Shop, and Nakayama's Shoe Repair before arriving at the schoolhouse on McComber Road. It was a U-shaped, green stucco building with a tar-paper roof, and inside the corridors were filled with students both Caucasian and Japanese. Ruth, excited and eager to make new friends, made her way to the second-grade classroom only to be told by a teacher to report to the *first-*grade homeroom. "I've already been to first grade," Ruth objected, but the teacher was adamant. She marched her into the first-grade room, where Ruth reluctantly took an empty desk next to a friendly Nisei girl, who said, "Hi, you new?"

Ruth nodded. "Just moved here."

"From where?"

"Hawai'i."

"Wow, I never met anyone from Hawai'i before! I'm Chieko Yamoto, my friends call me Cricket."

"Ruth Watanabe."

"How old are you?"

"Seven."

"Me too. I should be in second grade, but at the end of last year the principal demoted every Japanese student up to fifth grade, on account of our English wasn't good enough and we needed a year to make up."

"That's what they did to me," Ruth said, "even though I took first grade already in Honolulu!"

"Your English sounds good to me."

"So does yours."

A white girl in front of them turned in her seat and introduced herself to Ruth as Phyllis. "Yeah—goofy, isn't it?" she said, then to Ruth: "You're from Hawai'i? Can you do the hula?"

"No."

"You ever been to Waikīkī Beach?"

"Oh sure. Lots of times."

"Yeah? What's it—"

Just then the teacher entered and quieted the room: "Settle down now, class. I'm Mrs. Jenkins. I teach first grade."

"We know," Cricket called out. "We were here last year!"

The students laughed. Mrs. Jenkins smiled a nervous, ill-at-ease little smile. "Yes. Well. Before I take the roll, I need you to listen carefully." Looking as if she would rather not be doing this, she said: "Will all the *non*-Japanese students please stand up, take your schoolbooks, and line up at the door."

There were puzzled murmurs from everyone in the room.

"Class, please do as I tell you," Mrs. Jenkins said, more emphatically.

The white girl, Phyllis, turned to Ruth and Cricket, shrugged, and joined in as the white students obediently got up and formed a line at the door. Another teacher entered the classroom and asked, "Are they ready?"

"Yes," Mrs. Jenkins replied, voice quavering a bit.

"Good. Students, follow me."

As the teacher led them out of the room, Cricket leaned over to Ruth and whispered, "That's Miss Thomas. She's nasty. If she catches you speaking Japanese in class, she'll make you stay after school."

This was all baffling. Mrs. Jenkins tried to distract the Nisei students by asking them to open their English primers. This worked until they heard the sounds of students gathering on the lawn—at which point all of the remaining pupils rushed to the windows to look out, over Mrs. Jenkins' objections.

Ruth saw dozens of white children standing in a line that wrapped around the building, while teachers passed out little American flags on sticks to each one. Then, after roll had been taken, the teachers proceeded to march them away from the school, westward down Florin Road.

"Where are they taking them?" Ruth asked.

"They'll be fine, class, they'll be going to school somewhere else, that's all. Now, let's all get back to our—"

"Why?" Ruth asked.

"Why what?"

"Why are they going to another school and we're not?"

Her patience exhausted, Mrs. Jenkins declared, "Back to your seats, everyone, this minute!"

Ruth took one last look at her new friend Phyllis, disappearing down Florin Road, and wondered if she would ever see her again. She hadn't even gotten to tell her what Waikīkī Beach was like.

Chapter 5

1923–1930

ater, the parents of the Japanese students learned that their white classmates had been led across the railroad tracks to the Florin Community Hall, where they would attend classes for a few weeks until a new red-brick, two-story school building could be completed for them. They were shocked and anguished at this latest indignity. Issei—Japanese nationals—were already prohibited by law from ever becoming American citizens; the Alien Land Laws forbade them from owning land in their own names; and now their children were being treated as inferiors, undesirables, unworthy of studying alongside their white neighbors. The only consolation was that the Japanese and *hakujin*—white—children were, in fact, neighbors. Although segregated during the school day, the Nisei continued to play as they always had with their white friends—fielding softball teams on vacant land or sharing chocolate cones at Kato's Ice Cream Parlor. If the school board's goal had been to separate the races socially, it failed miserably.

Despite all this, Etsuko liked living in Florin. It was a close-knit, rural community not unlike the one she and Taizo had grown up in. Their closest neighbors—the Nobusos, the Kishabas, the Nakamuras, and the Isas—were hardworking, generous people. So were the people she and Taizo met at the Florin Buddhist Church. During one of the first services they attended, Reverend Tsuda quoted Buddha's words: "Do not dwell in the past, do not dream of the future, concentrate the mind on the present moment." This was wise advice, and Taizo and Etsuko sought to heed it by casting aside their *setsubō*—longing—for their old life and embracing this, the only life they had.

Surely the finest exemplar of this was their own daughter. Ruth was flourishing like a transplanted flower in the fertile soil of Florin, whether picking handfuls of juicy wild blackberries or patiently watching an orange-and-black monarch butterfly emerge from its chrysalis. Cricket, her ebullient new friend, eagerly showed her all the best and muddiest places to play. But Ruth never tired of the playground of their farm, whether she was feeding and watering the horses, Bucky and Blackie, milking the cow, or collecting eggs from the henhouse as she greeted each chicken personally: "*Konnichiwa*, Isabel. What do you have for us today? Oooh, what a big egg! Good girl!"

As her years in Florin piled up like eggs in a basket, they crowded out most of her memories of Hawai'i, including the four years she had spent at Kapi'olani Home. She still went to bed hugging her stuffed cow, and though it remained a source of comfort, she no longer remembered who gave it to her.

But there was one reminder of those days and Ruth thought of it each time she looked in a mirror or heard the voices around her at dinnertime: she neither looked nor sounded quite like the rest of her family. Yes, her eyes were the same, but her skin was slightly darker, her nose a bit wider, her whole face a little broader than anyone else's. That word, *hapa*, still stung, like a wasp in the fields. It wasn't until her tenth birthday—her actual birthday, February 8—when she could articulate her feelings that she asked Etsuko, "*Okāsan?* Why did my—Hawaiian mother give me up?" In a small voice: "Didn't she love me?"

"Oh, butterfly," Etsuko said, "I am sure she did. But she had no choice."

"Why not?"

"You are not old enough to understand, little one. But I am certain that she would have kept you if she had been able. Do not judge her for that."

"Did you know her?"

"No. But I know what is in a mother's heart, and I am sure she loved you." She took Ruth's hands in hers and squeezed them. "And wherever she is, I am sure she would be happy to know that you have a mother and a father and brothers who love you more than you can know."

Ruth smiled, mollified by her mother's assurances—for now.

For nearly seven years Taizo had done his best to trim the farm's expenses while increasing its yield. He succeeded in making the mortgage payments in full and on time, and slowly their bank ledger ceased bleeding money. Taizo still felt shame and anger for allowing himself to be duped into giving up everything they had in Hawai'i for this cruel lie. But at least their credit was now good and they were taking in more money than they were losing, even in the midst of the financial recession that had begun that year.

All of that progress came to an end on October 29, 1929.

The stock market crash was an earthquake felt first in New York City, but it wasn't long before its temblors radiated across the continent and shook the foundations of everything Taizo had been building. Public uncertainty about the economy reduced consumption, and food prices plummeted into a financial chasm.

Bank foundations were rattled too, as depositors demanded to withdraw their money, only to be faced with long lines and empty hands. Then, unthinkably, banks across the nation began to collapse into insolvency—financial sinkholes swallowing up the life savings of tens of thousands of working-class people. The banks that were still standing, desperate for cash, called in all their loans.

Sumitomo Bank in Sacramento called in the balance of Jiro's loan—$4,500—due immediately, or face foreclosure.

Panicked, Taizo and Jiro first sought an advance on their strawberry harvest from Mr. Nojiri, who distributed their berries through Nojiri and Company. He was a kind, generous man, always willing to help out a farmer when he could, but this went beyond his financial auspices.

They hastily tried to put together a *tanomoshi*—a kind of collective loan cooperative dating back to *samurai* days—but their neighbors, though sympathetic, were also struggling to stay afloat in the tidal wake of the crash.

Taizo and Jiro, desperate to spare their wives and children the specter of potential homelessness, kept their own counsel. Together they walked down to Elder Creek, a small stream lazing through lush woods of Douglas fir and spreading oak trees. The sheltering canopy of leaves and the whispering rush of the water afforded some privacy as well as a moment of needed serenity, reminding them both of their boyhoods in Hōfuna.

It did not take long for them to decide that there was only one man in Florin with the funds to purchase their debt, and that was Joseph Dreesen.

"He did offer us sixty-five hundred dollars for the land," Taizo noted.

"Seven years ago. He will not offer us that much again. Not in these times," Jiro noted. "And even if he were to offer us enough to pay off the debt, what then? Where do we go? What do we do?"

Taizo considered a moment, then suggested, "What if we . . . offer to sell him *most* of the land but hold back ten or twenty acres for ourselves to farm? To support our family, nothing more?"

"An interesting idea," Jiro allowed.

"Our *only* idea."

"True enough."

"And if he says no?"

Jiro sighed. "I worked as an itinerant laborer as a young man. I am not so old that I cannot do so again."

"Nor I, if we are even fortunate enough to find work. But condemning our children to such a life . . . that would break my heart."

Jiro nodded. He watched as a steelhead trout swam just below the surface of the creek, tail flicking as it followed the current.

"Like that fish, we can only go where the stream takes us," he said.

Taizo nodded, not happy to be reduced to a metaphoric fish.

The next day they met Dreesen in his rustic office in back of the Florin Feed & Supply Company. His hair was a little grayer, but his face and arms were still as tanned as an old leather hide, and he greeted them from behind his walnut desk with characteristic bluntness.

"Watanabe-*san*." He smiled like a wolf that had scented its prey.

"Mr. Ochida told me you tried to put together some kind of Jap loan association. I figured it wouldn't be long before you came crawling back."

Taizo and Jiro's spines stiffened.

"You once made us an offer, Sheriff," Jiro said, ignoring Dreesen's rudeness, "of sixty-five hundred dollars for our land."

Dreesen nodded. "I did, at that. But that was a long time ago. We find ourselves in a new world today, don't we?"

"Yes," Jiro agreed quietly.

"I keep up with local property values. And today I'd judge the value of your land as no more than—five thousand dollars. And I'm being generous."

Jiro looked to Taizo, who replied for him: "That is a fair appraisal, and we would be agreeable to such a sum in purchase of . . . ninety acres of land."

Dreesen raised an eyebrow. "Your spread's a hundred acres, ain't it?"

"Yes. We will sell you everything but the house, barn, and the ten acres of land surrounding it, which we would reserve for our own use."

Dreesen said flatly, "That wasn't the deal we discussed."

"As you say: We find ourselves in a new world," Taizo replied. "Only ten acres, but enough for us to feed our family. How else are we to survive?"

"Ain't my concern. Go back to Japan, I don't care. It's all or nothing."

Jiro and Taizo called upon every bit of Japanese reserve they possessed. "What you propose," Taizo said, "is little better than allowing the bank to foreclose on our property. And if that happens, you get nothing."

"Then the bank will put it up for auction and I can bid on it. Maybe get it for even less."

"You might not place the winning bid."

Dreesen smiled his lupine smile. "I'm a gambler. I'll take my chances."

Then Jiro suddenly spoke up. "What if I were to suggest a way—in which we *all* get what we desire?"

Dreesen snorted. "And what might that be, Watanabe-*san*?"

"We sell you all one hundred acres, buildings included—which you then lease back to us. We work the land *for* you—we Japanese are good farmers, you said so yourself. We do the work, you get the profits—less a percentage of the harvest you pay for our labor."

Taizo was as startled by this idea as Dreesen seemed to be. "You talkin' about sharecropping?"

"Leasing, sharecropping, whatever you wish to call it."

"Leasing land to Japs is illegal in California."

"And yet it is still done. You already have such an arrangement with Mr. Ochida, do you not? How did *you* get around the letter of the law, Sheriff?"—a mild barb sheathed in that last word.

Dreesen frowned. "Mr. Ochida and his son are managers, not tenants. Nothing illegal about it."

"There you are, then. We will be your managers. You may employ us only as long as the farm is making money. If it does not, you may end our employment and work the land yourself, or sell it for a profit. If it does make money, we work the land in exchange for fifty percent of the harvest."

Dreesen reflexively countered, "Forty percent."

"Forty percent, providing you supply us with feed and supplies. I believe that is customary in such arrangements."

Dreesen looked torn. Taizo judged that his greed had taken up arms against his hatred of the Japanese.

"You wily goddamn Japs," Dreesen finally spat out. But the expletive was followed by a grudging laugh. "Much as I'd like to, I can't argue with that. Saves me the trouble of hiring laborers. And forty percent of the harvest is probably less money than I'd pay in salary."

He stood up, all business now. "All right. I'll have contracts drawn up and a check cut. As long as you make money for me, you can stay. But the minute that farm goes into the red, I'll have you evicted faster than you can say *sayonara*. Do we understand each other?"

"Perfectly." Jiro held out his hand. To Taizo's surprise, Dreesen took it.

"You're a damn sight better businessman than I gave you credit for, Watanabe-*san*," he said.

Taizo was thinking exactly the same thing.

Outside, Taizo marveled, "It was an inspired idea, Jiro, but—where on earth did it come from?"

"My first job in California was as a laborer on a sharecropper's farm. I had forgotten all about Ochida-*san* and his arrangement with Dreesen until the sheriff mentioned him. I gambled that he would not pass up the chance to have us 'wily Japs' under his thumb."

"And you were right," Taizo said. "Well done, *Niisan*."

The honorific touched Jiro, and brought a smile to his face.

* * *

he Depression was terrible, of course, but Ruth was facing an even
more implacable enemy: puberty.

She stood in her bedroom, back flat against a wall as if facing a firing
squad, keeping her head level. With her left hand she raised a pencil to the
top of her head and made a little stroke on the wallpaper behind her.

"Dai?" came her mother's voice through the door. "Are you ready?"

"Not yet, *Okāsan*!"

She positioned one end of her mother's cloth measuring tape by the base-
board, holding it in place with her toe while her fingers raised the tape up
to the pencil mark—one of many made in previous years.

The cruel calculus of numbers decreed that Ruth stood sixty-four inches
tall, confirming what she already knew.

Angrily she hurled the tape onto her bed, tears welling in her eyes.

"You do not want to be late for your first day at school, butterfly," her
mother called out to her.

"I'm not going to school!"

A sigh from the other side of the door. "And what should I tell your
teachers?"

"Tell them I'm dead. Tell them I died of . . . colossalitis!"

"That is not a real disease, butterfly," came Etsuko's amused reply.

"It is and I'm dying of it!"

Ruth—all five feet four inches of her—threw open the door. She was
wearing a colorful print dress, knee stockings, and high-top shoes. "Look
at me!" she cried. "I'm a circus freak!"

"Dai, you are not a 'freak.'"

"Look!" She pointed at the height chart on the wall. "I grew an entire
inch this summer alone! Three inches since last year!"

Indeed, her mother—petite, like most Japanese women—had to crane
her head to address her. "You have gone through a growth spurt, that is all,"
Etsuko reassured her. "Your body is still growing."

"You mean like these?" Fruitlessly she adjusted her bra straps. "I've had
this thing on for ten minutes and I'm already sweating like a stuck pig."

"You are overexcited. Calm down."

"Why is this happening to me? Why won't I stop *growing*?"

Etsuko calmly took her hands in hers and squeezed them in the way that always made Ruth less anxious. "As I've told you before: it is probably your *hapa* half, your Hawaiian blood, that makes you a bit taller than most Japanese girls your age."

"I hate being *hapa*," she snapped. "I hate being half Hawaiian! Why can't I look like everybody else?"

"You are who you are, Dai—a beautiful young girl who will grow up to be a beautiful woman. Every girl your age goes through changes like these. Now put on your 'outside face' like a good Japanese girl and go to school."

"Outside face" meant the face she showed in public—quiet, not boisterous or emotional, to preserve the family honor. Ruth bowed her head, stoically accepting her fate, and went downstairs to get her box lunch and a thermos of tea. Ralph and Stanley, who had moved on to Elk Grove Union High—unlike Florin's schools, not segregated by race—were already in the kitchen. Ralph smiled at Ruth and said, "Good try, Sis. I'd be happy to take a couple of inches off your hands, if I knew how."

Ralph was short for a sixteen-year-old Nisei boy, barely five feet tall. Together they looked like Mutt and Jeff. "You're welcome to them, *Niisan*."

"Buck up, Sis. It won't be so bad."

"It'll be worse."

"Man, you've really got that Japanese fatalism jazz down pat. Ease up, Sis. It's not the end of the world." He gave her a fraternal pat on the back, then he and Stanley walked out to the main road to wait for the school bus.

Ruth met up with Cricket and they walked together to what was now known as Florin East Grammar School, its tar-paper roof patched over several times in the past few years, its green stucco walls fading in the bright sun to a pale lime. Cricket told her not to worry about what other kids thought, but that was easy for her to say—she was barely five feet tall.

They joined the crowd of students entering the school's courtyard. Ruth was now a whole head taller than most of the Nisei girls and half a head taller than most boys. She felt like a giraffe striding amid a herd of penguins.

Worse: the penguins took notice. Heads turned, faces tilted up, eyes stared, violating not just her privacy but all Japanese norms of propriety. Instinctively she slouched as she entered the school, navigating the corridors in search of the eighth-grade classroom and greeted with such *bon mots* as:

"Wow, Ruth, you got tall as a Maypole over the summer!" said a girl.

Ruth smiled. She always smiled. But she wanted to say: Yes, and from up here I can see that dandruff problem of yours.

"Hey, stringbean, what's the weather like up there?" said another.

This was invariably asked with a self-delighted laugh, as if he or she were the first human being on earth to conceive of this knee-slapper.

She wanted to dump the content of her thermos on his head and say: *It's raining*.

"Aw, shaddup, bigmouth!" Cricket yelled at the last boy, but this only attracted more attention. Ruth cringed.

"Cricket, don't," Ruth begged. "It just makes things worse."

Finally they reached their classroom. Now came the second most humiliating part of the day, as Ruth squeezed her gangly lower limbs under a school desk that seemed built for a Munchkin. She had not been able to cross her legs in class since fifth grade.

Recess was for most students a welcome respite, but for Ruth it was just another interlude in hell. Boys and girls alike played volleyball, tetherball, tag, or hide-and-seek. Ruth was no good at any of these. Hide-and-seek? Ha. Where did you hide when you were as tall as the Statue of Liberty? Tag? Her legs were long, so kids assumed she would be a good runner, but her still-growing limbs were slow to answer her brain's orders and she often tripped over herself, landing flat on her face. There was nothing funnier than seeing a giant being brought down. The one time she had played volleyball, her freakishly long arms launched the ball with such velocity that it zoomed straight across the net and hit Cora Okabe square in the chest, propelling her backward into Lulu Koizumi, both girls toppling like tenpins. Ruth was horrified but neither of them were seriously hurt and graciously did not blame her for it. Fortunately, no one ever asked her to play volleyball again.

Her first day back eventually ended and as she left the school building, there was more droll banter about her height. But the worst remark was delivered not at top voice but *sotto voce*, two girls giggling and whispering:

"I bet she's really a boy."

Tears sprang to Ruth's eyes and she ran all the way home. She entered the house weeping, and filthy from the dust she had kicked up along the way.

She kicked off her shoes and went straight upstairs. When Etsuko saw her, Ruth just gave her a look that said *don't comfort me*, her bedroom door slamming shut behind her. She fell onto her bed and wept into her pillow.

After a few minutes there was a familiar scratching at the door. Ruth opened it to admit Mayonaka. Ruth picked her up and brought her to the bed, where she curled up on Ruth's arm, offering warmth and comfort, as always, soothing Ruth's troubles with her purr.

Ruth skipped supper, but when the house was quiet she crept downstairs, pilfered some bread and jam from the kitchen, then slipped out the back door. She went to Bucky's stall and combed his mane, feeling calmer in his gentle presence. She gave him a kiss on his muzzle, then went over to the redwood split-rail fence that surrounded the corral, climbed it, and sat down on the top rail. It wasn't comfortable, but she didn't want to be comfortable right now. She sat there in the gathering twilight, eating her bread and jam, staring out at endless rows of green strawberry plants and painterly strokes of gold and purple in the sky above a distant treeline.

After a few minutes she heard someone behind her and turned to see Ralph. "Hi," he said, swinging his short legs over the top rail. "Rough day?"

"Yeah. You?"

"It was all right."

Now that he was closer, even in the dimming light, Ruth could see that he had a bruise above his left eye. "What happened to your eye?" she asked.

He shrugged it off. "Nothing. I'm swell."

"Give."

"Aw, just some guys horsing around. Kind of a . . . tradition."

"Did somebody hit you?" she said, alarmed.

"Naw, that's not it." He shrugged, as if it were nothing important. "There's these two *hakujin* guys. Every year, first day of classes, they got their little routine they go through."

"Routine? What are you talking about?"

"They pick me up, turn me upside down, and lower me into a big barrel with my feet sticking out. That's their little joke," he said matter-of-factly.

Ruth was shocked. "But that's . . . awful!"

"Eh, all the Nisei kids from Florin get picked on, Sis. Stanley got tossed into the showers once with his clothes on. Sometimes there's a fistfight."

"How—did you get out of the barrel?"

"Easy. I shift my weight—before I pass out 'cause I'm upside down—

and when the barrel rolls onto the ground, I crawl out backward. Banged myself in the forehead when I hit this time, that's why the bruise."

"And they do this to you *every* year?"

He nodded. "Yeah. I'm hoping for one more growth spurt. Just enough so I don't fit so easy in the barrel."

"You never told me any of this before," she said softly.

"And you better not tell anyone I told you—even Stanley."

"I promise."

She reached out and took his hand in hers. "I'm so sorry, Ralph." She felt suddenly ashamed. "I . . . guess I don't have it so bad."

"Naw, you do. We both do. But we'll live."

She squeezed his hand, the way her mother squeezed hers. He smiled.

Silently they watched the last traces of the sun's light retreating below the treetops, urgently waiting for puberty to end.

Chapter 6

1931–1935

By the time Ruth entered high school she had grown another inch, standing five feet five, certain that P. T. Barnum would be calling any day now. AMAZING! COLOSSAL! screamed the circus banners of her imagination. SEE THE ORIENTAL GIANTESS! HEAR HER TRAGIC STORY! STEP RIGHT UP!

At least this was what she envisioned on the school bus en route to her first day at Elk Grove Union High School. She was more than a head taller than most of the Nisei girls on the bus; even sitting down they all seemed like Lilliputians to her. Everyone on the bus shared some anxiety about going to a new school. But when Ruth stepped inside the large, red-brick building—so much more imposing than Florin East—her worries evaporated.

Elk Grove was not a segregated school, like Florin; the student body was made up of about three hundred whites, forty or fifty Nisei, and a few Hispanics. Walking its hallways for the first time, Ruth was astonished to find herself at eye level with most of the white male students. Even most white girls were only a few inches shorter than she; a few were nearly as tall. And to her wonderment, Ruth felt downright petite alongside the school's six-foot-tall basketball and football players. No longer was she a giraffe among penguins. She felt almost . . . *normal*.

Her coordination had even improved enough that gym class was no longer an obstacle course for her, and Mrs. Winter, the teacher, invited her to join the girls' intramural basketball team!

As pleased as she was, she reminded herself that this *was* the school where Ralph—now a senior and an inch taller—had been picked on by *hakujin* bullies, and he was not alone. It was not uncommon to hear the word "Jap" in use, either spoken directly to Nisei or behind their backs. It was not just traditional reserve that made Florin's Nisei shyer than their white classmates. The unspoken message they had heard loud and clear growing up was: You are different. You are less. You are second class. Here, among all these loud Caucasians, most of Ruth's Nisei friends could not help but shrink back a little, going out of their way to avoid any potential conflicts.

Which was not to say that many of the white students weren't friendly or kind—like Ruth's friend Phyllis Thomas, with whom she was reunited in school after eight years. And Ruth couldn't help but notice that some of the boys were quite handsome—especially one in her mathematics class, Will Lockhardt. He was tall, athletic, and had blond hair, a nice smile, and eyes as blue as a mountain lake—exotic good looks for a girl who had spent eight years at an all-Japanese school. He was also absolutely terrible at math—each time Mr. McGregor called on him for the answer to an algebraic equation, he flailed like a drowning man sinking in a sea of fractions and exponential numbers. Overcoming her shyness, Ruth quickly raised a hand and answered the question correctly, so when Will asked her after class, "How did you *know* that?" she happily offered to tutor him.

In study hall they wrestled quadratic equations to the ground, and over the next few weeks Will began picking up enough to get by in class. And Ruth had an excuse to gaze into those clear blue eyes, to laugh at one of his unfunny jokes, or to occasionally brush her hand against his while writing out an equation—the touch causing a most wonderful flurry of goosebumps.

She had been tutoring Will for about a month when she innocently brought up his name at home one day. Her parents were fairly liberal for first-generation Issei, allowing her to adopt American fashions and hairstyles and not objecting when Horace married a girl of his own choosing, Rose Ishida. But now they looked at her with barely concealed dismay as her father blurted out, "Has he tried to kiss you?"

Mortified beyond words, Ruth said quickly, "No, no, we're just friends, I help him with math, that's all."

Her parents looked visibly relieved.

"That is good," her father said, "because it is our feeling that Japanese girls should only marry Japanese boys."

Oh God, this was so embarrassing. "Papa, please! We're only fifteen!"

"It is not a question of race," her father stressed. "We lived in Hawai'i; as people of other races respected us, so we respected them. It is a matter of tradition. If you were to marry a *hakujin* boy, or even a Chinese"—Ruth sank into the cushions of her chair, hoping they would swallow her up— "how could he be expected to preserve our culture? How could he understand the importance of filial piety? These things that make us Japanese need to be passed on to the next generation, and generations after that."

"Yes, yes, I see, I understand, Papa," Ruth said, willing to say anything to end this conversation. "You're absolutely right. And we're only friends anyway, so there's nothing to worry about, is there? May I go now?" she asked, certain she would have a stroke if her father uttered another word.

Thankfully Papa just smiled with satisfaction, nodded, and Ruth fled.

The next day she informed Will that he had learned everything she had to teach and he was sure to pass Mr. McGregor's class with flying colors. In reality he scored a C for the year, but he seemed happy not to flunk out and she was happy—well, resigned—to trade those gorgeous blue eyes for no more skin-crawling discussions with her parents about dating.

Issei, especially those in rural communities, generally did not approve of American-style, unescorted "dating." For young Nisei, most of the opportunities to mix with the opposite sex came in group activities—classes, clubs, dances. The one time a boy had asked Ruth to dance, at freshman prom, the poor fellow was so much shorter than she that he wound up staring, with exquisite discomfort, into Ruth's bosom for the entire length of the song. Then he smiled, bowed, and vanished like smoke.

By junior year she had finally ceased growing, topping off at five feet seven inches—but now the Nisei boys were taller too. At the school New Year's party, when a studious-looking boy named Freddy Kurahara asked her to dance, she sized him up—he was only two inches shorter—and said yes.

He slipped his hand around her waist as they slow-danced to Bing Crosby singing "Shadow Waltz."

"I don't know if you remember," Freddy said, "but freshman year we both had Mrs. Barron for English."

She tried to conceal her surprise but he just smiled and said, "It's okay. I was just a little runt then, you wouldn't have noticed me. But I noticed you. You always had something funny to say when Mrs. Barron called on you."

Someone had noticed her? Two years ago? She had a secret admirer! Maybe his eyes weren't blue, like Will Lockhardt's—but there was a twinkle of humor in them that was equally appealing.

"Did you grow up here in Elk Grove?" Ruth asked.

"Yes, my parents own a grocery."

"I'm a farm girl. My parents raise—"

"Grapes and strawberries," they finished together. She laughed.

"What else is there?" he said. "Did you like growing up on a farm?"

"It's beautiful, especially in April when the white blossoms appear on the strawberry plants and the fields turn white as snow."

"Do your parents know you're here? At the dance?"

"Well, sure."

"You're lucky. My parents don't approve of dancing. They're very strict and traditional—they believe 'many temptations will come from the dancing pleasures.' They've forbidden my sisters and me from engaging in it."

"So, um, what are you doing right now?" Ruth asked, amused.

"I am enjoying New Year's festivities and good cheer with my friends. At least that's what I told my parents before I came. After all"—and there was that twinkle in his eye—"dancing may lead to temptation."

He laughed, and Ruth was smitten.

They began seeing each other at school—at lunch, in study hall, and at extracurricular functions. He came to her basketball games, though he had no interest in the sport; she joined the Drama Club because he was a member.

Their only physical contact, apart from dancing, was holding hands or a brief, stolen kiss; but that was enough to make her almost giddy with delight.

After two months of quietly not dating, they decided they were serious enough that they would tell their parents they were "seeing" someone at school. To their great relief, both sets of parents seemed pleased at the news. Freddy's parents invited her to dinner at their modest home in Elk Grove, where he introduced her not as Ruth but as Dai and she was careful to call him by his Japanese name, Hisoka. His parents were traditional but warm, and at the end of the evening Ruth rejoiced that they seemed to like her.

That night she lay in bed, fancying variations of what her new name might be: *Mrs. Fred Kurahara. Mrs. Hisoka Kurahara. Mrs. Dai Kurahara. Mrs. Ruth Kurahara.* Counting names as others counted sheep, she drifted happily asleep.

But the next day, when Ruth saw Freddy at lunchtime, his face was a blank slate. He asked her to go outside with him in a tone she had never heard before. "What is it? What's wrong?" she asked, but he would not answer until they were alone behind the school.

Now the blank slate cracked, and the pain revealed itself.

"I—I'm sorry, Ruth," he said softly, "but . . . my parents do not approve of us seeing one another."

"What?" She was stunned at this apparent reversal. "Why not?"

"They—do not believe in interracial dating."

"But I'm Japanese!" she said, almost laughing.

"Not 'pure-blood' Japanese."

The words struck her like a hand across the face.

"What?" she said in a small, disbelieving voice.

His anguish, she could see, was genuine. "I'm so sorry, Ruth. I love you. I do. But I must respect my parents' wishes."

As tears welled in his eyes, Freddy turned and hurried away.

Ruth felt light-headed, her legs wobbly. She slumped against the brick wall, sank slowly onto the ground, and cried for a long while.

She could not bear to remain at school and risk seeing Freddy again. She went to the principal's office, told his assistant she wasn't feeling well and had to go home, and left without waiting for a permission slip.

She walked all the way back to Florin and was exhausted and forlorn by the time she got home.

Papa was working in the fields near the house and asked her why she was home so early. She didn't answer, just hurried inside without even removing her shoes. Disturbed, Taizo followed her in, and when her mother asked, "Butterfly, what is wrong?"—Ruth turned on the stairs and snapped at them, almost savagely:

"Freddy's parents made him break up with me. Because I'm *hapa*. Because I'm not 'pure-blood' Japanese!"

She saw the expected shock, pain, and, yes, guilt in their eyes as that sank in. Fine, she thought bitterly. Let them stew in their own juices.

She pounded up the stairs and into her room. When Etsuko came in to comfort her, Ruth would have none of it, telling her to get out. She had never said this to her mother before, and the hurt in Etsuko's eyes was raw. But so was hers. Etsuko nodded and did as she was asked.

Ruth sat on her bed and cried. She hated being *hapa*. She hated being Japanese. Why couldn't she just be *herself*, like her white friends?

No one would ever want her or marry her because she wasn't "pure." She hated her Hawaiian blood. She hated her Hawaiian mother, whoever she was, for giving birth to her, for giving her *away*. Damn her—why couldn't she have loved her and raised her so she would have had a normal life? *Why?*

She said none of this to her parents, of course. By morning she realized how much that would hurt them and she remembered all the love they had given her over the years. It wasn't their fault the Kuraharas rejected her—but it still hurt to know that her own parents shared some degree of their prejudice and closed-mindedness. She had always seen them as perfect, and it pained her to realize they were only human, and products of their culture.

She and her parents never discussed the subject again, and when Ruth returned to school she did her best to avoid Freddy. She quit the stupid Drama Club and changed study halls. She made a point of eating lunch with Phyllis or Cricket or some other friend, and if she caught a glimpse of Freddy from across the room she quickly turned her attention elsewhere.

She skipped junior prom and throughout her senior year rebuffed every boy who showed the slightest interest in her. She wanted no more brush-offs, no more goodbyes.

But there was one goodbye she could not avoid.

Ruth was the first to notice, in that winter of 1934, that Mayonaka's appetite had decreased; all she did was drink water. She was old—exactly how old they didn't know, but she had been with them for fourteen years. When their veterinarian, Dr. Hoffman, came to treat an abscess on Bucky's left hoof, Ruth asked him if he would look at Mayonaka; he kindly agreed.

Mayonaka was lying stretched out beneath her favorite window, warming herself in a shaft of sunlight. It did not take long for the vet to diagnose that she was in the final stages of kidney failure. Blinking back tears, Ruth asked what could be done for her.

"Make sure she has plenty of fresh, clean water and a quiet place to rest," he said. "Looks like she's already found that. There's nothing else to do. She may live another few months, or another few weeks. I'm sorry, Ruth."

Ruth nodded and thanked him.

She nursed Mayonaka tenderly in her waning days, making sure she had enough water, sleeping beside her, stroking her. She held her and told her how much she loved her, as Mayonaka purred contentedly. Ruth marveled at how two souls—two completely different species—could make each other so happy. If you were kind to animals, they repaid that kindness a thousandfold. People disappointed; animals never did.

After Mayonaka had warmed herself in the last of her sunlight, fading away into the night for which she had been named, Taizo cremated her body and sifted her ashes into a small urn. Stanley and Ralph made a makeshift grave marker out of a large stone, writing her name on it in *kanji* characters, and her urn was buried beneath it. Beside the marker Etsuko placed a vase of flowers, a stick of incense, and a bowl filled with water. The water was traditional for Japanese graves, but it seemed especially fitting here and brought a small smile to Ruth's face. Etsuko chanted a *sutra* and thanked Mayonaka for the joy and grace she had brought to their home. The incense was lit, the sweet scent of sandalwood lofted on the wind.

Ruth thought: Goodbye, my true and tender friend. You will always be loved, and never be forgotten.

eleased from the crippling debt that had hobbled the farm's fortunes, Taizo and Jiro felt unfettered, weightless with freedom. The money that had gone each month to Sumitomo Bank could now be spent repaying other creditors like Mr. Noriji as well as on improvements in irrigation and even a good used truck. Fruit prices and market demand remained low, but Dreesen, as their landlord, provided feed and other supplies, and so by the end of the first year of their arrangement the farm had made a modest profit. Dreesen seemed satisfied. These days no farmers were getting rich, but thanks to Japanese farmers' intensive farming techniques they were at least faring better than most in the nation, where one out of every four farms was failing, or—as violent windstorms raked away topsoil in the Midwest, reducing entire farms to blizzards of blinding dust—simply disappearing.

Now a portion of the Watanabes' income could be saved for their children's education. Horace, Taizo's firstborn son, was content to stay on the farm with Rose and their two toddlers, so Stanley, next in line, was able to study engineering at Sacramento Junior College. Ralph also chose to remain at work on the farm, while Ruth had decided that she wanted to become a veterinarian. On his next visit she told Dr. Hoffman of her plans.

"Well, those are good intentions, Ruth," he said, "but being a vet's a pretty rough and tumble job. You've got to be able to lift ninety-pound hogs, treat cattle and horses that weigh *hundreds* of pounds—holding these big critters back while you treat them, keeping them from hurting you or themselves. Women just don't have the body strength for that kind of work."

Ruth was crestfallen. "Aren't there *any* women veterinarians?"

"If there are I don't know of any. I'm sorry, but those are the facts."

Ruth was disappointed and angry. She met with the school's senior advisor, Mrs. Householder, who presented her with the frankly limited career options for a Nisei girl in 1934. Teaching was a traditionally female occupation, and nursing or midwifery was a possibility, as was business school. Maybe she could become a bookkeeper, or a secretary. Assuming she could even *find* a job with eleven million people out of work in America.

Nursing came closest to being a vet—but when she raised the subject with her parents, her father became unaccountably vehement. "No! Absolutely not," he declared. "Nursing is not a—a 'clean' profession!"

"'Clean'?" Ruth repeated, without understanding.

"There is the danger from germs, disease—I will not allow it!"

Even her mother looked startled by how frankly emotional Papa seemed to be on the subject. "*Otōsan*," Etsuko said gently, "things in medicine have changed a great deal since—"

"Do not people still get sick?" he countered. "Do they not die?"

"But Papa," Ruth said, "nowadays there are antiseptic procedures—"

"No!" Her father remained adamant. "This discussion is over."

Baffled and angered by his old-fashioned obstinacy, Ruth stormed out of the house. Etsuko gently put a hand on Taizo's arm. "*Otōsan*, I understand your fear, but she does not. Perhaps it is time that we tell her the truth."

Taizo sighed, annoyed at himself for losing patience and control.

"No," he said, "it is better that she does not know. Anger passes, but knowledge can be a curse."

uth ran outside and into the barn. She was so sick of Papa's fussy old ideas about everything! She wanted to live in twentieth-century America, not nineteenth-century Japan. She saddled up Bucky and rode him out of the corral, down the bridle path between farms. She let him gallop full bore, his hooves kicking up whorls of dust that reminded Ruth of the tornado that plucked Dorothy out of Kansas. If only she too could be carried away to Oz!

But the path ended not at the Emerald City but at the endless emerald expanse of strawberry plants nearly ripe for harvest. She reined in Bucky and looked back. The parallel ribbons of green strawberry plants receded into the distance toward her family's farm, like arrows pointing the way to her future.

As if in confirmation of this, in mid-May came the customary week off from school for Florin's Nisei to help their families harvest the crops. Donning sun bonnets and gloves, Ruth and her family—with the aid of dozens of hired migrant Filipino laborers—toiled in the fields from dawn to dusk. It was grueling work—Ruth spent most of her time bent over the plants at a ninety-degree angle and by day's end her back ached like a sore tooth. Even her young knees were sore from so much stooping and squatting; she couldn't imagine how hard this must be for her parents, Uncle Jiro, and Aunt Nishi.

She did her duty without complaint, but by the end of the week she was determined that there had to be more to her life than this. Her father lived and breathed farming. But she would never be more than a workhand here.

At night she pored over the classified advertisements in the *Sacramento Bee* and the Japanese *New World-Sun*, looking for work, any kind of work. But their pages were bleak with heartbreaking pictures of long breadlines and places like "Pipe City" in Oakland, where the homeless lived inside six-foot-wide construction pipes—men, women, and children sleeping on cold concrete, eating only a thin mulligan stew made with water and whatever castoff or half-eaten vegetables could be salvaged from garbage cans.

The day after high school graduation she put on a pretty dress and began pounding the pavement—though in Florin the "pavement" was still largely wood and dirt. The town's business district was small, but she doggedly went from store to store, inquiring about work at Akiyama's Fish Market, Kato's Grocery, Tanikawa's General Store, Nishi Basket Factory, Noda's Ice Cream Parlor, Sasaki Tofu Shop, Ogata's General Store, and finally Nakajima Restaurant, where lunch patrons were eating dishes of steaming noodles, *teriyaki*, rice, and vegetables.

She noted a tall, lanky Nisei man in his early twenties, wearing a newly starched white shirt and black trousers, standing behind the cash register; she worked up her resolve, approached him, and asked to see Mr. Nakajima.

The young man said, "I'm sorry, he's not in just now. Can I help you?"

"I'm looking for a job."

"Ah," the Nisei said sympathetically, "I thought I recognized the look."

"What look?"

"No offense, I just meant that I've been in your situation myself. But I'm sorry to say we have all the staff we need."

Ruth sighed. "Are you sure? Do you need anyone to wash the dishes? Mop the floor?"

"No. Sorry," he said gently. Then: "Been doing this all morning?"

She nodded.

"Why don't you take a load off your feet. Would you like a cup of coffee? On the house."

She hadn't expected that. "Yes, thank you, that's very kind."

"Have a seat at that table for two by the wall and I'll get it for you."

Dispirited, Ruth went over to the table and slumped into the chair. The morning had been a total waste, and by the time she got home, word would probably have traveled back to her parents that she was out shaming them by looking for work. She was weighing whether to get a cab to Elk Grove's business district when the young man came over and put down a cup of hot black coffee in front of her along with a slice of strawberry pie.

"Thought you might like something to eat after your travels," he said.

She looked up at him. "That's really very nice of you, but—I'm not destitute, I can pay. I'm just looking for a job, that's all." That pie did look awfully good, though. "Thank you, Mister—"

"Harada. Frank Harada." He smiled. There was a kindness in his eyes, and a pleasing symmetry to his features.

"I'm Ruth Watanabe. You're not from around here, are you?"

"No, I hail from Fresno."

"Wow, you're a long way from home." She took up a forkful of pie. "What are you doing marooned in Florin?"

He laughed, then gestured to the chair opposite her. "May I?"

"Yes. Sure," she said, surprised but a little pleased.

He sat down and said matter-of-factly, "My parents had a farm outside Fresno—fifteen acres. We raised peaches, almonds, grapes. We lost it in the stock market crash. Bank foreclosure."

"Oh," she said softly, "I'm so sorry."

He shrugged. "It's worked out okay. Better than for most folks these days. My *otōsan* and my oldest brother got work at a vineyard in Visalia. My sisters were already married. The rest of us scattered like birds, finding work where we could. I've worked on farms in Salinas, Stockton . . . got jobs in hotels and restaurants in Walnut Grove, Loomis, and now here."

His voice was a mellow baritone, and it softened the hard edges and lonely spaces of the story he was telling.

"But you're so far from your family." Suddenly the notion of getting away from her father's old-fashioned ideas didn't seem quite so important.

"That was the hardest thing to get used to. I miss them every day. But you've got to go where the work is, not where you'd like it to be." He lowered his voice. "And I've managed to save some money. When the economy's a little better, I'd like to open my own restaurant."

"Maybe Mr. Nakajima will sell you this one," Ruth suggested. "He's about a hundred years old, isn't he?"

Frank laughed. "And he'll probably still be here in another hundred. But I don't want a restaurant like this. Look around this town, at how many

Nisei there are—do they only want to eat Japanese food? No, they like hamburgers and hot dogs and milkshakes, just like their *hakujin* friends."

"Yes," she agreed, "I was just thinking how I feel sometimes like I'm living in nineteenth-century Japan."

"So what about you? What do you want to do?"

Ruth started to say one thing, then decided on another:

"I'd like to . . . work at a restaurant like yours," she said with a smile.

"You're hired!" he declared with a smile and a snap of his fingers.

She laughed. It was the first time she'd laughed all day.

"Well. Thank you for the coffee and the pie, it was delicious. Are you sure I can't pay you?"

"Like I said, on the house."

She thanked him again and stood. He got to his feet as well.

She thrilled to realize that she was looking directly into his eyes.

They saw each other, surreptitiously, for several months before Ruth worked up her nerve to tell her parents—neither of whom, as it turned out, had been fooled. "We were wondering, butterfly, when you were going to tell us," Etsuko said with a smile, and Ruth was pleasantly reminded that although her parents may have been traditional in some ways, they were open-minded in other, more important ways.

Frank wore a brand-new suit to dinner and, coming from a large family, clearly felt at ease with the extended Watanabe clan: Stanley was away at school, but there were Horace and Rose and their two sons; Jiro and Nishi; Akira and Tamiko and their children; and Ralph. Jiro was gregarious, as ever, and Ralph joked, "So, the mystery man finally appears. I was beginning to think Sis was dating The Shadow." Ruth's parents mostly listened—to Frank's stories about taking work up and down the coast for the past four years—with expressions that were friendly and cordial. But Ruth had seen the same cordiality on the faces of Freddy Kurahara's parents, and she couldn't help fearing what hidden feelings might be lurking behind them.

But at the end of the meal, Taizo spoke up.

"It is not an easy thing to walk away from everything one knows and make a life for oneself far from family," he said to Frank. "I did the same in coming to America."

"I hope to make a new life—and family—with Dai," Frank replied boldly, "should that meet with your approval."

Ruth was afraid to breathe in the short silence until her father spoke.

"Dai is our only daughter," Taizo said, "and a daughter by choice. We feel we could not have chosen better."

He glanced at Etsuko, then back to Frank.

"It is good for us to see that she too could not have chosen better."

Her father smiled with more pride and happiness than Ruth had ever seen on his face, and her heart soared.

The wedding took place at Florin Buddhist Church, with Frank in his new suit and Ruth wearing a white American-style wedding dress her mother had sewn using bolts of imported Japanese silk—something they could not have dreamed of affording ten years before. The wedding colors were green and white, reminding Ruth of strawberry blossoms in April.

The wedding banquet was held, fittingly, at Nakajima Restaurant.

Within a year, Mr. Nakajima had some new competition in town.

Chapter 7

1941

"Frank's Diner" may not have met the dictionary definition of a diner—"a prefabricated restaurant in the shape of a railroad car"—but it measured up in every other respect. Prefabs were pricey, at least ten thousand bucks; it had been cheaper for Frank to rent a narrow, one-story building in downtown Florin and remodel it with the help of Ruth and her brothers. Frank painted the sign himself, red letters on white, and below the name, that ubiquitous imprimatur of the modern age, the Coca-Cola logo. Inside it boasted a modern curved marble service counter ringed by stainless steel stools with red vinyl cushions; behind the counter were gleaming panels of patterned chrome, a soda fountain, toaster, Sunbeam Mixmaster, glass displays showcasing five flavors of pie, and a blackboard listing the day's specials:

BREAKFAST SPECIAL, SERVED ALL DAY: BACON OR HAM & EGGS 30¢

BLUE PLATE LUNCH SPECIAL W/FRENCH FRIED POTATOES & COFFEE:
  RIB STEAK 55¢

LAMB OR PORK CHOPS 40¢, HAMBURGER STEAK 30¢

DESSERT SPECIALS, FROSTED MALTED 10¢, FRUIT PIES 20¢
  (A LA MODE 30¢)

On this busy afternoon, the first Saturday of December, the diner was packed: every seat at the counter was taken, as were the half dozen red vinyl booths along the wall, the patrons a mix of Nisei and Caucasian. The radio announced some rare good news from Europe: Hitler's offensive against Moscow was failing and German forces were in retreat. Frank was working the cash register as two Nisei waitresses took customers' orders and called them out to the fry cook in back, his ruddy, sweaty face intermittently visible through a small window behind the counter:

"Adam and Eve on a raft, java with sand, hold the cow!"

"Bowl of red, dog biscuits in the alley!"

"Zeppelins in a fog!"

The cook, Vince, swiftly prepared two poached eggs on toast with coffee, sugar, no milk; a bowl of chili, crackers on the side; and sausages in mashed potatoes.

Ruth sat at a small table in the back of the kitchen, going over the books—she served as the diner's purchase and inventory manager. She and Frank had found Vince in the desolation of Oakland's Pipe City, where they had gone looking to hire a couple of busboys. "If we're going to give someone a job," Frank reasoned, "I'd like to give it to someone who really needs it. Wouldn't you?" This was one of the reasons Ruth loved him, and she readily agreed. After they'd found two suitable busboys, the grizzled, unwashed Vince came up and mentioned he'd been a damn good short-order cook before the Crash. They brought him home, cleaned him up, and let him loose in the empty restaurant's kitchen, where he expertly juggled half a dozen common menu items simultaneously—and they tasted good too. They quickly found him a room in a nearby boardinghouse. The only thing he couldn't make well was coffee, so it fell to Frank to put on a decent pot of java before he opened up each morning.

Ruth closed the books and went up to Vince as he was sliding the chili bowl into the order window: "Vince, you make this look so easy."

"Yeah, I'm a regular Fred Astaire. So where the hell's my Ginger?"

She laughed and went to join Frank at the cash register.

"Profits up another three percent this week," she told him. "I'm beginning to think this may be a going concern."

"Yeah? Can I get a raise?"

"Sorry. All the revenues have already been invested in children's shoes." She gave him a goodbye kiss. "Speaking of which, I have to pick up Donnie and Peggy at my folks' place. See you at closing time."

"Y'know, lots of diners are open twenty-four hours a day."

"Honey, we've been operating in the black for two years; adding a third shift would put us right back in the red."

He shrugged. "Someday," he said wistfully.

Ruth drove their 1937 Oldsmobile to her parents' farm. Etsuko was standing on the edge of a strawberry field, holding one-year-old Peggy in her arms as three-year-old Donnie ran up and down the irrigation ditches— chased by none other than his Uncle Ralph, taking a break from work.

"Hard to say which one's the bigger kid," Ruth said. Etsuko laughed.

"Mama, mama!" Peggy cried, arms outstretched upon seeing Ruth.

Ruth took her from Etsuko and cooed, "Hey, sweetie pie, how are you? Did you have fun with *Obāsan* today?"

"Mom! Mom!" Now that he had seen her, Donnie came blowing like a gale toward her, followed close behind by Ralph, who arrived breathless.

"You've got yourself a budding Jesse Owens here, Sis," he said.

"Don't I know it." Ruth turned to Etsuko. "You and *Otōsan* are still coming for lunch Sunday?"

"Yes, of course. Church services start at nine-thirty. We will be at your house by eleven-thirty."

"Our services start a little earlier, we'll be back by ten-thirty." Ruth heard her mother's unvoiced sigh of disappointment that her grandchildren were being raised not as Buddhists but in Frank's Methodist faith. To them it represented another step away from Japanese tradition, but they were mollified that the children had at least been given Japanese middle names—Peggy Mei and Donald Naoki—and even respected Ruth and Frank's preference that the children be addressed by their American names. "They *are* Americans, after all," Taizo had told his wife, "and because they are, life in America will be easier for them than it has been for us."

Ruth kissed Etsuko on the cheek. "See you tomorrow. And thanks for watching the gremlins." She smiled at Ralph. "Get back to work, you bum."

"I think I liked it better," Ralph said, "when you called me *Niisan*."

Frank and Ruth were renting a two-bedroom house close to downtown Florin, in a neighborhood home to both white and Nisei families. As Ruth pulled into their driveway, their amiable next-door neighbor, Jim Russell—a salaried manager at the Florin Fruit Growers Association—was draping strings of Christmas lights from his eaves while his two young kids chased each other around the front yard, dueling with water pistols.

As Ruth got out of the car, Jim waved and unexpectedly broke into song: "On the sixth day of Christmas my true love gave to me—" And he held up a tangled snarl of wires and lights.

Ruth laughed. "Frank's getting that for Christmas too."

Donnie had nodded off in the backseat but awoke upon hearing the enthusiastic barking of their dog, Slugger. Ruth let the kids out of the car, then opened the gate in the fence, and watched with amusement as their sixty-pound black Labrador—as tall as Donnie and twice as heavy—leaped happily up and down while knowing enough not to tackle him to the ground.

"Okay, everybody inside!" Ruth gave Donnie a quick bath and tucked him into bed. Peggy was already fast asleep in her crib. Slugger was stretched out between them, a sentinel guarding them as he did every night. She gazed at her children's sleeping faces, still marveling that they were hers—that she now had a husband, a son, a daughter, a home of her own. Things that once had seemed so out of reach, now safely in her embrace.

As Etsuko finished dressing for church, Taizo, in his Sunday suit, looked out their bedroom window at the lush acres of green surrounding them, the house rising like an island on a placid inland sea. Two very different cycles of life coexisted in those fields, and this past week had been spent carefully tending each: pruning and weeding the slow-growing grapevines, whose life was counted in years, not months; and cutting back the strawberry plants' prolific runners that, left unchecked, would propagate new plants like weeds, leeching water and strength from the mother plants. It was a delicate balance, but if you maintained it correctly, the land flourished and repaid your stewardship richly. Taizo's heart swelled with pride: this was his land not by deed but by deeds, by right of the labor and love he put into it.

After church services, Taizo drove the truck to Ruth and Frank's house. He noted a car carrying several young white men coming from the opposite direction; as they passed the men glowered at them and one yelled:

"Goddamn Japs!"

The words, dripping in vitriol, hung in the air like an electrical charge after a lightning strike. Such overt racism was rare in Florin these days; even the elementary school had been reintegrated two years ago.

"Hooligans from Sacramento," Taizo said dismissively.

But when they entered the Haradas' home, Ruth and Frank's ashen faces shook Taizo even more than the racial epithet.

"Papa," Ruth said, "there's bad news. It just came over the radio. Japan has bombed Pearl Harbor."

Etsuko gasped. Taizo was incredulous: "Pearl Harbor? In Honolulu?"

Frank gestured for them to sit down in front of the console radio in the living room. "Where are the children?" Etsuko asked Ruth.

"Peggy's napping and Donnie's in the backyard playing with Slugger. I asked him to stay out there while we talked with Grandma and Grandpa."

The four of them sat listening as the CBS program *The World Today* brought the latest news from its correspondent in Washington, D.C.:

". . . attack was apparently made on all naval and military activities on the principal island of O'ahu. A Japanese attack upon Pearl Harbor naturally would mean war . . ."

Taizo sat, disbelieving, as the correspondent went on to report that Japanese warplanes were also bombing Manila in the Philippines and the Japanese Navy was invading Thailand. Taizo was not naive; he had read about Japan's brutal aggression in China and the South Pacific. But this was almost unimaginable. The country of his birth attacking not just his adopted home but the islands that had welcomed him with *aloha* and op-portunity.

Yet just as frightening to him were the words of the young white men who had passed them on the road.

"This is bad," he said gravely. "For us. For the Issei."

"What do you mean, Papa?" Ruth asked.

"Not for the Nisei. You and Frank, your children, you are American citizens. But *Okāsan* and I—we are Japanese nationals. We are the enemy."

"Papa, that's ridiculous. You're a farmer, not a soldier."

"The government could deport us as—what is the word? *Aliens.*"

"I think we could all use a stiff drink," Frank suggested. "Why don't I get us some *sake* while we—"

Taizo stood up suddenly. "No. No. We need to go home. *Okāsan?*"

Etsuko did not understand, but stood. Taizo made a small bow to his daughter and her husband. "Give our regrets to the children."

Taizo was silent on the drive home, where they found Jiro and the rest of the family—all but Stanley, who had taken an engineering job in Portland, Oregon—gathered around their own radio. Latest reports from Honolulu said bombs were falling not just on military targets but in parts of the city as well.

Etsuko began to cry, thinking of distant friends on Kukui Street and the kind Franciscan sisters at Kapi'olani Home.

Taizo declared, "We must burn everything Japanese in the house. What we cannot burn, we must bury."

Jiro said, "I was thinking the same thing."

"But Pop," Ralph said, "is that really—"

"*Moyashi nasai!*" Taizo snapped back: *Burn it!*

The urgency in his voice silenced and propelled them into action. Horace and Ralph went into the fields to dig a deep hole while Jiro and Akira prepared a bonfire in the backyard. Rose took the children and kept them occupied as Nishi and Tamiko collected anything that hinted at loyalty, or even affection, for their native land: from blatantly suspicious items like an antique ceremonial sword to Japanese books, musical records, even *origami* "good luck" paper cranes. *Tatami* mats were rolled up; the Japanese scroll in the *tokonoma* alcove taken down; porcelain teacups, tableware, jars, no matter how beautiful or cherished, were gathered up.

Horace and Ralph used spades to break through the layer of hardpan, digging a three-foot-deep hole in an irrigation ditch far from the house. Soon they were tossing in century-old family heirlooms. Even the small stone marker from Mayonaka's gravesite was interred.

With the bonfire ready, the *tatami* were thrown onto the pyre, the colorful straw mats quickly consumed by the flames. The *tokonoma* scroll incinerated instantly, as did the paper cranes, each barely making the fire flare. A beautiful bamboo basket used for flower arranging hissed and crackled as it died. The *bonsai* plants that Jiro had lovingly cultivated for twenty years were chopped into kindling and fed to the fire. Etsuko wept as she threw in family photos and a sheaf of letters, in *kanji*, from her mother in Japan.

Once the ashes had cooled, they were scattered across the fields. The blackened dirt in the backyard was turned over to leave no trace.

Exhausted, they shared a solemn supper. In the quiet normalcy of evening, Taizo began to wonder whether they had acted too precipitously.

Then, a little after seven o'clock, Jiro answered a loud rapping at the door, and three *hakujin* men in dark business suits introduced themselves as agents of the Federal Bureau of Investigation.

Taizo's heart pounded, but he stood, ready to join his brother for whatever fate awaited them.

One of the FBI agents asked, "Is Akira Watanabe here?"

Jiro and Taizo were taken aback. "Akira?" Jiro said. "My son?"

"You're Jiro Watanabe?" the agent said.

"Yes."

"Where is your son?"

Hearing his name, Akira came to the door. "I'm Akira Watanabe."

"Mr. Watanabe, you are a dual citizen of Japan and the United States?"

Akira replied politely, "Yes, but not by choice. The Japanese government grants all children of Japanese nationals the right of citizenship."

"And did you make a wire transfer of funds to the Japanese government in April of 1939?"

Akira appeared baffled a moment, then said with a laugh, "Oh, *that*. Yes, I paid them money or else they would have drafted me into their army!"

"So you admit you gave money to Japan's armed forces?"

"Yes, but that was the only way to avoid conscription."

The lead FBI man turned to a second one and said, "Escort Mr. Watanabe to the car. We'll look for contraband."

Another agent started to take Akira by the arm when Tamiko came running up. "But he's told you everything there is to tell!" she cried.

"We'll see, ma'am."

"I'll be fine, honey," Akira told his wife. He was barely able to kiss her on the cheek before the agent escorted him out.

"What is going on!" Jiro shouted. "Where are you taking my son?"

"Into custody, sir. For further questioning."

The remaining agents entered without the courtesy of removing their shoes and began ransacking the house. Jiro and Taizo could only watch as they opened closets, poked into cupboards, peeked under furniture. They blithely trespassed into bedrooms and pulled back sheets, searched inside pillowcases, rifled through wardrobe and underwear drawers. They confiscated Jiro's shotgun, binoculars, and a Kodak Brownie camera. All of these, the agents told them, were now forbidden items for Japanese to own.

The agents searched the barn and the backyard, and for a moment Taizo held his breath, afraid they might notice some faint revenant of the bonfire that had so recently blazed here. But they walked right over where the ashes had been, then walked back through the house, tracking in dirt as they did.

"What is going to happen to my son?" Jiro demanded.

"He'll be questioned at a secure facility, sir. Thank you for your cooperation." The G-man tipped his hat and the men left. Jiro and Taizo watched helplessly as they drove their black Packard—and Akira—away.

Tamiko wept inconsolably as Rose held her.

Horace and Ralph walked up, both looking stunned and guilty. "When we got that letter from Japan, we just ignored it," Ralph admitted. "I thought, hey, let 'em come after me, what can they do?"

"It seems they weren't the ones we had to fear," Horace said quietly.

Tears were rolling down Jiro's cheeks. "Why couldn't they have taken me?" he said softly. "Why did they have to take my son?"

*W*hen Taizo called and told Ruth what had happened, the uncertainty and dread she had felt all day metabolized into fear, and she shivered violently. She heard her father say, "Get rid of any guns, cameras, binoculars, and anything Japanese," but it all sounded like dialog from a radio play, the Martian invasion that had never happened. But this was happening, and as incredible as it seemed, *they* were the Martians.

Frank received the news with a stunned look. "My God," he said, softly so the children wouldn't hear, "he was serious? Everything?"

"Anything with *kanji* characters on it," she said.

Frank gathered a clutch of envelopes containing his parents' letters to him and stoically burned them in a trash can with old photos of his parents and grandparents in traditional Japanese dress. Frank gave his camera to Jim Russell, who expressed his astonishment at what was happening.

The next day the family learned that Akira was far from alone.

Beginning on the afternoon of December 7, FBI men in dark suits swooped down like crows on Florin, as they did up and down the West Coast. Their targets were leaders of the Japanese American community: Buddhist priests, businessmen with ties to Japan, teachers at Japanese-language schools, writers and editors for Japanese-language newspapers. In Florin they arrested Mr. Tanikawa, founder of the town's oldest general store, because he also acted as a go-between for arranged marriages and his frequent trips to Japan raised suspicions. Mr. Akiyama, owner of Akiyama's Fish Market, was arrested because he was an enthusiast of *kendo*—stylized Japanese swordplay, fought with bamboo sticks—and the FBI saw such games as "military training exercises." Mr. Sasaki, a local tofu manufacturer, was rounded up because he also served as secretary of the local Japan Association, a kind of chamber of commerce. A farmer named Iwao Tsuji had also been taken away, though no one understood why—least of all his terrified wife and two adolescent children, who were left to somehow run their forty-acre farm.

Frank walked to the diner at five A.M. as usual. The staff was as shaken as he was, but they buckled down and were ready to open by six. The breakfast crowd soon arrived, larger than usual—everyone wanted to talk about the attack and share whispered stories of FBI arrests. Later, Frank turned on the radio so everyone could hear President Roosevelt's address to Congress at nine-thirty A.M. asking for a declaration of war against Japan, which was quickly approved. The United States was now officially at war with the Empire of Japan. Frank studied his customers' rapt faces, only now realizing that all those faces were Japanese—there was not a single white face among them.

Ruth went about her usual Monday morning grocery shipping, driving with the children up Stockton Boulevard to Sacramento. But as she entered the city, she was jolted by the sight of handmade signs that had sprouted like fungi on fences, store windows, and telephone poles:

JAPS GET OUT!
NO NIPS WANTED!
ALL JAPS MUST GO!

She was grateful that the kids couldn't read and almost wished she couldn't either.

Shopping at the local Safeway, she was conscious of her Japanese features in a way she never had been before, flinching when a white customer merely glanced at her. She stocked up on toiletries, milk, bread, cereal, and meat, then worried, was she buying *too* much? Might it look as if she were hoarding food in advance of an impending attack? She took a deep breath and, in the candy aisle, when Donnie and Peggy begged for treats, Ruth surprised herself with her own whimsy and handed them each a Mars Bar.

She quickly paid and drove white-knuckled all the way back to Florin.

She stopped at her parents' farm, where Etsuko was quick to take the children outside to play while Ruth embraced Aunt Nishi and Uncle Jiro. "I'm so sorry, Uncle. Have you heard anything from the FBI?"

"No," he said bleakly. "I called their office in Sacramento, but no one will say anything other than that Akira is still being questioned. And now we have learned that the government has frozen the assets of Sumitomo Bank and other Japanese-owned banks. We cannot touch our savings; all we can do is live day to day." He blinked back tears. "Tamiko is beside herself with worry. She is taking the children and going to stay with her parents in Sacramento. She needs the comfort of her mother, and I cannot blame her."

At home, Ruth tried to hide her anxiety from the children. She knew she would eventually have to tell them what had happened, but they were so young and she wasn't ready to burden them with that knowledge yet.

Only one member of the household wasn't fooled. As Ruth was cooking dinner, Slugger padded into the kitchen and stood by her side as if protecting her from unseen forces. He looked up, making a little whining noise of concern. She bent down and ruffled his fur. "You can always tell when I'm upset, can't you, boy?" She reached up, picked up a slice of the carrot she had been chopping, and handed it to him. He wolfed it down, his tail wagging happily. "Fortunately," she added fondly, "you are also *highly* susceptible to bribery."

O n December 11, the Western Defense Command declared the entire West Coast of the United States a "prohibited military area." The following weeks saw hundreds more "enemy aliens" arrested amid unsubstantiated claims of a vast fifth column of "Jap" spies in the United States. There were fulminations of outrage from politicians and newspaper editorialists. Movie actor and Hearst columnist Henry McLemore wrote, "I am for the immediate removal of every Japanese on the West Coast to a point deep in the interior. I don't mean a nice part of the interior, either. Herd 'em up, pack 'em off and give 'em the inside room in the badlands. Let 'em be pinched, hurt, hungry, and dead up against it . . . I hate the Japanese. And that goes for all of them."

Prejudice against the Japanese was nothing new—it had even been enshrined in law in the so-called Oriental Exclusion Act of 1924, which prohibited further immigration from Asian countries. But now Japanese Americans were being seen as an existential threat, even by respected figures like California Attorney General Earl Warren and columnist Walter Lippmann, who added their voices to the call for "confinement," "removal," or "evacuation." Traditionally anti-Japanese organizations like the Associated Farmers lobbied for internment, as locally Joseph Dreesen once again opined to newspapers, "You can't trust a Jap."

In Florin, every public pronouncement sparked new rumors and speculation. Would only Issei—Japanese nationals—be removed? Nisei feared for their parents, but surely the government wouldn't do the same to them as American citizens? The very fact that the Farm Security Administration was encouraging Japanese farmers to continue working "for the war effort" indicated that the country needed them. To avoid appearing disloyal, the Japanese community enthusiastically embraced patriotic activities like selling war bonds and rolling bandages for the Red Cross.

The FBI continued to search homes with impunity, and on February 18, agents interrogated a local farmer named Hisata Iwasa. Iwasa spoke imperfect English, was recovering from a stroke, and, after the men left, became so shamed and agitated—fearing he had said the wrong things and thrown suspicion on innocent friends—that he took poison and killed himself.

The next day, President Roosevelt signed Executive Order No. 9066, "authorizing the Secretary of War to prescribe military areas . . . from which any or all persons may be excluded." Soon it became clear that "all persons" meant "all Japanese" and that "exclusion" meant "exile"—to one of ten "relocation centers" outside the "military areas," i.e., the entire West Coast of the United States.

On February 25, the Navy informed the residents of Terminal Island near San Pedro—mainly fisherman—that they had forty-eight hours to leave the island. Bainbridge Island in Washington State followed. In Oregon, Stanley Watanabe, his wife, and their children were sent to a hastily constructed assembly center in North Portland.

The mass evacuations had begun.

There was now a military curfew prohibiting anyone of Japanese ancestry from being on the streets between eight P.M. and six A.M. Vince had to open and close the diner because Frank couldn't risk violating the curfew. A travel limit was also imposed: Japanese Americans could venture no farther than five miles from their homes. But most of the stores and physicians that residents of Florin depended on were ten miles away in Sacramento. Exceptions could be obtained only from the provost's office in, of course, Sacramento. So in order to petition a waiver of the travel regulations, you first had to violate them.

"How could FDR *do* this to us?" Ruth complained bitterly, the children safely in bed, Frank at home after the nightly curfew. Franklin Delano Roosevelt was the first and only president that Ruth had voted for in her twenty-five years, and she had been proud of that vote, proud of the man who had labored so mightily to lift the nation out of the Depression. But now she felt angry, and betrayed: "God damn it, we're American citizens!"

"So are Negroes," Frank noted, "and what has it gotten them?"

"Is that all it comes down to in this country? The color of your skin? The shape of your eyes?"

"It won't be like this forever. But this is the way it is now, and we have to live with it. We have to show these bastards that we're loyal Americans and we will do our duty—and hope that someday they'll see us that way too."

Ruth's eyes filled with tears. "What about Donnie and Peggy? How many years will they be forced to spend in a . . . relocation center?"

"We'll be with them. That's all that matters to them."

"And what about the diner? What are we going to do with it?"

Frank winced. "Sell the inventory, I guess, and start all over again when we get back. That's more than your parents will be able to do."

"Oh God," she whispered, thinking of the farm, everything her father and mother had worked for since coming to California. "Poor Papa . . ."

Frank took her in his arms and she rested her head on his shoulder. He was more familiar with the world's injustices, the way people's lives could be uprooted like trees in a hurricane. But to lose his home twice, through no fault of his own—that was a bitter draft, and he almost choked on it.

A s the tidal wave of dispossession rolled into California's inland valleys, the Florin area was one of the last to be evacuated. It wasn't until late May that the grim heralds appeared, overnight, tacked up on telephone poles:

Pursuant to the provisions of Civilian Exclusion Order No. 92, this Headquarters, dated May 23, 1942, all persons of Japanese ancestry, both alien and non-alien, will be evacuated from the above area by 12 o'clock noon, P.W.T., Saturday, May 30, 1942.

One week's notice was standard. For supposed security reasons, the War Relocation Authority—or WRA—did not want news of which areas were to be evacuated to be made public more than seven days in advance.

The inland sea around the Watanabes' farmhouse had turned scarlet, the strawberry plants bursting with nearly ripe fruit. Bees buzzed amid the grapevines, like the sound of power lines on a quiet day—soothing, as long as you didn't get too close. Taizo, Jiro, Horace, and Ralph were out in the fields preparing for the harvest when they heard a discordant, unwelcome voice:

"Morning, Watanabe-*san*."

Joseph Dreesen—his hair as white as the document he held in his wrinkled hand—stood there smiling his wolfen smile, as Taizo knew he would be eventually.

"Ah. Sheriff," Taizo said. "Never one to waste time, are you?"

"Nope." He stepped forward, handed the document to Taizo. "And you don't have time to waste either."

Taizo glanced, unsurprised, at the eviction notice. "We have not breached our contract. We have made a profit for you every year since 1930."

"Technically. But you won't this year, because you won't be here to harvest the crop when the government ships you to hell and gone in six days."

"Surely you will not let it rot in the fields!" Jiro said, horrified.

"It's my land," Dreesen said. "I'll do with it as I like."

Jiro did not bother to conceal his fury. But Taizo remained calm, if not quiescent. "So, you have what you have always wanted. We Japanese will be gone from Florin. What shall you and your fellow *hakujin* do with it, Sheriff?"

"We'll farm it like you did."

Taizo smiled. "If you were able to do that," he said, "you would have done it before the first Japanese farmer tilled this unforgiving soil." He turned his back on Dreesen. "May you find the fortune you deserve, Sheriff."

Over the next two days the 2,500 Japanese residents of Florin presented themselves at the Elk Grove Masonic Hall to be registered. Ruth, Frank, and their children were each issued a manila identification card bearing a "family number"—2355—and each person was designated a letter: Frank was 2355-A, Ruth 2355-B, Donnie 2355-C, and Peggy 2355-D. Taizo, Etsuko, Jiro, and Nishi were assigned cards as well, but the ones for Issei—Japanese nationals—were colored red as a rising sun.

Ruth stared at the ID card in her hand and suddenly knew what it must feel like to be a Jew in Nazi Germany.

"All evacuees must bring the following items upon departure for the Assembly Centers," they were told. "Bedding and linens—no mattress—toilet articles, extra clothing, and essential personal effects for each family member, the total limited to forty-two pounds per person."

Everyone received inoculations against diphtheria, smallpox, and, most painfully, typhoid, which made the children howl. Then, after they had settled down, Ruth told them that they would be going to stay with Grandma and Grandpa for a few days.

"Why?" Donnie wanted to know. "An' what's this for?" he asked, holding up the card with his number on it.

"You're staying on the farm because we're going on a big adventure and we've got to get everything ready! And that card is so you don't get lost. So you be good and do whatever Grandma and Grandpa tell you to do, all right?"

"They will be just fine," Etsuko said, lifting Peggy.

The Federal Reserve Bank had been charged with assisting evacuees in the sale or storage of their personal property—in Florin the Community Hall and the gymnasium at the Buddhist Church served as warehouses for the Reserve. All property had to be crated and marked with the family's name and address. What couldn't be warehoused was usually sold for a fraction of its value to predatory "used furniture dealers" who knew their victims had no alternative but to sell, and quickly.

The Haradas needed to dispose of the diner's entire stock—grill, refrigerator, tableware, counter, booths. Anticipating this, the previous week they had placed an ad in the *Sacramento Bee*: "Diner, Florin, all appliances, sacrifice, evacuees." Grifters descended on them like carrion birds, offering one or two hundred dollars for ten thousand dollars' worth of inventory.

"Go to hell!" Frank snapped at them, but for days the opportunists flocked in, offering ten dollars for a new refrigerator or five bucks for a vinyl booth. Frank insisted on selling the diner as a whole, hoping that the buyer would keep it running and continue to employ Vince and the busboys.

Finally, a Sacramento businessman, Carl Clasen, offered a thousand dollars for the entire contents of the diner—and Frank and Ruth reluctantly agreed to take a dime on every dollar they had spent. Clasen promised to keep on Vince and the busboys—then reneged and fired them all the next day.

Frank felt sick inside. With Ruth's approval he gave Vince a hundred dollars and the busboys fifty apiece to get keep them afloat until they could find jobs, possibly in the suddenly booming defense industry.

Vince looked at the C-note in his hand, then up at Frank. "This—this is bullshit what they're doing to you," he said vehemently. "You and the missus—you're the best goddamn Americans I ever met." His voice broke, and all he could do was shake their hands. Ruth wanted to cry.

The day before evacuation, Florin's business district was a ghost town, the windows of Japanese-owned stores boarded up with wooden planks, the street empty but for those rushing to divest themselves of their possessions.

Ruth and Frank were required to sell their car to the Army for the war effort, but members of the Japanese American Citizens League—a.k.a. the JACL—helped them crate up their furniture and move it into the Community Hall. Florin was now divided into four districts, and residents of each would be sent to different temporary "assembly" centers, with no respect to the familial ties so important to the Japanese. "We have to move in with my parents," Ruth had said upon learning this. "We *have* to keep the family together."

Frank had agreed. That left only one problem, and he was waiting for them in their backyard when a cab dropped them off at their empty house. They heard the barks of pleasure at their arrival coming from behind the gate.

"Oh God," Ruth said under her breath.

"Bastards won't even let us take our dog."

"Should we bring him over to the farm, so the kids can say goodbye?"

"I think that will only make things worse," Frank said. "He'll be here when we get back—whenever that is."

They brought Slugger next door to Jim and Helen Russell's house. The couple was already standing in the doorway, waiting for them.

"You're going to stay here while we're gone," Ruth told the dog, hoping somehow he understood. She hugged him, kissed him on his snout. "You be a good boy for Jim and Helen, okay?" Her voice broke. "We love you, Slugger."

"He'll be fine," Helen said. "He's crazy about Cathy and Jeff."

"Thank you so much for doing this."

"Happy to help," Jim said. "If Bob Fletcher can look after the Okamoto, Nitta, and Tsukamoto farms, the least we can do is look after a dog."

"If you ask me," Helen said, voice quavering, "someday this country is going to regret what it's doing today. That's my opinion."

Jim said lightly, "Don't look at me, I voted for Wendell Willkie." They all laughed. "Come on, I'll drive you over to your parents' place."

Helen and Ruth hugged goodbye, then Ruth and Frank got into Jim's truck. As he backed it out of his driveway onto the street, Ruth looked back and saw Slugger standing there, his head cocked to one side as if puzzled.

Tears in her eyes, she had to force herself to turn away.

When they reached the farm, Jim promised to pick them up the next morning.

Etsuko was waiting for them on the doorstep. "Welcome home, butter-fly," she said with a sadness in her voice that alarmed Ruth.

"What's wrong, *Okāsan*?"

Etsuko, sounding shaken, told her, "Jiro received word today. Akira is being deported back to Japan."

"What!" Ruth cried. "That's crazy! He's never even *been* to Japan."

"Jiro fears he will be drafted into the Imperial Army. There is no consoling him."

Still reeling, Ruth and Frank entered the house, as bare as the Haradas' home. All that was left were a few mattresses to sleep on that night.

Donnie and Peggy rushed in to greet them, confused by all that was going on. "Where's Slugger?" Donnie asked.

"He's staying at Jim and Helen's house until we get back."

"When do we get back?"

"I don't know, honey," Ruth admitted.

"Where are we going?"

Frank said with false cheer, "To a camp, sport. Camps are fun, right?"

"And we'll all be together," Ruth assured them, even if it was a lie. "All" of them, she knew, might never be together again.

On Friday, May 29, Taizo woke before sunrise, washed, put on his business suit, then slipped outside to watch for the last time as the sun rose on what would always be, in his heart, his land—his and Jiro's. The fields were beautiful at dawn, the sun pulling back night's blanket on a bed of endless green and ripe red, the morning dew glistening like teardrops on the leaves. Taizo ached to stay here, in this moment, forever, one with the land he had loved and nurtured for almost two decades. But he forced himself to recall what was said, so long ago, after beloved Buddha had died:

Impermanent are all component things,
They arise and cease, that is their nature:
They come into being and pass away,
Release from them is bliss supreme.

Taizo's mind sought bliss but his heart found only loss.

The Elk Grove train station was busier than anyone had ever seen it at eight-thirty in the morning. Florin's Japanese had been leaving in daily shifts of five hundred per train; this group was the last to go. A ragged line of people—men in Sunday suits, women in dresses and hats, many openly weeping—was wrapped like a wilted garland around the tiny depot. A wooden ramp was piled high with rolls of bedding, suitcases, boxes, crates, duffel bags—so many lives and livelihoods, now reduced to a mountain of luggage and bundles of linen.

Jim Russell helped Ruth and Frank unload their luggage, and, sticking close to Taizo, Etsuko, and the rest of the family, they got in line for the nine o'clock departure. Jim's was not the only white face there—Jerry and Vivian Kara, who were taking care of the Yamada, Tanaka, and Tamohara farms, had ferried each family in turn to the train station—but they and a few others represented only a fraction of the Caucasian population.

"Helen made sandwiches for you to eat on the train." Jim handed Frank a big paper bag stuffed with food. "Ham and cheese for the adults, peanut butter and jelly for the kids. Write us as soon as you get an address."

"Are you sure?" Frank asked. "The FBI might consider you . . . suspect."

"Screw the FBI. You're not the enemy. You're our friends."

Frank and Jim shook hands; both men looked as if they wanted to cry. The line inched toward the Southern Pacific locomotive sitting on the other side of the depot. There was no platform at the station—passengers had to walk through knee-high weeds and sage scrub before they could board the train. Ruth asked herself, *How can this be happening? This is America.* Covenants of trust had been broken, faith in law betrayed.

Frank lifted first Peggy, then Donnie, into the railroad car. Ruth followed, her parents, brothers, uncle, and their families right behind.

They walked to the back of the car and found seats. They would not be separated, at least. When the last passengers had boarded, the train whistle blew with the shrillness of a scream and the train slowly moved down the tracks, picking up speed as they left the station. The landscape rolling by attracted the children's attention, curiosity getting the better of their tears.

And then suddenly two soldiers with rifles and bayonets were moving through the car, rolling down the blinds on the windows, shutting out the world. The car darkened, lights snapped on, but too late; Donnie and Peggy began wailing again, along with other children in the car.

"It's okay, sweetie, it's going to be all right," Ruth lied as she rocked Peggy, then, as one of the soldiers passed, she snapped at him, "Why did you have to lower the shades? Can't we even see where we're going?"

The soldier—barely out of his teens—looked at her and said, not without some chagrin, "It's not for you, ma'am. It's for the people outside. So they . . . can't see you."

Then each soldier took up position at opposite ends of the car and shouldered their rifles.

Ruth was thunderstruck. My God, she thought. We've had everything taken away from us—we're homeless; powerless—and yet we're so fearsome and repugnant that the whites have to be protected from the very sight of us?

Too angry to cry, Ruth held tight onto her children as the train hurtled blindly into an unknown future.

PART TWO

Gaman

Chapter 8

1942

The grandstand at Tanforan Assembly Center towered over the former racetrack like a half-completed ziggurat—once a temple of fortune, now a prison for those with the misfortune to have been born with a Japanese face. Tanforan Racetrack in San Bruno, California—twelve miles south of San Francisco—was coiled in a perimeter of steel, a high barbed-wire fence fortified by armed guard towers. Two soldiers opened the entry gates to admit busloads of hapless men, women, and children; they spilled out of buses, staggering under the weight of what was left of their lives. They gazed up at the two-story clubhouse beside the grandstand—where high rollers once followed the races from swanky box seats—with a mix of bewilderment and disbelief. They saw rifles pointed at them from watchtowers as well as dozens of tar-papered, military-style barracks squatting incongruously in the infield—like some absurd, unholy amalgam of sport and war.

Ruth shouldered Peggy and kept a tight grip on Donnie's hand. Her children's wide eyes took in the strangeness of their surroundings. Life had long since stopped making sense for them; by the time the family transferred from railroad car to Greyhound bus, the kids had gone silent and numb.

Beside her, Frank carried two heavy suitcases and a duffel bag slung over his shoulder. Behind them were Taizo and Etsuko, Ralph, Horace and Rose and their two sons, Jack and Will, with Jiro and Nishi taking up the rear.

"Everyone stay together," Ruth called out, seeing the way guards were herding evacuees into a long line snaking toward the side of the grandstand.

"Say, is it too late to put ten bucks on War Admiral in the fifth?" Ralph piped up, drawing at best rueful chuckles from his family.

A soldier approached the group. "Folks, if you'll just get into the intake line over there, we'll get you all registered and assigned quarters."

"Thank you," Frank said. Ruth rankled at his courtesy.

They got in line, but it took an hour before they even reached the entrance. Indeed, waiting in line would turn out to be the number one recreational activity at Tanforan: residents waited in line at the mess hall, at the post office, waited to use the latrine, the showers, the laundry. Now they inched their way toward one of the many cubbyholes under the grandstand and, once inside the cavernous interior, waited another half hour until reaching the front of the queue. Here men were separated from women and children from adults as everyone was searched from head to toe, frisked for contraband or concealed weapons. Straight-edge razors, pocket knives, and flasks of liquor were confiscated. Ruth's family carried none of these, so they were directed individually into small curtained compartments and ordered to undress. Ruth unbuttoned her blouse and a Nisei woman whose nametag identified her as NURSE MORI shined a flashlight into Ruth's mouth, listened to her heartbeat, made sure her vaccinations were up to date, then discreetly inquired whether Ruth had any "skin or venereal diseases." Mortified, Ruth said she did not, even as she heard a burst of laughter from outside; when she left the compartment, she found Ralph still chuckling.

"When they asked, I told 'em I had hoof and mouth disease and so they had to send me back to Florin. Got a rise out of 'em."

"I'm so glad you're enjoying yourself, Ralph," Ruth said sharply.

"Sis, this is all so nuts, you gotta laugh."

The family reunited at the registration tables, where Nisei clerks handed them forms to fill out and gave them yet another family identification number, 14793. But when they attempted to assign Ruth and her family to a different barracks from her parents, Ruth protested, "We are one family, we will not be separated!"

"Ma'am, I'm sorry, but we are limited by the availability of required spaces. We'll do the best we can to keep your family together."

Ruth, Frank, their children, Taizo, Etsuko, Ralph, Jiro, and Nishi were assigned to Barrack 9, Apartments 1 and 2. But Horace and his family were assigned to a different barrack on the opposite side of the track.

"Ruth, it's okay," Horace said. "We're in the same camp, it's not like we'll never see each other again. You take care of Mom and Pop, all right?" She nodded. "Unfortunately," he added dryly, "you also get custody of Ralph."

Ralph gave him a Bronx cheer, easing the tension.

One of the volunteer guides—a Nisei boy of fifteen named Ben—offered to show them to their quarters, escorting them out onto the racetrack. This was clearly Tanforan's Main Street; even in late afternoon there were hundreds of evacuees taking a stroll around the track, chatting with friends or just getting some exercise. All seemed to be smiling. Ruth couldn't tell if they were genuinely in good spirits or merely had on their "outside faces." Certainly Ben was chipper enough as he pointed out the sights.

"The main mess hall is back there in the grandstand, by the by. There are three dinner shifts, the first starts at four-thirty. Expect a wait." More barracks were being assembled in the infield. Ben led the Watanabes to the far end of the track. "Over there, that's one of our nursery schools—I see you've got little ones, ma'am, if you need some time alone to do housework, the preschool's open every morning from nine to eleven. Oh, and if you're partial to washing in hot water, I'd get to the showers early, by six A.M."

They veered off the dirt road, through a grove of eucalyptus trees that ringed the track, toward one of many long, green-roofed buildings, noticeably older than the other barracks. "There it is," Ben said cheerily. "Barrack 9."

Barrack 9 was only partly occupied, but the barrack opposite it held a full complement of evacuees. All of its doors were propped open and the residents were outside their apartments, sitting in handmade chairs or working in victory gardens. The carefully tended flowers, pretty window boxes, and leafy vegetable patches lent it color and a homey touch, and many doors bore whimsical names like "The Bel-Air Arms" and "Ritz Apartments." But there was no mistaking—at least not to a farm family—what the original purpose of the buildings were.

"These are stables," Taizo said in astonishment and dismay.

"Yeah," Ben allowed, "the first evacuees got most of the new housing. This is what's left. But we've all got to pitch in for the war effort, right?"

Stunned, the Watanabes walked down to the far end of "Barrack" 9. Some wag had painted on the exterior wall: SEABISCUIT SLEPT HERE.

"Heh." It was the best even Ralph could manage.

Ben opened the door and led the way inside.

As soon as Ruth entered, she choked at the smell of horse manure, which explained why all the neighbors had their doors open.

The "apartment" was nearly dark, the sunlight barely sifting through two grimy windows on either side of the door. Ben reached up to switch on the single bare light bulb dangling from the ceiling.

Illumination did not beautify the interior. The original horse stall had been divided into two rooms, each about ten feet by twenty feet. A pair of Dutch doors, gnawed over with teeth marks, marked the point at which the original equine tenant's accommodations had ended; the front room, once intended for fodder, had been extended to create more space. The ceiling sloped down from a height of twelve feet in the rear to seven in the front, but the partitions between the one-room "apartments" didn't extend all the way to the ceiling—so one could easily hear, from the other apartments in the barrack, the tinny blare of radios and the susurrus of people murmuring, talking, or just rustling back and forth.

"Oh my," Etsuko said softly, running her hand along a wall. It had received a slapdash whitewashing, creating a chalk-white frieze of spiderwebs, horse hairs, bits of hay, and insects, all shellacked to the wall in bas-relief. The floorboards were covered with linoleum of indeterminate color beneath a two-inch layer of dust and wood shavings—but there were places where the original manure-stained boards were exposed, and still pungent.

Ruth felt the bile rising in her throat and struggled to keep it down.

The only furnishings in either room were half a dozen Army cots, their steel frames and bedsprings spray-painted yellow, folded up against the wall. The only light fixtures were the bare bulbs, one to a room, dangling on their cords from the ceiling.

"Where are the mattresses?" Jiro asked Ben.

"Oh, just go to the mattress department—one of those big buildings we passed on the way here. When the block manager makes his rounds, he'll get you some cleaning supplies to spruce up the place. And there's plenty of scrap lumber around, enough to build tables, stools, whatever furniture you want."

The family stood there, silently aghast, until Frank finally thanked Ben for his help and the young man jauntily went on his way.

Donnie wrinkled his nose and said in a small voice, "Mama, it smells bad in here."

Etsuko began to weep.

Ruth wrapped her arms around her children and told them, "Don't worry, we'll clean this up and get rid of that nasty smell, I promise."

Taizo went to Etsuko and let her bury her face in his chest as she wept. "It will be all right, *Okāsan*," he said with a gentle reassurance he did not truly feel. "We will *gaman*, and all will be right in the end."

Gaman was a word rooted in Buddhism that meant "enduring the seemingly unbearable with patience and dignity." Ruth had heard her father use it often after they moved to California. And now, after they had endured so much already, here they were, once more forced to *gaman*.

There was a tap on the open door. Ruth turned to see an Issei woman standing on the threshold, holding two brooms and a dustpan in her hand. "*Konnichiwa*," she greeted them. "Welcome to Tanforan. I thought you might wish to borrow these. We did not have any when we first moved in."

Etsuko quickly recovered herself and smiled. "Thank you, that is so kind of you. That is exactly what we need."

The neighbor introduced herself as Shizuko Kikuchi. She was tiny even for a Japanese woman, but radiated strength and composure. After Etsuko introduced herself and her family, Shizuko gazed into Etsuko's eyes—did she notice the redness around them?—and quietly assured her, "You and your family will be fine. If you need anything else, do not hesitate to ask."

She bowed and left, but with this simple act of grace Shizuko seemed to bequeath a part of her strength and calm to the Watanabe clan. Etsuko began sweeping with a welcome purpose, as Nishi took the other broom in hand.

The men went to the "mattress department," which turned out to be a stable filled with bales of hay where they were given empty mattress tickings and told they could fill them with as much as straw as they needed. Someone would sew up the tickings for them once they were full.

Taizo looked down at the empty ticking in his hand and the shame he had been trying to hide from his family cut like a *tantō* blade to his heart. But he had no choice but to provide for his family as best he could, and *gaman*.

Peggy and Donnie needed to go the bathroom, so Ruth took them to the nearest latrine—a small, tar-papered building, men's on one side, women's on the other. Unwilling to let Donnie go into the men's room alone, she took them both into the ladies' room, which, to Ruth's shock, was equipped with communal toilets lined up in two rows, back to back, with no partitions or curtains between them. Afterward she lifted the kids up to wash their hands in a long tin "sink"—like a feeding trough—that ran the length of a wall. Halfway through washing Ruth noticed a handmade sign, written in Japanese, that had been taped onto the mirror above the trough. Ruth's Japanese was a bit rusty because her parents spoke more English these days, especially around Donnie and Peggy, but she had no trouble reading:

PLEASE DO NOT EMPTY BEDPANS INTO THE SINK!

Ruth blanched and quickly scooted the kids outside, where she said cheerily, "Let's have some fun and go for a walk!"

These were just the words to nudge Donnie out of his stupor: "I wanna see the racetrack again!" Ruth lifted Peggy and followed her son through the thicket of eucalyptus trees. The track was still crowded with pedestrians making way for the occasional Army supply truck. Inside the track's oval, young men were playing baseball, which captivated Donnie; they watched the game a while, then wandered down to listen to the Tanforan Band practice "America the Beautiful." Once again, everyone around them was smiling, as if they were taking in the county fair. Ruth wondered if they had been issued regulation smiles from the Army and hers had yet to be requisitioned. Or maybe, she admitted, they were just trying to make the best of a bad situation.

Ruth and the kids returned to their barrack to find the door and windows open, the floor dust-free, and the linoleum revealed to be an odd reddish mahogany in color. Etsuko told her, "The house manager came by with Army blankets. Tomorrow he'll bring us mops, soap, and buckets so we can wash the windows and give the walls and floor a good scrubbing."

"If there's still horse poop on the floorboards under the linoleum," Ruth said, "that might not help much."

"Then maybe it will help a little," her mother replied stubbornly.

Ruth laughed but was pleased by her mother's spirit.

The men returned, sheepishly delivering eight lumpy, straw-filled mattresses. "There are only six cots," Frank said, "but we made two extra mattresses. Ralph and I can sleep on the floor and the kids can share a cot."

"Tomorrow we will build some chairs and table," Taizo said. "We can make the necessary tools from scrap metal."

They further divided the two rooms with bed sheets hung from the rafters. Jiro insisted that Taizo, Etsuko, and the Haradas occupy the front room. "The children need fresh air. We will make do in back."

By this time they were all starving—the last food they'd eaten were the sandwiches Helen Russell had made for their train trip. Mess Hall 5 was closest to them; they arrived to find at least a hundred people standing in two lines. The Watanabes waited for the better part of an hour to get inside, where the line then inched and squiggled between steam counters and scores of internees eating at picnic tables. At the head of the serving counter, there were stacks of plates and bins of silverware—no chopsticks.

It was Etsuko's turn to feel shame. All these people holding out their plates for food—it reminded her of the breadlines during the Depression, vagabonds begging in soup kitchens. Now she was holding out a plate—homeless, like many on those breadlines—and she couldn't help but feel as if she, too, were begging. Her shame and embarrassment was almost greater than her hunger; she nearly walked away, preferring to starve. But when she reached the first steam counter she fought back her pride and held up her plate, her hands trembling. A cook reached into the metal pan, took out a plain boiled potato with his fingers, and put it on her plate. The second man also used his fingers, picking up two Vienna sausages and dropping them next to the potato. The third used a ladle, at least, to scoop up a wad of yellowish-green spinach, and a girl at the end of the counter gave her two pieces of sliced bread. Etsuko looked at her plate in dismay: She had debased herself, and for what? Canned sausage and overcooked vegetables?

"No rice?" Taizo asked the last of the cooks.

The man shook his head. "Not today. Maybe later this week."

The family found a table and sat down to desultorily eat their supper. "What *is* this?" Donnie asked, poking a sausage with his fork.

"It's just a hot dog without a bun, silly!" Ruth improvised. This changed everything, and he attacked the sausages with gusto. The same could not be said for the rest of the family. Nor did the mess hall lend itself to relaxing dining: it echoed with the clatter of dishes, the clangor of pots and pans colliding in the kitchen, and the cacophony of hundreds of people conversing all at once.

Frank went away for a few minutes to speak with one of the cooks, and when he returned he said, "The kitchen staff is overwhelmed preparing three meals a day for eight thousand people; they need all the help they can get. Tomorrow I'll apply for a job; maybe I can even help improve the fare."

By the time they finished dinner it was dark out and a chill, cutting wind flung dirt into their faces. There was no outdoor lighting, so they stumbled blindly over tree roots, felt the sting of eucalyptus branches, and walked into a webwork of clotheslines strung between barracks. Finally they reached Barrack 9, stepped inside, and immediately breathed in the stench. The atmosphere was poisonous, but it was too cold to open the windows. So they turned on the single light in each apartment, Ruth got the children into pajamas, and the adults prepared for bed as well. Donnie sat on his prickly bed of straw and said what everybody was thinking:

"Mama, I want to go home."

Ruth's heart ached. She couldn't find the words.

"Please, Mama, let's go home," he said plaintively, and began to cry.

Peggy echoed, "Home, Mama," and also started to cry.

Frank lifted her up and rocked her, saying "Shh, shh, it's all right, baby. It's all right . . ."

Ruth took Donnie in her arms. "We—we can't go home yet, honey. We have to stay here for a while. But remember the fun we had today? Watching the baseball game? And that big track—you can run all the way around it tomorrow, if you want! Will you do that? Show Mama how fast you can run?"

"Okay," Donnie said uncertainly, sniffing back tears.

"Good boy." She tucked him into bed, his sister next to him, covered by the same Army blanket. She kissed them both on their foreheads. "G'night."

Frank bent down and kissed them too. "We love you, babies."

"I'm not a baby," Donnie said, pride trouncing sorrow.

Taizo and Jiro turned off the lights. There was no heat in the stall, and they all shivered under thin blankets as the wind gusted through cracks in the thin walls. The combination of manure and the sickly-sweet smell of hay made them all want to gag. Almost as bad, there was no privacy, no quiet. Through that foot of open space between the ceiling and the top of the partitions, the Watanabes could hear their neighbors' snores, the chattering of teeth in the cold, the colic of babies . . . but most unnervingly, they heard weeping. The weeping of grown men and women, cries of hopelessness and loss, separation and misery. And in that collective lament, Ruth heard one closer by, muted in its shame: the sound of her own father's sobs, shocking in its newness, his familiar strength and solidity, like a once-sturdy oak, now riven with such grief and despair that it broke his daughter's heart.

They finally fell asleep, only to discover during the night that they shared their quarters with other tenants: tiny horse fleas with a vicious bite, flies drawn to the manure under the floor, mice that could be heard scuttling from room to room in the dead of night. Ralph and Frank quickly came to regret their decision to sleep on the floor. By morning the family was covered with flea bites and grumpy from what felt like sleeping on cacti. Ruth took the kids into the ladies' latrine to brush their teeth; others were doing the same as water streamed from the spigots down the length of the trough. One woman spat out a gob of tooth powder and Ruth watched in horror as a chalky tendril of saliva came floating downstream past her.

Oh my God, she thought. Are we really expected to live like this?

After breakfast Etsuko and Nishi began mopping the floors and scrubbing the walls with Ajax cleanser as the men went foraging for scraps of metal and lumber. Ruth wanted to help but all she could do was get the kids out of the way long enough for the apartments to be whipped into something fit for human habitation. She could at least return the borrowed brooms to their neighbor, and when Shizuko came to the door she invited Ruth and the children in for tea made on their little hot plate. Ruth was pleasantly surprised by their apartment, which was cheerfully covered in linoleum liberated from the bar at the former Tanforan Clubhouse and furnished with attractive handmade furniture—chairs, table, benches, shelves, closets—as well as a radio and a phonograph. The Dutch stable doors had been taken down and replaced with a curtain separating the two rooms; colorful maps, painted scarves, and college banners adorned the walls.

Shizuko introduced Ruth, Peggy, and Donnie to her husband, Nakajiro, and her daughters and sons, including Charles, an affable graduate student the same age as Ruth. "Welcome to the *neighh*-borhood," he said with a laugh. "Say, this just came out, you might find it useful." He gave her the latest issue of the camp newsletter, the *Tanforan Totalizer*, for which Charles was a staff writer. One of the headlines announced MEMORIAL DAY SERVICE SET.

"I have nothing against Memorial Day," Ruth said, "but isn't this a little . . . paradoxical? Saluting the flag as we're surrounded by barbed wire?"

"I understand how you feel. But we have to show we're loyal Americans. We have to be better than the way they're treating us."

"Do we? Why?" Ruth asked sarcastically.

"Because there's a war on, and in the end there is more hope for us in America, with its democratic traditions—and all its flaws—than under the dictatorship of Imperial Japan or Nazi Germany. And if we're to have a place in postwar America, we have to show that we *are* Americans."

Ruth thought bitterly: Why don't the damn Germans and Italians have to prove that they're Americans?

Everyone was doting on Donnie and Peggy, and Ruth thanked Shizuko again for the loan of the brooms. "Did you make them yourselves?" she asked.

Shizuko shook her head: "Montgomery Ward catalog."

"We can order things by mail?"

"Sure," Charles replied wryly, "the Bill of Rights still guarantees us the freedom to shop." Ruth had to laugh. He explained that copies of the Montgomery Ward and Sears, Roebuck catalogs were available at the post office, as were postal money orders. "Some of us still have a little cash in hand, and those who don't can work jobs here and make enough money to buy little amenities like gardening equipment, clothing, small appliances . . ."

She thanked Charles for the information and left with the kids to check out the nursery school Ben had pointed out yesterday. She was impressed by what the teachers had wrought there out of scraps: orange crates covered over in wallpaper were used as tables and colorful cut-outs of flowers decorated the windowpanes. There were sandboxes, a homemade seesaw, beanbags, blocks, and other toys to occupy the children. Donnie and Peggy seemed to like it so she enrolled them, starting the next day.

It was a foggy Bay Area morning but the weather was mild and the wind kinder than it had been during the night. As they explored the camp Ruth found herself surprised by the ingenuity of the residents, who—even knowing their stay here was only temporary—had opted to lend their homes as much grace and beauty as they could. There was an artificial pond in the infield where residents sailed boats or practiced fly-casting, as well as a little park decorated with flowers, a bamboo fence, and an old Japanese lantern—an oasis of serenity in a desert of drab utilitarian buildings, dusty roads, and military green. Ruth could see it was a favorite of the Issei, many of whom came to sit and meditate in this small semblance of a homeland they might never see again. For recreation there was also a six-hole golf course, baseball diamonds, basketball, tennis, football, boxing, badminton, and *sumo* wrestling.

Ruth took the kids to lunch in the main mess hall in the grandstand. They didn't care for the egg foo yung but gobbled up the pork and beans. Ruth thumbed through the *Tanforan Totalizer* and read about the latest war news, art lessons being taught by the well-known painter Chiura Obata, as well as something of potential interest to Jiro.

After lunch the fog lifted and Ruth took the kids up into the grandstand. Donnie tackled the hundred-odd steps eagerly. The stands were a popular place to while away the time: some residents dozed or sunned themselves on benches; others played dice or board games like *go* or *shogi*. When they reached the top Ruth put Peggy down on a bench, forced Donnie to sit still for one minute, and looked out at the surrounding city.

To the north, what appeared to be rolling green hills were actually the grassy ridges of San Bruno Mountain, with tracts of multihued houses coloring the lower slopes like wildflower fields. To the south, cars streamed past on Bayshore Highway, their drivers mostly oblivious to the eight thousand souls interned at Tanforan. Less oblivious, perhaps, were the pilots of the military aircraft that took off from Moffett Field, the sound of their engines a muted growl from afar. To the east, San Francisco Bay, cupped between mountains and city, dazzled blue in the afternoon sun.

"Gee whiz!" Donnie cried out.

"Oooh, high up!" Peggy agreed.

For a moment it *was* exhilarating, taking in the sweeping expanse of the world outside. Then Ruth's gaze fell on the curtain of steel around the camp, the watchtowers with their guns pointed inward, and was reminded that the world outside was just that: out of bounds. The view only confirmed her loss of freedom: freedom that everyone outside took for granted, for their birthright. What should have been *her* birthright, and her children's.

When she returned "home," Ruth was amazed at the improvements her mother and Aunt Nishi had wrought. The once-gray windows matted with grime and horsehair were spotless, admitting welcome shafts of afternoon sunlight into the front room. The walls had been scrubbed to a fare-thee-well, the embalmed insects excavated from the dried whitewash—with the result that the whole room seem lighter, brighter, larger. Both floors and walls had been cleaned with bleach, and the smell of manure was no longer pervasive. The holes and cracks in the walls were now stuffed with wadded paper or tacked over with cardboard.

"Wow," Ruth said, "you two did the work of seven women!"

"I think eight," Nishi replied, "but who is counting?" They all laughed.

The children were tired so Ruth put them to bed in the back room. This freed her to help Etsuko and Nishi unpack. Inspired by Shizuko's apartment, Ruth suggested hanging some colorful scarves on the walls and removing the stable doors and replacing them with something pretty. Resourcefully, Ruth began unscrewing the hinges of the Dutch doors with the flat edge of a coin. There were also several layers of paint covering the hinges that she chipped away with a nail file. Within half an hour she had removed the doors and each woman sacrificed one of her scarves to stitch together a lovely curtain between rooms, one that could be pulled back during the day to admit light and closed for privacy at night.

When Frank, Taizo, Jiro, and Ralph returned, they were greatly impressed with what the women had achieved—and vice versa. Using only scraps of lumber, pieces of iron, and discarded nails from a construction site, the men had built two sturdy chairs and had begun work on a table and a pair of wardrobe closets for each room. Ruth thought that her father looked particularly pleased and proud with their handiwork, and she was glad to see this after last night. As long as Taizo had something to do, as long as he felt useful, his spirit would meet the challenge.

"Uncle?" Ruth showed Jiro the *Tanforan Totalizer*. "There's something here that might interest you." She pointed out the headline MESSAGES VIA RED CROSS and read aloud, "'Residents wishing to send messages to Japan or other foreign countries may do so through the American Red Cross by applying at First Aid headquarters in Mess Hall 3.'" She suggested, "Maybe you can write your family in Hōfuna, asking whether Akira has contacted them. Or write the Japanese draft board to find out if he was . . . inducted."

Jiro took the paper excitedly. "Yes. Yes, that is exactly what I will do. I will do so at once! Thank you, Dai, thank you." He embraced her in a bear hug. "You have given me hope, my sweet niece!"

That night they went to bed tired but with a sense of accomplishment.

Around midnight it started raining. The rhythm of the rain on the roof, even the rumble of distant thunder, was soothing at first—then Ruth began to hear a steady *plop, plop, plop* distressingly close at hand. She looked up. A flash of lightning briefly illuminated dozens of holes in the roof, like constellations in the night sky. In minutes all the adults were up, moving beds, using pots and buckets to catch the myriad of leaks.

"*Shikata ga nai,*" her father said with a shrug: Can't be helped.

The next day he and Frank were up on the roof, patching the holes with bits of plywood and tar paper collected from the lumberyard (after first trudging through the ankle-deep mud of the wet track). Ruth looked up at her father and marveled—a man of sixty, doing the work of a twenty-five-year-old. She had never felt prouder, never loved him more, than at this moment.

The only lifeline connecting the closed universe of Tanforan with the outside was the daily mail delivery. Residents had to stand in long lines at the post office to receive their mail, but what else was new? Here they received letters from home—from white neighbors who were looking after their houses or belongings—or from friends and family at other relocation centers. Evacuees were given "letterforms"—lined greenish paper on which no more than twenty-four lines of text could be written, then folded into quarters for mailing, no postage necessary. To the mortification of everyone concerned, the address side of the form announced in large, boldfaced letters that it came from an INTERNEE OF WAR. Letters to correspondents outside the camp were subject to the Office of Censorship, which deleted any derogatory comments about camp conditions, though correspondence between evacuees in different camps was not. Jiro and Nishi received letters from their three daughters, who were interned in Poston, Arizona, and Ruth was happy to see a letter from Stanley, whose family was safe and living in not-dissimilar surroundings. The Portland Assembly Center had been hastily built on the site of the Pacific International Livestock Exhibition, fragrant with the same aromas as at Tanforan:

At first the placement of the camp baffled me, Stanley wrote, *until I realized it was probably thought up by some horse's ass and then it all made sense.*

Ruth laughed out loud. She would have to share this with Ralph.

Like all evacuees, Taizo had sent change of address forms to his friends on the outside, and in response he received a letter back from an old friend, Mr. Hioki, who had owned a dry goods store next to the Watanabes on Kukui Street. When he saw the Honolulu postmark, Taizo's heart sank, wondering how much more terrible life must be for his Japanese friends back in Hawai'i; Taizo had heard that martial law had been declared after Pearl Harbor. But Mr. Hioki's letter was nothing like what he expected.

His friend told him that, unlike on the West Coast, the vast majority of Japanese living in Hawai'i had not been forced to relocate. Out of the 158,000 Japanese living in the islands—both Issei and Nisei, foreign nationals and American citizens alike—only two thousand individuals deemed "potentially dangerous" had been sent to internment camps at Sand Island and Honouliuli. Because the Japanese made up thirty-seven percent of the islands' workforce, it was feared that the economy would collapse if they were all removed in a mass evacuation. And so the majority of Hawai'i's Japanese residents were allowed to stay in their homes and, in most cases, retain their businesses.

Taizo was stunned. How was this possible? The mere possibility of a

Japanese attack on the West Coast had been enough to justify evicting 110,000 Japanese from their homes and dumping them into stables reeking of horse manure. Hawai'i *had* been attacked, but the majority of its Japanese residents had been allowed to remain in their homes and continue their lives as if nothing had happened! How was this fair? How did this make any sense?

Sitting on the edge of his cot as Etsuko gathered laundry to be washed, Taizo revealed none of the shock and anger he felt. Once again his shame at having been duped by Jiro boiled up in him. Had he and his family stayed in Honolulu, they would not have lost their home and business. They would not be imprisoned. Taizo quickly folded the letter and stuffed it into his pants pocket. Etsuko must never see this; his family must never know of the life that might have been theirs had they remained in Hawai'i. It would only make them feel even worse over what they had lost. And selfishly, he could not bear the shame of seeing that loss in their eyes.

And so he left the barrack, disposed of the letter in a pile of leaves being burned near the grandstand, and bottled up the secret inside him.

But his anger at Jiro was not so easily contained. Each time he saw his brother he felt a festering rage and resentment. He may not have shown it on his face but, despite himself, his manner toward Jiro became colder; he rebuffed offers to play *go*, spoke barely a word to him during meals. Jiro read the change in Taizo's body language; baffled, he finally approached him alone outside and asked, "Taizo, have I done something to offend you?"

Taizo snapped, "Have you *done* something? We are here because of what you have done, because of your lies! It is because of *you* that my family is living in a horse stall!"

Jiro hung his head. "I know. You are right. I am so sorry."

"You *are* sorry," Taizo said, "a sorry excuse for a brother!" Jiro looked deeply wounded. "For the moment we share living quarters, and out of respect for family harmony, we will speak no more of this. But know that in my heart, you are no longer worthy of respect, and I no longer consider you my brother!"

Taizo turned and stormed away. Shattered into silence, Jiro made no attempt to disguise the shame and sorrow in his face.

*　*　*

radually life at Tanforan improved: the dirt roads were covered in gravel; the mess halls began serving Japanese foods like rice, tea, and pickled vegetables. Frank worked long hours for all of sixteen dollars a month, leaving in the morning and not returning until after the last dinner shift—which was why Ruth, as she helped Etsuko with the ironing one day in late July, was so surprised to find him back home after having just left a half hour before. "Forget something?" she asked.

"No. I, uh, stopped at the post office before going to work."

She could see he was holding a letter in his hand, and immediately feared the worst: "Is Stanley all right? Akira?"

"It's not about either of them. But . . . it is bad news." He turned to Ruth's mother. "Etsuko? Could you give us a minute?"

"What is it? What's wrong?" Ruth demanded.

"It's from Jim and Helen Russell."

Ruth's heart skipped a beat. "Slugger?"

Frank nodded. "After we left, he . . . spent a lot of time in our old driveway, like he was waiting for us to come home." His voice caught. "Then he started running away. Looking for us, I guess. The first time they found him at your parents' old house, and brought him back."

"Oh God," Ruth said, tears welling in her eyes.

"Jim and Helen tried to keep him indoors, but he clawed at the doors and draperies, desperate to get out. So they did the only thing they could, they tied him up with a rope in the backyard and brought him in at night. But one day he chewed through the rope and leaped the fence again. They searched everywhere. All over Florin. Elk Grove. All the way to Sacramento." He added quietly, "They tried, Ruth. They did their best."

Ruth began to sob. All she could think of was her good boy, lost, lonely, and perhaps starving somewhere, and all because of . . .

"God *damn* it!" she shouted in a burst of fury.

"Honey, calm down—"

But Ruth was not to be placated. To Frank's shock, she pushed over the ironing board, which crashed to the floor, then gave it a violent kick.

"God *damn* it! *Slugger*—" It was a howl of grief unlike anything Frank had ever heard from her. She grabbed the water jar they used for the iron, but before she could throw it Frank grabbed her by the wrist.

"Honey! Stop it, before you hurt yourself!" He had never seen her like this. "I loved him too, honey. But—for Chrissake, he's only a dog."

Only a dog. Why did those words only fuel her rage?

"Let me go!" Her voice raw, anguished, she threw off his grip, losing her own grasp on the water jar, which struck the wall and shattered.

Ruth sank into a chair, covered her face with her hands, and wept uncontrollably, as if she had tapped some deep well of sorrow and loss. She ached to see her good boy one last time, his brown—no, *black*—furry face, his loving eyes, or just to know that he was safe. But somehow she knew she never would.

Chapter 9

In August it was announced that Tanforan would shut down in October and its residents would be transported to new relocation camps beginning September 15. These camps—collectively and whimsically dubbed "Shangri-La" by the *Tanforan Totalizer*—were in Gila River, Arizona; Poston, Arizona; Topaz, Utah; and Manzanar, California. Many Issei, who could not bear hot climates, were convinced they were being sent there to die; rumors spread like measles among the children that they would find rattlesnakes and scorpions curled up in their beds. And some evacuees were simply sad to say goodbye to the little community they had built in the shadow of the grandstand.

The train waiting on the railroad siding that day was an antique that looked as though it had not seen service since World War I. Shades were drawn inside, and in place of electric lights there were gas lamps. Armed soldiers again stood guard at either end of the car. The Watanabes—

including Horace and Rose and their sons, Jack and Will—settled in, and though the children were restless at first, the tedium, dim light, and rhythmic motion of the train eventually lulled them to sleep. Ruth found herself dozing too until, after ten hours, the train whistled, slowed, and stopped.

The evacuees stepped into bright sunlight beside a tiny train depot whose sign read, somewhat forlornly, LONE PINE. But it was what loomed behind the depot that commanded their attention: a chain of towering granite mountains, their lower slopes green with the last breath of summer, their jagged summits serrating the blue desert sky. No one getting their first glimpse of the Sierra Nevada could fail to be awed by its beauty and grandeur. But they had little time to appreciate it before guards herded them onto buses.

There were no shades on these windows so Ruth was able to enjoy her first taste of Outside in four months. Lone Pine's Main Street was populated with storefronts refreshingly familiar in their ordinary, small-town way: Hopkins Hardware, Safeway, Bank of America, Dow Hotel, and Sterling Service Station. A rider on horseback trotted past Buicks and flatbed trucks parked at the curb. A drugstore advertised MALTS and SODAS, and in that moment Ruth would have traded her left kidney for a chocolate milkshake.

And to the east, standing like a Pharos on some inland shore, Mount Whitney rose majestically almost two miles above the desert floor. Ruth pointed it out to Peggy and Donnie, who *ooh*ed and *aah*ed at its heights.

But within minutes they had left Lone Pine behind like a mirage of gentler times and were traveling north on U.S. Highway 6.

The town of Manzanar, Spanish for "apple orchard," was what much of the surrounding Owens Valley had once been—a thriving community of apple, pear, and peach growers and cattle ranchers—until the city of Los Angeles, rich and thirsty, began guzzling up land and water rights all over the valley. It wasn't long before the farmers' irrigation water was being siphoned out of the Owens River via the Los Angeles Aqueduct. Eventually even the groundwater was pumped right out from under those property owners who had not sold out to the rapidly expanding metropolis to the south. By 1935 most of the parched land had reverted to sage-covered desert. Then, after Pearl Harbor, Los Angeles was persuaded to lease six thousand acres of land to the U.S. government, which proceeded to bulldoze the long-abandoned site, stripping away any remaining topsoil and laying the foundation for a new Manzanar.

Manzanar Relocation Center was a sprawling city on the sand that resembled a huge Army base: five hundred wood-and-tar-paper barracks housing some ten thousand displaced Japanese Americans. There were also schools, churches, warehouses, stores, thirty-four mess halls, a fully equipped hospital, libraries, a canteen, fire and police departments, baseball diamonds, and athletic fields. The press liked to say it was "a typical American city," but this was only true if five-strand barbed-wire fences and guard towers armed with .45-caliber Thompson submachine guns could be considered typical.

The Watanabes' bus came to a stop just inside the stone entry gate, which was crowned by an odd pagodalike roof. The bus door folded open to admit a gust of hot dry air, like an oven door being opened. But it wasn't until Ruth disembarked and got a good look at her surroundings that she understood, with a queasy feeling, why the camp had been built here.

A few miles west rose the eastern wall of the Sierra Nevada—its lofty summits more than ten thousand feet tall, Mount Williamson a giant among giants at fourteen thousand feet. The mountains extended as far south and as far north as the eye could see: the rocky spine of California, four hundred miles long, its granite peaks at once breathtaking and forbidding.

Opposite the highway were the rugged brown flanks of the Inyo Mountains, their peaks also thrusting ten thousand feet into the sky, forming a second line of ramparts from north to south. The two mountain ranges seemed to merge into vanishing points at each end of Highway 6, as if pinching off any hope of escape. They were bulwarks, Ruth realized, walling off the evacuees from the rest of the state, which had to be shielded from the likes of her and her family.

"It's like . . . God's own prison," she said under her breath to Frank.

Frank nodded. "Guess there wasn't room at the bottom of the ocean."

Taizo had similar thoughts as he gazed up at the summits: Do the *hakujin* really fear us this much? Or do they *hate* us this much?

Etsuko sensed his unease and slipped her hand into his.

"We are together, all else can be endured," she said.

Guards directed them to the registration office, where a clerk gave out housing assignments. "You've come at a good time," he said. "When the camp first opened there weren't enough barracks and we were assigning eight or more people per apartment. Now, with new construction almost finished, we can accommodate a family of four to each one. But since there are thirteen in your family . . ." He asked Ralph, "Mr. Watanabe, you aren't married?"

Ralph said dryly, "No, thanks for mentioning that, Mom forgot today."

Etsuko blushed and scolded, "Ryuu!"

"I'm afraid we're going to have to assign you to the bachelors' quarters."

Ruth started to object. "Now, wait—"

"It's okay, Sis," Ralph said with equanimity. Then, to the Nisei: "I'll take the penthouse. With a view of the tumbleweeds if possible."

The clerk laughed. "I'll see what I can do." He found Ralph a suitable spot and gave the family directions to their new living quarters in Block 31. They walked out into what felt like the mouth of a blast furnace but was only First Street. The town hall and post office were on one side of the street, the police station and offices of the *Manzanar Free Press* on the other. It felt at least ninety degrees in the shade as a hot wind raked sand across their faces.

"Well, it may be isolated," Ralph noted, "but on the bright side, it's also hotter than hell."

Manzanar was laid out in a grid pattern of thirty-six blocks, each clearly enumerated; finding their assigned barrack was not difficult. Each block contained fourteen barracks plus a mess hall, recreation hall, latrines, and laundries. The blocks were widely spaced with large open areas every four blocks that served as firebreaks in an arid environment packed with combustible timber. The monotony of the grid pattern and the drab tar-paper construction was occasionally relieved by colorful "pleasure parks"—green spaces alongside barracks or mess halls where residents had dug *koi* ponds, planted trees, and decorated with fragments of clear quartz, red amethyst, and silver-gray hematite foraged from the surrounding mountains.

Ruth was surprised to see scores of children in the streets, shooting marbles or tossing softballs back and forth. To the children, it seemed, Manzanar was an adventure, a giant sandbox to play in. Ruth couldn't help but smile at their energy and innocence, while Peggy, Donnie, Jack, and Will were excited to see so many potential playmates.

Ralph found his quarters in Block 20, Barrack 2, Apartment 1, which he was to share with five other bachelors. One of them, Satoru Kamikawa, was also from Florin, and wrote for the *Manzanar Free Press*. He and Ralph hit it off immediately, and Ralph told his family he would catch up with them after they were settled in.

They went on to their new home: Block 31, Barrack 3, Apartments 1–3. There was a construction crew of Nisei men working on Barrack 5, and Frank asked them whether these buildings were new construction.

"Not new," the foreman said, "but a helluva lot better. These shacks were put up in a hurry—no insulation, no flooring other than wood planks. We've been putting in drywall and Celotex lining, laying down linoleum . . ."

"You a contractor by trade?" Frank asked.

The man laughed. "I've got a degree in history from USC. The WRA trained us. It's up to you to decide how well."

Each "apartment"—a single room—was twenty by twenty-five feet, furnished with the requisite single light bulb dangling from the ceiling, four steel cots fitted with mattress covers (to be filled later with hay), two brown Army blankets per person, and a large Coleman oil heater. The walls and ceiling had been newly lined with plasterboard and buttressed with Sheetrock, and the linoleum floor was a cheerful red.

"Compared to the horse stalls," Horace's wife, Rose, observed, "this is like something out of *Good Housekeeping*."

"Are we gonna live here, Mommy?" Donnie asked.

"Yes we are, sweetie. You like it?" Ruth asked.

"Yeah. It doesn't smell like poop."

They all laughed, then heard, from behind them, the voice of another child: "Hi!"

Ruth turned to see a grinning boy, maybe twelve years old, standing in the open doorway of their apartment.

"Well, hi," she said, "who are you?"

"Akio," he answered, but before he could say anything more, the boy's mother—a dignified-looking woman wearing round eyeglasses—appeared beside him in the doorway. She bowed to the new arrivals. "My apologies for my son's intrusion into your privacy."

"If this place is anything like Tanforan," Ruth said, "I'm not sure there's much privacy to intrude on."

The woman laughed and introduced herself as Teru Arikawa; she and her family lived in Barrack 4, opposite them. She invited her new neighbors over for tea and rice cakes, where they met her husband, Takeyoshi; sons Akio, Burns, and Robert; and their two daughters, Alice and Helen. In addition there were two framed photos of sons James and Frank, who were both serving in the United States Army.

"I thought the Army wasn't accepting Nisei," Ruth said, confused. "Aren't we all classified as . . . enemy aliens?"

"Frank joined before the war and James enlisted after Pearl Harbor, before the ban went into effect," Takeyoshi said proudly. "They cannot go into combat, but they are still serving their country, at Camp Shelby, Mississippi."

Ruth took in their neat and comfortable apartments and asked, "This is lovely. How long have you all been here?"

"Since June," Teru said. "Oh, you should have seen it then! There were holes in the walls, in the floor, in the ceiling—the wind blew right through them. At night, even with the heater on, it was freezing cold."

"*Below* freezing," her husband corrected. "We had to go to bed with our clothes and coats on. And in the morning we woke up with sand all over our blankets, our faces, in our mouths . . . you are lucky to have come now."

The families exchanged stories of their internment and of their roots in Japan until a panel truck drove up with the Watanabes' furniture and other household items. "Thank you so much for the tea and rice cakes," Etsuko told Teru. "We are fortunate to have such gracious neighbors."

"As are we," Teru said with a small bow.

Ruth, Frank, Donnie, and Peggy settled into the first apartment; Horace, Rose, Jack, and Will into the second; and Taizo, Etsuko, Jiro, and Nishi into the third. Taizo was unhappy at having to share a room with Jiro, but there was simply no alternative arrangement. His family knew only that there had been a falling out between them and that Taizo blamed Jiro for their being here. Ruth could hardly blame her father; his fraternal devotion had cost him dearly.

They hung up window curtains, nailed shelves to the walls; tapestries and silk scarves softened the drab edges of the barrack. At five o'clock the family was summoned to dinner by mess hall bells that pealed three times a day. The meal was decent enough—fish, rice, and *uri*, a yellow Japanese melon—and that night the oil heater kept them mostly warm. But to be safe, Etsuko ordered some heavier blankets from the Sears, Roebuck catalog.

After breakfast Frank applied for a job at their mess hall while Ruth, Peggy, and Donnie braved another dust storm—handkerchiefs held over their mouths to avoid breathing in the sand—to enroll in one of the camp's eighteen nursery schools. It was bright and airy, with simple homemade furniture. Most girls wore summer dresses and the boys overalls, but several boys were in short pants—understandable in this heat—and Ruth made note to sew Donnie a pair. "You two be good, okay? I'll see you this afternoon."

The dust storm had passed and as she walked back along B Street, Ruth felt mildly encouraged. At least the accommodations here were an improvement over Tanforan. Then, as she neared the intersection with Eighth Street, she heard voices raised in argument.

About a block away a trash truck was idling near the curb, manned by three bellicose men—she would later learn they were Kibei: born in America but educated in Japan—shouting at two Nisei men nearby.

"Do not believe the lies the *hakujin* feed you!" one Kibei yelled. "The Americans are being beaten at Guadalcanal! They have no more warplanes left, no aircraft carriers!"

"Ah, bullshit," the first Nisei shot back.

"You are fools," another man on the truck shouted, "throwing your lot in with the *hakujin*! When Japan wins this war, they will kill traitors like you!"

As if this wasn't alarming enough, Ruth now noticed that the garbage truck was flying two flags: a black pirate flag, of all things, replete with a white skull-and-crossbones, and another banner proclaiming, in Japanese, MANZANAR BLACK DRAGON ASSOCIATION.

"Screw you and Tojo too!" the second Nisei spat out, as he and his friend turned and walked away.

This inflamed the Kibei, who gunned the engine. The truck lurched forward, nearly sideswiping the two Nisei, who reared back just in time.

The truck came roaring down the street, oblivious, it seemed, to Ruth. She jumped back as it barreled through the intersection, honking its horn.

She leaned against a barrack wall, her heart hammering, not knowing whether to scream or to laugh. A garbage truck flying the Jolly Roger? Really? And yet there were other people on the street who seemed to take no undue notice of the truck. What just happened here?

Back home, she decided not to mention what she had seen. Ralph dropped by to tell the family that Satoru had gotten him a job with the *Manzanar Free Press* as a copy boy. "Eighty percent of the people here work," he said. "Only sixteen bucks a month, but that buys a lot of gum and cigarettes. There's even an agricultural project south of the camp—farmlands where we grow our own food." Horace decided on the spot to apply for a job on the farm crew. Taizo felt a stirring of hope and excitement for the first time since evacuation, and he surprised Horace by announcing he, too, would apply. "Why not?" he asked. "I am a farmer; why not farm here?"

Only Jiro had no interest in work, intending to occupy himself by writing to his daughters and to anyone in Japan who might know of Akira's whereabouts. "I am sixty-four years old. I consider myself reborn," he declared airily, referring to the tradition of *kanreki*, when a man reaches the age of sixty-one and is "reborn" into another cycle of life.

Taizo shook his head in evident disgust. "Some of us," he said coldly, "are not afraid of a hard day's work." He and Horace left to sign up.

At which point Nishi—displaying a moxie quite uncharacteristic for her—dropped her husband's dirty laundry into his lap and countered, "Reborn man may change his own diapers."

Jiro looked down at the wrinkled underwear in his lap—and then roared with laughter.

Even more surprisingly, he got up and took it to the laundry shed.

Nishi, watching him leave, actually seemed saddened by this.

"His spirit is broken," she said softly. "He loved to work. He loved our son. They are both gone from his life now."

And for the first time any of them had seen, Nishi began to weep. Etsuko folded her arms around her and let her mourn her missing child.

*M*anzanar was always intended to be self-supporting, with the desert adjacent to the camp cleared of sagebrush and leveled for farmland. The fierce wind had carved out sand dunes worthy of the Kalahari; internee crews did the hauling of sand and leveling by hand. They also reconditioned eight miles of irrigation ditches dug back in the 1900s, with water to be drawn from mountain streams flowing down from the heights of the Sierra Nevada. The soil was light and sandy, so fertilizers were required to make the land arable again. As water flowed into the arid soil, the land drank it in like someone abandoned for dead in the desert. In May a late planting was done, and now, in late September, Horace and Taizo—part of an internee crew of men in denims and wide-brimmed hats, carrying *bentō* lunches and canteens of water—walked through the camp's south gate, past the barbed wire, to reap the fall harvest.

Fanning out from the base of majestic Mount Williamson were 120 acres of cultivated farmland as green and fertile as any Taizo had ever seen: fields of lettuce, red ripe tomatoes, and small yellow peppers; radishes for pickled *daikon*; rows of tall cornstalks; the *uri* melons that had tasted so good at dinner; and the dark green rinds of *kabocha*, Japanese winter squash.

The crew was entirely Nisei, with a handful of Issei. Taizo was frankly amazed that they had been let out of camp without Army supervision. As they crossed Bairs Creek toward the farm fields, Taizo said as much to the foreman, a farmer from Fresno, who laughed: "Wasn't always like this. Up until June we had five *hakujin* foremen overseeing us. Knuckleheads didn't know a goddamn thing about farming."

"What happened in June?" Horace asked.

"A hundred of us quit in protest. That got the Army's attention, and now the only *hakujin* in the Agriculture Section are the farm superintendent and his assistant, who know enough about farming to let us go do our jobs."

"And they are not afraid we will run away?" Taizo asked.

"We convinced them that no Japanese would dishonor himself by running away after committing to do a job. They decided to trust us."

"Most honorable of them," Taizo said wryly.

"Careful," the foreman joked, "saying anything good about the administration can get you branded an *inu*."

"A dog?" Horace said, puzzled.

"A spy. FBI informant."

"Do such informants actually exist?" Taizo asked.

"How do you think the Feds knew who to arrest after Pearl Harbor? They had help." He let it go at that and Taizo did not inquire further.

Horace and Taizo were assigned to harvest the *daikon*, which had to be picked before the ground froze. The foreman continued, "Up here it can drop to twenty-two below zero by the first of October, and drop fast. Use the small trowels to check the roots, and don't forget to drink plenty of water—it'll be over ninety degrees by noon."

Taizo had done this so often that he had no need for the small trowel. With his fingers he gently scraped away soil around the radish's leaves, enough to expose the roots: they were at least an inch long, ready to be harvested. He grabbed the plant by the leaves, wiggled it a little to gently loosen it from the soil, then pulled. Taizo smiled at the fine white tuber, placed it in a wooden crate, and moved on to the next one.

He worked his way down the row, only occasionally finding a root too small to be harvested. He was surprised by how quickly he worked up a sweat in this dry heat, but paid it no mind. He paused and gazed up at the soaring peaks of the Sierra—at the "purple majesty" of these American titans—and paradoxically felt almost as if he were back in Japan.

"Hey, Pop, slow down and stop showing me up, huh?"

Taizo wiped perspiration from his brow and glanced back at Horace's teasing smile. Taizo was truly happy for the first time since he left Florin, but as the hours wore on he was bothered by brief but painful cramps in his calves and thighs—muscles twitching as if they were the strings of a *shamisen* being plucked. At first he thought he was simply out of shape, but by the end of the day the spasms had spread to his shoulders, something he had never experienced even when shouldering a heavy wooden yoke. After one particularly painful cramp he could not stop himself from grunting; the foreman heard this and approached him.

"Watanabe-*san*, are you all right?"

"Yes, fine," Taizo lied. "Just a little cramp. I must have pulled a muscle."

"Where does it hurt?"

Embarrassed that he had betrayed his discomfort, Taizo told him.

"That's all, just cramps? No dizziness, fatigue . . . ?"

"No, no."

The foreman nodded. "Heat cramps," he said, without undue concern. "Working in this broiling sun can bring them on."

"I have been drinking water, as you told us to—"

"Dr. Goto says it's got something to do with not enough sodium. Go home, rest in a cool place if you can find it. Maybe drink some water mixed with salt. If you're not better by tomorrow, go to the hospital."

"And if I am better?"

"Get some salt pills to bring to work and I'll see you at six."

Taizo was relieved that the cramps were something ordinary and common. Trying not to limp, he made his way back to the camp's south gate.

At home, Etsuko mixed a tablespoon of salt with a quart of water and poured her husband a glass. Taizo took a swallow and tried not to blanch.

"Is it that bad?" Etsuko asked.

"Not quite as bad as the carp's blood I was given for pneumonia when I was twelve." But he drank two full glasses, then lay down on his cot. "I think I will rest here for a while. Go to dinner without me."

"I will bring something back for you."

"If they have more *uri*," he said, "that would not be amiss."

Etsuko said worriedly, "Perhaps you should wait a day or two before going back to work . . ."

"I shall be fine, *Okāsan*."

He closed his eyes. Within minutes he was asleep.

And he was right: the next morning he felt strong and refreshed, free from cramps. Horace went to the dispensary to get his father some salt pills, and together they headed back to work.

After dropping off the children at nursery school, Ruth made the long walk to the post office in Block 1 to pick up the family's mail. Standing in line behind a Nisei woman about her age, Ruth watched as a military policeman inspected a package the woman was picking up. Ruth squirmed a little as she recognized its contents: several bright orange tins of Sheik Condoms. Satisfied there was no illegal contraband in the package, the MP handed it to the woman.

As she turned, the woman saw Ruth staring at the open package. "I— I'm sorry," Ruth said, blushing in embarrassment. "I didn't mean to—"

The woman looked at her with eyes like black ice, said bluntly, "I refuse to raise children in a concentration camp," and walked out.

Was it the bitterness in her voice or her use of the words "concentration camp" that so disconcerted Ruth?

She picked up her mail—a postcard from Stanley informing her that he and his family had been transferred to the relocation center at Minidoka, Idaho—and stepped outside. Still thinking of the woman's words, Ruth started to cross the street and nearly collided with Ralph, on his way to work at the *Free Press* across the street.

"Sis!" he said. "Hey, take it easy, you'll mow somebody down!"

"Sorry." Ruth laughed in chagrin and noticed that Ralph was not alone; with him was a Nisei woman in her late twenties, her hair pulled back in a bun, wearing glasses and a man's shirt, tails out, over her khaki pants. She was puffing away on a Lucky Strike. Despite herself, Ruth was shocked: hardly any Nisei women smoked cigarettes, much less in public.

"Ruth, this is the editor of the *Free Press*, Chiye Mori. Boss, this is my sister, Ruth Harada."

Miss Mori—Chiye—extended a hand. "A pleasure to meet you."

"And you," Ruth said. "Ralph's family is honored that he's working at the *Free Press*."

"Well," Chiye said with a chuckle, "it's free in the sense that it doesn't cost anything, I guess. But we do our best. How are you and your family settling in here at Manzanar?"

"Oh, it's . . . fine. But the . . . atmosphere is a bit different from Tanforan."

"Yeah, the atmosphere has way more sand in it," Ralph joked.

"You seem disturbed by something, Mrs. Harada," Chiye noted.

Ruth told them about her encounter with the Black Dragons—she was hesitant to discuss the delicate matter of the woman and her condoms—and Chiye nodded knowingly. "You've arrived at a tense time for Manzanar, Mrs. Harada. There's a lot of conflict and distrust these days, even between Nisei and Issei—the elders feel that their traditional authority is being undermined by the young Nisei leaders, and the Nisei—"

"Sis," Ralph jumped in, "why don't I swing by your barrack after lunch? When I have more time to talk?"

"Sure, that would be swell," Ruth said, aware of the uncharacteristic gravity in his tone. "Good meeting you, Miss Mori."

"You too, Mrs. Harada."

Ruth walked home along A Street, trying to puzzle out what Miss Mori had meant and why Ralph seemed so anxious to cut off the conversation. Passing the intersection with Fourth Street, she received yet another shock.

"Miaow?"

Ruth stopped short. Had she really heard that, or just imagined it?

"Miaoowww . . ."

No, it was real—and coming from somewhere up Fourth Street. Ruth followed the plaintive little cries to the corner of Block 19.

Leaning up against a garbage can was a small cat.

No—a kitten. Brown—or maybe white; it was covered in dust—no more than four or five weeks old.

But this was impossible—pets were prohibited in the camps. Was this a stray? Where did it come from, in the middle of the Mojave Desert?

"Oh, you poor baby," she said. Its big green eyes—almost comically too large for its head—gazed up at her with part fear, part supplication.

"Miaowww?"

Ruth bent down and gently picked up the kitten. She cradled it in the crook of her left arm while she stroked its head with her right hand. It purred faintly and Ruth's heart melted. She didn't give a damn if it was prohibited—she hadn't been able to save Slugger, but she *could* save this sweet baby. "It's okay, honey, you're safe now."

She turned with the cat in her arms—only to flinch at the sight of a Nisei policeman standing about six feet away, watching her.

Her heart quickened; she prepared herself to run if necessary. But the officer made no move, just said, "S'okay, ma'am. We get these all the time. Sometimes they wander in from Lone Pine or Independence. That a kitten?"

"Yes," Ruth said, uncertain of where this was going.

"Somebody probably dumped a litter on the side of the road."

Ruth was aghast. "People *do* that?"

"They dumped *us* on the side of the road, didn't they?" he said mordantly. "Cute little guy—or is it a girl?"

"Girl, I think. Hard to tell at this age."

"She looks thirsty. Better take her home and give her some water."

"But . . . I thought dogs and cats weren't allowed here."

"Officially, no. Unofficially—cat? What cat?"

He tossed her a grin and walked casually away.

Ruth felt a thrill of relief. She gazed into the kitten's beseeching eyes and suddenly everything she had been worrying about dwindled in significance. She hurried home, where she filled a teacup with water from the outside tap. The cat lapped it up as if she hadn't had a drop in days. Ruth took some dried tuna she'd bought at the canteen, let it soak in water to soften up, and offered a little piece of it in the palm of her hand. The kitten sniffed it—then quickly gobbled it up. Ruth smiled at the familiar sandpapery feel of her tongue on her skin. She fed her a little more tuna.

Sated, the cat lay on the floor and dozed, her chest rising and falling as she slept. Ruth was smitten.

Fortunately, when Frank came home around one o'clock—he was working first shift in the kitchen—he too fell in love with the ball of fluff. "What's a little angel like her doing in a place like this?"

"Abandoned. I've been brushing her with a fine comb. She was *covered* with fleas."

"We'll need to order cat food and flea powder from the Sears catalog," he said, and with that, the cat was a member of the family.

When she picked up Donnie and Peggy from nursery school, Ruth told them that there was a surprise waiting for them. They tried guessing all the way home, but their wildest guesses did not anticipate a tiny white kitten padding around the apartment, exploring her new surroundings.

"Oooh! A kitty, a kitty!" Peggy cooed.

"Can we pet him?" Donnie asked eagerly.

"Her. Yes, but you have to be gentle and not frighten her."

Ruth picked up the kitten and the kids gently stroked her back. She immediately began purring like a well-tuned car engine.

"What's her name?" Peggy asked.

"I thought maybe you and Donnie could pick one for her."

"She's like Mary's lamb," Peggy said. "White as snow!"

"Like a big snowball!" Donnie said.

"Snowball. That sounds good."

"Snowball," Donnie addressed the cat sweetly, "you sure are cute."

"I love her so much, Mommy, can we keep her?" Peggy implored.

"You bet," Ruth said. "But it's our little secret, okay? Except for family."

Frank smiled, thinking: A snowball in hell, how appropriate. But the happiness on his children's faces was lovely to see, and it wasn't just them; he saw the tenderness in Ruth's eyes and knew this filled a void in her as well.

*T*hat morning Taizo was tasked with picking hot chili peppers and was provided with gloves to prevent any contact with the capsacin oil, which burned like a firebrand if it touched the skin, mouth, or eyes. Harvesting peppers also required a delicate touch, since the branches were fragile and liable to break if tugged too hard. Taizo used hand pruners to snip the ripe peppers from the branch, then deposited them into a basket. By ten o'clock the temperature had climbed to ninety degrees, and Taizo had to stop himself from using his gloved hand to wipe the sweat from his brow. He remembered to drink water and take his salt pills, which seemed to be working: by midday he hadn't experienced much muscle cramping.

The crew ate lunch in the cool shadow of Mount Williamson and then it was on to the cornfield. Taizo was told how to judge whether an ear was ready to be harvested—the end of the ear should be rounded and blunt, not pointed—but it took him a few tries to find the right angle to twist the ear off the stalk, then toss it into the wagon following alongside. He had to find his rhythm quickly to keep up with the wagon—a fast look, twist, snap off the ear, toss it into the wagon, then repeat the process for the next ear of corn. After ten minutes he hit a good pace—look, twist, snap, toss—and used his sleeve to wipe away the sweat that was dripping from his brow.

After an hour Taizo began to tire but—seeing the Nisei workers around him not slackening their pace—he pushed on.

*R*alph came by that afternoon and was as surprised and charmed by Snowball as the kids and Etsuko had been. But it didn't take long for him to turn to Ruth and Frank and suggest, "You two want to take a little walk?" At Manzanar, walking the camp was the closest thing to privacy you could find. Etsuko agreed to stay with the children and Snowball, who was now rambunctiously jumping from cot to cot as if they were trampolines.

They walked down to B Street and, safely out of earshot, Ralph said,

"Sorry, Sis, about cutting you off with Chiye this morning. But trust me, you don't want to spill a lot of loose talk around reporters."

"What's this about?" Frank asked. Ruth told Frank about her close brush with the Black Dragons as well as her experience with the woman at the post office.

"Yeah, I can believe that," Ralph said, nodding. "There's a ton of anger and resentment in this place. Grievances against the administration over living conditions, shortages of meat and sugar . . . and Christ, there are more political factions than at an anarchists' convention!"

"No kidding," said Frank. "On my first day I had to choose between two different kitchen worker unions."

"Yeah, a surprising amount of dissension comes out of the mess halls. Harry Ueno, the head chef at Mess Hall 22, founded the Mess Hall Workers' Union, while Fred Tayama at Mess Hall 24 started a competing group that's very pro-administration. Fred also belongs to the Japanese American Citizens League—they're so gung-ho America they probably shit red, white, and blue turds." Ruth and Frank laughed. "And you've met the Blood Brothers, a.k.a. the Black Dragons. They hate the JACL because they claim JACL leaders in Los Angeles like Tayama were working with the FBI, ratting out innocent Issei to the Feds. They claim he's still informing at Manzanar."

"How do you know all this?" Ruth wanted to know.

"Because with my usual half-assed luck, I find myself smack in the middle of *another* faction—many of the *Free Press* staff are Communists, but they're rabidly antifascist and pro-America Communists. How do you like *them* apples?"

"It sounds," Frank said, "like what you get when you rip ten thousand innocent people out of their homes, put them all in one square mile of desert, and surround them with a barbed-wire fence."

"Is there anything we can *do* about any of this?" Ruth asked.

"Not a damn thing, Sis. Just keep your head low and watch your step. You never know when you'll step on a goddamn landmine."

By midafternoon Taizo was still keeping up the bruising pace—look, twist, snap, toss—but was breathing harder, his pulse pounding in his temples. His skin felt hot, but at least he wasn't sweating as much. None of the younger workers seemed to be having any difficulty, so he refused to betray his own. Look, twist, snap, toss. The sun was too damned bright, it was giving him a throbbing headache, and . . . Suddenly he felt nauseous and dizzy, as if he were seasick; he struggled to keep his balance. Twist—snap—

He stopped, the ear of corn still in his hand, momentarily disoriented. *"Pop!"*

Horace's voice. He turned toward it. Horace was running toward him and Taizo's head was suddenly spinning on some new, terrible axis—

And then night covered him like a black tarpaulin.

uth, Etsuko, and Ralph hurried into the hospital, a two-story, 250-bed facility in the northeast corner of the camp. At the nurses' station in the men's ward, they were told that Taizo was in Room 3—but the room was empty. They returned to the nurses' station and this time a different nurse—a pretty young woman with a warm smile whose nametag identified her as NURSE ETO—told them, "I know where he is, come with me."

They followed her to the bathroom, where a young, handsome Nisei doctor was bent over a bathtub—the first bathtub Ruth had seen in four months!—with a stethoscope pressed against her father's chest. Next to him stood another nurse—and Horace. "Mom!" he called out. "Come on in!"

Etsuko went to him as Ruth and Jiro watched from the doorway. All but Taizo's head was immersed in water, a damp cloth covering his forehead.

"Is he all right?" Etsuko asked anxiously.

"He's suffering from heatstroke," Nurse Eto explained. "He's being immersed in cool water in order to lower his body temperature."

The doctor took away the stethoscope and said, "Heartbeat is back to normal, and his temp is down to a hundred and one." He stood, held out his hand instinctively to Etsuko. "Mrs. Watanabe, I take it?"

"Yes. Will he be all right?"

He nodded. "Yes. I'm Dr. Goto, chief of medical services. Your son says Mr. Watanabe had heat cramps yesterday. It's not unusual to see that progress to heat exhaustion or heatstroke." As he spoke, the second nurse gently dabbed Taizo's face with a wet sponge. "We see this especially with older patients who aren't used to temperatures in the high desert."

"Is he awake?" Etsuko asked. "May we speak with him?"

"Sure, for a couple of minutes."

Etsuko went to her husband's side at the bathtub, sat down on a stool. "Otōsan? Can you hear me?"

His eyes half opened. He took in the sight of his family with mild alarm. "Have I awakened at my own funeral?" he said weakly.

Everyone laughed. "You are going to be fine," Etsuko said. "It was too hot out there for you, that's all."

Taizo nodded. His eyes drooped closed as he drifted back to sleep.

"I think that's all for now," Dr. Goto said. "Nurse Eto, will you assist Nurse Sasaki?" He took the Watanabes into the ward and told them, "We're going to keep him for a day or two to make sure the sunstroke hasn't done any damage to his brain or other organs. Then after he's discharged, he needs to stay inside, rest, and avoid the sun and further exertion for at least a week . . ."

"Doc," Ralph said, "should a man his age really be out there working the fields in this kind of heat?"

"If he were my father, I'd advise against it." Ruth's heart sank at the doctor's words. "I know how much pride Issei men take in working, but . . . that's a conversation you might have with him once he's recovered."

Taizo was discharged two days later and had no objection to resting at home for the rest of that week. When Ruth brought Snowball over to meet him, her father seemed quite taken with her; as a cat lover he heartily approved of the new addition to the family.

When Ruth and Horace gingerly brought up the subject of whether Taizo should stop working in the fields, he was surprisingly unresistant. "Yes," he agreed, "I suppose that might be for the best." He did not tell his family of the intense shame he felt, having fainted in front of all the younger workers. Surely they must have thought him a weak old man, unfit for hard labor. He could not bear the thought of going back among them, of seeing the naked pity in their eyes.

Do not dwell in the past, do not dream of the future, concentrate the mind on the present moment.

His days as a farmer were over; he knew that now. He spent his time playing *go* with Etsuko or sitting outside in the shade, Snowball dozing in his lap, watching the passing parade of other people's lives—like so many Issei men with too much time and no work to do. His small smile belied the sorrow in his eyes. Ruth saw this and ached for him, for all he had lost— his farm, his livelihood, his role as provider. It made her angry; it made her want to weep. The sturdy oak was now old and bending in the wind.

Chapter 10

eat lightning lit up night skies above the Sierra as crisscrossing searchlight beams from the eight guard towers spun a luminous spiderweb across the darkened camp. Eluding that web were six men wearing dark blue Navy peacoats, black caps pulled down low, black scarves obscuring all but their eyes—and carrying wooden clubs as they approached Fred Tayama's apartment in Block 28.

It was eight o'clock in the evening on Saturday, December 5, 1942. Tayama had just returned—with permission of the administration—from the national JACL convention in Salt Lake City and was stretched out on his bed, working on a speech, when there was a rapping on the door. Expecting a friend, he called out, "Come in." The door banged open and the six masked men burst in, three rushing to each side of his bed. One of them began beating Tayama in the head with his club while the others pummeled his body and legs. Despite the drubbing he was taking, Tayama somehow managed to roll out of bed, scramble to his feet, and grab a chair, using it as a weapon to defend himself.

Outside, a little girl saw the fight through the open door and screamed. Tayama's assailants panicked and fled back into the dark pockets of the camp. A neighbor called for an ambulance, and Fred Tayama, blood trickling from his scalp, had just enough time to consider himself lucky before he collapsed.

hree blocks away, in Block 31, Ruth heard the ambulance's siren as it arrived at Block 28—and by the time Tayama was on his way to the hospital, word of the attack had spread, like ripples in a *koi* pond, throughout camp. There was shock, but no overwhelming sympathy, for the injured man. Tayama was widely disliked at Manzanar; he was seen as an *inu*, an informer and collaborator with the camp administration. Just recently, it was said, he had met with the FBI, and a short time later an internee at Manzanar, viewed as an "agitator," had been arrested and spirited away.

Ruth didn't know Tayama but hoped he would be all right. At the moment her hands were full caring for Donnie, Peggy, and Frank, all of whom shared the same winter cold and fever. Frank's cough was so bad that Dr. Goto had prescribed him cough syrup with codeine.

Around ten o'clock that evening there was a knock on the door. It was Ralph, standing on the doorstep, looking unusually sober. "Can I come in?"

"Why would you want to? Everyone's sick."

"I promise not to breathe." He stepped inside as Ruth closed the door. "Tayama's okay. He's got a bunch of bruises and lacerations, but he'll be fine."

The children were sleeping and Ruth motioned Ralph to the other side of the apartment, where Frank was sitting on his cot. "Keep your voice low," she said, "I don't want the kids hearing this if they wake up."

"Who"—Frank coughed mid-question—"assaulted him?"

"The MPs have arrested Harry Ueno. Tayama claims he can identify him as one of his attackers. Says he recognized Harry's eyes."

Harry Ueno had recently become quite the folk hero in camp when he accused an administration official and the chief steward of stealing war-rationed sugar and meat—rarer than gold and intended for the residents—to sell on the black market. The FBI even came to investigate, giving the official a grilling he could not have appreciated even though ultimately no charges were brought.

Frank was doubtful about the assault charges. "I've met Harry a few times. He's always seemed sincerely concerned about the welfare of the evacuees."

"He is," Ralph said, "but he also thinks Japan is going to win the war and probably expects them to pin a medal on him when they 'liberate' Manzanar."

"But why would Harry attack Tayama?" Ruth asked.

"Rumor is the men were members of the Blood Brothers and they were pissed off Tayama had introduced a motion at the JACL convention urging the U.S. government to draft Nisei men into the Army."

"What!" Ruth was taken aback. "Who gave him the right to do that? As if he speaks for everyone at Manzanar?"

"Ah, you begin to perceive the problem. Even worse, the motion passed. Well, if I get drafted, it's not like the housing's going to be any different," Ralph added with a halfhearted smile. "Anyway, I just wanted to tell you to stick close to home tonight—the camp is even more tense than usual."

"So much for our plans to go out jitterbugging," Frank said hoarsely.

"Sorry, twinkletoes," Ruth said, "the only items on your dance card tonight are aspirin and sleep."

He nodded. "Thank God tomorrow's Sunday."

But it was far from a peaceable Sunday, despite an almost unnatural calm that morning, broken only by the seven o'clock mess hall bells. Ruth—up half the night tending to the kids—slept right through breakfast, as did Frank, so her parents brought them back some fish, rice, and coffee. "Did you hear anything more about the attack last night?" Ruth asked her father.

"Ueno has been taken to jail in the town of Independence," Taizo told her. "People are very angry about this, they think he is being punished for— *Okāsan*, what is the phrase in English?"

"'Blowing the whistle.' On the administration's theft of meat and sugar. They believe that is really why he was removed from camp."

The children woke up coughing and Ruth had no more time for camp politics until ten o'clock, when she was surprised to hear the mess hall bells ringing—too late for breakfast, too early for lunch. She assumed a meeting was being called to discuss the jailing of Harry Ueno.

Then, at eleven-fifteen, all the lunch bells in camp began ringing forty-five minutes earlier than usual. Ruth had just warmed up some Campbell's chicken soup for Frank, Peggy, and Donnie; Frank felt well enough to look after the kids and told her, "Go get a good meal for yourself." She pecked him on the cheek and left for lunch with her parents.

When they entered the mess hall Ruth saw Jiro and Nishi eating alone at a table and knew better than to approach them with Taizo there. Jiro had decided that peace in the family was best served if he and Nishi ate their meals apart from the rest of the family. Ruth had not been able to dissuade him from this view and his absence at the table saddened her.

They were, however, joined by Ralph, who confirmed that there had been a meeting to discuss the arrest of Harry Ueno: "A Committee of Five was appointed to demand that Harry be returned to camp. If not, there was talk of a camp-wide mess hall strike. There's going to be a second meeting at one—that's why lunch was called early today, to allow for bigger attendance."

"You are going to this meeting?" Etsuko said.

"As a reporter. For the paper."

"Is that wise?" Taizo asked. "Wasn't one of your coworkers on the newspaper assaulted not long ago?"

"Joe Blamey, yeah, he was beaten up by some pro-Axis teenagers, but they were just stupid kids."

"Just be careful, Ralph, okay?" Ruth asked.

She spent the afternoon tending to family but around four o'clock heard that Harry Ueno had been returned from Independence, was now in the jail inside the Manzanar police station, and the Committee of Five was trying to secure his release. There was to be another meeting at Mess Hall 22 at six P.M. This information came from a neighbor, not Ralph, whom Ruth imagined was at the *Free Press* reporting what he'd seen to his editor.

At seven o'clock there was a knock on their door and Ruth, assuming it was Ralph, opened it in relief—only to find that her visitor was Koji Ono, the forty-something Issei who served as their block manager, one of the internee-elected representatives on the advisory council to the WRA.

"Mrs. Harada, there's a phone call for you in my office." There was no apartment-to-apartment telephone service at Manzanar, just service between offices. "It's Dr. Goto. Sounds important."

"Dr. Goto?" She was at first perplexed, then worried.

She and Koji hurried to his office—it was already near freezing outside—and she picked up the phone. "This is Ruth Harada."

"Mrs. Harada, James Goto." He sounded breathless, quite at odds with his usually calm bedside manner. "Am I correct in recalling that one of your brothers works for the *Manzanar Free Press*?"

She felt a chill of premonition. "Yes. Ralph."

"There was a—well, frankly, a mob here, just a few minutes ago," he said. "They wanted to kill Frank Tayama. We hid him and when they couldn't find him, they broke into two groups—one going to the jail to free Harry Ueno and the other, I heard them say, bent on killing staff members on the *Free Press*."

"*What?*"

"They had a list, a 'death list'—God knows who all could be on it. I wanted to warn you, tell your brother to hide, just in case."

Ruth was nearly hyperventilating but managed to stammer, "Thank—thank you, Doctor. I'm so grateful you called."

"Good luck. We're all going to need some tonight." He hung up.

Ruth thanked Koji and hurried back to the apartment. The kids were asleep and Frank, sedated by the codeine, was not remotely conscious. She could hear, in the distance, the sound of people running in the street, and knew there was only one thing she could do. She grabbed one of the heavy Navy peacoats that had been distributed to every household in Manzanar, put on a wool cap, and went next door to her parents' quarters. "*Okāsan*, would you look after Frank and the children while I run an errand?"

"Right now?" Etsuko asked.

"What kind of errand?" Taizo asked.

"I won't be long," she said, ignoring the question. "Don't worry."

She tried to keep the fear out of her voice and rushed out.

It was a cold, moonless night as Ruth headed south on C Street. There was a light wind at her back but at least the sand and pebbles it stirred up weren't flying directly into her face. It wasn't long before she was in Block

20, knocking urgently on the door to Barrack 2, Apartment 1, the bachelors' quarters. "Ralph? Are you in there?"

The door opened. Ralph's friend and roommate Satoru Kamikawa stood in the doorway. "Mrs. Harada, hello. I'm afraid Ralph's not here."

"Do you know where he is?"

"Probably still covering the demonstration. He and I were at the meeting in Block 22 when it broke into two groups, one headed for the police station to free Ueno, the other to the hospital to—"

"To kill Fred Tayama, I know. Dr. Goto says the mob couldn't find Tayama and were going after staff members of the *Free Press*."

"Yes, we heard Joe Kurihara's 'death list' at the mess hall meeting. But I'm sure Ralph's not on the list, Mrs. Harada. I might be, but not him."

"Not yet, maybe."

"We get these death threats at the *Free Press* all the time. Whenever Chiye writes a pro-American editorial someone threatens to kill her."

"Forgive me if I'm not as blasé about it as you," Ruth said, irritated. "Is Ralph at the police station?"

"Yes, he wanted to see it through."

"And you didn't?"

Satoru admitted, "No. Things were starting to look pretty bad. I tried to talk Ralph into coming back with me, but . . . your brother is a very determined young man."

"Yes," Ruth said, "and I'm going to kick his determined head in if somebody already hasn't. Thank you."

She turned and wended her way through Block 20 to B Street, where she turned right. She heard increasing noise and commotion ahead of her, and the probing of searchlights from on high made her feel like a criminal on the lam. She pulled her cap lower over her ears against the chill, then turned on Third Street until she reached A Street. She turned right, then stopped short, her heartbeat skipping like a stone across water.

There were at least five hundred people gathered in front of the police station; like her, most were bundled up in Navy peacoats. Cautiously she made her way around the back of the crowd. The protestors were separated from the police station by a buffer zone of about a hundred military police armed with machine guns, rifles, and shotguns; but the soldiers were significantly outnumbered by the protestors.

One man was standing on the roof of a parked car, declaring in a loud angry voice: "We will kill all the dogs in Manzanar, starting with the biggest dog, Tayama! Then George Hayakama and Tom Imai and the rest of the stooges on the camp police force! And those Communist dogs at the *Free Press*, Chiye Mori, Tad Uyeno, James Oda——"

Those last names quick-froze Ruth's blood more than the biting cold. Her gaze swept across the building that ran parallel to the police station—where she saw, in a window, a familiar pair of eyes peeking out between curtains.

Her heart skipped again, this time with relief.

Slowly she made her way toward First Street, trying not to attract any undue attention; fortunately the crowd was focused on the speaker atop the car. She glanced up the street. Hanging from the very first door on the right was the sign: DEPARTMENT OF REPORTS / FREE PRESS.

She backed up, reached the door; it was locked. She waited until there was a burst of applause from the crowd to the oratory, then rapped as quietly as she could on the clapboard door. When no response came, she waited for more covering crowd noise, then rapped again and whispered as loudly as she dared, "Ralph! For God's sake, it's me, Ruth! Open up."

The door quickly opened, Ruth rushed in, and a surprised Ralph locked the door behind her.

"Sis! What are you doing here?" he whispered.

"What are *you* doing here?" she whispered back. "The protesters are out to kill *Free Press* staff, and here you are in the first place they'll look!"

"Oh hell, I'm not on any death lists," Ralph assured her. "I'm strictly small fry. The big fish went into hiding after the afternoon rally."

"You're taking a hell of a chance!"

"It's my job. Satoru and I were here this afternoon, watching the crowds, and no one thought to look for us here."

"Ralph, please come back to our barrack, you'll be safer——"

"Sis, I'm a newsman. Somebody has to report what's happening."

"And you seriously think the administration will let you *print* that?"

"Maybe not. But I'll still try." He nodded to the side window. "C'mon, I think that looney tune on the car has finally stopped talking."

Ruth reluctantly followed him to the window. From outside now came the sounds of—voices raised in song? In Japanese? Ruth understood the words—*Kimigayo wa, chiyo ni yachiyo ni*, "May your reign continue for a thousand, eight thousand generations"—but Ralph had to identify it for her as "Kimigayo," the Japanese national anthem.

"What's going on inside the police station?" Ruth asked.

"The Committee of Five went in a while ago. They brokered the deal to get Ueno back to Manzanar, but now the crowd wants him released. And they want *inus* killed. I think the committee's lost control of the mob."

Indeed, the protestors were becoming more belligerent—inching closer to the soldiers, hooting at them. A few yelled *"Banzai!"* and in response some MPs shouted back, "Remember Pearl Harbor!" A sergeant barked at his men, "Hold your ground!" Most of the soldiers looked young and scared, flinching when people threw stones or lighted cigarettes at them. An Army captain ordered the crowd to disperse, but they ignored him and kept needling the soldiers like little boys poking sticks into a nest of scorpions.

Satoru was right. This was looking very bad.

The captain tried to reason with the protestors, speaking at some length, but when protestors threw large stones at him, he retreated behind the line of MPs. He repeated the order to disperse, but the crowd only jeered.

At the captain's signal the soldiers started putting on gas masks, then began throwing tear gas canisters into the crowd. Stormy clouds of white smoke erupted behind the protestors and within seconds they were choking on the gas filling their lungs and stinging their eyes. The crowd dispersed, scattering in all directions—but some at the front of the crowd surged forward in panic, *toward* the line of soldiers.

Suddenly the air was torn by the jackhammer noise of machine guns and shotguns—at least two dozen rounds ripping into the crowd.

"Jesus Christ!" Ralph shouted.

Shotgun rounds tore into a young man—he looked like a teenager—a red fog briefly enveloping his torso as he fell, facedown, onto the ground. At least ten other people, most of them running away, also fell.

"Oh God!" Ruth cried. "No!"

Most protestors were fleeing for their lives, but a few were fighting back. They opened the driver's side door of a parked car, released the parking brake, then pushed it forward, sending it speeding toward the military police. The car clipped off the northeast corner of the police station but kept bearing down on the line of soldiers. An MP fired a short burst of machine gun fire that blew out the car's tires; it veered and crashed into an Army truck.

The remainder of the crowd now fled, leaving behind almost a dozen broken bodies beneath a wreath of smoke.

Ruth and Ralph stared in shock.

"Shit," Ralph said softly.

Soldiers hurried to the fallen and began carrying them into the police station, presumably for first aid.

"We'd better get out of here," Ruth said. "If we're found in here, everybody in camp will think we're spies—*inus*."

They hurried up First Street, along with scores of others fleeing the violence. At the first intersection they turned right onto B Street. The wind carried the distant wail of an ambulance siren. But though most people were trying to escape, there were also angry groups shouting "Kill the *inus*!" Ruth and Ralph gave these a wide berth. Ruth wondered how it had come to this, how it was that they could be running for their lives from both the U.S. military and *their own people*?

A searchlight beam swung toward them and they ducked, missing it by inches. An Army jeep bristling with armed soldiers barreled up Fifth Street, causing Ruth and Ralph to fall back until it passed; when it had, they ran across the next firebreak until they reached Fourth Street, where Ralph had to stop, prop himself up against a barrack wall, and catch his breath.

"Where the hell are we?" he said between gasps. "The Russian front?"

"It's cold enough," Ruth agreed. "Are you going to be okay?"

He nodded, took a last gulp of air, and they continued running.

Mess hall bells began pealing all over camp, summoning people to meetings, even now. There was a very wide firebreak between Sixth and Seventh Streets and as they raced across it, Ruth felt exposed and vulnerable.

They made a beeline for Barrack 3. Ruth yanked open the door to her apartment and she and Ralph rushed in, slamming the door shut behind them.

The lights were off but everyone in the room—Etsuko, Frank, the children—were wide awake. How could they fail to be, Ruth realized, with the world turned upside down outside their walls?

"Mommy, Mommy!" Peggy cried, running to her mother and wrapping her arms around her legs. "You're back!"

Donnie, too, ran up and embraced her. "Where were you, Mommy, why is there so much noise?"

"It's all right, sweeties," she said, wrapping her arms around them.

Snowball sidled up and rubbed her head against Ruth's leg.

"Honey, thank God," Frank said softly. "Where *were* you? I wanted to go look for you but didn't know where to begin."

"Later," she told him, then, to the kids: "You two are up way past your bedtime. Time to go to sleep, okay?"

But though she tucked them in, the commotion outside, the constant knell of kitchen bells and the keening of ambulance sirens, kept them awake and afraid. Finally, Ruth gave them each less than a teaspoon of Frank's cough syrup, and the codeine in it had them kayoed within minutes.

The adults went to the other side of the small apartment, Ralph and Etsuko sitting in chairs, Ruth and Frank side by side on the cot. Ruth and Ralph explained where they had been and what happened, tears again filling Ruth's eyes as she recounted the shootings. "I'm sorry," she told Frank, "I know it was dangerous, but I *had* to find Ralph."

But Frank just nodded and draped his arm across her shoulders. "Of course you did. I'm just glad you're both safe." He looked at Ralph. "*Are* we safe? Do you think they might come after you?"

"I don't know," Ralph said. "I don't think so, but after all I saw tonight, I don't know anything for sure."

Frank looked thoughtful, then got up, picked up a makeshift crowbar fashioned out of scrap metal, and gripped it firmly. "Someone should stand guard, just in case," he said. "I've been asleep for nearly half the day, so I'll take first shift."

Etsuko stood. "I will tell Taizo and Jiro and Horace. They will want to arm themselves as well." She gave Ruth a kiss. "You are a good sister, butterfly."

Ruth tried to sleep, but as exhausted as she was, she couldn't. Every time she closed her eyes she saw that young man, wrapped in a shroud of blood and falling, falling forever in her memory.

His name was James Ito: seventeen years old, from Pasadena, shot through the heart and abdomen and pronounced DOA at the Manzanar hospital. The other fatality was Katsuji "Jim" Kanagawa, twenty-one, from Tacoma, Washington. Dr. Goto had labored to repair the perforations in Kanagawa's stomach, lung, and pancreas, but he died of bronchial pneumonia five days later. Nine other men, ranging in age from twenty to fifty, recovered from bullet wounds. Dr. Goto's report stated that all of the wounded but for James Ito were shot in the side or back, indicating they were running away. When the Army told Goto to change his findings, the doctor refused—and was summarily fired and transferred to another camp.

Two soldiers—privates Ramon Cherubini and Tobe Moore—had been the ones to start shooting, firing their weapons into the crowd as parts appeared to be advancing on them. Authorities determined that they acted in self-defense, and they were not prosecuted.

Well into Monday morning, Manzanar was in a state of barely contained chaos. Martial law was declared; meetings were broken up by MPs with tear gas. Throughout the night there were attacks on suspected *inus*.

Army reinforcements and California State Guard troops were called in to keep order. There were scattered work strikes. Schools closed. Many pro-American Japanese sought protective custody in MP headquarters, and by Wednesday sixty-five people—including Fred Tayama and *Free Press* staffers Chiye Mori, Satoru Kamikawa, Joe Blamey, and Ted Uyeno—were removed from Manzanar for their own safety. Jobs were found for them in nonmilitary zones in the Midwest and Northeast as part of the WRA's "work furlough" program that allowed evacuees out of the camps if they relocated from the West Coast. Fifteen men thought to be the prime instigators of the riot—including Harry Ueno, who had been sitting in a jail cell the whole time—were ultimately sent to Tule Lake Relocation Center in Northern California.

The *Free Press* suspended publication for twenty days, and when it returned no mention was made of the revolt of December 6.

On December 21, a Buddhist funeral was held for James Ito and Jim Kanagawa in the woods outside the camp. Only 150 internees were permitted to attend. The rest of the camp's residents, most wearing black armbands in honor of the fallen, observed a two-minute prayer and moment of silence at one P.M.

As she stood silently among the mourners inside the camp, Ruth grieved not just for the two young men but for everyone in Manzanar. This was insanity, all of it. Valid grievances had turned into senseless brutality, on all sides. In her heart she was deeply afraid—afraid that the violence and death had marked everyone at Manzanar as suspect, as potentially dangerous subversives. She feared that even if the war ended tomorrow, the authorities would never permit the ten thousand souls imprisoned here to leave—and that the mountainous walls surrounding them would be the farthest horizons that they would ever know.

Chapter 11

1943

aizo liked to sit in the wooden chair outside his apartment, gazing at the Japanese rock garden an ambitious neighbor in Barrack 4 had wrought from the blistering forge of the desert. It was a *karesansui*, a Zen or meditation garden, at its center a "lake" of white sand—artfully raked to mimic gentle waves combing the surface—with stones of quartz floating on the lake like crystalline islands. A miniature footbridge connected the "shore" to the largest island, a pyramid of granite rocks that represented Mount Horai, the mountain paradise of Shintō legend and symbol of a natural world of perfect harmony. During Taizo's first months here this garden was a solace to his spirit. He could stare at it, meditating, for hours, and the reality of life at Manzanar did not disappear but lost its power to affect him.

But now he could find no solace in the white waves of sand. The loss of his farm and home was a bitter harvest not of his own sowing; all that was left to him was his dignity. Now he had been shorn of even that, and by his own daughter's hand. When Dai had feared for her brother's life and both Frank and Haruo lay abed, had she come to her father? Had she shown him the respect he was due as head of the family and asked for his help in the search? No; she had gone off her own, dismissing her *otōsan* as a fragile relic too old to be of any assistance. Ever since his collapse in the fields the family treated him as if he were made of porcelain and with one bump might shatter like an old plate. But he was still a *man*. He was happy Dai and Ryuu were unharmed, but she should have shown the proper respect to him *as* a man.

Tears were trickling down his face and he wiped them away before anyone could see. He was proud of Dai, her courage and spirit; all he had wanted was one last chance to make her proud of *him*.

"Hey, Pop!"

Ralph came running up, holding a folded-up newspaper. Taizo concealed his sadness with a smile. "Ryuu, what brings you here so early?"

"Big news!" He rapped on the apartment door. "Hey, Sis! Frank!"

Ruth and Frank came out, equally surprised to see Ralph. "FDR just announced it," Ralph said, opening the paper. "The Army's going to form an all-Nisei infantry battalion!"

A few days earlier, the War Department had unexpectedly announced that it was rescinding its ban on Japanese American citizens serving in the armed forces and they were now free to volunteer for military service.

"It's going to be called the 442nd Regimental Combat Team, and the Army is calling for volunteers from both Hawai'i and the mainland."

"Looks like the JACL is getting what it wanted," Frank noted.

"But get this," Ralph went on. "Now FDR says, quote, 'Americanism is not, and never was, a matter of race and ancestry. A good American is one who is loyal to this country and to our creed of liberty and democracy. Every loyal American citizen should be given the opportunity to serve this country . . .'"

Ruth looked incredulous at that. "Americanism isn't a matter of race and ancestry? Then what the hell are we all doing in this sand trap?"

"It's a first step," Ralph said. "At the *Free Press* we've heard rumors that the government's started to have second thoughts about this whole internment. They're already speeding up the work furlough program. And now there's this."

"I think it is an excellent idea," came a voice from behind them. They all turned to see their neighbor, Takeyoshi Arikawa, a proud smile on his face as he walked toward them. "Our son Frank is going to be part of this regiment. It will be his chance to show his loyalty. They will represent us all, all of us who love America."

"Congratulations, Arikawa-*san*," Taizo said, knowing what this meant for his friend and neighbor. "I am sure your son will acquit himself nobly."

Ruth had to admit to herself, she was surprised. After the riot, she never thought the government would trust any Japanese again.

But of course, it would not be as easy as all that.

A week later an Army team descended on Manzanar, and two separate "registration forms" were distributed to all households. The first, for Nisei men, was a Selective Service form, "Statement of United States Citizen of Japanese Ancestry." The second, given to Nisei women and all Issei, was a War Relocation Authority form, "Application for Leave Clearance"—"leave" as in relocation via the work furlough program. The questions were mostly innocuous, asking for the registrants' sex, age, marital status—but two were far from innocuous, requiring unambiguous, unqualified yes/no answers:

Question 27 asked Nisei men:

Are you willing to serve in the armed forces of the United States on combat duty wherever ordered?

The equivalent for Nisei women—and, oddly, Issei of both sexes—was:

If the opportunity presents itself and you are found qualified, would you be willing to volunteer for the Army Nurse Corps or the WAAC?

Question 28 was substantially the same on both forms:

Will you swear unqualified allegiance to the United States of America . . . and forswear any form of allegiance or obedience to the Japanese emperor, or other foreign government, power, or organization?

Question 28 exploded like a grenade in all ten relocation camps, and the uneasy peace in the wake of the Manzanar riot was shattered in a blast of anger, bewilderment, and indignation. Worse, it broke the bonds of family, and the Watanabes were no exception.

After Pearl Harbor, many Nisei men wanted to defend their nation, only to be told that their ancestry marked them as potentially suspect. Now the Army, represented by a team holding informational meetings in Manzanar mess halls, told them, "Signing this statement will give you the opportunity to prove your loyalty to the nation on the field of battle."

"We didn't prove it when we *peacefully agreed* to leave our homes and come to this damn place?" a man shouted back. "You didn't ask Germans or Italians to prove their loyalty—how many times do *we* have to?"

The Army officers had no ready answer for this.

"Yes," said another Nisei, "why do you ask for our loyalty *after* you've done all the damage to our lives?"

"If we answer 'yes' to these questions, will our privileges and rights as citizens be restored? Can our families go back to our homes?"

The Army team allowed that that was not yet possible.

"Would I be considered disloyal if I answer 'no' only to Question 27?"

"Why can't we serve alongside white soldiers?"

"Will we receive restitution for the loss of our homes and businesses?"

Again, the officers had no ready answers.

In the absence of clarity from the Army, many families had to puzzle out the meaning and consequences of the questions for themselves. The Watanabes gathered for this purpose one morning while all the children were in school, all eight adults squeezing into Taizo and Etsuko's apartment.

The first comment was Jiro's, and typical Jiro it was:

"Do you think," he asked, "I should volunteer for the Army Nurse Corps or the WAACs?"

Everyone but Taizo laughed. Etsuko said dryly, "I do not see you in a nurse's uniform. The WAAC uniform might flatter you more."

"What a damnfool question!" Taizo snapped, as irritated by Jiro's flippancy as by the question itself. "It is almost as foolish as Question 28. The same government that denies me citizenship because of my race wants me to forswear any allegiance to Japan? To renounce my Japanese citizenship? Am I to become a man without a country, with no allegiance, no home, no rights?"

Ruth had never heard such outrage in her father's voice.

"And if we do answer 'no' to these questions," Jiro said, "what can they do to us? Put us in a concentration camp?"

Ralph answered grimly, "They can put you in a *worse* concentration camp, like Tule Lake—or they might deport you back to Japan."

Jiro sighed. "Would that be so awful? My son is over there somewhere— perhaps I *should* return and look for him. Nishi, do you agree?"

Nishi said quietly, "I am more afraid that if we answer 'yes,' they will send us to some *hakujin* community where we will be feared and attacked. The stories in the newspaper are terrible, full of hatred toward Japanese—"

"Yes," Horace agreed, "a coworker of mine went to Idaho last year, on work furlough, to help the farmers harvest their beets. He was told that helping the war effort would be proof of his loyalty. But when they went into a restaurant to eat dinner, the owner called them 'damn Japs' and threw them out! They were American citizens, yet they were treated like Japanese soldiers!"

"Why are they even *asking* Nisei this question?" Ruth said, puzzled. "If we answer 'yes,' the Army could interpret it as an admission that we *have* loyalty to the Japanese emperor, that we *are* disloyal."

"They might even take away our citizenship," Rose pointed out.

"And if Japan wins the war," Jiro said, "such a statement of loyalty to America could be considered treasonous."

Frank asked, "If we say 'yes,' will that be as good as volunteering to enlist? I'd consider enlisting, but I don't want to be tricked into doing it."

Finally, Ruth addressed the group: "All right. Let's take a poll, see where we all stand. Who's thinking of saying 'no' to Question 27?"

Jiro, Nishi, Taizo, and Etsuko raised their hands—reasonably, since all were well past draft age. Rose and Ruth herself, both of whom had small children to care for, also raised their hands.

"Now, who's considering answering 'no' to Question 28?"

Again Jiro and Nishi raised their hands—and, to the surprise of his children, Taizo. Etsuko asked him, "*Otōsan*, are you sure?"

"I am sure of nothing," Taizo answered honestly. "I do not wish to return to Japan. But I do not wish to be a man without a country."

"Pop," Ralph said, "if you answer 'no-no,' they'll either deport you or send you to Tule Lake. Then the only way to avoid us being separated as a family is for the rest of us to say 'no-no.'"

"No! That is not necessary. This is my decision alone."

"I will not abandon you, husband," Etsuko said with steel in her voice.

Ruth glanced at Frank, who nodded and said, "We won't either."

"Nor we," Horace agreed.

Taizo took that in. The idea of saying "no-no" was a seductive vent for his anger, but he could not allow his children and grandchildren to suffer the consequences of his anger. He sighed and relented. "Very well. I will answer 'yes-yes.' I will even join the WAACs if they ask me."

Laughter eased the tension, but Jiro, atypically, did not laugh. "Ryuu," he asked, "will the government allow us to repatriate to Japan voluntarily?"

The laughter receded, leaving a silent tide of sadness in the room.

"Yes, Uncle, if that is what you want," Ralph said softly. "You'd have to wait until a prisoner exchange is available through the Spanish Consul, who acts as a humanitarian intermediary between the American and Japanese governments."

Taizo was as shocked and saddened by Jiro's decision as the rest of the family but he would not allow himself to show it.

"It is what *we* want," Jiro said with a nod to his wife. "Our daughters have lives and families here. After the war—whoever wins it—surely we can come back and visit them. But for now, Japan, and Akira, call to us."

Jiro and Nishi were not alone. To avoid registration, in February almost a thousand people in all ten relocation centers chose to apply for repatriation to Japan. The next month saw a similar number, and in April the requests for repatriation mushroomed to over fifteen hundred internees.

Unlike Taizo, many Issei fathers answering "no-no" exerted great pressure on their sons to do likewise and many Nisei did so of their own volition, unwilling to abandon their aged parents; filial piety demanded nothing less. Those who answered "yes-yes" risked public shame by those who vehemently disagreed. Nisei who wished to enlist in the Army often had to leave the camp under cover of night.

Registration began on February 10 and was conducted block by block in a progressive sequence, in mess halls or recreation buildings. Nisei men of draft age were registered separately from women and aliens and were also required to formally answer Questions 27 and 28 in front of an Army colonel.

By the time the Army team reached Block 31, Taizo had had ample time to ponder his dilemma. Despite his assurances to his family, he still feared the consequences of answering "yes" to Question 28, renouncing his ties to Japan while receiving nothing in return. Sitting at one of the mess hall tables alongside other Issei, he again went over the questions. He was suspicious of the phrase "Application for Leave," as if by signing he was requesting leave to go . . . where? To some white community where his family would face prejudice and hostility, to "start over"? Everything he and his children had worked for all their lives had been sold, confiscated, *stolen*. They had little money to start new businesses. Haruo and Frank would likely find new jobs, but Taizo knew he was too old, too *Japanese*, to be hired by any *hakujin* firm.

His gaze fell, for the hundredth time, upon the last question, the words having lost none of their frightening implications:

Will you swear unqualified allegiance to the United States of America . . .
and forswear any form of allegiance or obedience to the Japanese emperor,
or other foreign government, power, or organization?

He felt like a man drowning at sea, adrift midway between two ships. The first ship, a Japanese trawler, had thrown him a life preserver that was floating nearby, close enough to him to grasp. The other was an American naval vessel; the captain and crew were yelling at Taizo not to take the Japanese ship's life preserver but refused to throw out one of their own.

Tears trickled down his face. How had the ship of his life, which had found such welcome shores in Hawai'i, foundered and run aground on the rocky shoals of this damnable California? What if he *was* deported to Japan? Would his own people regard him as a traitor for immigrating to America?

Or might they treat him as a human being?

That would be a welcome change.

Fueled by rage, loss, and a fever to strike back in the only way he could, Taizo picked up his pencil, answered *No* to Question 27 and an even more emphatic *NO* to Question 28, and handed in his questionnaire.

He did not wait for Etsuko, Dai, and Rose to finish their questionnaires, and he did not tell them how he had answered. This was his decision alone; he would not allow them to follow his example out of filial piety. Outside the mess hall, it was ninety degrees in the shade and blustery winds blew hot from the north; but when he took in a deep breath of the air, it still tasted sweeter, purer, than it had to him since he had left Florin.

As the WRA had hoped, the relocation program began picking up speed almost immediately, with a hundred internees departing Manzanar in March for work furlough jobs in Grand Junction, Colorado; Chicago, Illinois; Madison, Wisconsin; and scores of other communities. Ruth's neighbor, Alice Arikawa, left for a job as a civilian clerk for the Army in Washington, D.C.—clearly with two brothers in the military, her loyalty was not in question. That number grew to three in June, when nineteen-year-old Burns Arikawa also enlisted. Mrs. Arikawa was sad to see them go but obviously very proud as well. None of this surprised Ruth—this family was more patriotic and sacrificing than most white families she knew—but what did surprise her was, on the same day Burns enlisted, Ralph dropped by to tell Ruth and Frank that he, too, had volunteered for the Army.

"What!" Ruth was flabbergasted. "You're kidding!"

"Nope. I leave for the recruiting center in Salt Lake City on the twelfth."

"Well—congratulations," Frank said brightly. "We had no idea you were even considering this."

"Been thinking about it for a couple months. Writing all those flag-waving stories for the paper just started to feel so goddamn hypocritical. I really do believe the U.S. has to win this war, but I wasn't willing to put my money where my mouth was. It may not be fair that Nisei have to prove our loyalty by fighting for this country, but if that's what it takes to convince the *hakujin* that we're Americans too, then somebody's got to do it."

Ruth was badly shaken. "But why does that somebody have to be *you*?"

"Why not? I'm single, no dependents. What good am I doing in Manzanar, writing for a government-censored newspaper in a concentration camp? At least I'll get the hell out of here. And if I die, I'll die a free man."

Ruth suddenly burst into tears, jumped to her feet, and ran outside.

Ralph, genuinely nonplussed, looked to Frank. "Wow. I didn't see that coming. Um, which one of us goes after her?"

"I think you do." Frank smiled. "You've known her longer."

Ralph followed the sound of weeping to the ladies' latrine, where he paused at the threshold.

"Sis? It's gonna be okay. I shouldn't have said that, I'm not gonna die."

The weeping stopped, and in a few moments Ruth came out, looked at her brother—and punched him in his left arm, just below the shoulder.

"Oww!" he cried out. "What the hell was that for?"

"Damn it, Ralph, why are you are always getting yourself into trouble?"

Ralph rubbed his arm. "That hurt. You're mean."

"Sorry. Reflex action."

Ralph said gently, "I won't always have my sister to help bail me out of trouble. It's time I started doing that for myself."

"But it's *you* who've always helped *me*. From my very first day, when you showed me how to use chopsticks."

He laughed. "Didn't think you remembered that."

"I remember you helping me with chopsticks and later walking with me to my new school. Everything important." She dried her eyes on the sleeve of her blouse. "God, I could use a stiff drink right now."

"One of my roommates has a still. He brews a pretty decent beer."

"Sold. Get some for Frank too. We'll toast to your enlistment." She hugged him, and as she did she said softly, "You'd damn well *better not* die."

*T*aizo and Etsuko greeted the news as stoically as they could manage, with a mix of pride and fear. Burns Arikawa and Ralph left Manzanar together. Burns's mother, Teru, added a third blue star to the service flag hanging in their barrack window, as Etsuko quietly hung up her first.

But by late summer it became clear that there had been an additional purpose to the registration program.

Beginning in August, a review board began "segregation hearings" in Manzanar and the other nine internment camps for those who answered "no-no," in order to determine those who were disloyal to the United States. The aim was to isolate them, along with other "troublemakers"—the latter including many who simply had stood up for their civil rights—in a single camp: the newly rechristened Tule Lake Segregation Center in Northern California.

Manzanar's Project Director, Ralph Merritt, stressed to the residents that everyone would have an opportunity to clarify or recant his or her answers to Questions 27 and 28; the people sent to Tule Lake would not be mistreated in any way, but removing them from the general population would allow the "loyal" residents of Manzanar to live here free of insecurity and unrest.

Taizo's notice came on August 20. At first he tried to hide it, but when Etsuko finally saw it he tried to dismiss it. "Many men are being asked to appear. They cannot send us all away, can they?"

"*Why* are they asking you to appear, *Otōsan*? You did answer the last two questions 'yes-yes,' did you not?" When he failed to respond she snapped, "Taizo, answer me! Did you say 'yes-yes'?"

"Everything will be all right, *Okāsan*. Trust me. And do not tell anyone else of this. There is no use worrying over a hearing before it has happened."

Etsuko did not like this but honored his wishes, saying nothing to Ruth or Horace at dinner and sleeping barely a wink that night.

The next morning Taizo put on his business suit and reported to Block 31's recreation building where the Segregation Board—consisting of Ralph Merritt and three other administration officials—greeted him and asked him to sit down in front of the rec table where the board sat.

Merritt said, "Mr. Watanabe, our records show that you answered 'no' to Question 28. Was that, in fact, your answer?"

"Yes," Taizo replied, "it was."

"Do you believe you understood the question when you answered it?"

"Yes."

A woman, Miss Adams, spoke up: "Did you make the answer of your own free will without influence, threats, or pressure from others?"

"Yes."

"Did your answer mean that you were not loyal to the true principles of the U.S. government as you understand them?" she asked.

"No. I believe in those principles. Or . . . I used to."

"So was your 'no' answer, then," Merritt said carefully, "intended merely as a protest against what you considered unfairness and discrimination against you like evacuation and detention, and *not* intended to indicate that you were either loyal to Japan or disloyal to the U.S.?"

Taizo considered that a long moment, then answered, "If I swore loyalty to America, would America repay my loyalty with citizenship?"

Merritt sighed. "Not at this time."

"And if I swear allegiance to America and Japan wins the war, will the Japanese government then brand me a traitor because of that?"

Merritt said, "I can't answer that, Mr. Watanabe."

"We Japanese value fidelity and honor above all, Mr. Merritt. If I reject allegiance to Japan, I will become a man without a country, and possibly a traitor to be executed. If I reject allegiance to America, I will either be segregated or deported. The second choice seems less fatal."

"Mr. Watanabe, would you like to answer Questions 27 and 28 today in the affirmative? Say 'yes' to them? There's still time to change your answers."

Taizo shook his head and said, "No."

"Do you wish to make any statement?"

"Yes. I do."

Taizo sat straighter in his seat as he weighed his words.

"I came to America forty years ago carrying nothing but a bedroll, because I heard it was a place that welcomed all who were willing to work hard. I labored on the plantation ten hours a day, six days a week, for ninety cents a day. I saved enough to move to Honolulu and start my own business. I paid taxes like everyone else. I came to California, and even though I was denied the rights of a citizen, I believed in 'American principles.' I believed my children would have even more opportunities. I listened to them practice the Pledge of Allegiance for school and I was proud. They were Americans!" He smiled at the memory of his children's bright faces, but the smile quickly faded. "Then war came, and America was quick to cast aside its principles. Can you tell me, Mr. Merritt, that that pledge still means something? 'Liberty and justice for all'?"

Frustrated, Merritt said, "We are *trying* to give you back that liberty."

"And will I get back the life America took away from me? Will there be justice for me and for my family?"

This was met by embarrassed silence from the board members.

"For me it is a question of honor, Mr. Merritt," Taizo said in conclusion. "If America is not willing to honor its own principles . . . how can I?"

Merritt looked genuinely saddened. He glanced at the three other board members, each of whom nodded wordlessly. Merritt turned back to Taizo and said, "I respect your view, Mr. Watanabe, and that *is* your choice. Unfortunately you give *me* no other choice but to order your transfer to Tule Lake Segregation Center. If members of your family wish to join you there, they may apply for transfer. You will have all the same rights at Tule Lake that you have in Manzanar, except for the right to apply for leave clearance. You will be there for the duration of the war. Do you understand?"

Taizo said he did, and with that, the hearing was over.

"Why, Papa, why?"

Ruth struggled to understand the inexplicable. She was not the only one. The family was gathered again in Taizo and Etsuko's apartment—all but Rose, who was looking after the children—and their shock at what Taizo had told them was matched only by their heartache.

"A man is nothing without honor," Taizo said simply. "They have taken everything else from me, but they will not take away my honor."

"'Everything'? What about *us*?" Ruth shot back. "Doesn't your family matter more than your honor?"

Taizo smiled. "On the contrary—it is for all of you that I do this. As the proverb says: *Ikka no memboku to naru*, 'To bring honor to the house.'"

"Proverbs!" Ruth was as incredulous as she was angry. "Good God! They're putting you in a *stalag* and you're quoting *proverbs*?"

"I do not expect you to understand, Dai," Taizo said gently. "You are American. I do not expect anyone else to agree with or follow me."

"*I* will follow you," Etsuko said flatly. "I am your wife."

"*Okāsan*, that is not necess—"

"*I am your wife*." Etsuko laid down the words like a gauntlet. Taizo knew better than to pick it up. He simply nodded.

"We'll *all* go with you," Horace declared. "I'll tell the WRA I want to change my answer to 'no-no'!"

"No, you will not," Taizo replied.

"So will I," Ruth said stubbornly.

"No. You. Will. *Not!*"

Ruth flinched; she had never heard her father truly shout before.

"You are *all* Americans," Taizo said. "That is what we raised you to be—to be accepted in this country. These old Issei who demand their children answer 'no-no' out of loyalty are fools. You must go your way, and I must go mine. We can only be true to ourselves. And I will not see my grandchildren raised in a '*stalag*,' if that it is what Tule Lake turns out to be."

This last arrow found its mark. Ruth began to see how hopeless this was. How could she take her children somewhere that might be even worse?

"Dai—Haruo—do not worry," Jiro said. "Nishi and I will also be at Tule Lake, at least until a prisoner exchange is arranged for us. We will be there to help Taizo if needed."

"I do not need any more of your *help*," Taizo said sharply.

"And tomorrow," Etsuko declared, "I will apply for permission to accompany my husband."

Tears sprang to Ruth's eyes at the thought of losing both her mother and her father for the duration of the war. But she knew not to try to dissuade Etsuko once she had reached a decision.

Etsuko slipped her hand into Taizo's and said, "What is done is done."

He nodded. "We shall *gaman*."

The first contingent of 288 evacuees was scheduled to leave Manzanar on October 9, 1943, Taizo among them. Etsuko had applied for transfer to Tule Lake, but she would have to wait. Ten thousand "disloyals" from the nine other internment camps had been sent to Tule Lake in the first month of the program. The camp had originally been designed to house some fifteen thousand people, and adequate housing was at a premium. Etsuko was frustrated to learn she would have to wait until more barracks were constructed at Tule.

That morning in October the Watanabe family rose well before dawn, even the children, who had been told that their grandfather and Uncle Jiro and Aunt Nishi would be "going away for a while." For their sakes Ruth did her best to stay calm and be brave in the face of the thing she had feared the most her entire life: losing her family. Ralph's leaving was a jolt; this felt like an earthquake, and Ruth struggled to maintain her balance.

One by one everyone said their goodbyes. The children, still drowsy with sleep, each hugged Taizo in turn.

Ruth embraced her father. "I love you, *Otōsan*."

"And I have loved you, Dai, since the moment the sisters brought you to us and you told us excitedly how you went to the zoo and saw a bear and a monkey and an elephant and a lion."

"Did I say that?" Ruth said, smiling.

He nodded. "And your eyes were so full of love and tenderness that I knew you would grow up to be a fine woman."

Tears streamed down Ruth's face, and Taizo's glistened as well. But before she could reply, there was a knock on the door.

It was Taizo's WRA escort. Idling behind him was the panel truck that would take him and 287 other "segregees" to the Lone Pine railroad station, where a special train bound for Tule Lake would be leaving at ten A.M.

Unembarrassed by the presence of the escort, Etsuko gave Taizo a tender kiss. "I will be with you soon, my love. My place is always with you."

Taizo followed the escort to the truck. Watching him, Ruth felt sorrow, loss, but also, she had to admit, an ineffable pride as he walked forward with dignity and grace—hewing to a path she feared she would never fully comprehend.

tsuko now found herself alone in the apartment, and that night the twenty-by-twenty-five-foot room seemed larger than it ever had—and achingly empty. Etsuko resolved to be brave and curled up on her cot, her back turned to her husband's empty cot. But her resolve soon crumbled and she began to weep, wishing that this was all a terrible dream she could rouse from and find Taizo beside her, back in their old bedroom overlooking the strawberry fields. Her Buddhist faith told her she had to let go of what was and face what is, but how could she let go of a man who was a part of her, a man she had lain beside and loved for forty years?

She wept as softly as she could, but after five minutes she heard the *click* of the door opening, the sound of someone padding toward her, then lying down in Taizo's cot. For an instant she allowed herself the fantasy that it was he, that he had changed his mind and returned to her. But the reality was almost as comforting. She heard her daughter's voice whispering "Sssh, sshh, it's all right, *Okāsan*," and then Ruth's body inched over and held Etsuko, comforting her as Etsuko had comforted Ruth as a child. And now Etsuko wept in gratitude for the welcome warmth of her daughter's arm draped across her, for her gentle assurances, and for the gift that Ruth had always been to her.

Chapter 12

1943–1944

Tule Lake Segregation Center was a two-and-a-half-square-mile city resting on a dry lake bottom; the sandy soil was stubbornly resistant to green growth and yielded little in the way of shade. Unlike the mountainous walls surrounding Manzanar, here there were only low hills, an ancient volcanic crater the internees dubbed Abalone Mountain, and the broken crown of a volcanic butte known as Castle Rock. The camp was secured with a battalion of a thousand military police on a base outside and twenty-eight guard towers with search beacons ablaze at night like the burning eyes of God.

The registration clerk tried to assign Jiro, Nishi, and Taizo to the same apartment, but Taizo insisted on rooming apart from Jiro. He ended up sharing an apartment—filthy and reeking of cigarette smoke—with two bachelors more interested in gambling than housekeeping. The block manager, a man in his thirties named Yamasora, brought Taizo a broom and fresh bed linens. Yamasora, like Taizo, came from Okayama-*ken* and the two hit it off, chatting about their old home, soon to be Yamasora's home once more (he was at Tule because he had applied for repatriation to Japan). After Taizo's corner of the apartment was made more habitable, Yamasora offered him a tour of the camp's facilities, including the well-stocked canteens, and invited him to dinner. Standing in line at the mess hall, they were strafed by the cold knife's edge of a wind that set Taizo to shivering so badly that, once inside, it took two cups of hot tea to thaw him.

"Hah! And this is a *warm* night," Yamasora told him.

Later, Taizo composed a carefully worded letter to Etsuko:

I find myself in comfortable surroundings. In many ways Tule Lake is superior to Manzanar: there are three well-stocked canteens that sell everything from Hawaiian shirts to fresh shrimp, sashimi, crab, and tuna. There is also excellent daikon grown here at the camp. Housing is still scarce as more "disloyals" arrive each day, but I am assured that when you are given clearance to come to Tule we will be assigned quarters together. I miss you and Dai and Haruo and the children very much, but this war will not last forever and I know that someday soon we shall all be together again.

Less than a week later, a truckload of internee farm workers overturned on the way to the agricultural fields outside camp—killing one man, injuring twenty-eight others. Tempers flared in the "colony"—as internee housing was called by administrators—when it was revealed the truck driver had been an inexperienced minor. Aggravating the tragedy was grievance over the fact that eight hundred farm workers had not been paid back wages. As laborers refused to return to the fields, meetings were called to discuss the matter.

It was resolved to form an organization, Daihyo Sha Kai—"representative body"—to lobby for safer working conditions. One person was elected to this organization from each block; Yamasora was elected from Block 17.

Daihyo Sha Kai then elected a committee of seven to negotiate with the administration—but Tule Lake's Project Director, Ralph Best, refused to negotiate, fired the striking workers, and shipped in strikebreakers from "loyal" camps to reap the fall harvest. WRA trucks removed thirty-two thousand pounds of food supplies from camp warehouses to the tent city where the "scabs" were quartered. Not only did residents suspect the scabs were getting the best food, the strikebreakers were also earning as much in two days as the striking workers had been paid for a month's work.

R uth and Frank invited Etsuko to live with them until her transfer was approved, but Etsuko, not wishing to be an inconvenience, declined. So one evening Ruth asked Donnie and Peggy, "Would it be all right if Snowball went to live with Grandma for a while so she won't be lonely for Grandpa? You can go over and play with her anytime." They readily agreed to help Grandma, who accepted their kind gesture. Snowball, still bursting with energy, amused Etsuko with her antics and kept her company through the long nights. The grandchildren visited every day after school and the sound of their laughter, though occasionally raucous, was infinitely preferable to the haunting silence of one lonely person in a room full of ghosts.

Ruth also took Etsuko along to the baseball games that Frank and the kids enjoyed. The World Series had just ended in St. Louis with the Yankees victorious over the Cardinals 4–3, but at Manzanar there were numerous off-season games to keep the crowds happy. The one thing everyone in Manzanar could agree on was baseball. The camp boasted a hundred men's teams and fourteen women's teams; the sport, enthusiastically embraced in all the camps, helped knit together the evacuees' fractured lives with a thread of community identity, morale, self-esteem, and much-needed normalcy.

Etsuko understood the game but it hardly mattered to her who won, whether it was the Manzaknights vs. the Solon Nine or the Dusty Chicks vs. the Zephyrettes. She was thrilled by the roar of the crowd and delighted in the cheers of her grandchildren. Their joy helped fill the absence in her heart.

Also welcome were letters from Ralph, who was in basic training at Camp Shelby, Mississippi, and reported on tensions that existed in the 442nd between the Hawaiian-born Nisei and the mainland Nisei:

The Hawaiian Nisei talk island pidgin, which the mainland Nisei don't understand, and they call the mainlanders "Kotonks"—"the sound you get when you knock the mainlanders' empty heads together"—and the mainland Nisei in turn call them "Buddhaheads." First time anyone tried calling me a Kotonk I shot back in pidgin, "Why, boddah you? Like beef?" That shut them up. Since I was born and raised in Hawai'i but lived on the mainland, neither side knows what to make of me. For once the bullies are afraid of picking on me, hah!

While weather still permitted, Ruth arranged picnics along the banks of Bairs Creek, which meandered through the southwestern corner of the camp on its way to the ever-thirsty Los Angeles Aqueduct. Paths wound through a small wooded glade and rustic bridges spanned the creek; here picnickers feasted on everything from *yakitori* and rice to hot dogs and potato salad.

Taizo was never far from Etsuko's thoughts, and as they walked the arbored pathways she told Ruth stories she had never shared before, of her childhood in Hōfuna, of her marriage to Taizo: "Our families were neighbors. I knew Taizo's face across the border of our two farms and long before we reached maturity our families had arranged our marriage. I remember being grateful that our homes were close—unlike some brides, who moved so far away they never saw their families again."

She laughed. "How naive I was! When Taizo's father died and his eldest brother inherited the vineyard, I had no idea I would end up moving across an ocean and never see my mother and father again."

That sounded so cruel to Ruth, but she just said, "When you and Papa married, did you know each other well?"

"Not well, but I like to think he found me as pleasing as I found him. He had grown from a sickly child into a strong, kind man. Kindness is scarce in this world, Dai; that is why we were so happy that you found Frank. In Honolulu I knew 'picture brides'—who had only seen a photograph of their betrothed—who came to the grocer's with blackened eyes or broken teeth. I shuddered and was grateful I had Taizo, whose only touch was tender."

Ruth slipped her hand into hers. "You'll be with him again soon."

"At the start, we were apart for two years—only men were allowed to emigrate from Japan to America. I had to wait until the law was changed to allow women. At least I know today that I will not have to wait *that* long."

* * *

On Monday, November 1, WRA Director Dillon Myer visited Tule Lake on an inspection tour and was greeted by a crowd of at least six thousand internees outside the administration building, peacefully protesting working conditions. The protestors gradually dispersed without incident. But the size of the crowd alarmed the *hakujin* staff, their fears stoked by another incident occurring at the same time: a group of fifteen internees stormed the camp hospital and assaulted the widely disliked chief medical officer, Dr. Reece Pedicord, blaming him for the recent death of a Japanese baby.

Two evenings later, Taizo was awakened past midnight by a rumbling noise that sounded as if the earth itself were tossing in its sleep. He went to the window, looked out, and was astonished to see Army tanks lumbering through the streets. Soldiers inside announced through bullhorns: *"Stay indoors! Do not leave your barracks, stay inside!"*

Taizo could not go back to sleep, but those who did woke the next morning to find three hundred military police occupying the camp. There were armed soldiers stationed on every corner as radio patrol cars and tanks prowled the streets. The thunderous roar of jeeps, cars, and tanks was a deafening display of power orchestrated to strike fear into the internees.

Compounding this was a racket of construction as a barbed-wire fence was being erected between the colony and the administrative area: no internees, even ones employed in administration, were permitted inside, and those who tried to report to work were rewarded with tear gas fired by military police. This was a tactic the Army would continue to exploit: tear gas to break up small groups of unarmed internees peacefully waiting in line at latrines, showers, or coal piles—harassing them for the sole purpose of intimidating the populace.

Tule Lake was now under martial law—and ninety-nine percent of the internees, including Taizo, had absolutely no idea why.

That same morning, as she was grocery shopping at the Manzanar canteen, Ruth was greeted by the front page of the *Los Angeles Daily Mirror*:

ARMY TAKES OVER TULE LAKE CAMP

Seizure Follows Disclosure of Aliens' Sabotage at Segregation Center

TULE LAKE, Nov. 4. (U.P.)—The Army tonight took over the Tule Lake Japanese's segregation center at about 10:30 P.M., according to Lt. Col. Verne Austin . . .

Accounts of sabotage and openly avowed loyalty to Japan came to light today in further revelations of just what happened Monday . . . Ernest Rhoades, the resigned fire chief at the camp, asserted that all fire alarm telephones had been destroyed, sand and broken glass were tamped into hydrants, and automobiles were damaged, one having been scratched with the words: "To hell with America."

Ruth found herself standing at an intersection of horror and disbelief, knowing only one thing for certain: this news had to be kept from her mother.

But the camp was already buzzing with conflicting stories about what was happening at Tule Lake, and when she returned Ruth found a shaken Etsuko standing on her doorstep, a tremor in her voice.

"Dai, have you heard? There were ten thousand rioters at Tule Lake! They threatened to kill Mr. Myer and the Army had to come in to save him!"

"*Okāsan*, it's not that bad, I've seen the papers."

"I knew your father should never have gone there!"

Ruth embraced her mother. "I'm sure he's fine. He's not the sort to be part of any violence. He's probably having breakfast in the mess hall right now. We'll write him a letter and he'll write back saying he's all right."

"Good. Yes. Oh, that stubborn old man!"

The mess hall was thick with rumor, speculation, suspicion, and fear. Why had the Army taken over the camp? Why couldn't people go to work? What had happened during the night to so drastically alter life at Tule Lake?

Yamasora, glancing nervously around the room as he ate breakfast with Taizo, confided, "From what I heard, last night some *hakujin* drivers signed out a truck from the motor pool and used it to deliver more stolen food to the strikebreakers. Some Japanese from the motor pool got into a scuffle with white security officers, and when a small crowd gathered around Director Best's house, wanting him to intervene in the theft, he got the idea they were planning to abduct him and he called in the Army.

"The military police arrested eighteen internees, mostly members of Daihyo Sha Kai. They're in the stockade and nobody is allowed to see them. This could be the excuse Best needs to get rid of us so-called trouble-makers."

"Are *you* safe, Yamasora-*san*?" Taizo asked, concerned.

"Oh, I'm pretty low on the totem pole," he said hopefully. "I'll be fine."

The next day the Army began the first of many barracks searches for contraband, confiscating such legal and illegal items as liquor, paring knives, scissors, carpenters' and gardeners' tools, wooden canes, binoculars, cameras, and radios with short-wave capability. They also took away human "contraband," arresting anyone they suspected of being involved in the events of November 1 or 4, or anyone with a reputation for "agitation"—like members of Daihyo Sha Kai.

Taizo was alone in his apartment when the soldiers came to search; as he stepped out of their way and into the doorway, he overheard sounds of a scuffle outside. He turned to see Yamasora being dragged out of his office by two MPs. One of the soldiers twisted his arm so violently that Yamasora shrieked in pain. Taizo ran toward his friend.

"What are you doing!" Taizo yelled. "There is no cause for that!"

"Go home, Grandpa," one of the men said with offhanded contempt, turning away. This young, cocky, contemptuous American soldier seemed to embody every indignity Taizo had endured these past eighteen months.

Taizo reached out and took the soldier's arm in an attempt to get his attention. "What has he done? Are you—"

As casually as he might use a flyswatter, the soldier brought his rifle up and slammed its butt into the side of Taizo's head, which exploded into fireworks behind his eyes. He fell in a daze to the ground.

He was groggily aware of being pulled to his feet, a gun pressed into the small of his back, as the soldiers marched them toward a waiting jeep.

Taizo's head began to clear as he and Yamasora were led into an empty office in the administration building, where they were handed over to two big *hakujin* men in shirtsleeves—not Army, perhaps internal security—who quickly got down to business. They pushed the two prisoners up against a wall, told them to raise their hands above their heads, and "stay that way."

"Okay, Tojo," one of the men said to Yamasora, "we know you were part of the dirty business on Sunday night, so you might as well come clean."

"I wasn't even there!" Yamasora protested.

The security man coldcocked him, driving his fist into Yamasora's face. Yamasora's nose spurted blood as his body began to fall sideways.

"I said stand up, Jap!" the other man snapped, and Taizo now noticed he held something in his hand.

A baseball bat.

"I swear, I wasn't there!" Yamasora pleaded.

The man grabbed him by the collar of his shirt and viciously slammed him into the wall. "Don't give us that shit!"

The man with the bat swung it with cruel velocity into Yamasora's side. His ribs fractured with a sound like a string of firecrackers popping.

Yamasora collapsed like a stringless marionette.

"Stop it!" Taizo shouted. "This is inhuman!"

"Inhuman? That's funny. Tell that to the fifteen hundred GIs you Japs just butchered at Tarawa."

The other security man bent down beside Yamasora. "C'mon, Nip, this doesn't have to be so hard. Tell us what you know about the leaders of your Daihyo Shit Kaka or however the fuck you say it."

Yamasora responded in kind: "Fuck you."

The man with the bat bent down and rested the bat on his shoulder like Babe Ruth aiming for a ball—but in this case the ball was Yamasora's face.

Taizo ran at the man as he swung, grabbing the bat before it connected.

"Goddamn!" the other security man said with a laugh. "This old Jap's got more balls than the young one."

The man with the bat yanked it away from Taizo, then swung it into the side of Taizo's head. Mercifully he would not recall the moment of impact.

aizo woke to exquisite agony; he reached up to touch the side of his head, which was swollen, tender to the touch, and caked with dried blood. Hazily he became aware of his surroundings. He felt a chill in the air and heard a moaning that sounded like the cry of an *obake*, a ghost. Taizo's head throbbed like a beaten drum, but the cries of the wailing man bespoke pain far greater than his own.

"Taizo? Good, you're awake. You all right?"

Taizo looked up. Yamasora was sitting beside him, his face battered and bloodied, his arm in a sling made of old rags. Taizo looked around. He was lying on a thin pallet resting directly on the cold ground, his body covered by two even thinner blankets. He and a number of other men were squeezed into a single Army tent; there was no oil heater, and judging by the light it seemed as if night would not be long in coming.

"Where are we?" Taizo asked.

"They call it the 'bullpen.' The stockade. Taizo, you shouldn't have tried to help me. Now you're in the same miserable boat I'm in. I'm sorry."

Taizo sighed and said with what he thought was commendable stoicism, "I fear I shall never be able to enjoy a baseball game again."

Yamasora laughed. "I think that goes for all of us."

"Who is moaning?"

Yamasora nodded to a man, big as a *sumo* wrestler, two beds down. "That's Tom Kobayashi. Officer Martin hit him with a bat so hard that the bat broke in two. He has an open wound on his scalp and is in constant pain."

"Has he had medical attention?"

"Nope. None of us have. Dr. Mason from the hospital was there at the interrogations, in case a doctor was needed, but he didn't lift a damn finger."

Taizo was introduced to his fellow prisoners—all younger than he, most arrested on the night of November 4 and beaten by security officers. Tokio Yamane's mouth was in bad shape after repeated punches, with only four teeth remaining. Another man was told, "Confess or I'll make your eyes come out of your head" and then struck brutally in both eyes, each now blackened and as swollen as puffer fish. "They laughed as they hit us," said Bob Hayashida, who worked at the motor pool. "There were WRA officials there watching and a security guy told one of them, 'It's open season on Japs, like to try your hand? It's like shooting ducks!'"

It was all more than Taizo could take in. His head was still throbbing and he lay back onto his pallet, which was cold as an open grave. He closed his eyes and woke to the sound of mess hall bells ringing.

An MP entered the tent and escorted the prisoners to the Army mess hall for dinner. As Taizo walked, he saw that the "bullpen" was surrounded by a barbed-wire fence covered by wooden boards—so no one could see in?—with armed guards in each corner. In the mess hall Taizo was surprised when told to take a tray and help himself to the ham, eggs, sausages, and hot coffee—and even more surprised that the prisoners sat surrounded by white soldiers who seemed unperturbed by their presence.

That night the wind yowled like a cat, the gusts rippling the canvas of the tent's walls and causing the tent poles to wobble like fragile saplings. Cold drafts of air blew in through the cracks and the temperature inside plunged below freezing. Taizo wrapped himself in his two blankets, for what little good it did, and did his best to sleep.

The headlines in the Los Angeles papers only grew more histrionic: PLAN OF TULE LAKE JAPS TO BURN BUILDINGS RELATED, with the story asserting that the internees "heaped oil-soaked sacks of straw about the administration building where they were holding 150 whites" in an attempt to "burn the place down." Another claimed that TULE LAKE RIOTS MAY HAVE BEEN TOKYO-INSPIRED, "staged by ringleaders on direct orders from Tokyo." Etsuko was beside herself with fear for Taizo's safety, exacerbated by the lack of a reply to the letter she and Ruth had written.

The *Manzanar Free Press* was silent on the subject, so Ruth went straight to the administration office and insisted on seeing the Project Director himself, Ralph Merritt. After ten minutes she was ushered into his office. "My father was one of those transferred to Tule Lake," she explained, "and we haven't heard from him in over a week. We're very concerned for his safety, and according to the papers—"

"Don't believe the newspapers, Mrs. Harada," Merritt told her. "Most of what they've printed about the incident is just hysterical nonsense. I spoke with WRA Director Dillon Myer about that mass demonstration the papers claim was violent and threatening, and he said that couldn't have been further from the truth. Yes, there's been some violence, but the internees didn't take anyone hostage and no one tried to burn anything down."

"Then why did Mr. Best call in the Army to take over the camp?"

"I'm not clear on that myself," he said with a frown. "I can certainly call Colonel Austin and inquire about your father, though I can't guarantee I'll get a straight answer. But I can try."

"Thank you," Ruth said. "I appreciate that."

"I remember your father's case," Merritt said sadly. "I didn't want to send him to Tule, but he gave the board no choice. He seemed like a good man hamstrung by his own sense of honor. I'm sorry."

Taizo dreamt of his farm in Florin, the fields white with strawberry blossoms in the spring; but then, no, the white wasn't blossoms, it was snow, and Taizo began shivering in his sleep. He woke to the bitter cold of a late November morning and was grateful when the breakfast bells rang, so he could go inside the heated mess hall and warm himself with food and hot coffee. As they were escorted to breakfast, Taizo noted that the Army had begun expanding the stockade by erecting a barbed-wire fence around five Army barracks. Apparently the soldiers in the barracks were being relocated and these buildings would house the ever-growing number of "detainees," now approaching two hundred. Taizo longed for the day they would vacate the flimsy tents and sleep on real cots on a real floor surrounded by real walls.

Days in the bullpen were tedious but tolerable—there was a weekly delivery of cigarettes and newspapers, something to read at least. Taizo was stunned to see the lurid lies they printed about Tule Lake while blissfully unaware of the bloody truth. Mail service also resumed, though outgoing mail was heavily censored; Taizo finally received the letters Etsuko and Ruth had been writing, as well as a note from Jiro, worried and frustrated because the Army refused to allow him to visit his own brother.

He replied to Jiro first, saying that under no circumstances should he tell Etsuko her husband was a prisoner: he was deeply ashamed to be here and refused to have his family dishonored. Then Taizo wrote Etsuko, telling her not to worry; the stories about Tule Lake were overblown. He apologized for not replying sooner but he had a cold—true enough; he had begun coughing yesterday—and that all was well.

*R*uth felt immense relief upon receiving the letter, but Etsuko fixated on Taizo's cold and on a subtle unsteadiness in his handwriting. "He is still not well, I can tell. We should send him some cough syrup and lozenges." Ruth agreed—it gave her mother something to do—and at the camp's co-op store bought him cough medicine, Vicks VapoRub, and a pair of long underwear. They boxed it up and sent it with a long letter from Etsuko and two shorter ones from Peggy and Donnie that consisted of crayon drawings of Grandpa, a bright sun shining in a paper sky, and two valentine-red hearts.

December arrived in Manzanar bearing an unexpected gift: snow. Manzanar's children—many of whom had never seen the stuff before—bundled up in peacoats and happily jumped into snowdrifts, learning quickly how to pack and toss snowballs, construct snowmen, and use scraps of plywood as passably good sleds.

December brought snow to Tule Lake as well, as well as a frigid mass of blustery air that kept people indoors during the day and at night seemed to rest on Taizo's chest like a block of ice. His cold had worsened, his cough now a deep rattle in his chest, and the medicines from Etsuko did little to alleviate it. The long underwear made scant difference when those wintry gusts bellowed through the tent at night.

Finally, at least, the prisoners were receiving proper medical attention. When Dr. Mason took Taizo's temperature—103 degrees—and saw his blood-streaked sputum, he immediately had Taizo transferred to the camp hospital and put him on penicillin, though the new antibiotic was in short supply, as was much else. Due to the Army's demonstrated inability to manage a camp the size of Tule Lake, there were now frequent shortages of medicine, milk, food, hot water, fuel—some children were even barefoot for lack of shoes.

Inside a heated building, lying on a soft bed, Taizo was perversely grateful to the cold that brought him here. But Dr. Mason told him it wasn't a cold but bacterial pneumonia (brought on, he neglected to mention, by the squalid, freezing conditions in the bullpen). The word "pneumonia" sent a shiver through Taizo as he recalled his six months abed with the "winter fever" when he was twelve.

"Am I"—his shortness of breath punctuated the question—"allowed visitors?"

"It depends on their age and health," the doctor replied.

In the end, there was only one person he could ask for.

"Jiro," Taizo said, chest rattling as he took another breath. "Brother."

The doctor allowed a short visit. When Jiro arrived the next morning, he paled to see Taizo in bed with the same illness that he, Jiro, had inflicted upon him fifty years ago. But his brother looked so much worse now.

"Taizo," he said softly. "How are you feeling?"

"Better," Taizo said. He took a breath. "Warmer."

"It is unconscionable what they did to you in that stockade," Jiro said angrily. "Everyone in camp knows what they did. They are only putting prisoners in barracks now because they are afraid of being found out!"

"What is done—" Taizo burst into a wracking cough, and Jiro flinched to see bloody spittle trickling out of his mouth.

A Nisei nurse hurried over and wiped his chin with a towel. "Don't make him talk too much," she advised Jiro, who nodded.

"Taizo, answer me with a nod or a shake of the head. Shall I tell Etsuko that you are sick, in the hospital?"

At first Taizo shook his head, then thought better of it and nodded.

"But I should not mention the stockade—*how* you fell sick?"

Taizo shook his head vehemently. "Tell her," he said, then, out of breath, waited for some more air and went on, "caught—outside. Must never—know—" He paused, then, summoning the strength and will to go on: "She would—blame herself. For not—being here. It would—haunt—her."

"I understand."

"Tell her I love her."

"I will. I promise."

Taizo nodded gratefully.

Tears welled in Jiro's eyes. "My brother. Twice I have brought this fever upon you. I would give up my own life to take back the letter I wrote, selfishly asking you to join me. I am not asking for your forgiveness; I don't deserve that. I only ask that you believe me when I say: I am *so* sorry, Taizo."

Taizo was touched by Jiro's contrition and by the obvious love in his eyes. It reminded him of something, an old proverb . . .

He said, *"Koi to seki to wa kakusarenu."*

Jiro laughed. He knew the proverb:

"Love and a cough cannot be hidden."

Taizo smiled and put his hand on Jiro's, unafraid to show his own love. Nothing else mattered anymore.

hen word of Taizo's death arrived in that first week of January, it came as a cold, cruel shock after the sunny letter he had sent just weeks before. Had she not been given that false hope, Etsuko might have borne the news with some measure of composure; now she simply broke down, shudders of grief wracking her small body. Ruth had to rein in her own anguish to offer what strength she could to her mother. That night she stayed again with Etsuko, though neither of them fell asleep for hours; they spoke of the man they had both loved, his strength, his kindness, his humor. Snowball seemed to sense their shared sorrow and kept her distance, curled up on a pillow on the floor. Finally Etsuko drifted to sleep, leaving Ruth still wide awake. Her grief was a storm, a driving rain falling too fast to be absorbed; but beneath the sodden earth roiled a core of fiery lava, her anger at the actions of the country that had taken everything from her father. The storm would pass, but the anger would continue to burn like lava within the hard mantle of her heart.

Chapter 13

1945

*M*itsuye Endo was a twenty-two-year-old Nisei woman fired in 1942 from her position as a clerk with the Department of Motor Vehicles in Sacramento due only to her Japanese ancestry, then interned at Tule Lake and, later, Topaz War Relocation Center. She was an American citizen who had never been to Japan, did not speak Japanese, and had a brother in the United States Army. Civil rights attorneys James Purcell and Saburo Kido (then president of the Japanese American Citizens League) persuaded her to be a legal "test case" and filed on her behalf a writ of habeas corpus holding that as a loyal citizen, her evacuation and detention were unconstitutional.

On December 18, 1944, the Supreme Court issued their opinion that "whatever power the War Relocation Authority may have to detain other classes of citizens, it has no authority to subject citizens who are concededly loyal to its leave procedure." The Roosevelt administration, given advance notice of the Court's ruling, sought to preempt it by rescinding—the day before, December 17—the exclusion order for Japanese on the West Coast and announcing that all relocation centers would close by the end of 1945. Secretary of War Henry L. Stimson announced the news on the radio that night, and the next evening, at Manzanar, meetings were held in every block to elaborate on the new policy and to answer any questions residents might have.

Ruth, Frank, Horace, and Rose were among the skeptical populace gathered in their local mess hall, listening to a WRA official wearing hornrim glasses read a statement from Director Myer explaining that "all persons of Japanese ancestry, unless there are reasons in individual cases, can return to the West Coast effective after midnight, January 20, 1945."

Applause and cheers erupted from the crowd.

The official went on to stress that the relocation centers will "remain in operation for several months" and that school "will be continued through the current school year. This will enable families with school-age children sufficient time to plan their relocation so that the pupils may reenter school in their new communities at the beginning of the fall term." He noted that the lifting of exclusion came at an opportune time since "there is a good demand for workers in war plants, in civilian goods production, and on the farms.

"Special funds have been provided by Congress for the assistance of needy people who have been displaced from their homes by restrictive governmental action . . ." He finished: "The WRA feels wholly confident that no evacuees will be deprived of adequate means of subsistence by reason of the closing of the homes. Signed, D. L. Myer, Director."

After further applause, the official opened the floor to questions.

Ruth shot to her feet before anyone else and raised a hand.

"Yes," she said, "I have a question."

Something in her tone made Frank think: *Uh oh.*

"Yes, ma'am, go ahead."

Ruth asked, "Is that all?"

The official blinked like a startled owl. "Pardon me?"

"I said, is that all?" she repeated. "No apology? No 'We're sorry we tore you from your homes and destroyed your businesses'? No 'We're sorry we put you in prison camps with machine guns pointed at you and your children twenty-four hours a day'? Or"—and here her voice broke—"'we regret the death of your loved ones who would still be alive today had they not been brought to this godforsaken, *goddamned pisshole in the middle of nowhere?*'"

Her shouted words—and her use of profanity, quite indecorous for a Nisei woman—shocked and silenced everyone in the room.

Frank took Ruth gently by the arm, saying quietly, "Okay. You've made your point. Let's go home."

Moving like a sleepwalker, Ruth allowed herself to be escorted outside into the chill winter night. The frigid air quickly sobered her, bringing with it a cold draft of embarrassment. She started for their barrack, but only got as far as the latrine before she broke down weeping. Frank wrapped his arms around her, whispering softly, "It's okay. You've had to hold it all in—for the sake of the kids, your mother—but you can let it go now."

Between sobs she said, "I—can never—let him go. Never!"

Frank knew there was nothing he could say or do but to hold her. He felt the same grief—for Taizo, for Slugger, for their old lives left shattered at the side of a road none of them had ever expected to travel—but fought back his tears so he could remain strong for Ruth. He would cry those tears later, and knew that Ruth would be there to be strong for him.

The residents of Manzanar now found themselves unexpectedly free—but to do what? The war was still on, Japan had yet to be defeated, and anti-Japanese feeling still ran high, especially in California. This was luridly illustrated, in January of 1945, by newspaper accounts of one Sumio Doi, a young Nisei whose family was the first to return to California from Amache Relocation Center in Colorado. With two brothers in the U.S. Army, it was up to Sumio to ready the family farm in Auburn in time for harvest. Four men and three women—one himself a soldier, AWOL from the Army—attempted to burn down, then dynamite, the family's property. Shots were also fired into the Doi home. The local sheriff posted a guard at the Doi farm, suspects were arrested—but despite signed confessions from all defendants, two juries, one state and one federal, chose to acquit them.

Is it any wonder that many of the remaining internees at Manzanar actively resisted the idea of leaving the camp that had become a safe harbor?

Among these were Ruth's neighbors, the Arikawas. There was now a gold star above two blue stars on the white service flag that hung in their window: in July, Frank Arikawa had been killed in action on the Italian front, the first service casualty from Manzanar. Though they grieved for their son, Teru and Takeyoshi were proud he had died serving his country. Every day as Ruth passed their window, she thought of the courageous soldier in the photograph whose face she would never see in life. She also thought of Ralph, whose 442nd Regiment was distinguishing itself in battle—three months ago, in France, the 442nd had rescued more than two hundred members of the Texas "Lost Battalion"—but was paying for it with such a tragically high number of casualties that it was sometimes called "the Purple Heart Battalion."

Every day Ruth thought of this. Every day she repressed her dread. Now she asked Takeyoshi Arikawa about his family's plans to relocate.

"I would like to take my family home," he admitted, "but there are too many people in Los Angeles who would resent our return. These are troubled times for America. Why should I cause this country any more trouble?"

That response was so Japanese in its self-effacement that it almost made Ruth laugh. She herself did not give a damn about troubling a country that had exiled her family to a concentration camp.

But Ruth and Frank did decide, for the kids' sake, to wait until after the end of the school year in late May. Meanwhile they applied for "relocation subsistence grants"—twenty-five dollars per person, plus three bucks a day for travel expenses, and the WRA picked up the tab for transporting their personal property. It wasn't much compared to all they had lost, but Frank and Horace had worked jobs at Tanforan and Manzanar at sixteen dollars a month and had saved about three hundred dollars apiece. Etsuko's frozen assets in Sumitomo Bank would soon be wired to her too. And the men hoped to find employment as quickly as possible.

Regrettably, there would be two fewer friends to go home to; their one-time neighbors, Jim and Helen Russell, had moved to San Jose, California, where Jim had taken a new job. In a letter Jim offered to drive all the way to Sacramento to pick the Watanabes up at the train station there; Frank thanked him for his generosity but told him they would manage on their own.

At the end of February, WRA Director Dillon Myer himself came to Manzanar to address a capacity crowd. Ruth promised Frank that she would absolutely, positively not swear at anyone. She was expecting only more of the same dry policy statements, but Myer surprised her with his candor about anti-Japanese prejudice in California:

"These are the people who have been working against you for the past forty years," he said bluntly. "They are the ones who are now occupying your homes, operating your farms and other types of business, and making plenty out of it. And they are the ones who fear your competition." He said "race-baiters" like these were trying to intimidate evacuees into remaining in the camps and were hoping for "eventual deportation of all Japanese after the war." He said such campaigns were just so much "bluffing" and encouraged the evacuees not to give in to their bullying.

It was a very heartening talk for many, Ruth included, and it had its effect. In March of 1945, 158 people left Manzanar to relocate, while another 603 made plans to do so.

It was in March, over lunch at the mess hall, that Horace unexpectedly brought up the possibility of leaving sooner rather than later.

"It's just that if we wait to leave until the end of May," he pointed out, "the harvest season will be over. If we leave, say, in mid-April, I might stand a chance of finding harvest work, in Florin or elsewhere."

"I don't like the idea of taking our kids out of school either," Rose conceded, "but at this age, it won't make much difference to them, and the money Horace might be able to make could make a big difference to us."

Ruth considered that. "Well, we do have to go back sometime. And Myer was right: the Japanese helped make Florin what it is today, and we have every right to go back. It's as much our town as it is Joseph Dreesen's."

"I heard the old coot finally died," Horace noted.

"Good riddance," Etsuko said with indecorous contempt, prompting laughter all around the table.

A little after three P.M. on April 12, 1945—two days before the Watanabes were set to leave—Manzanar was rattled, as was the nation, by the shocking news that President Roosevelt had died in Warm Springs, Georgia. Flags across the camp were lowered to half staff; shortly after, all the block managers stood outside in silent prayer, paying tribute to the man who had guided America out of a Depression and through forty months of a war more brutal and global than any other in human history. Usually stoic Japanese wept openly—even Ruth, who still harbored conflicted feelings about the man who had given the order to send them here and who was, directly and indirectly, responsible for so many of the losses they had endured. But he was still the president, and she wept for him and for Mrs. Roosevelt, whose sympathy for the plight of the internees was well known (she had visited the Gila River Camp in Arizona in 1943).

The morning of April 14 was clear, bright, and mild; high clouds floated in a pale blue sky above the saw-toothed ridges of the Sierra Nevada. The Watanabes' luggage was placed aboard a Greyhound bus bound for Northern California as Donnie and Peggy, thrilled to be going anywhere, raced up the steps just ahead of their father. Ruth was holding a small wooden crate from which Snowball was emitting a variety of unhappy sounds. The Arikawas had come to bid the Watanabes farewell and good luck; Ruth and Etsuko thanked them for the welcome they had extended on their first day in Manzanar: "'One kind word can warm three winter months,'" Etsuko quoted, before she and her family boarded the bus.

Ruth felt an unaccustomed thrill, too, as the bus passed through the open gate, beyond the barbed wire, and onto Highway 6, heading north. There were no shades on the bus to shield the outside world from their Japanese faces, and Ruth felt a weight lifted from her soul, a buoyancy of spirit she hadn't known in three long years. Even the speed of the bus—all of forty miles an hour—was exhilarating after the stasis of life in Manzanar.

She was free. Her children were free. That joy of release kept her weightless as a cloud for the next eight hours.

They arrived in Sacramento in late afternoon and took a cab to the city's *nihonmachi*. Once a thriving community of Japanese-owned grocery stores, tailors, hotels, Japanese baths, lodging houses, and homes, it was now a multihued tapestry of varied races: whites, Hispanics, Chinese, and Negroes. Housing was scarce, but the local branch of the JACL had converted several houses into hostels for returning evacuees, and it was at one of these that the Watanabes and Haradas would spend a comfortable night (and possibly longer, if they couldn't find accommodations closer to Florin).

The next morning they browsed several used car lots (technically, every car in the U.S. was a used car ever since the auto plants had converted to war production in 1942). The most practical choice was a nine-passenger Chrysler station wagon. According to the young Chinese salesman, it retailed four years ago for fourteen hundred dollars, had only eighty thousand miles on it, and he was selling it for the bargain price of nine hundred dollars. Etsuko astonished them all by negotiating him down to eight twenty-five, then reached into her purse and withdrew the exact amount in cash.

Painted olive green and with a huge wheelbase, the car could almost have passed for a military vehicle. The men, of course, each wanted to drive it first; they flipped a coin, Frank won, and soon the Chrysler was tooling off the lot, heading south down Stockton Boulevard.

Within half an hour they were turning left onto Florin Road. Etsuko gazed out the window with a wistful pleasure and Ruth spontaneously took her hand, gave it a squeeze, and smiled. They were coming home at last.

But as they entered Florin's downtown clustered along the railroad tracks, Ruth's smile faded. In 1942, Florin's downtown had been busy and prospering; now many of the stores had yet to reopen, their windows soaped over or boarded up. But that wasn't the worst of it.

"Oh my goodness," Etsuko said, "look. Akiyama's Market—is *gone*."

It was true. There was only a soot-stained foundation and the charred stumps of a building frame where Akiyama's Fish Market once stood.

"What happened to it, Daddy?" Horace's son Will asked.

"Looks like . . . fire, Will. Must've burned to the ground," Horace said.

"And Nishi Basket Factory," Rose said, "it burned too."

"Even Mr. Nakajima's restaurant," Ruth said quietly. So many fondly remembered pieces of their past, now just blackened slabs.

Frank pulled the car over to the curb and parked.

The family got out and found themselves standing at the center of not quite a ghost town, with only a handful of stores still open. Among these was Florin Feed & Supply—the late Joseph Dreesen's company. Of course.

"I'd heard there was arson in Taishoku and Auburn," Horace said, "but I hadn't expected—"

"There's one place that's still doing business," Frank said in a strangely flat voice. Ruth followed his gaze and recognized, with a sick feeling, a long, narrow building, with a red sign atop advertising itself as NICK'S DINER.

Without even thinking, Frank began walking toward it.

Ruth quickly handed the children over to Etsuko and hurried to keep pace with her husband.

"Honey," she said, "is this a good idea?"

"Probably not." He opened the door to the diner.

They entered and saw the familiar red vinyl booths, chrome counter-top, and daily specials posted on the chalkboard. A jukebox was playing a Frank Sinatra song. Everything was almost exactly as it had been when they last saw it three years before. It was lunchtime and the diner was doing good business, most of the booths full, the customers mostly white, as was the man behind the cash register.

Frank went up to the cashier and said, "Hi. You the owner here?"

"Since last year," the man replied proudly. "Nick Castellano. You folks back from the . . . camps?"

"Yes, we just got back."

"I gotta say, I thought you people got a raw deal. Hey, you want a couple slices of pie, on the house?"

Frank smiled. He couldn't help liking this guy, but . . . "No thanks, but it's swell of you to offer. You seem to be doing well here."

"Yeah, the train station pulls in a lot of customers—passengers grabbing a square meal before their train leaves."

"You bought this place from Carl Clasen?"

"Yeah, how'd you know?"

"Do you mind my asking—how much did you pay for it?"

Nick looked puzzled by the question, but answered it. "Well, the building's a lease, but I got a good deal on the inventory—thirty thousand bucks."

Frank felt as if he had been sucker-punched in the gut. Thirty grand for inventory he and Ruth had been forced to sell for a thousand dollars.

Forcing a smile, he said, "Thank you. Good luck," then turned on his heel and hurried for the door.

"Frank?" Ruth followed him out, concerned when he didn't respond, just ran into the alley alongside the diner. Once out of sight of anyone on the street, Frank doubled over and vomited up his breakfast.

"Oh, honey . . ." Ruth placed a hand on his back. He remained bent over, waiting to see if the nausea would start again, but finally straightened. Ruth took out a handkerchief and wiped his mouth. As she did she saw that his eyes were glossy with tears.

"I'm so sorry, honey," she said. "It's not fair. None of it was fair."

"I know. I thought I knew that. But this—this I wasn't expecting." He sighed. "You were right. I should never have stopped at this goddamn place."

"What's done is done," Ruth said, realizing only after she'd said it that she was echoing her parents' words in similar times of grief and helplessness.

None of the adults asked them what had happened; they could clearly see the shame and distress in Frank's eyes. Peggy saw it too but had no qualms about asking, "Daddy, what's wrong?"

He managed a smile and ruffled her hair. "Nothing, sweetie." He turned to Horace. "You want to take the wheel for a while?"

"Sure."

They drove out of the business district and down Florin Road. Soon farmland was rolling past on both sides, but the scenery was only slightly more encouraging than what they'd seen downtown. Some of the land—like the Yamada, Tanaka, and Tamohara farms, which had been left in the care of Jerry and Vivian Kara, and the Okamoto, Nitta, and Tsukamoto farms, looked after by Bob Fletcher—were flourishing, their fields lush with trellises of green grapevines and acres of green strawberry plants.

But here, too, there had been arson, writing its black signature on the land: the charred remains of farmhouses, only brick chimneys and cement foundations still standing. The fields were ashen shadows of themselves.

Sadder still were the farms—presumably left in someone's care—that had seemingly been abandoned and left to die.

As Horace turned up French Road, toward what used to be the Watanabe farm, Ruth began to feel the same queasiness that Frank had at the diner. The car pulled into the driveway, parked, and the Watanabes got out to survey what had once been their home, their green inland sea. The structures were still standing but the grounds had been looted of anything of value: tractor, tools, animals, even the wooden posts of the corral. The fields were filled not with ripening fruit but with thickets of weeds and the dried tendrils of grapevines clinging to rotting trellises. Even the buried family heirlooms had been unearthed and stolen.

Etsuko's eyes filled with tears. Perhaps, she thought, it is better that Taizo did not live to see this; it would have broken his heart.

"But . . . wasn't Dreesen planning on working this?" Frank said.

"He did not want the farm," Etsuko said bitterly. "He only wanted us not to have it. To keep it out of Japanese hands."

They stood staring into this wasteland, this embodiment of Dreesen's hate reaching out to torment them, unfettered by the constraints of death.

At last, Horace spoke up. "I . . . think I'd like to drop by Bob Fletcher's place. See if he could use some help on one of the farms he's looking after."

Etsuko turned from the empty shell of the home she had loved, walking with quiet determination back to the car. "I have seen enough here."

ob Fletcher was delighted to see the Watanabes again and told Horace that he could indeed use his help harvesting the Tsukamoto farm: "Al and Mary have been living in Kalamazoo, Michigan, you know, but they're planning on coming back here this summer. I've got migrant workers from Oklahoma working their farm and the others, but I could always use an extra hand with the harvest. And if you need a place to stay, I don't think Mary and Al would mind if I put you up in their house until they got back."

After they'd thanked Bob for his generosity, Frank drove to the Tsukamoto farm, dropping off Horace, Rose, Jack, Will, and their luggage. Then Frank, Ruth, Etsuko, Peggy, and Donnie headed back into town to check on the belongings they had left in the Florin Community Hall. Members of the JACL were there to help them locate their things, and everything was accounted for and undamaged—not that they had anywhere to take it.

They left the Community Hall and were halfway to their car when they heard a familiar voice:

"Ruth! Ruth!"

Ruth turned and saw, across the street, her old friend Chieko— "Cricket"—her always-expressive face full of delight.

Ruth felt the same joy. Cricket ran across the street and the two women embraced. "Oh, Ruth, it's so good to see you! Welcome home!"

"It's so good to see you too." This was truly the only decent thing to happen today. "I heard you were sent to Rohwer."

"Oh yeah, *that* was fun. Marooned in the middle of a swamp. Mosquitoes the size of crows, I swear! But we made it back okay, give or take a few pints of blood, and I even got my old job back at the post office."

"You remember my mother, and Frank and the kids . . ."

"Oh my gosh, look how big they are! Hi, Donnie, Peggy, remember me?"

"No," the kids said, in indifferent unison.

Cricket laughed. "That's okay, you were little guppies then. Not big fish like you are now." She turned back to Ruth. "I saw what happened to your old place, I'm so sorry. Do you have somewhere to stay?"

"No, we just arrived."

"Then you're staying with us," Cricket decided. "We've got plenty of room. Oh, what a beautiful cat!" She poked her finger into Snowball's carrying crate; Snowball hissed. "I know, honey, you don't like it in there, do you? Well, we've got plenty of room for you to roam around, you'll love it!"

"Cricket, we don't want to impose—" Ruth began.

"Oh, for gosh sakes, you're not. Stay with us however long you need to get your bearings. That is *all*, I am not taking no for an answer! I'm almost done at the post office—I work first shift, so I can pick up Abby from school at three. Meet me at my folks' place, it's still standing and we're all living there!"

She raced back across the street and into the post office building.

"I am glad some things remain the same," Etsuko said with a smile.

ricket, her husband, Mitch, and their daughter, Abby, lived along with Cricket's widowed father in the family farmhouse off Gerber Road, which had been conscientiously looked after by George Feil. Though Cricket's *otōsan*, Nobu, was the same age as Taizo would have been, he did not hesitate to join his hired migrant workers in preparing the fields for harvesting. Etsuko watched him work from her bedroom window and wanted to cry. She was not comforted by the lush fields and familiar terrain surrounding it; in truth, she did not enjoy being there. But Cricket and her family were so generous and kind that she would have died rather than betray her feelings in any way.

Frank spent his time looking for jobs at cafes, lunch counters, or diners anywhere from Florin to Walnut Grove, but few Japanese restaurants had reopened yet and the *hakujin* eateries were still wary of hiring "Japs."

Meanwhile, half a world away, Soviet troops launched their final assault on Berlin, Mussolini was executed by Italian partisans, and on April 30, Adolf Hitler committed suicide in his bunker before Allied troops could capture him. Each evening the two families would gather around the big console radio to hear the good news from Europe—culminating, on May 7, with the German army's unconditional surrender to Allied forces. The next day America and the world celebrated V-E Day, the end of war in Europe.

But in the wake of the Nazi defeat, new horrors unlike any the world had ever seen were exposed: the Nazi extermination camps, where six million Jews were starved, tortured, and gassed to death. Pfc 1st class Ralph Watanabe—whose field artillery battalion was attached to the U.S. 4th Division—was outside the city of Dachau when he and his unit liberated a satellite slave labor camp, Kaufering IV Hurlach. As Ralph wrote his sister:

Sweet Jesus, Sis, we never expected anything like this. We shot the locks off the prison gates and all these people struggled to get to their feet. They were wearing black and white striped prison uniforms and round hats, just like you see in the movies—but you never saw this in a movie. They were walking skeletons, nothing but skin and bones, with sunken eyes that bored right into your soul. They were so weak from hunger they could barely shuffle out of the camp, and you could only give them tiny bits of food or water because they'd been starving so long their bodies had forgotten how to handle solid food.

One Polish woman was afraid, she'd never seen people with Japanese features and she couldn't understand the pidgin some of the guys used. One of my buddies got down on his knees in front of her and said, "From my God to your God, we are your liberators."

Too many of them died, even with medical attention. I cried myself to sleep that night.

But by the time she received this letter, Ruth had already seen the Nazi atrocities for herself—in the movies.

At the Alhambra Theatre in Sacramento, Ruth, Frank, and Etsuko watched the first newsreel footage out of the death camps, luridly titled NAZI MURDER MILLS!—and yet that was not hyperbole. The Watanabes and a mostly white audience took in grisly images of what the narrator called Nazi "hellholes." First they saw American POWs—emaciated, starving, with ugly untreated wounds—rescued from a German POW camp. Then came the slave labor and extermination camps, like Buchenwald. Ruth flinched at the sight of burned corpses stacked like kindling and a single lifeless foot extruding from a lime pit. The handful of survivors bore the livid scars of torture racks. And then there were the furnaces, many no bigger than bakery ovens, where both the dead and the living were cremated. "Don't turn away, look!" the narrator demanded of his audience, the oven door open to expose the skulls inside, skulls that once had human faces and housed human souls.

They said nothing to one another on the drive back to Florin, and only years later would they realize that they all shared the same thought at the same time: whatever they had suffered at Manzanar, it could not compare to the suffering and brutality they had witnessed that night. Ruth resolved never to gripe again about what she had endured in the war. It seemed . . . disrespectful. So many millions dead, but she was alive. Her mother, her children, her husband, they were alive. Her father was gone, but felled by a bacterial infection, not gassed in an oven. That night she buried her anger deep inside and put on her outside face tight enough to choke her.

And judging by the silence of everyone in the car that night, Frank and Etsuko had come to a similar conclusion, for neither of them would so much as mention the names Manzanar or Tanforan again—not for many years.

By midsummer more evacuees had returned to Florin, some to flourishing farms and some to ashes. Slowly the town began to regain a bit of its prewar character, with new stores readying to open and old neighbors returning to greet one another. After working the Tsukamoto farm, Horace was able to negotiate a fire-sale purchase of an abandoned farm nearby.

But aside from a few odd jobs, steady employment eluded Frank. After mentioning this in a letter to Jim Russell—now a superintendent with a dried-fruits cannery—Jim wrote back urging Frank and his family to come to San Jose:

> I can get you a job, easy, in the packing shed, and there could be room for advancement. The company's on solid ground and now that the war's almost over they're looking to expand. And there seems to be a more welcoming attitude here toward returning Japanese—a group called the Council for Civic Unity of San Jose has even converted the Japanese Language School into a hostel for temporary housing of all the families returning to Santa Clara County, though you're welcome to stay with us until you find a place of your own.

Ruth was moved by Jim's offer but a little dubious about the nature of the work. "They sell dried prunes?"

"Among other things. Their products are in all the national stores; the brand name is Sunsweet."

"But Frank—owning a restaurant, that was your *dream*."

He just shook his head at that. "No. My dream—from the moment my folks lost their farm—was to have a *home* again. And whatever job gets us a roof over our head and food on the table is what I want. My dream is you and Donnie and Peggy and Etsuko, too, if she wants to come with us."

Ruth kissed him. "I love you. I'm willing to take a flyer if you are."

Frank seemed genuinely happy to write Jim and accept his offer.

This put Etsuko at a crossroads, but she had little difficulty deciding which path to take. When Horace and Rose invited her to live with them, she replied politely but candidly:

"Haruo, I love you and your family. But I cannot live in Florin. There is nothing here for me but grief." She promised to visit often—San Jose was only a hundred miles away, after all.

Once again the Haradas prepared to move, but before they could, the Japanese community was rocked by one more seismic shock.

* * *

ixteen hours ago," President Truman announced in a radio address to the nation on August 6, 1945, *"an American airplane dropped one bomb on Hiroshima, an important Japanese Army base . . . The Japanese began the war from the air at Pearl Harbor. They have been repaid many fold.*

"It is an atomic bomb. It is a harnessing of the basic power of the universe. The force from which the sun draws its power has been loosed against those who brought war to the Far East . . ."

Hiroshima Prefecture had been a major source of Japanese immigrants to the United States and many had settled in Florin—including Cricket's father, Nobu, who came from Onomichi Town in the southeast corner of the prefecture. Nobu was concerned for his relatives in the city of Hiroshima, but the scope of the damage done to it did not become apparent for days, until a thick pall of dust caused by the massive explosion finally lifted. What was left standing—and what wasn't—stunned the world.

Newspaper headlines shouted:

HIROSHIMA POSSIBLY WIPED OUT—BLINDING FLASH VAPORIZED BUILDINGS

BOMB ERASES 60 PER CENT OF HIROSHIMA—

4-SQUARE-MILE AREA COMPLETELY WIPED FROM MAP

150,000 KILLED BY ATOM BOMB

For many, the first reaction was one of utter disbelief.

"How could one bomb do all that damage?" Cricket's husband, Mitch, scoffed as his family and the Haradas gathered around the radio for the latest news. *"Vaporizing* buildings? That's like something out of Buck Rogers!"

"This is all propaganda designed to cow Japan into surrendering!" Nobu insisted, refusing to consider the terrible alternative.

Three days after Hiroshima, a second atomic bomb leveled the port city of Nagasaki, home to a quarter of a million people. The headline in the *San Francisco Examiner* declared:

NEARLY ALL IN CITY KILLED

Now there were no denials from Nobu, only tears. He feared for what might have happened to a beloved aunt and uncle who lived in Hiroshima.

Six days later, the Empire of Japan surrendered unconditionally. The front page of the *Los Angeles Times* featured a drawing of a tattered Japanese flag and, in a headline almost as large:

PEACE!

But so many in Florin could feel no peace. Soon letters began arriving from Japan telling of the unprecedented destruction to Hiroshima—and of deaths unlike any in human history. The men and women who were outside were incinerated instantly, the heat of the blast etching their silhouettes in concrete, leaving behind only wraithlike shadows. Many of those who survived the initial blast were soon soaked in a "black rain" that stormed down soot, dust, and invisible roentgens of radioactivity that first sickened, then killed them all.

Nobu's aunt survived, but his uncle died in the blast; there wasn't even a shadow left behind. Dying with him in Hiroshima were thousands of American-born Kibei—children sent to Japan for their education, a common and now-tragic practice among the Issei.

Florin's disbelief and shock gave way to grief, sorrow, and anger. Some Issei cursed America and "the damned *hakujin*" for what they had done. Some blamed Japan for starting the war. All grieved for cousins, sisters, brothers, nieces, and nephews they had lost.

Ruth still felt disbelief, as well as horror, at the magnitude of the devastation. "Jesus," she said to Frank, "all those people. All those *civilians* . . ."

"They're far from the first," he noted grimly.

He was right. This war had seen more civilians targeted for mass slaughter than in any previous war: Nanking. Dresden. London. Manchuria. Auschwitz. Dachau. In her heart Ruth wept for them all. But *this* . . .

"My God. What kind of world has this become, where someone can press a button and an entire city vanishes in a single flash of light?"

While doing their best to console Cricket's family and other neighbors, the Haradas were also preparing for their move to San Jose. With Horace's help, they transferred their household belongings from the Florin Community Hall and into a rented truck for the drive south.

The night before the trip, as Ruth and Frank lay in bed, exhausted and overwhelmed, Ruth spoke into the darkness:

"Is it wrong for me to feel relief that at least the war is over?"

Her husband took her hand in his.

"No. It's not," he said gently. "The war *is* over, and we can move on with our lives. We're owed that much. To live a quiet, ordinary life again."

She smiled. She liked the sound of that.

"You promise?" she said, teasing. "A quiet, ordinary life?"

"I promise."

It was a promise, they both knew, he had no power to keep—but Ruth loved him for it, and, starting with a long kiss, showed him how much.

PART THREE

'Ohana

Chapter 14

1948

*D*onnie, now ten, and Peggy, eight, were playing ball, normally a fine thing for children to be doing on a warm, sunny day in August—if they were *outside*. Not in the living room, where a pop fly ricocheted off the ceiling and fell toward Peggy. She reached up to catch it, just as Max—a sixty-pound golden retriever—jumped up, snatching the ball in his mouth. "Good catch, Max!" Peggy took the ball, now dripping with dog slobber, and pitched it to Donnie, but it spun wildly astray and into the kitchen, where it crashed into what sounded like the refrigerator. Max eagerly galloped after it, but even he stopped dead when he heard:

"Peggy! Donnie!" And moments later: "*Yuck!* Did you *spit* on this?"

"Not me, Mom!" Donnie called.

"Me neither!" Peggy said.

Ruth held the slimy ball with two fingers as if it were a giant booger. "How many times have I told you *not* to play ball in the house?"

Donnie and Peggy were silent. They knew this was a trick question.

"Go out in the backyard and play, that's what it's there for!"

"It's too hot outside," Donnie protested.

"It's a zillion degrees," Peggy added helpfully.

"Yeah? You want to see how hot things can get in *here?* Out! Out! You too, Max." Ruth wedged the ball between the dog's jaws and marched them—in steely, Mommy-means-it silence—to the back door. Reluctantly the kids ran out into a perfectly nice grassy yard graced by pink-blossomed azalea bushes and a tall palm tree whose long shadow was ticking toward high noon.

As the sunlight hit her Peggy moaned, "I'm *melting.*"

Ruth suppressed a chuckle. "Don't worry, sweetie, that only happens to wicked witches. So *be good* and have fun!"

She shut the door and returned to their brand-new Kelvinator, now defaced by a small ding in the door. Peggy really had quite an arm; maybe they could trade her to the San Francisco Seals. Only two weeks of summer vacation left, Ruth told herself. If I could get through three years in internment camps, I can get through this.

Snowball, having observed the chaos from the sanctuary of the second-floor landing, rested her head on her paws and went to sleep.

Ruth smiled despite her aggravation. The Haradas had been lucky to find this place—a small, two-story stucco house on North Fifth Street, a block from Jackson Street, the heart of San Jose's thriving Japantown. They had spent two years in a one-bedroom shoebox of an apartment on First Street, but fortunately Frank was promoted to foreman of the packing shed just as the housing shortage began to ease. Etsuko generously contributed to the down payment from her bank funds; she had her own bedroom, the kids each had small rooms of their own, and the Haradas had a real home for the first time since Florin. Ruth was especially happy that her mother had adapted well to their new community—she was currently out enjoying *dim sum* with church friends at Ken Ying Low restaurant. Etsuko still grieved for Taizo, as did Ruth, but seemed content with her new life.

The chime of the doorbell found their chatty mailman, Mr. Ng, on the doorstep. "Lots of letters today, Mrs. Harada," he said, handing Ruth a bundle. "Another one from Japan."

"Oh, that must be my Uncle Jiro." Jiro and Nishi had returned to Japan in 1946, where they were relieved to discover Akira, wounded but alive, in an Imperial Army hospital in Tokyo. Upon his deportation to Japan, Akira had indeed been drafted into the Japanese army—but in combat he could not bring himself to shoot at American troops. He was branded a coward by the soldiers in his unit, several of whom gave him a beating so severe it came close to puncturing his left lung. Jiro and Nishi took him back to Hōfuna, where he slowly regained his health. And as soon as she was permitted to travel to Japan, Akira's wife, Tamiko, joined him with their children.

After Mr. Ng left, Ruth glanced at the envelope from Jiro and one from Stanley in Portland, feeling a pang of regret that her once-close family was now so widely scattered. They did see Horace and his family at least once a month; Ralph was the nearest, studying journalism at UC Berkeley on the G.I. Bill.

But as she flipped through the packet of letters, bills, and circulars, she was surprised to see an envelope addressed to her parents—both of them—at their old rural route in Florin. The latter address had been crossed out and someone—most likely Cricket—had handwritten below it FORWARD TO: 659 N. FIFTH STREET, SAN JOSE, CALIFORNIA.

Even more surprising was the postmark—*Honolulu, Territory of Hawai'i*—and the sender's name: "R. Utagawa."

She could have waited until Etsuko returned and handed the letter to her. But the Honolulu address seemed to signal bad news—the death of an old friend, perhaps, though Ruth had never heard her parents mention any "R. Utagawa." Etsuko was still fragile emotionally—they had only recently succeeded, after much stress and bureaucracy, in getting the federal government to return Taizo's cremated remains from Tule Lake—and Ruth hesitated to add another death to her mother's burden of grief.

Or perhaps Ruth was simply curious. In any event, she didn't think her mother would mind if she took a peek inside. She opened the envelope and took out a piece of folded notepaper. The letter was handwritten with an odd leftward slant, as if the writing had been an awkward task. But as she focused on what the words actually said, Ruth's curiosity turned to shock:

Dear Mr. and Mrs. Watanabe:

My name is Rachel Utagawa. My late husband and I gave Ruth up for adoption. A day has not gone by since that I haven't thought of her. I wonder how she is. Is she married? Does she have children of her own? Sister Mary Louisa Hughes has told me what good people you are, and how much you love Ruth. I'm happy to know she had such good parents. I would give anything in the world to hear her voice or see her face, even once. It is a longing, a setsubō, which has never gone away. I intend no disrespect to you. I am her mother by blood, but you are her parents by law and by love. I hope you will look kindly on this request. Thank you.

> *Sincerely yours,*
> *Rachel Utagawa*
> *1726 S. King St.*
> *Honolulu, T.H.*
> *ph. HON 68412*

Nothing on earth could have prepared Ruth for these words. Now it was she who felt fragile, and burdened with a knowledge she had never anticipated. This woman—Rachel Utagawa—was her "natural" mother. Up until this moment she had never been more than a concept to Ruth, an empty phrase—*natural mother; Hawaiian mother*—with no face, no name, no voice, no part in Ruth's life other than the leaving of it. Now, knowing her name, reading her plea, Ruth felt only anger that this woman should intrude herself into Ruth's life, at a time when that life had returned to something resembling normal. After all these years, *now* she wanted to be part of her life?

Ruth's pulse was racing. She sat down on the living room couch, trying to regulate her breathing. On her last visit to their family doctor, Dr. Higuchi, he had warned her that she was in danger of becoming hypertensive.

"Mom!" Donnie yelled from outside. "Can we come in? I'm hungry!"

"I'm *starving*," Peggy amplified.

Grateful for the distraction, Ruth hid the letter inside a book. She made three tuna fish sandwiches and ate lunch with her children. Watching them eagerly devour their food, the indoor baseball paled in significance and she was reminded of how adorable they could be. Their presence reassured her of all that she had in life—and no slip of paper could take that away.

After lunch the kids went out to play again and Ruth reluctantly reread Rachel Utagawa's letter. Her anger had ebbed and she allowed herself to see the sorrow and regret written, not so invisibly, between the lines. *Setsubō*: she had heard her parents use this word at Manzanar.

Ruth heard her ten-year-old self ask Etsuko why her "Hawaiian mother" gave her away: "Didn't she love me, like you do?" She remembered Etsuko's response: "Oh, butterfly, I am sure she did. But she had no choice." At the time Ruth didn't understand that. As she grew older, she assumed it meant her mother was underage, or unmarried. She had never asked again.

Maybe she hadn't wanted to know—or to let go of her resentment.

Could she ignore this woman's *setsubō*—knowing that her parents had felt the same longing for something lost to them?

She hid the letter on the top shelf of her bedroom closet and did not mention it to Etsuko for fear it might upset her; the last thing she wanted to do was cast any doubt on how much she loved her mother. But over the course of the next three days she came to realize that she could not gainsay her "Hawaiian mother" what she said she longed for: *"I would give anything in the world to hear her voice."* It might turn out to be nothing more than that—Ruth certainly didn't want more—but that much, at least, she could give her.

On Sunday morning Ruth feigned illness—an upset stomach, not far from the truth—and let Frank take the kids on the short walk to the Japanese Methodist Church, about a block and a half down Fifth Street. Etsuko had an even shorter walk: San Jose's beautiful Buddhist Temple stood almost directly across the street. Once alone in the house, Ruth took the letter out of the closet. She read it over again, took a deep breath, then picked up the telephone and dialed the phone number given in the letter.

She heard the hiss and crackle of the radio-telephone connection between the mainland and Hawai'i—God only knew how much this call would cost—followed by a ring. Ruth fought a sudden, panicky impulse to hang up. Another ring—and then Ruth heard, across a gulf of three thousand miles, a woman's voice, still groggy with sleep:

"Yes?"

She sounded a bit irritated, actually. Ruth belatedly remembered the time difference between California and Hawai'i. Damn. Well, no turning back.

"Is this . . . Rachel Utagawa?" she asked.

For a moment the only answer was the hiss of static.

"Hello?" Ruth repeated.

All grogginess was quickly gone: "Yes, this is she."

"My name is Ruth Watanabe Harada." Then, apologetically: "It's three hours earlier in Hawai'i, isn't it? I must've woken you up."

"That—that's all right," the woman's voice said. "I'm sorry, I . . . wasn't quite . . . prepared for this."

"Well," Ruth said dryly, "that makes two of us."

Good God, she thought. Her voice—it sounds so much like *mine*.

"Are you calling from . . . California?" Rachel asked.

"Yes. San Jose." Desperate for something to say, Ruth started to explain how Rachel's letter had gone to her parents' old address in Florin, "but a girl at the local post office went to high school with me, and—"

"I named you Ruth," Rachel suddenly declared, a seeming non sequitur.

"Did you?" Ruth said, not knowing how else to respond.

There was a brief pause, then Rachel asked, "Did you speak with your . . . parents before you called me today?"

The way she hesitated a second before saying "parents" annoyed Ruth.

"My father passed away several years ago. My mother's very frail, I didn't want to possibly upset her." A note of her old anger and resentment crept into her tone: "Anyway, it was me you wanted to talk to, wasn't it? Though isn't it a little late to decide you want to get to know me?"

There was a deep, sad sigh on the other end of the line.

"Ruth," Rachel finally replied, "I gave you up for adoption because I had to. Because I was forced to . . . by the government."

Ruth was completely thrown by that. "What?"

"Have you ever heard of . . . Kalaupapa?"

"Kala . . . no."

"It's on Moloka'i. Where Father Damien died."

Ruth had definitely heard of Father Damien: the Catholic priest who went to a remote leper colony to tend to the afflicted, only to himself contract, and die from, the disease. The implications of what Rachel had said now sank in, as did Etsuko's words of thirty years ago: *"She had no choice."*

In a small, shocked voice, Ruth said: "You're a leper?"

In the silence that followed, Ruth could almost see Rachel flinch.

"They call it Hansen's disease now. And I've been paroled. They found a cure. A treatment. I've been released, I'm no danger to anybody."

Feeling numb, Ruth could only repeat dully, "Hansen's disease?"

"It's not hereditary. It doesn't pass from mother to child unless the baby remains with the parents for an extended time. That's why we had to give you up."

The numbness was giving way to panic. She didn't know what to say except, "I . . . think I'd better have a talk with my mother."

"Yes," Rachel agreed, "that's a good idea."

"I'll call back tomorrow," Ruth said, desperately wanting this conversation to be over before her heart exploded. "Or the next day."

"Ruth—"

"I'm sorry. I can't talk right now. I'll call back, I promise."

She was not certain if that was true or not.

hy in God's name didn't you *tell* me?"

In the privacy of Etsuko's bedroom, her mother sat on the edge of her bed, her head lowered in embarrassment.

"I wanted to. Many times. But your father thought it best you did not know all the facts of your parentage."

Ruth was dumbfounded. "But why?"

Etsuko looked up. "In Japan, having leprosy is a terrible thing. It is seen as sinful—in Shintō the word *tsumi* means both sin and leprosy—and Buddhism says it is a punishment for sins in a previous life. It is the blackest of black marks on a family's lineage. The shame is so great, no one will marry into the family." She added pointedly, "Had Frank's parents known about your mother's illness, it is unlikely they would have blessed your marriage."

Ruth labored to understand. "Then why on earth did you go to Kapi'olani Home? Weren't there other orphanages in Hawai'i?"

Etsuko sighed and patted the bed. "Sit with me. As we used to."

Ruth sat down beside her mother and waited.

Etsuko asked, "You have heard the story of how your father nearly died of pneumonia when he was twelve?"

"Many times. Did he really drink the blood of a carp?"

Etsuko nodded. "I have no idea if it helped him, but it surely did no good for the carp." Ruth had to laugh. "The doctor prescribed remedies, but it was not he who saved his life. Taizo was nursed back to health by a woman—a midwife friendly with Taizo's family. In those days there were no such things as nurses in Japan, only midwives. But they often knew as much as doctors did, and this one came over almost every day for six months—applying warm poultices and hot mustard plasters, making sure he had fresh air, feeding him nourishing soups and broths—until the winter fever passed.

"When he was well enough to leave the house, he went to the midwife's home to thank her for all she had done. But when her mother answered the door she declared, 'I have no daughter.' Taizo persisted, and she admitted that her daughter had left because she was . . . 'unclean.' The last thing this mother said to her daughter was 'Never come back. And die quickly.'"

"My God." Ruth flinched at the cruelty. "She—she had leprosy?"

Etsuko nodded. "She must have contracted it from one of the women she had midwived. Back then, there were no leprosy laws in Japan and no public hospitals that would take them; it was not uncommon to see homeless lepers wandering from town to town, living hand to mouth. Your father searched for her, but it was fruitless. Years later he learned that she had died at Kaishun Hospital in Kumamoto-*ken*, a private sanitarium for lepers opened by an Englishwoman, Hannah Riddell. He never had the chance to thank his benefactor for what she'd done for him."

A tingle of intuition ran up Ruth's spine as she asked, "This woman —what was her name?"

Etsuko said, "Her name was Dai."

Of course, Ruth thought. Of course.

"Taizo felt he owed her a debt he could never repay—until he read about the Kapi'olani Home. And so we found you and named you Dai to honor her." She squeezed Ruth's hand. "I know you found your father's ideas about honor difficult to understand. But you owe your life with us to that sense of honor."

Tearfully, Ruth embraced Etsuko. "I understand now," she said softly. "I understand, *Okāsan*."

They sat there, interlocked in their love and grief for Taizo, until Ruth pulled away and asked, "So what should I do? About my . . . Hawaiian mother?"

"She is part of your life, Ruth. She *gave* you life. Call her back."

"What if she asks to come here? How would that make you feel?"

"I am secure in the knowledge that I am the mother of your heart," Etsuko said, smiling. "But she is the mother of your blood. She deserves to see what a fine woman you have become . . . if that is what you wish as well."

"I wish I knew what I wished," Ruth said. "This is so . . . overwhelming."

"It is your decision, butterfly," Etsuko said gently. "But I have never known you to make a bad one."

That night, while Donnie and Peggy were in the living room listening to the music and adventure from *Gene Autry's Melody Ranch*, Ruth closed the door to the bedroom she and Frank shared and told him everything. He read Rachel's letter and was as stunned as Ruth was by Rachel's admission and by the history Etsuko had revealed. His first thought was "What about the kids? Are they going to—" He couldn't bring himself to complete the sentence.

"She said it wasn't hereditary. But I'm going to call Dr. Higuchi tomorrow and ask him what he knows about leprosy."

"That's good. Jim was an Army doc, he might've encountered this. Ask him whether it's safe for us—and the kids—to be around her."

"I called her a leper." Ruth felt ashamed. "She sounded hurt. But that was the only word I knew."

"You couldn't know. This is beyond the experience of most people."

"What do I do, Frank?"

He smiled. "I think that may be the first time you've asked me that since we've been married. You don't usually have trouble figuring that out."

"I do now. I feel so . . . confused about this woman. For years I've been angry at her, at my *hapa* half, but when we spoke I couldn't help marveling at how alike we sound. And there was such longing and sadness in her voice—"

"You don't have to decide right away. And you don't have to commit to do anything you don't want to do."

Ruth nodded. If only she *knew* what she wanted to do.

It took her several days to assimilate all that Dr. Higuchi told her about Hansen's disease; she even went to the public library to read whatever she could find about Moloka'i and Father Damien. There wasn't much other than a couple of biographies of Damien, and she was impressed by the courage of this man who had given his life to help people who had been forgotten, abandoned. But the graphic descriptions of the physical effects of leprosy—tumors, disfigurement—made her queasy, anxious. It took more days to work up her nerve, but that Sunday Ruth again dialed Rachel's number in Honolulu (though a few hours later).

This time Rachel answered it on the first ring:

"Hello?" The fear and anticipation in her voice was palpable.

"Hi," Ruth said. "It's me again."

Simultaneously they said, "I'm sorry—"

Simultaneously they laughed.

"You first," Ruth said.

"I'm sorry if I alarmed you last week," Rachel said. "I'm sure it was enough of a shock, hearing from me, much less the rest of it."

"I'm sorry it took me so long to call back," Ruth said. "I guess I panicked a little. My first thought was for my children; what it might mean to them."

Ruth heard the barely concealed delight in Rachel's voice: "How many children do you have?"

"Two. Peggy's eight and Donald is ten."

"That's wonderful."

"My doctor says you're right, leprosy isn't hereditary," Ruth said. "But that children are more susceptible to it."

"Did he also tell you that you don't get it from casual contact? From touching someone, or breathing the same air they do?"

"Yes. But he did say that children are more susceptible."

There was a pause as Rachel seemed to consider her words. "Ruth, it's

212

you I want to see. I'm willing to do it under any conditions you name. If you don't want me near your children, I won't go near them."

Ruth ginned up the courage to ask, "How . . . bad . . . is your leprosy?"

"You mean, am I disfigured?"

"I didn't say that."

Rachel said candidly, "My right hand is deformed. And my feet. Other than that, my main complaint is neuritis."

Dammit, Ruth thought, why do I keep putting my foot in my mouth like this? "I'm sorry. I didn't mean to sound . . . tactless—"

"It's all right. Not many people know much about leprosy. Even in Hawai'i it's something most people would prefer not to think about."

There was a long silence, and then Ruth admitted, "I used to wonder about you. Who you were. Why you . . ." She paused. "I think it's only fair to tell you. I love my *okāsan*, my mother. I loved my father."

"Of course you do. They raised you. Raised you well, to judge by what I've heard. I'm not trying to replace anyone in your affections, Ruth."

"Then what do you want from me?"

"Just what I said in the letter. To see you." Here Rachel's voice caught. "You were the only baby I ever had, and you were taken from me after less than a day. If someone had taken Peggy or Donald from you right after they were born—if you hadn't seen them in thirty years—what would you want?"

Ruth heard and was moved by her words, but even more clearly she heard Rachel's voice. It was a voice that sounded like family.

"We're not rich," she told Rachel. "I can't afford to come to Honolulu."

"I don't expect you to," Rachel said, sounding relieved. "I have savings. And Social Security—I worked at the Kalaupapa Store for almost twenty years. The government paid for my food, housing, and clothes, so I've got a few dollars in the bank . . . and a list of places I want to see before I die. But nothing as much as I want to see you, Ruth."

"You worked for twenty years? How long were you at Kalaupapa?"

"Let's see—I was sent there when I was seven years old, and I left last year, so . . . fifty-four years."

Ruth was thunderstruck. *Seven years old?* Suddenly the contours of Rachel's life seemed larger, and sadder, than Ruth had ever imagined.

But there was only happiness in Rachel's voice now. "Ruth—*mahalo nui loa*. In a nutshell that means 'thanks a bunch.'" Ruth laughed at that. "I'll be in touch when I know my travel plans."

That evening, after the kids had been put to bed, Ruth told Frank and Etsuko of her decision. "I think it's best I meet her alone, away from the kids."

"I agree," Frank said. "How do *you* feel about this?"

"Afraid. Excited. Part of me can't wait to see what she looks like. Part of me wants to drive the hell away, as far and fast as I can."

"Hawaiians and Japanese have something important in common," Etsuko noted. "We both revere our ancestors. In Hawai'i I was honored to hear long, beautiful *mele*s—songs, or chants—joyously singing the history of an *'ohana*, a family, going back twenty generations or more. It is like hearing a chorus of voices singing across time itself.

"You have a Japanese legacy, Dai, but our blood is not your blood, no matter how much we love you and you love us. You have songs to hear from your Hawaiian mother, and songs to be revealed, perhaps, of your Japanese father. I am excited for you. I cannot wait to hear the songs you sing back to us."

Chapter 15

The Hotel Sainte Claire, built during the last great roar of the 1920s, was a lavish, six-story palace whose extravagant cost earned it the nickname "the Million Dollar Hotel." It was still the finest hotel in San Jose, and Ruth had been frankly startled when Rachel wrote saying she would be staying there. Either her Hawaiian mother really did have money to spare or she was trying a bit too hard to show she did not need money from Ruth.

Ruth had never even been inside the hotel's lobby before and couldn't help feeling intimidated—both by the opulent Spanish Revival decor and by the fact that hers was the only nonwhite face there. The lobby was chiefly populated by businessmen in dark three-piece suits. In her sunshine yellow dress, Ruth felt like a canary among a flock of blackbirds.

She hadn't anticipated being as nervous as she was. Even after their several phone conversations, none of this seemed quite real. She took the elevator to the sixth floor, then stood at the door to Rachel's room— collecting both her thoughts and her composure—and knocked.

A few moments later the door opened and Ruth found herself staring into the face of the woman who had given birth to her.

Rachel was tall and slim, her broad face and amber skin resembling Ruth's own. Her graying hair was styled in fashionable waves. She looked to be in her early sixties. She was quite beautiful, with warm brown eyes and a smile that, upon seeing Ruth, lit up her face like a sunrise.

Ruth's smile was more nervous.

"Hello," she said. "I'm Ruth."

Rachel's eyes glistened.

"Ruth," she said softly. "Oh my baby, you're so beautiful."

As Ruth blushed, Rachel reached out in an embrace. By Japanese standards, hugging a total stranger was well outside the norms of polite behavior, and Ruth couldn't help tensing up as Rachel held her. Rachel seemed to sense this and let go before it became too discomfiting.

She took a step back, wiped at her eyes. "I'm sorry," she said with a smile. "I'm a blubbering old woman. Take me out and shoot me."

Ordinarily this would have made Ruth laugh, but she had barely heard the words. Her gaze had fallen on Rachel's right hand, which—as Rachel had warned her—was deformed, contracted into something like a claw.

It was true. It was all true.

Ruth felt suddenly unsteady on her feet. "May I . . . sit down?" she asked.

Rachel stepped aside. Ruth wobbled precariously on her heels and gratefully sat down on the edge of the bed.

"Can I get you some water?" Rachel asked with concern.

Ruth shook her head and took a few deep breaths. She looked at Rachel and said in quiet amazement, "You . . . really do have leprosy."

Rachel seemed understandably puzzled. "Well, yes."

With an embarrassed laugh, Ruth confessed that until that moment, "part of me didn't quite believe you. I'm sorry. I shouldn't laugh, but . . ."

She explained what Etsuko had told her about her Hawaiian mother having no choice but to give her up. "But I couldn't help it, I'd still wonder. How you could have given me up. Why you didn't—love me enough—to keep me."

"Oh, Ruth," Rachel said with a sigh, sitting down beside her.

"Please don't be offended by this," Ruth said, "but in a strange way . . . it's almost a relief to learn that you have leprosy. To know that you gave me away because you had to, because you really didn't have any other choice."

"Nothing else in this world could have made me give you up."

All at once Ruth felt self-conscious, having shared so much, so soon. She stood, smiling sheepishly. "Why don't we go downstairs to the restaurant and get some coffee," she suggested. "Or maybe something stronger."

*T*he gin and tonic she ordered in the hotel's palm-bedecked atrium restaurant helped relax the tension in her body but did nothing to relieve the tension of the conversation. Rachel had ordered a Danish pastry and a cup of coffee. She took a sip. "So . . . your parents adopted you when you were five?"

Ruth nodded. "Mama always wanted a daughter, but after my brother Ralph was born she learned she couldn't have any more children. So they decided to adopt a girl." She did not bring up her namesake, Dai; she was still coming to terms herself with her *okāsan*'s revelations.

"Do you recall anything of Hawai'i?"

Rather than go into the few scraps of the past she recalled from her parents' home in Honolulu, Ruth said, "I'm afraid not. My earliest memories are of Florin, our farm there."

"What brought your parents to California?"

"Well, Papa always wanted his own farm. And in Hawai'i, I guess, there weren't many opportunities of that kind for an Issei. You know what that is?"

Rachel smiled, nodded. "My husband was Japanese."

Mortified, Ruth shaded her eyes with her hands. "Yes, of course he was. You had no idea you'd given birth to such an idiot, did you?"

But Rachel only laughed. "No, you've just either had too much to drink or not enough." She sliced off a piece of pastry with her fork. "You were talking about your father?"

Ruth understood that Rachel was only trying to show an interest in her life, but her Japanese reserve made her hold back anything she feared would embarrass her family. So she omitted mention of the subterfuge on Uncle Jiro's part that brought them to California and merely said that her father had gotten a lease on land in Florin. "I lived on our farm till I was eighteen, when I met Frank."

She opened her purse and spread a fan of photographs on the table. She pointed to one of her husband. "That's Frank."

Rachel smiled. "He's very handsome."

"And this is Donald, and Peggy." She pointed out photographs of Donnie in cowboy garb and Peggy posing shyly in a candy-striped blouse.

"As you can see," Ruth said, "Donald wants to be Roy Rogers when he grows up. Peggy wants to grow up, period."

Rachel asked, "May I . . . ?" At Ruth's nod she picked up the photos and, gazing at them, her smile blossomed with wonder and elation.

"They're beautiful," Rachel said softly.

"Thank you. I think so too, when they're not driving me to drink." Surprising herself, she asked, "Your husband. What was his name?"

Pleased, Rachel answered, "Kenji. Charles Kenji Utagawa."

"Do you have a picture?"

Rachel took a snapshot from her purse, handed it to her, and Ruth saw her "natural" father for the first time: a handsome, smiling Nisei in his mid-thirties. In his face Ruth saw traces of her own—the same cheekbones; an echo of a smile—and in his eyes she unexpectedly saw something of Frank.

"He loved you so much, Ruth. He called you his baby, his *akachan*. The day you left Moloka'i he told you, 'Papa loves you. He'll always love you, and he'll always be your papa.'" Her voice broke like glass on the last word.

Ruth's tone was tender. "He looks . . . very kind."

"He was. A very kind, sweet man."

Ruth glanced up. "So he's not—"

Rachel shook her head. "No. He was killed five years ago, in a fight with another resident named Crossen. A bigoted *haole*—white man—who hated Kenji because he was Japanese. Hated everyone and everything, really. Kenji tried to intervene when Crossen was beating his girlfriend, and died in the attempt."

"I—I'm so sorry," Ruth said. "That makes two fathers I lost to the war."

"What do you mean?"

"My papa died at Tule Lake." When she saw the blank look on Rachel's face, Ruth elaborated, "The relocation camp."

"Relocation?" Rachel repeated, as if not comprehending.

Ruth stared at her incredulously. "You don't know? Where have you—" She stopped short, realizing too well where Rachel had been. "But—you had them too, didn't you?"

Rachel, looking truly abashed, meekly shook her head.

"I don't think so. Not in Hawai'i," she said. "I . . . believe the Japanese made up too large a part of the workforce."

Ruth said bitterly, "That sure didn't stop them here! All those farms, no one to work them—"

"You went too?"

Ruth's temper flared at what seemed an annoyingly dense question.

"Of course I went!" It was louder than she intended. At adjacent tables heads turned, diners glared. Ruth flushed in embarrassment or anger or both.

"We all went," she said, lowering her voice. "The signs went up on May 23, and we were evacuated by May 30."

"One week? They gave you one week?"

This was the last thing Ruth wanted to talk about, but she clearly couldn't avoid it. She told Rachel about her family's dispossession, about their months at Tanforan and years at Manzanar. She tried to keep a calm tone, but as she recounted the details, the fury in her heart reignited and the wound of her father's death bled as if freshly cut. Rachel stared in disbelief, then horror. Ruth looked down to avoid meeting Rachel's eyes.

As if reliving it all again, she explained about the loyalty questionnaire, her father's transfer to Tule Lake, and his death there from pneumonia. Finally Ruth looked up—and was shocked to see that Rachel was weeping.

Ruth instantly regretted discussing this. Instinctively she took Rachel's hand—her right hand, folded in on itself—and tried to stem her tears.

"I'm sorry," Ruth said, "I shouldn't have told you all this—it's okay, *we're* okay, really—"

"It's not right. It's not fair."

"It wasn't right. But it's over."

Rachel shook her head. "No. No." There was torment in her eyes.

"You were supposed to be free," Rachel said in a whisper. "You were never supposed to know what it was like to be taken from your home— separated from your family—to be shunned and feared." Then, so softly Ruth could barely hear: "That was all I had to give you."

The desolation in her voice felt like the sere emptiness of the high desert, where the keening wind echoed human despair.

Ruth got up without hesitation and folded her arms around Rachel, tenderly holding her as she would a frightened child and, in soft, consoling tones, told her, "It's all right. Everything's all right. It's all over. I'm free. *You're* free. It's all"—and she said the word she knew she had to say, even if she didn't feel it, not yet—"It's all right, Mother. Everything's all right . . ."

A s Ruth escorted Rachel back to her room, her mind was a jumble of conflicting emotions: she felt profound pity for this woman's tragic life, reluctant pleasure at the mystery of her *hapa* half at last revealed—and guilt that any emotional bond she might be forming with Rachel was a betrayal of the parents who had raised her. Unable to reconcile her love for them with her growing, traitorous affection for this woman, Ruth panicked. After returning Rachel to her room and making sure she would be all right, she invented somewhere she had to be, started to say her goodbyes . . .

"Wait," Rachel interrupted, a bit desperately, "just a minute. Please. I . . . have something for you."

With her left hand she removed a large suitcase from the closet, hefted it one-handed onto the bed, and asked Ruth to open it.

With some trepidation—as if she were opening an inverted Pandora's box that might suck her love for her parents forever inside—Ruth opened it.

Whatever she was expecting to see, this wasn't it.

The suitcase was packed with gift boxes—dozens of them, in every shape and color. There was one the size of a pillbox, wrapped in pink and crowned by a bright red bow almost bigger than the box itself; another wrapped in lavender, ornamented with a yellow ribbon teased and curled into something resembling a flower; and a large box covered by light blue foil that shimmered like the sky on a hot August day. Too many to take in all at once. Christmas had never been celebrated in her parents' home, but Ruth imagined this is what it would have felt like—sneaking downstairs on Christmas morning, overwhelmed by a glittering pile of gifts under the tree.

Rachel seemed to take great pleasure in saying, "Happy birthday," and when Ruth stammered a reply, Rachel prompted, "Open them, if you like."

One by one Ruth opened them. Each gift was modest yet chosen with impeccable taste: a baby's rattle that might have captivated her attention as an infant; a Raggedy Ann doll she would surely have loved when she was three; an elegant fashion doll that six-year-old Ruth might have proudly shown off to her friends; a set of combs and hair brushes for a thirteen-year-old's vanity table; and many more. Thirty-two years, thirty-two presents.

Ruth unwrapped the last one—a copy of *Tales of the South Pacific* by James A. Michener—and held it in hands that were suddenly trembling.

Her family had always celebrated birthdays on New Year's Day, but on her actual birthday Ruth sometimes found herself wondering whether there was someone, somewhere, thinking of her. Now she was presented with proof that there had been, and she was speechless with emotion.

"My God," she said. "You did this every year? For me?"

"We did," Rachel said. "Kenji and I."

Ruth cleared a spot on the now-crowded bed and sat.

"Tell me about him," Ruth said. "Kenji. My . . . father."

Ruth did not leave for home. She listened to a life's story that was, she discovered, richer than it was sad. She learned about Kenji, who on his first day of work at a Honolulu bank was arrested for being a leper, his career gone in an instant; her grandfather, Henry, a merchant seaman who brought Rachel dolls he found on his travels and inspired her own thirst to see the world; her brother Kimo, who also contracted leprosy; and her grandmother, Dorothy, who hid her son in Kula, in the wilds of upcountry Maui, and tenderly cared for him for the rest of his short life. She learned of Rachel's *hānai* auntie, Haleola, a Native Hawaiian healer who opened up for Rachel a world of magic and myth out of Hawai'i's past; her friends Leilani and Sister Catherine and Francine, Rachel's cherished *'ohana* at Kalaupapa, all but Catherine now gone. She learned what *'ohana* truly meant, and that she was a part of it. She began to understand that none of this could replace or usurp the family she had always known, but only enriched what she already possessed. With wonder and a growing absence of fear she realized: *I am more than I was an hour ago.*

She returned home late that evening and in her excitement repeated almost all of what Rachel told her to Frank, and of how longingly she had looked at the photographs of Donnie and Peggy. "I'd—like to bring her home to meet them," she said nervously. "If that's all right with you."

Frank was cautious but not dismissive. "Dr. Higuchi said the sulfa drugs reduced the bacteria in a patient's body to noncontagious levels?"

"Yes. Rachel says she's shown no sign of the disease for almost two years. The risk to us—to the kids—is basically nonexistent." She added earnestly, "Oh, Frank, she's lost so much in her life. She deserves to meet her grandchildren. They deserve to meet *her*."

Frank let out a breath. "Okay. What about Etsuko?"

"I'll ask her first thing tomorrow."

Etsuko readily agreed and Ruth explained to the kids that they had a third grandmother—a Hawaiian grandmother—who was coming for a visit. Donnie said enthusiastically, "She's from Hawai'i?"—though he pronounced it "*How ah ya*," the way Arthur Godfrey did on his radio show. "Oh boy! Does she live in a grass shack?"

"Uh, no," Ruth said. "She lives in an apartment building. One thing, though. She hurt her hand, years ago, so it looks a little scary at first. You two be good and don't say anything to make her feel bad about it, okay?"

They nodded soberly and promised that they would not.

She called Rachel at her hotel and told her only that she would be picking her up for lunch in Japantown. Rachel seemed happy just to be seeing Ruth again—but when they pulled up in front of the house on Fifth Street, Rachel seemed confused: "I thought we were going to lunch?"

"We are," Ruth said with a smile. "Frank is a great cook."

The astonishment and joy in Rachel's face was lovely to see.

Frank and the kids came out to greet Rachel. But preceding them was Max, who eagerly raced down the flagstone path to the sidewalk, barking a welcome. At first Ruth feared he would bowl Rachel over, but she just squatted down to his level as he approached, allowed him to sniff her left hand, and said, "Well now, I hadn't heard about you, what's your name?"

"This is Max. He's still a puppy."

"He certainly is." Rachel scratched under his chin and allowed Max to lick her face, which both impressed and delighted Ruth.

"Did you have a dog at Kalaupapa?"

"Two. Hōku and Setsu. Pets were the only children we were allowed."

Frank pulled Max away as Donnie and Peggy ran up to Rachel.

"Are you really our grandma from Hawai'i?" Donnie asked breathlessly.

"I am," Rachel said, her eyes bright with the wonder of this boy. "Are you really my grandson from California?"

"Sure I am!"

She looked at Peggy. "And you're my granddaughter? Peggy, isn't it?"

"Yeah!"

There was such happiness in Rachel's face that Ruth wanted to cry.

"You're both so beautiful," Rachel said softly. "More beautiful than I could ever have dreamed."

She stood up just as Etsuko, moving a little more slowly these days at sixty-three, came down the flagstone path and, to Rachel's surprise, draped a homemade *lei* of pink azalea blossoms around her neck.

"Aloha," Etsuko said warmly.

Rachel, moved, made a small bow to her and said, *"Konnichiwa."*

"My name is Etsuko. May I call you Rachel?"

"Of course. I'm honored to meet Ruth's mother."

"As am I," Etsuko replied graciously.

The words brought tears to Rachel's eyes.

"And I'm Frank." He smiled and extended a hand. Rachel took it in her left hand as she gazed into his face.

"You have very kind eyes," she told him.

The minute they were inside Peggy ran upstairs and came back holding up a recalcitrant Snowball to meet Rachel. "This is Snowball, she's my best friend in the whole world," Peggy said. "She even sleeps with me at night."

Frank had prepared a delicious meal of sautéed sea bass, rice, and green beans. Over lunch, Etsuko peppered Rachel with questions about what Hawai'i was like these days and reminisced fondly about her days in Waimānalo and Honolulu's Chinatown.

"If there was only one place I could revisit in this life," Etsuko said wistfully, "it would be Honolulu. Some of the happiest years of my life were spent there." Etsuko also solved a nagging problem of nomenclature for Ruth by inquiring of Rachel, "What is Hawaiian for 'Mother'?"—and henceforth as Etsuko was *Okāsan*, Rachel was *Makuahine*. The kids called her "Grandma Rachel," which seemed to please her greatly.

"What's Hawai'i like?" Donnie wanted to know. "Are there cannibals and headhunters?"

"Donnie!" Ruth admonished.

Rachel just laughed. "Wrong hemisphere, I'm afraid. Though it's said Hawai'i did have human sacrifice at one time, many centuries ago."

"Neat!" Donnie declared. Peggy agreed enthusiastically.

Ruth sagged in her seat. "And you thought they were such angels."

"Oh, you should've met me when I was their age," Rachel said with a chuckle. She told her grandson, "Hawai'i is a place of gentle trade winds and crashing surf. Of sweet ukulele music and erupting volcanoes. Of peace and serenity and restless ghosts that march across the night."

"Ghosts?" Peggy gasped.

"Volcanoes?" Donnie marveled. "Do they shoot lava into the air?"

"Sometimes." Rachel told them a little of her childhood, the trolleys she used to ride, of body-surfing at Waikīkī and of her father Henry, the sailor. "He visited some of the most spectacular and beautiful places on earth," she said, "but he always came back to Hawai'i because he loved Hawai'i best."

When she mentioned the dolls he brought her from exotic ports, Peggy announced, "I have dolls!"—and immediately took her new grandma by the hand, up the steps, and into her bedroom, where she introduced her to her dolls. "This is Elsa, this one is Reiko, this is Maggie."

"Oh, they're very pretty," Rachel told her. "It's good to have friends, isn't it? Ones who love you and stay with you no matter what?"

"Yeah. 'Specially at night, when it's dark."

"Yes," Rachel agreed, "especially then."

Before the day was out Ruth and Frank invited Rachel to check out of her hotel and stay with them. There was a *futon* that Ralph slept on when he came over for the weekend, and Etsuko slept on that—rather happily; she had never quite taken to Western mattresses—while Rachel slept in her bed.

That first night, when Rachel took off her shoes and stockings, Etsuko couldn't help but see that her feet were fleshy stumps—the toes having been resorbed back into the body. She looked away before Rachel noticed, but she thought: This woman has endured. She knows what it means to *gaman*.

Rachel stayed in California for two weeks, playing dolls and *go* and even cowboys and Indians with Donnie and Peggy. Ruth, watching them play, saw glimpses of the mother she might have had, even as Rachel delighted in the chance to be a grandmother as well as a mother for the first time.

One day Ruth drove everyone to San Francisco, one of the distant ports Rachel's father had visited. They corkscrewed down Lombard Street, strolled along the Embarcadero, and rode cable cars. Ralph came over from Berkeley to join them for lunch at Fisherman's Wharf, and after being introduced to Rachel he said with feigned puzzlement, "Okay, so you're Ruth's Hawaiian mother. But what does that make you to me? 'Half mother'? No, that's not right. 'Mother once removed'? No, that's not it either. There's only one thing to do, Rachel: I'm going to *hānai* you."

Other than Ralph, the only ones present who understood that were Rachel and Etsuko, and they both laughed.

"What does ha-nigh mean?" Peggy asked.

Etsuko said, "It is Hawaiian for 'adopted by family'—and I think it is a fine idea, Ralph."

"Then it's official," Ralph declared. "Rachel, you are now my *hānai* mother. This entitles you to worry about whether I'm eating right, do I have enough money, and ask me twice a week when my girlfriend Carol and I are going to get married. Welcome to the *'ohana*."

"I'm honored, Ralph," Rachel said, genuinely touched. But she couldn't resist adding, "And when *do* you and Carol plan on getting married?"

Everyone laughed, no one harder than Ralph.

Rachel later told Ruth it had been one of the grandest days of her life.

On the day of Rachel's departure, Ruth helped her *makuahine* aboard the S.S. *Lurline*, tipping the porters and making sure Rachel was properly settled in her tiny cabin. They walked the length of the ship together, Hawaiian music playing over the loudspeaker system, until fifteen minutes before the scheduled departure time of four o'clock, when the ship's horn sounded two blasts—final call for all visitors. Ruth hugged Rachel, kissed her, and said, "Thank you. For giving me life, and health, and freedom."

"Thank *you*. Meeting you has been a gift I could never have imagined five years ago."

"Neither could I. Well, I did think about it when I was fourteen."

"You did?"

Ruth grinned. "I used to fantasize about meeting you and demanding to know, *Why did you have to make me so damn tall?*"

They shared a laugh, but Ruth added soberly, "But now I know why."

"Yes? And why is that?"

Ruth said, "Because I had some pretty tall shoes to fill."

Speechless, Rachel could only smile happily as Ruth kissed her again, then turned and walked down the gangway to the pier. Rachel watched her go and silently gave thanks—to God, to her *'aumākua*, to whoever had allowed her to live long enough to be in this place today. Even if she never saw Ruth again, she could someday tell Kenji that his little *akachan* had grown up to be a woman to make them both proud.

Chapter 16

1951

As the twin-engine Beechcraft C-45 approached the eighteen-hundred-foot airstrip on the tip of the Kalaupapa peninsula, the pilot, Happy Cockett, turned to his only passenger, Rachel Utagawa, and advised, "Might be a little bumpy on landing. Slight crosswind, and this strip is still sod on sand. The territory keeps saying they'll pave it someday, but for now, hang on to your teeth."

"It's not my teeth I'm worried about," Rachel joked. This was her first trip back to Kalaupapa since her "parole" four years ago. The chartered Cessna that had taken off from this same airport, bound for her new life in Honolulu, had been smooth and exhilarating; today she watched as the grassy airstrip loomed larger in the cockpit window while also appearing alarmingly short. Crosswinds buffeted the plane like a Hawaiian musician pounding an *ipu* drum, but the landing gear touched down with only a small bounce.

Happy helped Rachel out onto the low-set wing of the aircraft, steadying her as she walked nervously across the wing and onto a stepstool that deposited her on familiar ground. "I hope your friend feels better," he said, returning to the plane to gather his main cargo: one of two daily airmail deliveries to Kalaupapa that had been inaugurated the previous year.

Rachel felt the sea spray on her face as the surf crashed against the rocky coastline, and like that, she was a child again, body-surfing the swells rolling into the white sands of Papaloa Beach; then a teenager, standing strong on a surfboard riding the surging crest of a wave; and years later, sitting on the sand with Kenji, his arm around her, as they watched Hōku and Setsu playfully dart in between fingers of foam lapping up the beach.

"Mrs. Utagawa? I'm Dr. Kam, we spoke on the phone?"

She turned to face the settlement's young, sober-looking resident physician. "Yes, of course, *mahalo* for calling me. How is she?"

"Not well. I'm afraid her condition continues to deteriorate."

They walked toward a makeshift parking lot. In the distance, white-tailed tropicbirds soared high atop the *pali*, their cries lost to the wind.

"You said on the phone she fell about six weeks ago?" Rachel asked as they got into a car.

"Coming down the front steps of the convent. Fractured her left hip. That limp of hers didn't help. How did she get it?"

"It was . . . an accident," Rachel said. "A long time ago."

They drove onto the narrow road that followed the coastline into town. "When I examined Sister Catherine after her fall," Dr. Kam said, "I suspected that she had a fairly advanced case of osteoporosis. I prescribed three to four months' bed rest, to allow the hip to heal."

"I don't think Catherine has had more than three *days'* rest since she arrived at Kalaupapa," Rachel said.

"She's not the most docile patient in the world. After one month she tried to get out of bed when no one was looking. She fell again, worsening the fracture. She's been on a slow decline ever since."

"What does that mean, exactly?"

"At seventy-nine, her body doesn't have the reserves of strength to cope with two traumatic injuries. She picked up an infection, and her immune system is so weak that even penicillin hasn't been able to knock it out."

Rachel felt herself trembling. Quietly she asked, "Is she dying?"

Dr. Kam hesitated before replying, "I'm sorry, but yes."

"How much longer?"

"Not that long."

Rachel blinked back tears. "Is she awake? Lucid?"

"Both, on and off. I wouldn't have arranged for the air transport if I didn't think there was some purpose in your coming." He glanced at Rachel. "The other sisters say you two were very close when you were here."

"She's . . . my best friend," Rachel said, and her voice broke as she steeled herself for what lay ahead.

S ister Catherine lay in bed, eyes shut, the pain in her hip having abated for the moment—she had received a morphine shot that morning. She had resisted taking the morphine at first, a reflexive reaction borne out of her mother's addiction to the opioid laudanum. But then her years of nursing told her that her sisters would not be offering her morphine unless her prognosis was terminal—and with that, a weight was lifted from her. She finally allowed herself to think of her own pain first, because there was no longer anything she could do to ease anyone else's.

But letting go of life was not the same as embracing death. Though she still wondered what might be awaiting her on the other side, she told herself that whatever fate God had chosen for her would be her just due.

"Catherine?"

Catherine opened her eyes. She knew that voice as well as her own.

Rachel was standing next to her bed, and suddenly all of Catherine's fatigue, the drowsiness from the morphine, faded in a rush of joy.

"Oh, Rachel!" She reached out her hands to clasp her friend's.

Rachel took them, trying to hide her shock at how thin Catherine had become. Once her arms had lifted children and scrubbed floors at the Bishop Home for Girls, where Rachel had spent her childhood; now they felt as light, as fragile, as crepe paper stretched over bone. But the sister's eyes were bright and happy.

"It's good to see you, Catherine."

"I'm so glad you're here, Rachel. And I can't thank you enough for sending me those photographs of Ruth and her family, all so happy and healthy. I remember my last night with her at Kapiʻolani Home—I wanted that night to never end, but I knew it had to, because the next day was the start of Ruth's life of freedom."

Rachel slid a chair closer to the bed and sat down. "She's everything I could have hoped for in a daughter, Catherine. Everything *we* could have hoped for. And her children—I still can't believe I'm a *tūtū*, a grandmother!"

"We were both so young when we came here." With a resurgence of her youthful excitement she added, "Oh, Rachel, you should see Bishop Home today! There are no more children there, only young women. There are so few children being sent to Kalaupapa at all these days, thanks to the sulfa drugs. What would Mother Marianne say if she could see this?"

"Amen," Rachel answered, and Catherine laughed.

The laughter turned into a cough, and the cough became a struggle to catch her breath. Rachel was on the verge of calling a nurse when the sister found her voice: "Are you—going back to California this year?"

Rachel nodded. "Next month." Her friend's erratic breathing continued to alarm her. "Catherine, are you all right?"

"Yes, I'm just . . . tired," she said. "I tire very easily." Indeed, the rush of happiness that had buoyed her upon seeing Rachel now was ebbing as quickly as the years had ebbed away. "How long will you be here, Rachel?"

"As long as you need me to be."

Catherine smiled faintly. "Thank you." Her eyes closed.

Rachel remained by her side. When a nursing sister came later with Catherine's dinner—little of which she ate—she brought food for Rachel as well. Catherine chatted as she picked at her meal, reminiscing about Rachel's auntie, Haleola, and her father, Henry. "Such good people. Such good souls."

Catherine soon nodded off again. When Dr. Kam made his rounds, Rachel asked if she could spend the night in the empty bed beside Catherine's. "Of course," he said. "From what the sisters tell me, you're *'ohana*."

She thanked him and, exhausted by the trip and the strain of seeing Catherine in this state, fell into a dead sleep by ten o'clock.

In the middle of the night she was awakened by:

"Rachel?"

She opened her eyes and saw Catherine gazing at her.

"Thank you," the sister said softly. "For being here."

"Where else would I be?"

"Do you remember the last time we were together like this?"

"Yes." Rachel didn't elaborate.

But Catherine did. "That night we spent in the dispensary," she said. "The day I . . . jumped into the sea. Tried to . . . kill myself."

She had not spoken these words aloud for many years, and hearing them now, they did not seem as frightening as she imagined they would.

"You told me God would understand my pain and forgive me, as He forgave my parents their own pain and . . . sins."

"I still believe that," Rachel said.

Catherine hesitated, then confided, "Two nights ago I saw my father. Sitting in that chair you were sitting in today."

"Were you happy to see him?"

Meekly Catherine admitted, "Honestly? It scared the hell out of me."

Rachel laughed. "Well—did *he* seem happy?"

"Yes. Oddly enough, he did. He was smiling at me. Happy to see me."

Rachel asked, "Do unforgiven souls smile, Sister?"

A thin crescent of a smile lit Catherine's face.

"No," she conceded, "I suppose they don't."

As her eyes shut, she said tenderly, "I love you, Rachel."

"I love you too, Catherine."

Rachel lay there for an hour, listening to Catherine's shallow breaths like sighs in the darkness, before she finally drifted into a restless sleep.

The next morning Catherine continued to recall bygone days at Kalaupapa, but she was awake and alert for a shorter period of time. Her pain increased, and the sisters upped the dosage of her morphine. The following day she spoke even less, before falling into a deep slumber.

The day after that she did not awaken at all.

Rachel kept vigil for another three days, holding Catherine's hand, talking to her in hopes that she could hear; but Catherine never regained consciousness. A priest administered the last rites. Dr. Kam or the nurses checked her vitals frequently, but other than this brief activity, there was a calm surrounding Catherine that was like a *mouo*, one of those lulls on the ocean when Rachel would float in the water without a wave in sight. Rachel prayed Catherine was feeling that kind of peace. When she finally stopped breathing it was almost unnoticeable, the passage between life and death barely a flutter; all that separated them was the single beat of a heart.

Rachel held Catherine's lifeless hand and stayed there for some time, weeping for her friend, her last connection to her youth at Kalaupapa.

Two days later, the Sisters of St. Francis held a Requiem Mass in St. Elizabeth's Convent for their cherished colleague:

May Christ receive thee who has called thee, and may the Angels lead thee into Abraham's bosom . . . Eternal rest grant unto her, O Lord, and let perpetual light shine upon her.

Sister Mary Catherine Voorhies's casket was taken to the Catholic cemetery, where according to her wishes she was laid to rest alongside the scores of girls and young women who had blossomed under her care only to die after a few short seasons. In a long life marked by grace, compassion, dedication, grief, and courage, Catherine had loved them all.

A month later, as Rachel's plane landed in San Francisco, she resolved to keep her mood sunny and make no mention of the death of her old friend. She wanted to enjoy this trip, not have people feeling sorry for her. And in fact Ruth greeted her in such high spirits that Rachel couldn't help having her own uplifted. In the car, Ruth revealed why she was in such a good mood:

"I have a job!"

Rachel was startled. "I didn't know you were thinking of getting one."

"I hadn't, not for a while," Ruth said. "After the war I was just so relieved that life was *normal* again, I was content to be a mother and a homemaker—content to have a *home*, and a normal life."

"And now?"

"I got over it." Ruth laughed. "I woke up one day realizing my entire life consisted of cooking, cleaning, packing lunches, doing laundry, getting the kids up in the morning, and getting them to bed at night."

Rachel would have given anything to have lived a life like that, but she heard Ruth's frustration and nodded her understanding.

"I'd see ads on TV—all these happy white women wearing pearls and pleated skirts as they scrubbed down the kitchen—and I'd think, well damn it, if these *hakujin hausfraus* can do it, so can I. Except whenever I'd go to see Helen Russell, she was as bored and restless as I was and we'd sit drinking vodka gimlets at eleven A.M., wondering why we weren't happy too.

"Then I'd think about how it was before the war, when I was helping Frank run the diner, and I realized: I was happy then. I had the kids, I had Frank, but I also had something new to challenge me each day. Normal, I decided, is highly overrated. Is it normal to drink vodka gimlets at eleven A.M.?"

"No," Rachel agreed. "So where are you working?"

"Bill's Shanghai Restaurant. I have *Okāsan* to thank for it. She's friends with Mr. Dobashi of Dobashi Market, who was putting up a new building on Jackson Street. He told her he'd asked Bill Dair, a leader in the Chinese community and the owner of a Chinese grocery, if he'd be interested in opening up a restaurant in the building."

"I was wondering who the 'Bill' in 'Bill's Shanghai Restaurant' was."

"A very nice man—he even gave me time off while you're in town. So before anyone else could submit a résumé, I applied for a job. I'm doing what I did at Frank's Diner—bookkeeping, managing inventory. I work from nine A.M. to three P.M. and have time to get home and cook dinner too."

"I take it Frank approved?"

"His exact words were 'Good, we can use the extra money.'" She laughed. "Always practical."

When they arrived home, Donnie and Peggy—now thirteen and eleven, respectively—came rocketing out the front door and into Rachel's arms, filling her with renewed wonder that she was holding *mo'opuna*—grandchildren—of her very own.

"I'm happy to see you too," she said. "Look how tall you are! Peggy, you're almost as tall as your brother!"

"She gets that from me—you *and* me," Ruth said. "But unlike me, she's very coordinated and athletic. She plays point guard in girls' basketball."

Donnie was not to be outdone: "I won the class swim meet this year!"

"Really? Well, you're going to be another Duke Kahanamoku!"

"Who's that?"

"He's an Olympic swimming champion, and he's Hawaiian, like me."

Frank and Etsuko greeted Rachel with more hugs. Frank carried her bags upstairs and as soon as she was settled sharing Etsuko's room, Rachel was shanghaied into a game of Parcheesi with the *keiki*. Throughout the game they chattered away nonstop—Peggy about sports, Donnie about his favorite TV program, *Space Patrol*—and Rachel happily listened to every word.

For dinner the family was joined by Ralph—now a cub reporter for the *Oakland Tribune*—his wife, Carol, and their two-year-old son, John Taizo Watanabe, or "John T." as his father sometimes called him. Even Rachel was touched by this quiet tribute to a man she had never met.

Frank cooked a delicious dinner of chicken and dumplings and Ruth baked, in honor of Rachel's visit, a pineapple upside-down cake.

"So you don't live in Honolulu anymore?" Ralph asked Rachel.

"No, I'm living with my sister, Sarah, on Maui now," Rachel said. "I would never have imagined this happening—Sarah and I were always at each other's throats as children. When I tracked her down in Lahaina, she fainted dead away because she thought I'd died long ago. But she welcomed me into her home and invited me to share it with her."

"That was lovely of her," Carol said, smiling.

"Yes. And my brother Ben also lives on Maui, in Hana. When I left Kalaupapa I was afraid my *'ohana*—my family—was either gone or wouldn't want to see me because I had leprosy. I never dreamed I'd be reunited with my sister and brother, or get to meet my nieces and nephews." She looked around the table and smiled. "Or all of you. My California *'ohana*."

Her eyes misted over, as did those of a few others at the table.

After dinner the adults shared coffee in the living room, chatted about John T. and Ralph's new job with the *Tribune*. "I read your story about the Korean peace talks," Frank said. "You think they're going anywhere?"

"It's still early. I hope so."

"Lowering the draft age to eighteen doesn't show much faith in the negotiations," Ruth noted.

There was a sharpness in her tone Rachel had heard only once before.

"I think the Army just wants to be prepared, Sis."

But this only seemed to raise Ruth's hackles.

"Eighteen years old, Ralph?" she said. "Horace's son Jack is nineteen, he could be drafted tomorrow—you think he's ready for that?"

Gingerly Ralph replied, "There were guys in the 442nd who were only eighteen, nineteen years old, and they served with distinction."

Ruth countered, "'Served' or 'died'?"

Ralph frowned. "Both."

"So they're too young to drink but not too young to—"

"Dai," Etsuko said gently, "Rachel did not come all this way just to hear you and Ryuu argue about politics."

Ruth was suddenly embarrassed by this very un-Japanese breach of decorum in front of a guest.

"You're right, *Okāsan*," she admitted. "I'm sorry, Rachel . . . Ralph. I just . . . worry about Jack, you know? All the nephews."

"So do I, Sis. So do I."

Rachel admired Etsuko's graceful handling of the situation, even as she made a mental note that despite what Ruth had told her, her daughter was clearly not "over" all the wounds the war had inflicted on her family.

The next day, in a quiet moment together in the living room, Ruth asked her *makuahine* whether she had done any traveling other than these trips to California. "Just back to Moloka'i. For a visit," Rachel said, trying to keep her sadness over Catherine's death out of her voice. "But Sarah and I are taking a cruise to Hong Kong next year. I've wanted to see China ever since my father brought me a pair of Mission dolls when I was four."

Rachel reached for her purse, took out an envelope. "You asked me in your last letter if I had any photos of my Kalaupapa family."

"Oh yes, I'd love to see them!"

Rachel took out a handful of old, sepia-toned photographs. She handed one to Ruth. "This is my father, Henry, at my wedding."

Ruth gazed into the smiling eyes of a tanned Hawaiian man in his fifties, his broad face aglow with pleasure. Beside him was Rachel, young and beautiful in her hand-sewn wedding dress, and her groom, Kenji, in a dark suit. Henry Kalama looked like a good man, a loving man; Ruth wished she could have met her grandfather. "He looks almost as happy as you do."

Rachel smiled seeing her father's face. "Papa was very happy I'd found someone. He loved me so much, and I adored him. When the Board of Health put me on the boat to Moloka'i, I thought I would die at the thought of never seeing Papa again. But he visited me at Kalaupapa, even though the trip back then wasn't easy or cheap. He would have lived there if the authorities had allowed it." Her smile faded. "This was the last time I saw him."

"I see a lot of him in you," Ruth noted.

"Thank you. I like to think that's so." Rachel handed her daughter another photo. "You'll enjoy this one."

Ruth laughed as she took in a snapshot of two terriers looking eagerly up at the camera, big dog-smiles on their scruffy faces. This was a later, color photo, and Ruth could see their markings—one was mottled black and white, the other mixed with a light brown—and their big brown eyes.

"The salt-and-pepper one is Setsu, the tricolor is Hōku," Rachel said.

"Do they have some beagle in them?" Ruth asked.

"Yes, they were the product of a mixed marriage." Ruth laughed at that. "They brought us such joy," Rachel said wistfully. "So much spirit and energy. And digging! I could never plant a garden because they'd dig a hole to China before anything even sprouted. But they were so loving and loyal. At the wake, Hōku never left Kenji's casket, guarding him to the very end."

"They're adorable."

"I still think of them every day." She took out another photo. "And these are my Bishop Home friends. I think I was sixteen here."

This was a formal, posed photo of young Rachel, as yet showing no signs of leprosy, standing amid three rows of girls, in uniform dresses, ranging in age from eight to eighteen. Many smiled despite open sores on their faces. Rachel had forgotten that Catherine was in this picture too, she and Sister Leopoldina flanking their young charges. Rachel felt another pang of grief but fought it, trying to keep her tone light:

"That's me, right here. Beside me is my best friend, Francine." Ruth saw a short Hawaiian girl with black, pixie-cut hair and a mischievous grin. Her left hand was contracted into a claw, as Rachel's right hand was today. "She was a jockey in horse races after Kalaupapa got a racetrack."

"You had a racetrack?" Ruth said, amazed.

"Yes, Mr. McVeigh had it built after he became superintendent. He believed we should live and enjoy life, not just wait for death. He did more for Kalaupapa than any man since Father Damien." Rachel pointed out a half-Chinese, half-Hawaiian girl with long black hair: "This is Emily, and behind her, that's Cecelia"—Ruth saw a bright-eyed Filipino girl—"and this is Hina. She was from 'topside' Moloka'i, and one Saturday night she led us all on a . . . well, 'jailbreak' is the only word for it."

"You *broke out* of Kalaupapa?"

"Yes, but only for the night," Rachel said with a grin. "We went to a party in Kaunakakai. We were young and rebellious, Hina's friend was having a party, and we were damned if we weren't going to go to it!" She laughed as she recalled, "It took us hours to climb the *pali* and another hour by wagon to get to Kaunakakai. At the party Cecelia—oh God, I haven't thought of this for years—Cecelia got absolutely stink-eyed and we had to practically pour her into the wagon to take us back to the *pali*." Ruth laughed at the image. "Mother Marianne caught us coming back, but she was so astonished that we *had* come back that she let us go without even a punishment."

"Why *did* you go back?" Ruth asked.

"There was some debate about that at the time. But in the end it was worth it for the look on Mother's face."

Rachel gazed at these faces from her youth and thought of the other friends who hadn't lived long enough to be in the photo: Josephina, Hazel, Noelani, Bertha . . .

"All of them gone now. They passed away and I lived to see a cure. Why? I was no different from them, no better. Why was I spared?" Her voice was soft, but even after all these years she still grieved for them. "Why did the *ma'i pākē* take my brother Kimo after a year, and here I am, still standing at sixty-three? *Why did I live when they all died?*"

Ruth winced at the sudden anguish in her voice and gently put a hand on hers.

"I don't know why, Rachel," Ruth admitted. "I've asked those kind of questions too. I was raised Buddhist, but as I grew older I found it too . . . . fatalistic. Whenever someone died I was told, 'Everything is impermanent.' When Frank asked if I'd consider becoming Methodist, I did it partly for his family and partly to see if Christianity held any better answers for me. But whenever I asked those question of my minister, he would just say, 'God has His reasons,' and that didn't seem like a very good answer either."

Her fingers closed gently around Rachel's deformed hand.

"Why did you live? Maybe so your grandchildren could know their *tūtū*. So I could know my mother, and you could know your daughter. I don't know why some people die and others don't. I'm just happy you didn't.

"And you know what? I think your friends at Bishop Home would be happy too—happy that one of them finally made it out, like you did when you all went to that party."

Rachel thought of her friends—saw them again in that rickety old wagon going to Kaunakakai, their faces bright with the exhilaration and delight of being *free*—and she smiled, knowing that Ruth was right. She heard Emily and Hina and Cecelia, cheering for Francine as she won a horse race—and cheering for Rachel even now. They had been with her all along.

Chapter 17

1954

$\mathcal{T}$he Pan Am Strato Clipper *Golden Gate* was a double-decker colossus of the air that flew higher than any commercial plane before it—25,000 feet—and faster too, San Francisco to Honolulu in just nine and a half hours. The amenities were grand, even the "thrifty" Rainbow Service where Ruth and her family enjoyed comfortable reclining seats and a sumptuous breakfast, lunch, and seven-course dinner. There was even a cocktail lounge on the lower level for those who wanted some conversation or tropical drinks.

The price was steep—$255 per passenger, or $1,275 for the whole family—but that included hotel accommodations and was comparable in cost to a windowless cabin, no bath, on a lower deck aboard a Matson ocean liner. Two years ago Frank had been promoted to superintendent of Sunsweet's Plant #1, and with Ruth's income and a lot of scrimping and saving, they were able to splurge on airfare. The trip was being made as much for Etsuko, who longed to see Hawai'i for what could be the last time, as it was for Rachel, who happily flew from Maui to spend nine days with them all.

As they approached Honolulu, Etsuko peered out the window excitedly. "Oh, from the air O'ahu is even lovelier than I ever knew!"

All the islands Ruth was able to see were beautiful, covered in lush greenery, ringed by exquisitely clear turquoise waters, huddled together in a vast, forbidding ocean. Ruth had never realized before how truly remote they were: half a million Americans living in the middle of the Pacific Ocean.

On landing, Ruth stepped into the moist, hot tropical air, her hair tossed back into her face by a cooling trade wind, and was startled to find it— *familiar.* There was a sweet floral scent carried on the wind that was like the forgotten perfume of an aunt only dimly recalled. She had not expected to remember anything. Among her handful of memories of Hawai'i was one of Ralph walking her protectively to her new school; previously that memory had always been flat, one-dimensional, like a movie playing in her mind. Now it turned tangible as she recalled the balmy touch of the wind, the humidity in the air, the quality of light itself. Now the memory felt *whole.*

"Look! There she is!" cried Peggy, waving.

Rachel was part of a small crowd waiting for arriving passengers behind a chain-link fence. She wore an *aloha*-print dress and stood beside a Hawaiian woman with garlands of pink-and-white flower *lei*s draped over her arm. As the Haradas passed through the gate, the woman proceeded to drape a plumeria *lei* around each of their necks.

"Aloha!" Rachel said as she hugged Ruth. *"E komo mai*—welcome!"

The heady fragrance of the *lei* jogged something else in Ruth's memory. "Didn't we have flowers like these once?" she asked Etsuko.

"Yes, in back of the store on Kukui Street we had a yellow plumeria plant. I tried growing one in Florin but it was too cold." Etsuko looked around her with a smile of wondrous delight. "So many more houses on the mountains! And this airport was not even here when we left in 1923!"

"Hiya, *tūtū*," Donnie said warmly as he embraced Rachel.

"My God, look at these *keiki*," Rachel said wonderingly. Sixteen-year-old Donnie was as lanky and handsome as his father, and fourteen-year-old Peggy, as tall and beautiful as Ruth. "You're almost too big to be called *keiki*!"

Peggy hugged her too. "Grandma, I'm so happy to finally be here."

Following Rachel's directions, Frank drove their rental car onto Nimitz Highway, the most direct, if hardly picturesque, route to Waikīkī—but the kids didn't care, they were thrilled to be anywhere this new and different. They drove through a screen of wind-blown palm trees on both sides of Kalākaua Avenue to their destination: the Moana Hotel.

Waikīkī's first luxury hotel, opened in 1901, the Moana—Hawaiian for "open sea"—was also second to none in Old World charm and hospitality. From the moment the Haradas drove up to its portico entrance they were made to feel special by the staff (as all guests were). Their comfortable, tropically decorated rooms had an ocean view, motivating Donnie and Peggy to unpack, change into bathing suits, and half ask, half declare, "Time for the beach?"

The adults were happy to change into their swimwear—all but Rachel, who wore a sundress and closed-toe sandals—but on the way to the beach, they stopped by the Kama'āina Bar for some mai-tais after the long trip. Prodded by impatient offspring, they were finally herded toward the Moana's choice oceanfront location. Beachgoers had flagged their pieces of paradise with gaudy umbrellas; in the distance the green caldera of Diamond Head crouched like a stone lion at the far end of Waikīkī.

Donnie and Peggy dove enthusiastically into the surf.

"Wow, this water is *warm*!" Peggy called out. "You sure this is the same ocean we have back in California?"

"A few degrees south makes a big difference," Rachel called back.

"The tradewinds are as cool and soothing as I remembered them," Etsuko said happily, looking out from beneath a wide-brimmed hat.

Rachel had not been here since moving to Maui and was relieved to see that—while it scarcely resembled the more rural Waikīkī of her childhood—it still retained its beauty. The Moana was one of only eight buildings on the beach: the Waikīkī Tavern; the windowless back wall of the Waikīkī Bowling Alley; the Surfrider Hotel; the Outrigger Canoe Club, famous for launching the career of Olympian Duke Kahanamoku; the Royal Hawaiian Hotel, in whose palatial pink buildings Rachel once briefly stayed; the Halekūlani Hotel; and the old Wilder family beach home. At the 'ewa end of the white crescent, only a thick grove of coconut palms covered Cassidy's Point.

Frank and Ruth joined the kids in the ocean, which was warm as bathwater. Ruth felt a gentle swell pass under her and took in the dazzling white beach fanning out on either side of her. The warmth of the water, the briny smell of the sea, the brightness of the sun, and the blue clarity of the sky—Hawai'i truly engaged all of one's senses.

After an hour they all came out of the water to rest. Frank, sitting in a beach chair and looking out to sea, suddenly blinked. "Was that mai-tai more potent than I thought, or does anyone else see what I'm seeing?"

Ruth looked out to sea and saw a dark-skinned figure not just standing but playfully *pirouetting* on a long, fire-engine red surfboard. Even more remarkably, at the forward "nose" of the board, sat . . .

"My God," Ruth said, "is that a *dog*?"

A small brown-and-white dog was, in fact, perched calmly on the board's nose, smiling happily.

"Oh, sure," Rachel noted casually. "That's Sandy. He's famous."

"Sandy? Is that the dog or the guy behind him?" Frank asked.

"Dog. Surfer is Joseph Kaopuiki, but everyone calls him Scooter Boy. You want to meet them?"

"You know him?" Peggy asked.

"When I was living in Honolulu, I liked to come here and watch the surfers—it brought back good memories. I became friendly with a few of the beachboys: Chick Daniels, Poi Dog Nahuli, Scooter Boy . . . come on."

She escorted the Haradas down to where Kaopuiki was shouldering his impressively large board—fifteen feet long—as Sandy shook off seawater.

"Scooter!" Rachel called.

Scooter was a slender part Hawaiian in his mid-forties. "Rachel? Hey, where you been, haven't seen you in a long while."

"I moved to Maui to live with my sister," Rachel explained. "Scooter, I'd like you to meet my daughter and her family."

Sandy sniffed Ruth and Peggy, instantly pegging them as suckers for a dog, allowing them to stroke his wet matted fur and scratch behind his ears.

"How did you teach him to surf?" Ruth asked.

"Like I teach everyone. He's a smart little guy, picked it up fast."

"Could you teach me to surf?" Peggy blurted out.

"Peg," Frank said, "I'm sure Mr. Ka—Scooter has better things to . . ."

"Be glad to," Scooter said, "for Rachel's *'ohana*."

Frank asked, "She's only fourteen, is it safe?"

"I started surfing a lot earlier than that," Rachel said, "and as good as my papa was, he wasn't a master waterman like Scooter."

"Hey," Donnie piped up, "how do I learn to use one of those canoes?"

Scooter nodded toward the turquoise building next door to the Moana. "Outrigger Club Services can set you up. Ask for Sally Hale, she's in charge." He turned to Peggy. "Come on, let's get you started and onto that board."

After showing Peggy how to go from belly-down to popping up on the board, Scooter had her paddle out to the first break, turn around, and wait for a wave. They were small swells, and Peggy actually managed to hop to her feet on the first try and ride a wave for all of four seconds—before she fell off the board into waist-high waters. This only spurred her to get back on. Within an hour she was riding waves for close to a full minute before wiping out.

"She has good form," Rachel noted.

Frank smiled. "She doesn't get this from *my* side of the family."

Rachel beamed with pleasure and pride for her granddaughter.

Later, Frank tried to give Scooter a tip, but he demurred. "Professional courtesy," he said with a wink to Rachel, who was touched and flattered.

Donnie enjoyed canoeing but complained, "I wanted to take a closer look at a coral reef but the instructor said no, the water was too shallow."

"He did that because you could've scraped the bottom of the canoe on the coral and damaged it," Rachel explained. "Coral reefs are living creatures, Donnie. They're hard skeletons that form around tiny animals called coral polyps, and if you step on one, or scrape it, you can kill it."

"They're *alive*? They look like stone."

"The skeleton is made of limestone, which the polyps secrete. If you want a closer look, you could go snorkeling one day at Hanauma Bay."

"That sounds great!" Donnie said, and Frank promised to look into it.

The next morning the family enjoyed a leisurely breakfast in the hotel's Banyan Court Lānai, under the spreading green canopy of the hotel's fifty-seven-year-old banyan tree. Everyone was happy with the food, especially Peggy, who loved her hotcakes with macadamia nuts and coconut syrup.

Ruth sipped her coffee, marveling at how the restaurant and banyan tree had seemingly grown up together, accommodating one another's needs. She watched the morning sun peek through the tree's tangle of branches. It was so beautiful here; so serene. She had no conscious memory of going to Waikīkī Beach as a child, though Etsuko told her that she had; but there was still a comforting familiarity about the sweet fragrance of orchids and jasmine and the salt breeze off the ocean. Now she knew why Etsuko missed Hawai'i.

"*Okāsan*," Ruth said, "would you like to go to Chinatown today? Frank and the kids want to stay at the beach, so it'll just be you, me, and Rachel. Maybe we can do a little shopping afterward."

"Oh yes, that would be wonderful. To see Kukui Street again."

"Etsuko," Rachel cautioned, "there's still a Chinatown here, but it's not necessarily the one you remember. A lot's changed in thirty years."

"I understand. It is just for—what is the phrase?—'old time's sake.'"

After breakfast, Ruth drove, as Rachel navigated, to the streets *'ewa* of Fort Street and what remained of Honolulu's once-thriving Chinatown. Ruth parked and they explored the area on foot. There were some newer shops and markets here—China Silk House on Fort Street, Chinese Bazaar on Nu'uanu Avenue—but these were unfamiliar names to Etsuko. The fish market near A'ala Park was still operating, the reek of the day's catch still competing with the sweet smell of soap from nearby laundries. But she searched in vain for the Chinese Mission School, Komenaka's General Store, or any of the family groceries she'd frequented.

The shabby condition of the buildings, the flaking and fading of their paint, discouraged her even more, as did the relative quiet. She recalled Kukui Street as bustling with conversation and commerce in at least three languages. The silence saddened her.

"*Okāsan*. Look," Ruth said suddenly.

Etsuko stopped. They were standing in front of a two-story building with a barber shop and grocery store on the first floor, shaded by yellow-and-white awnings from the sun; the second floor was fronted by a long plantation-style *lānai*. "Isn't this where . . . Papa's store was?" Ruth asked.

Etsuko looked up at the building's street number: 216.

"Oh!" she cried. "You're right. How did I not recognize it?"

"I can't believe I *did*," Ruth said, pleased and surprised by these fragments of her past that were surfacing from some deep fathom of memory. "Does it look like anyone's living up there?"

Rachel looked up at the windows. "Hard to tell in this light."

Etsuko went around the corner of the building and into the alleyway behind it. Here their *furo* bath had stood awaiting Taizo at the end of a long workday; now there were clotheslines strung across the alley, adorned with shirts, trousers, dresses, and a pair of white underwear flapping like a surrender flag in the breeze. "It would appear, Goldilocks," Etsuko joked, "that the three bears are at home."

Then Etsuko's gaze fell onto something else—something that astonished and delighted her.

"Oh, Dai. Look," she said.

Standing next to the rear entrance to the shop was a five-foot-high plumeria tree whose branches brimmed with star-shaped yellow blossoms.

Etsuko went to the tree, cupped a cluster of flowers in her hands as if she were holding faerie dust, and breathed in their rich perfume.

"I planted this when we first moved here," Etsuko said proudly. "It was just a cutting, but look at it now!"

"Do you want to knock on the door?" Ruth asked. "See if we can go inside and take a look?"

Etsuko considered for a moment, then shook her head and smiled.

"No, I don't wish to impose. We enjoyed many happy years here; I hope the present tenants shall as well. It is enough for me to know that I left something of beauty behind and that it has thrived. I am content."

After Chinatown, Ruth, Rachel, and Etsuko shopped for clothes in local stores like Take's at Waikīkī and Gem's of Honolulu, and in a souvenir shop Ruth bought a bottle of the coconut syrup that Peggy liked so much.

The next day they drove to Hanauma Bay, an extinct volcanic crater whose south wall had been eroded by ocean waves, creating an underwater refuge teeming with exotic marine life. Rachel would have dearly loved to join Ruth, Frank, and the kids in the water, but though she wore a bathing suit, she just sat on the sand with her feet covered, keeping Etsuko company.

After an hour, Donnie emerged from the water, suitably impressed. "This place is incredible! The coral comes in so many different shapes—some look like trees, some like flowers, some like human brains—and in so many colors! And I didn't touch a single one, *tūtū*, just like you said."

Rachel smiled. "Your ancestors would be proud. There's an old Hawaiian saying: 'The land is the chief, man is its servant.'"

Donnie considered that. "Does that include the ocean?"

"Yes. Haleola told me that to ancient Hawaiians, the *'āina*—the land, sea, and air—were all interconnected. The *'āina* provided all the basics of life, and so they respected and cared for it."

"Are you sure you don't want to go in the water?" Peggy asked Rachel.

"I wish I could, but it's hard to swim with my feet like this."

"Then use my fins." Peggy held out her mask, snorkel, and swim fins. "And they'll cover your feet."

Rachel tried to recall the last time she'd been in the ocean. *Years* ago . . .

"C'mon, *tūtū*," Donnie said. "You know you want to."

Rachel took the snorkeling gear from Peggy and grinned.

"Anything for my *mo'opuna*." But as she took off her sandals she felt a thrill that had nothing to do with her grandchildren.

Gingerly Rachel walked down the sand and into the water, and when it was waist-high she put on the swim fins with her good hand. Then she leaned back and let herself float, kicking a little to propel herself backward. Like most Hawaiian children she had learned to swim before she could walk, and now the waters washed over her like the welcome embrace of an old friend.

On shore, Etsuko and the *keiki* cheered as Rachel waved to them.

Rachel turned over in the water and reentered a glorious kingdom of color, life, motion, sensation. A school of yellow tangs swam swiftly past her, as if late for an appointment. Blue-and-black striped butterflyfishes nibbled on plankton on the rocky bottom, as an electric-blue unicornfish munched on a strand of seaweed. Rachel gently kicked herself forward to take in the brilliantly hued array of coral below her. Haleola once told her the names of all of these and she was pleased to find she still remembered: huge mounds of yellow lobe coral, *pāhauku puna*; a beautiful purple-blue mushroom coral, *ko'a kohe*; treelike branches of black coral, *ēkaha kū moana*. It all came back to her, the feel of being gently rocked by the waves, the weightless delight of flying above mountain ranges of coral. She took a deep breath and, as she had done so often in her youth, jackknifed her body, and dove to the bottom. The fins propelled her down as if her feet had no infirmity at all. She hovered above the elegant black coral and saw, wedged between its branches, a speckled orange scorpionfish sleeping the day away. She looked around her, at the breathtaking topography of this magical realm beneath the waves. She felt wonderful. She felt at home. She felt young.

The next day, at breakfast, Donnie and Peggy were still talking about Hanauma Bay and asking their *tūtū* about all she saw. Finally, after the *keiki* left for the beach, Rachel leaned in to Ruth and said, "I have a surprise for you today. Somebody wants to meet you."

"Here? Who?"

"Someone who knew you a long, long time ago. Her name is Sister Mary Louisa Hughes."

This *was* a surprise. "She's the nun who helped you find me?"

Rachel nodded. "She worked at Kapi'olani Home, and you were her favorite. When I told her you were coming to Honolulu, she mentioned she would dearly love to see you again. Do you mind?"

"No, not at all," Ruth said. "I don't remember her, but then, I didn't remember what Papa's store looked like until I saw it again."

Soon Ruth was driving up twisting roads to the lush Mānoa Valley, where green mountain slopes sheltered residential homes as well as many private and public schools. It was one of these, St. Francis School on Pāmoa Street, that they sought. Ruth drove onto the grounds, away from the girls' school and toward St. Francis Convent.

"She's in Room 117," Rachel said as they made their way down the carpeted corridor, a younger nun passing by with a nod and a smile. Rachel knocked twice; Ruth felt unaccountably anxious. The door was opened by a short, stocky woman in her seventies, her broad, open face cowled by the white veil of her vocation. It took her only a moment to recognize who was on her doorstep.

"Oh my heavens," she said. "Rachel! And . . . Ruth?"

Reflexively, Sister Louisa stepped forward and embraced Ruth, who tried not to betray her discomfiture.

"Oh, Ruth," the sister said happily, "it's so good to see you again!"

Ruth was chagrined to discover that nothing about this woman—her face, her voice, even her touch—seemed at all familiar.

Louisa put some coffee on to brew and produced teacups from a cabinet. "I was so sorry," she told Rachel, "to hear about Sister Catherine. I can't remember where I put my shoes some mornings, but I still vividly remember the night she came to Kapi'olani Home with Ruth. She said to me, 'Sister, I would count it a great favor if you would do something for me.' I said of course, what? She said, 'Take care of her?' And her voice broke as she said it, broke with love and with the heartbreak of having to give you up, Ruth."

Ruth could hardly fail to be moved by this. "I wish I had met her—well, I did meet her, but I was a little too young to remember."

"Of course. Do you remember the Home? Do you remember the cow?"

"The cow?" Ruth said blankly.

"We had a cow from a nearby pasture that regularly came by to graze on our lawn, and one day you went out to greet her. 'Hi, cow!' you said."

Ruth laughed. That sounded like something she would have done, but she didn't *feel* it the way she had felt the memory of Papa's store or the aroma of plumeria; it was just a story being told to her by a nice old woman she couldn't recall to save her life.

"You loved all animals, especially—" Louisa stopped, as if accidentally stepping off a walkway into a briar patch, then went on, "On your sixth birthday, I gave you a toy cow."

"I remember *that* cow!" Ruth said excitedly. "I had it with me in Florin. I used to sleep with it."

Louisa seemed pleased by that. She served them coffee and asked about Ruth's life in Florin. Ruth relaxed and told her about the farm, about her brothers, about meeting Frank. She skipped over the war and brought out photos of Donnie and Peggy from her purse. Louisa took the snapshots and smiled. "Oh, they're beautiful, Ruth. You must be so proud."

They chatted about Ruth's life and her meeting Rachel, and despite her lack of recollection, Ruth felt a growing warmth for this kind-hearted woman.

Finally, after an hour, Louisa stood and said, "Well, you probably want to get back to your family. Thank you for coming to see me, Ruth. It's so good to know that you grew up healthy and happy and loved. God bless you."

"God bless you, Sister," she said, hugging her, "for taking care of me. You and Sister Catherine both."

Driving back to Waikīkī, Ruth had to admit she didn't recall "Sister Lu" or Kapiʻolani Home. "I don't understand why I should recall the scent of a flower and not this woman who obviously loved and cared for me."

Rachel considered that. "I think you remember your family's store because that was a place of great happiness for you. An orphanage, even when one is looked after by a loving nun, is not usually a happy place. I grew up in one too, and even though I had friends, it still wasn't home. Home, for you, started the day Etsuko and Taizo adopted you.

"But whether you remember her or not, you made an elderly woman very happy today." She added, smiling, "Make that two elderly women."

After several days of sightseeing—including ʻIolani Palace, home to Hawaiian royalty before the kingdom was overthrown by greedy *haole*s and later annexed to the United States—the seventh day of their trip found them all back on the beach, ready to go into the ocean when they heard:

"Mr. Harada?"

A bellhop, his uniform looking somewhat outlandish on the beach, approached them. "Yes?" Frank said.

"There's a phone call for you, sir. You can take the call in the lobby."

"Probably somebody from work," Frank said, and left.

But when he returned several minutes later, his expression had turned somber.

"What's wrong?" Ruth asked.

"It was Betty Oda." Betty was the teenage daughter of their next-door neighbors, who was looking after the pets. "She had to take Snowball to the vet."

Peggy's alarm was immediate. "What's wrong with her?"

"She wasn't eating for the past few days, and today, when Betty came over to clean the litter box, she found . . . blood," Frank said grimly.

"Oh God," Peggy gasped.

"Dr. Nealey says she has tumors—cancer—in her stomach." Frank was at pains to say the words. "He says she may only have a—day or two left."

"But she was fine when we left!" Ruth said.

"No, she wasn't," Peggy blurted. "I—I could tell something wasn't right. You know how she loves to jump up onto the windowsill and sun herself? She stopped doing it last week. I thought she was getting old, I never thought—" The words ended in a sob. "I should've *known*, should've *said* something—"

"It's not your fault, Peg," Ruth consoled her.

"They—they can't *do* anything?" Donnie asked.

"All they can do is end her suffering," Frank said gently. "Betty doesn't know what to do. I told her I had to talk with all of you first."

"We can't just let her die *alone*!" Peggy said.

Ruth thought of Slugger. She knew exactly how Peggy felt.

"I'll go back," Peggy said, "to be with her when they do it. She's been with me every night for the past twelve years—now *I* need to be with her."

"You can't go by yourself, honey, you're only fourteen," Ruth said. "I'll go with you." Ruth turned to her *makuahine*: "I'm sorry, Rachel, but—"

"I'd do the same thing," Rachel said. "Go."

In San Francisco they took a cab from the airport directly to Dr. Nealey's veterinary clinic in San Jose. One glimpse of Snowball brought tears to Peggy's eyes: she lay in a cage looking lethargic and weak, eyes closed, a small bald spot on her white head.

"Oh, Snowball," Peggy said. At the sound of Peggy's voice the cat opened her eyes, looked up, and managed a faint *miaooww*.

"Can I pick her up?" Peggy asked.

Dr. Nealey nodded. "Gently. Don't put any pressure on her stomach."

Peggy took Snowball and nestled her in the crook of her arm. "I'm so sorry, baby, I should have *known* you were sick . . ."

"No, Peggy, don't think that," Dr. Nealey said. "Animals do their best not to show their pain. In the wild it would be a sign of weakness. By the time you noticed her symptoms, it would have been too late to do anything."

"You're sure it's too late, Doctor?" Ruth asked.

"There are too many tumors in her stomach to remove surgically. And she's bleeding internally. All we can do is end her suffering."

"Can we have a few minutes alone with her? To say goodbye?"

"Of course."

Dr. Nealey left. Peggy raised Snowball up and the cat managed to brush her head against Peggy's cheek in one last show of affection.

"I love you too, Snowball," Peggy said. "I always have and I always will."

Ruth gently stroked the cat's head. "Our little angel of Manzanar. We needed you as much as you needed us."

Ruth and Peggy got a ride home from Betty Oda. Betty brought Max over from her house, where she had been looking after him, and he greeted them with a happy bark. But once inside the Haradas' home he began to seem confused. He followed Ruth and Peggy from room to room, sniffing and poking around as if searching for something. When he got to Snowball's litter box, he lay down on his haunches and whimpered plaintively. Peggy petted him with tears in her eyes. Ruth called Frank in Honolulu to tell him; he sounded like he was crying too.

Their exhaustion catching up with them, Ruth and Peggy both napped for a while. When it was time for dinner, Peggy sat down at the table, and a small smile came to her wan face as she looked down at her plate.

"Hotcakes?" she said in surprise.

"With coconut syrup." Ruth put the bottle of syrup by Peggy's plate. "If we can't be in Hawai'i, we'll bring Hawai'i here."

Peggy tucked into her pancakes and after a minute said, "Mom? If I tell you something, will you promise not to laugh?"

"Of course. What is it?"

"I think I know what I want to do, after I graduate high school. I want to be a vet, like Dr. Nealey."

Ruth felt a bittersweet rush of pride, gladness, and a little envy.

"Why would I laugh at that, Peg?" She smiled and squeezed Peggy's hand. "I think that's a *wonderful* thing to want to be."

Chapter 18

1957

ncle Jiro, now seventy-seven, with thinning hair and a thickening paunch, leaned back in Frank's easy chair. "When your aunt and I brought Akira back to Hōfuna in 1946," he told his audience of Ralph, Horace, and Stanley, "we found the family fortunes in decline. My elder brother Ichirō, who inherited the farm, had died of a heart attack three years before, and his sons had been conscripted into the army. Ichirō's wife made do with hired labor, barely breaking even. Only one son, Eiji, returned from the war, and so she was broken-hearted as well. I offered to take charge in exchange for room and board. Once Akira had recovered from his injuries he helped with the spring planting, and within two years the farm was again turning a profit."

Jiro took a sip of *sake*, his listeners aware that any narrative their uncle told inevitably made him the hero of the tale.

"But you're not returning to live here, *Ojisan*?" Stanley asked.

"No—Akira, Tamiko, and their children are all happy in Hōfuna, as are Nishi and I. And Japan is becoming something it has never been before: a democracy. I always admired America for its democratic principles, even though those principles were not extended to me."

"But the McCarran Act changed all that," Ralph pointed out. "You could be an American citizen now, just like Grandma Etsuko."

"I am glad America is living up to its ideals," Jiro said, "but I am happy being a citizen of Japan at a time when that means more than it ever has."

The Harada house was bursting with family on this Sunday afternoon. As Jiro held court in the living room, Frank and Ruth were preparing a supper of *nori* soup, beef *sukiyaki*, rice, green bean *shiraae*, and *mochi*. Peggy, now seventeen, was playing softball in the street with her teenage cousins; in the dining room, Etsuko doted on Ralph and Carol's newborn daughter, Susan. At the other end of that table, nineteen-year-old Donnie—or Don, as he now preferred to be called—was quizzing his Grandma Rachel about her travels: "So you finally got to see the Great Barrier Reef?"

"Yes, and on the way I stopped at Rarotonga in the Cook Islands, where my father made port as a sailor. But the highlight was Australia. I took a tour of the Great Reef on a glass bottom boat—it was so beautiful!"

Don said enviously, "I would *love* to see that someday."

"How was your freshman year? Have you decided on a major yet?"

"Yeah, I think so. I had this great biology professor who talked about the similarities between plants and animals. I thought about what you said in Hawai'i about how the land, sea, air, living things, how it's all interconnected. So I'm thinking about a major in biological science."

"Don, can you help me set the table?" Ruth asked her son.

"Sure. We'll talk more later, *tūtū*, okay?"

Rachel felt privileged to have been included in this gathering. The Watanabes all knew she had leprosy, but if they harbored any cultural fear of the disease they did not betray it and graciously accepted her as part of the family. She couldn't help but wonder if this was what life with Kenji's family might have been like, had they both not had Hansen's disease and been ostracized by his relations. But then, had they not been sent to Kalaupapa, she and Kenji might never have even met, much less married, on O'ahu.

Before dinner began, Jiro rose, held up his third glass of *sake*, and declared in a tone both sober and tipsy: "Thank you all for this warm welcome back to your shores. But there is one who could not sit among us today, and I must honor his memory. To Taizo—my brother, my family, my friend."

Ruth would have preferred not to be reminded of an absence that still stung, even today—but, like everyone else, raised her glass in honor of her *otōsan*.

A s dusk fell, the teenagers gathered around the television set, watching *The Jack Benny Program*, followed by Steve Allen's comedy-variety show. In the backyard, the adults stood or sat in lawn chairs to drink—beer, wine, or *sake*—or to smoke or make small talk. Etsuko sat at the far end of the yard chatting with Stanley and his family; Frank stood with Ruth's other brothers, talking sports; and Ruth, Jiro, and Nishi were chatting near the kids' old swing set, now rusting in place. Jiro was on his fifth glass of *sake* and even more voluble—and sentimental—than at supper.

"Ahhh, Dai," he sighed, "I would give my left arm to have your father here today."

"I know, *Ojisan*. That was a lovely toast."

But Jiro's rush of sudden guilt could not be quelled. "I failed him at Tule Lake as I had failed him too many times before."

"Uncle, I'm sure that isn't—"

"On my honor, Dai, I wish it had been *me* they had taken away that day, *me* they had put in that stockade—"

"What?" Ruth said with a gasp.

"Jiro! Be quiet!" Nishi said, poking him in the side.

"What do you mean, taken away? What . . . stockade?"

"Five weeks they left him in that hellhole! Cold blustery winds by day, freezing temperatures at night—it should have been *me*, not Taizo . . ."

"When he is drunk," Nishi said urgently, "he makes up nonsense—"

No—whatever her uncle was talking about, Ruth had the chill instinct that it was far from nonsense. She thought of Etsuko and felt a flush of panic, but was relieved to see her mother sitting at the opposite end of the yard, laughing with Stanley, apparently not having heard any of this.

Before Jiro could compound his mistake, Ruth quickly took him by the arm. "Uncle, come, let's go for a walk," she said, pulling him away.

"No, no," he drunkenly resisted, "I must tell you, I must apologize—"

She yanked on his arm hard enough to make him wince. She half whispered, half hissed, "You're so damn eager to lose that arm? I'll take it off *for* you if you don't shut up and *come with me!*"

Ruth walked Jiro and Nishi down the block until they were far enough from the Harada home for no one there to hear.

"All right, *Ojisan*," Ruth said, "what do you mean, my father was 'taken away'? He was arrested?"

Jiro nodded.

"Your father did not want you or your mother to know," Nishi said.

"My mother's *not* going to know. But I have to know what I'm protecting her from. *Why* was he arrested?"

Jiro's response was to start sobbing again, so it fell to Nishi to tell Ruth the truth: how Taizo had been arrested trying to help a friend; how he was beaten, interrogated, thrown into a flimsy tent and left there for seven weeks in the bitter cold; and how he was removed only when he fell ill with pneumonia.

"They killed him," Jiro spat out between sobs. "Bastards!"

Ruth was stunned; overwhelmed. It was bad enough that her father had died at Tule Lake, but now to learn that it hadn't been just a random event, an act of God, but the direct result of brutal mistreatment . . .

She told Nishi, "Take him to Taketa's Coffee Shop and pour as much coffee into him as it takes to sober him up."

Nishi nodded. "I am so sorry, Dai. You were never supposed to know."

And I wish to God I didn't, Ruth thought. She walked back home and into the backyard as casually as she could manage.

Frank came up to her. "There you are. Where are Jiro and Nishi?"

"Jiro had a little too much to drink. Nishi took him to get some fresh air."

Ruth hurried inside, into the empty kitchen. She braced her arms against the sink, her rage growing like a fast-moving wildfire. She went to the fridge and pulled out a bottle of Pabst Blue Ribbon. After a few swallows she began to relax a bit. After five minutes she had finished the bottle and felt composed enough to go back outside and socialize with her guests. Things will be fine, she told herself. Her mother would never know. *Never.*

Within the hour the party began to break up, just as Jiro and Nishi returned. Jiro's face looked ashen, as if he might have thrown up along the way, but he was sober. He and Nishi were staying with Horace in Florin, and before they left, Jiro found Ruth and privately, respectfully, bowed to her.

"My apologies, Dai," he said. "For everything."

She nodded and tried to smile.

That night, once she and Frank were alone in their bedroom, she closed the door and locked it—something she never did—and Frank knew at once something was wrong. "What is it, hon?"

She didn't reply, just held onto him and wept without words, wept for her father and the tortures he had gone through—the old wound of his death, barely healed, now torn open again, bleeding rage and grief and sorrow.

ry as she might, Ruth could not banish from her thoughts Jiro's drunken, but accurate, words: *They killed him. Bastards!* It was like knowing a murder had been committed but being helpless to tell anyone, to do anything to right the wrong. But she could not exhume the crime without grievously hurting her mother. She just had to learn to live with it.

So she beat back the rage that was pounding in her temples and covered it with a smile and a cheerful tone. Frank had taken vacation time during Rachel's visit and they took her on day trips to Sausalito, Santa Cruz, and the Napa Valley. The only one who couldn't join in was Peggy, who was volunteering full-time at Dr. Nealey's veterinary clinic this summer; the work experience would help when she was ready to submit her veterinary school application.

But wherever they went, Ruth felt irritable—impatient in traffic crossing the Golden Gate Bridge, or annoyed at the crowds jostling her on the Santa Cruz boardwalk. At the end of each day she returned home drained and exhausted. But she lay awake for hours, feeling the rapid fire of her own heartbeat, finally sinking into anxious slumber.

She woke at seven, barely rested. Frank said, "I'll make breakfast, go back to sleep if you want," but she couldn't, everything had to seem normal. Peggy was feeding Max as Ruth came downstairs to the kitchen.

"We're not going anywhere today, are we?" Don asked as he tucked into his bacon and eggs.

"Nope. Today is a free day," Frank said, pouring coffee for Ruth.

"Trish wants to go see *Tammy and the Bachelor*." Trish was Trish Messina, Don's girlfriend and also a student at San Jose State.

"You need a lift?" Frank offered. "I'm headed in that direction myself. Car needs filling up after all that driving."

"Sure, thanks."

Both Don and Peggy shoveled down their food and were out of the house, along with Frank, before Ruth had finished her second cup of coffee.

"We are abandoned," Ruth said with an amused sigh.

"At their age, butterfly," Etsuko noted, "you and your brothers were seldom found in great abundance at home."

Ruth smiled. "You seem quite stoic, by the way, at the idea of Don dating a non-Japanese girl."

Etsuko shrugged. "I no longer care about such things. She has a good heart. I have decided that is all that matters."

Ruth stood and started to clear the kids' place settings. "You and Rachel sit and relax. I'll do the dishes."

Etsuko and Rachel sat chatting in the dining room, and in the kitchen, over the sound of running water, Ruth could make out their conversation:

"—confess that I still wake up at night, expecting to hear the sound of Taizo's breathing. Even today I find the silence . . . alarming."

Ruth's eyes teared up and she felt her face grow flushed, not from the heat of the water but the seething temper she was laboring to control.

"The silence," Rachel agreed, "can be terrible. When I lived alone in Honolulu, sometimes I would go to the supermarket even if I didn't need to buy anything—just to be among people, to hear their voices."

"I tell myself," Etsuko said, "that Taizo might have died of pneumonia when he was twelve. He would never have married me, never had sons and a daughter and grandchildren that he loved. But the pneumonia did not take him that day, it let him live a full, rich, loving life, before finally claiming him in the end. I tell myself those years were a gift of fate."

Ruth's rage erupted in a muscle spasm that made her hands clench.

She heard a sound like the tinkle of wind chimes—then looked down and saw glass splinters falling into the suds like icicles into snow.

She heard Etsuko call out, "Dai?"

Moments later, Etsuko and Rachel hurried into the kitchen to find Ruth, blood dripping into the soapsuds.

"What happened?" Rachel asked as Etsuko ran to Ruth's side.

"I . . . dropped a glass," Ruth lied.

Etsuko took Ruth's left hand by the wrist and gently put it under the faucet, the stream of water washing away blood and small fragments of glass. The suds in the sink turned redder than clouds at sunset.

Etsuko pressed a dish towel against Ruth's bleeding palm. "Is your right hand hurt, Dai?"

"No, I don't think so. The dishrag must have protected it."

"Then use that hand to hold this as firmly against your palm as you can until we get to Dr. Higuchi's."

"*Okāsan*, it's nothing, I'll be—"

Rachel said, "Just keep pressing. Listen to your mother. To both of us."

*D*r. Higuchi cleaned out all the glass fragments and sewed five stitches in Ruth's left hand. The other cuts were small enough to simply bandage. Ruth's shock had worn off by the time the kids got home; she held up her swathed hand and quipped, "Look, I'm Boris Karloff in *The Mommy*." They all laughed, even Frank and Etsuko.

Rachel didn't laugh.

Frank grilled flank steaks and made French fries for dinner. Afterward the kids washed the dishes, prompting another joke from Ruth: "Dr. Higuchi says I need to keep this bandage on until Peggy leaves for college."

Again, everyone but Rachel laughed.

Etsuko, exhausted by the day's emergency, went to bed by nine o'clock. Rachel was with Frank and the kids in the living room, watching Perry Como, when she noticed that Ruth had slipped out of the room. She went into the kitchen, where she saw through the window that Ruth was outside sitting on one of her children's old swings, slowly rocking herself back and forth.

Rachel followed her into the backyard, sitting down on the swing next to Ruth's. "Hi."

"Hi. Just needed a little quiet."

Rachel asked gently, "What's been bothering you, Ruth?"

"Just feeling rattled by the accident, that's all."

Rachel shook her head. "No. You've been irritable all week, ever since the party for your Uncle Jiro."

"I'm fine," Ruth said, irritated.

"And you didn't 'drop' that glass. If you had it would've broken in the sink, not in your hands. How did you cut yourself?"

Ruth's eyes flashed with annoyance. "What is this? Am I on trial for breaking a glass?"

Rachel replied calmly, "I saw your father—Kenji—do something similar once. He was drinking a can of beer, trying not to hear the sounds of our neighbor Crossen hitting his girlfriend. When the girl cried out, Kenji tensed up and crushed the beer can. There was Schlitz everywhere, even on the ceiling. Took us hours to wipe it all off, and even then the house stank like a brewery for two days."

Despite herself, Ruth's curiosity was piqued. "You've never mentioned he had a temper."

"Oh, when we first met he was angry all the time—angry at being in Kalaupapa, angry that he had his career, his future, taken away from him. I couldn't blame him. After we married the anger went away—until Crossen moved in." Rachel turned and looked at her. "So what are you angry about, Ruth?"

Ruth winced. "I—I can't tell you. My moth—Etsuko can't ever know."

"It's about your father? Taizo?"

"I can't say. I just *can't*."

"All right," Rachel said quietly. "I don't need to know. But whatever it is, you're bottling it up inside and not doing a very good job of it."

"What do you know about it?" Ruth said sharply.

"You think I haven't been just as angry as you are now?" Rachel said. "I saw Crossen beat my husband to death. I watched as he was convicted of manslaughter, only to be sent not to jail but to another room at Kalaupapa."

There was a fierceness in Rachel's voice Ruth had never heard before.

"Do you know what I did on the day I left Kalaupapa? Before I left? I went to Bay View Home, where Crossen was serving out his sentence because no jail in Hawai'i would take a 'leper' for a prisoner. I walked right into his room. I looked him straight in the eye and said, 'I'm leaving.'

"Then I smiled and said, 'But you never will. Even if the sulfa drugs cure you, you'll either be put in prison on O'ahu or just left here, in Kalau-papa . . . for the rest of your life.'"

"Wow," Ruth said softly.

"It was the cruelest thing I'd ever done in my life. That's how angry I was. But it felt like a weight had been lifted off me." She paused, looked down, haunted by what came next. "At least for nine days."

"What do you mean?"

Rachel sighed.

"Nine days later, Kalaupapa's superintendent, Lawrence Judd, called to tell me that Crossen's body had been found floating in the waters of 'Awa-hua Bay. He might've been drunk, or it might've been a suicide. Maybe both. All at once I felt a different kind of weight. I still do."

Ruth was astonished by everything she had heard but managed to say, "But . . . you don't *know* that you were the reason he did that!"

"Just some kine coincidence, eh?" Rachel said, lapsing into Hawaiian pidgin for emphasis. "A nice thought. But I know."

"Even so, you could never have foreseen he'd kill himself."

"No, I couldn't. And if I had the chance to do it over again, would I still do it?" She looked unflinchingly at Ruth and said, "*I don't know.* You un-derstand? You see now what anger does to you, where it can take you?"

Rachel took Ruth's hand in hers and said, "Today it just got you some cuts in your hand. Tomorrow, who knows?"

Ruth said softly, "They killed him. The Army killed him." And she poured out the story Nishi had told her. Rachel winced at the details, as bloody and brutal as what Crossen had done to Kenji.

"I'm so sorry, Ruth," Rachel said, squeezing Ruth's hand. "That's a ter-rible burden to have to bear. But there's a word in Hawaiian that might help you bear it: *kala*. It means 'to forgive' but also 'to let go.'"

"How the hell do I forgive the bastards who murdered my father?"

"You don't. I never forgave Crossen for murdering Kenji. But I finally forgave myself—for not being able to prevent it. Let go, Ruth. *Kala*."

Ruth wept, not just for her father but for herself, the daughter she had wanted to be, the one who could rescue him the way he had rescued her.

Sumimasen, Otōsan, she apologized. *Sumimasen.* She could not save everyone she loved. But she could, and would, save Etsuko from this.

Chapter 19

1960–1961

The house was too damn quiet. Ruth stood in the living room, longing for one more indoor baseball game with Donnie, Peggy, and Max. She felt a twinge of loss, even two years later, thinking of Max. She consoled herself with the knowledge that he had lived a long life—eleven years—for a dog his size, and that he had been loved every day of that life.

The kids, of course, were a happier matter, as much as she missed them. After two years of pre-veterinary classes at the University of California at Davis, Peggy had been accepted to their School of Veterinary Medicine. She had studied hard and spent the summer between freshman and sophomore years working with large animals on Horace's farm in Florin. Don graduated from San Jose State with a B.S. in Biological Science and was accepted to the Scripps Institution of Oceanography—affiliated with UC San Diego—for its Master's Program in Marine Biology. Tuition at public universities in California was free, but Frank and Ruth were nevertheless both working overtime to pay the registration fees and room and board.

"Dai, I'm ready to plant."

Etsuko, in gardening gloves and apron, entered the room carrying a small cellophane bag with a plant cutting inside.

"This was very thoughtful of Rachel," Ruth said. Etsuko had wanted a tropical plant that could survive in a colder climate; Rachel's sister, Sarah, had suggested a bird of paradise, and Rachel sent a cutting from their own garden.

"Yes, I wrote her that it will provide our garden with both a touch of Hawai'i and a warm reminder of her."

They went out to the garden, where Etsuko kneeled down, the arthritis in her knees keenly protesting. Ruth was hefting a large bag of mulch out of the house. Etsuko opened the cellophane bag and took out a three-inch length of tuber sprouting a fan of green leaves.

Ruth deposited the bag of mulch on the ground beside her mother.

"You're sure it doesn't get too cold in San Jose for these things?"

"It's true they grow best in warmer climates," Etsuko said, taking up her spade, "but our winters are relatively mild; mulch should provide enough insulation from the cold. Should temperatures drop below freezing, we can cover the plant with burlap to protect against frost."

Etsuko happily dug a shallow hole, placed the cutting in it with the crown of leaves pointing upward, then backfilled the hole with topsoil. "Rachel recommends watering it twice a week and feeding every two weeks," Etsuko said, adding, "I am so glad, Dai, that you saw fit to make her part of our lives. Knowing her has enriched us all, in one way or another."

Etsuko dipped her hand in the mulch and began spreading it lightly around the base of the plant. "Did you know the bird of paradise is also called a crane flower? Because its blossom resembles the head of a crane."

"I remember the paper cranes we had back in Florin," Ruth said. "Weren't they supposed to be good luck?"

"Yes. In Japan the crane is revered—legend says it lives a thousand years and brings good fortune and longevity to a home. We had to burn those paper cranes on December 7. And bad luck quickly followed."

Etsuko started to get up—only to find her head spinning like a *beigoma*, a child's top. What was happening to her?

"Dai—" she started to say, before a wave of nausea struck her.

Her legs buckled and she collapsed into darkness.

*W*hat seemed like only a moment later, Etsuko opened her eyes to find herself in a strange bed, wearing a thin cloth gown, a blood pressure cuff wrapped around her left arm. At her bedside were Ruth, Frank, and Dr. Higuchi, all of whom appeared relieved to see her eyes open.

"What happened?" she asked. "I—I was just in the garden."

"That was an hour ago, *Okāsan*." Ruth took her hand. "You lost your balance and fell. You were unconscious, I had to call for an ambulance."

"Oh no," Etsuko said, her face showing its first flush of color. "Did the neighbors see me taken away? What must they have thought?"

"It's nothing to be embarrassed about, Etsuko," Jim Higuchi told her, "and Ruth was right to call the ambulance. What do you recall happening?"

"I—I started to get up from my gardening and my head began spinning. My legs collapsed under me. That is all I remember."

"Have you felt short of breath at any time recently?" Higuchi asked.

"No."

"Yes, she has," Ruth said. "*Okāsan*, every time you climb the stairs to the second floor you're out of breath, remember?"

"Only for a few moments," Etsuko objected. "It's nothing."

"Have you experienced any chest pains?" Higuchi asked.

"No," she answered truthfully.

"Your blood pressure's high," Higuchi said, "and listening to your heart I heard an irregular rhythm. It could just be stress-related, but I'd like to get an electrocardiogram and a chest X ray to be sure."

"This is silly. There is nothing wrong with me. I just had a dizzy spell."

"*Okāsan*, please, do as the doctor suggests," Ruth implored.

The concern in her daughter's tone outweighed Etsuko's unvoiced fear; she agreed to the tests. But being out of bed for even half an hour tired her, and after the tests she fell asleep as soon as she was back in her room.

When she awoke, Ruth and Frank were sitting by her bed. They called for Dr. Higuchi, who came in a minute later and sat down.

"This is going to sound worse than it is, Etsuko," he said, "but you do have an irregular heartbeat, and the chest X rays indicate a partial blockage in the left side of your heart. Technically you're in the early stage of congestive heart failure, but don't let that alarm you. You haven't experienced any chest pains and we're going to do our best to keep it that way. Your condition can be managed effectively with rest, medication, and small changes in diet. If you take care of yourself, you can continue to live a good long life."

"How long?" Etsuko asked warily.

"Everyone's case is different, but I've had other patients your age live up to another ten years."

That sounded both reassuring—in ten years she would be eighty-five, a long life by any measure—and frightening. Ten years could go by in a flash.

Frank said, "Jim suggests we move your bedroom from the second floor to the first, so you can avoid climbing stairs."

"And I'm going to take a leave from my job while you recover. Everything's going to be all right, *Okāsan*." Ruth squeezed her hand as her mother had done for her many times. Etsuko chose to believe her.

Only a week later, Ruth walked into her mother's newly relocated bedroom—formerly occupied by Don—to find Etsuko tucking her pillows under the bedspread and smoothing out its folds. "*Okāsan*," she said, "why are you doing that?"

"I have not forgotten how to make a bed, butterfly."

"But you're not supposed to. Remember Dr. Higuchi's chart?"

The chart in question was a table of calories burned per minute for various daily activities: Washing & dressing was 2.6 cal/min; Washing face & combing hair, 2.5 cal/min; Sitting was 1.6 cal/min while Standing was 2.0, and Climbing Stairs a whopping 6.0–10 cal/min.

"Oh, that silly chart," Etsuko scoffed. "Look at me, do I appear to be exhausted? Or in pain?"

"No, but you're supposed to be avoiding chores like cleaning and washing dishes to conserve your energy for things you enjoy, like gardening."

"I am not yet an invalid, Dai. I can make my own bed, wash my own dishes. As for cleaning, at Manzanar I must have swept out a lifetime's worth of dust and sand in three years, so I am more than happy to retire my broom."

Ruth smiled at that. "Good, we'll have it bronzed. In the meantime, breakfast is ready. Did you take your diuretic pill this morning?"

"Yes, yes," Etsuko said with a sigh, "and I was up at least ten times last night. Is this pill so necessary?"

"That's the whole idea—flushing the sodium from your body."

"A little too much flushing, in my opinion," Etsuko muttered.

Ruth laughed.

After breakfast, Ruth left for the supermarket. "Promise me you won't go do any gardening until I get back," she asked.

"I plan on doing nothing more strenuous than sewing," Etsuko said. "I need to finish the dress I'm making for Susan's birthday." Ralph and Carol's daughter was turning three in two weeks.

"Thanks. I'll be back within the hour, okay?"

"I will try not to die while you are gone," Etsuko teased.

Ruth found her mother's sense of humor taxing at times.

After her daughter left, Etsuko went to her bedroom to retrieve her sewing kit. The fabric for Susan's dress—dark blue, patterned with white seagulls—was in the top drawer of her dresser. But the pattern she had been planning to use was not. She must have left it in the old shoebox in which she kept her patterns. It was probably still upstairs, in her old room.

She did not relish climbing those stairs any more than she did acting against her daughter's wishes. But she needed to finish that dress in time for Susan's birthday party. She could wait an hour for Ruth to return, but it irked her to feel so dependent upon others.

She took the steps slowly, keeping her hand on the banister, but with each breath she felt as if she were ascending Mount Fuji. When she reached the second floor she was breathless and rested for a moment.

The shoebox was indeed in her closet, but had been placed on the top shelf alongside boxes of Donnie's old sneakers. Etsuko dragged over a chair, but the memory of her fall in the garden gave her pause. *Should* she wait until Ruth came home? No, that was ridiculous; she was here now, wasn't she?

She got up onto the chair, standing there for a moment to make sure the dizziness did not return. When it did not, she reached up and took the box from the shelf. She felt a rush of pride and satisfaction—

And then felt a spasm in her chest, as if something had reached inside her and squeezed her heart like a sponge.

She gasped for breath—felt a shudder in her pulse—but the dizziness didn't return and the spasm eventually subsided. She stood on the chair, breathing hard, then slowly got down. She waited, dreading another stab of angina—Dr. Higuchi had warned her of these and insisted he be told if she experienced one—but fortunately there was no further pain. She walked over to her grandson's bed and lay down. After what seemed an hour but was probably only fifteen minutes, she got up, tucked the shoebox under one arm, and returned to the stairs. It was a long, frightening descent, but at the end she was merely out of breath, nothing worse. She gratefully lay down on her bed and fell asleep.

She woke when Ruth returned home with the groceries.

"Sorry. Were you taking a nap?" Ruth said as she paused by the room.

"Yes," Etsuko said, as matter-of-factly as she could. "I felt a bit tired."

"Good. I'm glad you're taking Dr. Higuchi's advice to heart."

Over the next few months, Etsuko felt the occasional brief angina pain but told no one and simply endured it. Then one Sunday in the midst of church services she felt a spasm so painful that she cried out and fainted. Reverend Hojo called O'Connor Hospital as his wife hurried across the street to inform the Haradas. Within minutes Etsuko was being carried into an ambulance, which Ruth and Frank followed to the hospital.

After examining Etsuko, Dr. Higuchi came out of the ICU and told the Haradas, "She suffered a heart attack, but a relatively mild one. When she came to, she admitted that she's been having chest pains for months but didn't want to tell you."

Ruth felt equal measures relief and anger. "She *hid* them from us?"

"You know what it's like with the Issei—they endure the pain, they *gaman*. And she didn't want you to worry."

Reflexively Ruth began kicking herself—how could she not have noticed, not have *known*, that her mother was hurting?

"What's her prognosis?" Frank asked.

"Generally good. We'll have to keep her a few weeks for observation. I have her on Demerol, she's in no pain; when she's ready to go home I'll prescribe digitalis as needed for angina. She should regain most of her strength, though she'll have to be even more careful about exerting herself."

When they went to see her, Etsuko seemed weak and contrite for concealing her pain from Ruth, who was careful not to show any irritation: "The important thing is you're going to be fine."

When Etsuko returned home two weeks later, still a bit unsteady on her feet, the first thing she wanted to do was check on the bird of paradise in the garden. She was pleased to see that it had sprouted several new shoots. "Perhaps it will bloom this fall or winter," she said, and Ruth—happy to hear her mother looking forward to something—encouraged the notion.

When winter came, alas, there was no bloom on the plant; but the season brought something else, just as welcome.

When Rachel walked through the front door on December 23, Etsuko's face lit up with pleasure. "Oh, Rachel! I'm so glad you could join us," she said. Rachel wrapped her arms around Etsuko—and was shocked by how thin and bony her small body felt. This reminded her, disturbingly, of Sister Catherine as she lay abed in the Kalaupapa hospital. But Rachel didn't betray her unease and said with a smile, "I'm glad to see you too, Etsuko."

"How was your trip to South America?"

"It was wonderful. I brought pictures." Rachel sat down beside her. "Thank you for inviting me to share your holidays with you."

"*My* holiday is next week—New Year's Day," Etsuko said lightly, "but I have come to enjoy Christmas. Mostly for the delight it brings the *keiki*."

Don and Peggy, no longer *keiki* but adults in their early twenties, were on break from school and were equally happy to see their *tūtū*. Each was eager to tell her about their lives and studies.

Over supper, Rachel noted idly that though Ruth filled her plate with yams, string beans, and other vegetables, she was avoiding the main course. "Ruth, aren't you having any of this delicious ham you've cooked?"

Ruth sighed. "I'm afraid not. Lately I've been trying not to eat meat of any kind. I'm not squeamish about cooking it for others, but growing up on the farm I could never understand the difference between dogs and cats, who we treat as pets, and cows and chickens, who we see as food. First rule of farming: never name the livestock. I never did eat chicken at home."

"True," Etsuko confirmed.

To avoid wearing Etsuko out, houseguests were carefully scheduled: on Christmas Eve, Ralph, Carol, John T., and Susan visited; on Christmas Day, it would be Horace and Rose's family. Etsuko loved seeing the joy in the children's faces as they opened their gifts; she even enjoyed listening to Bing Crosby's velvet voice sing "Silent Night" and "White Christmas" on the hi-fi.

She was unable, of course—and unwilling, in any event—to join the Haradas at Christmas Day services at their church. Ruth stayed home to look after her and Rachel kept them company.

Sitting in the living room beside Etsuko, Rachel said, "Kenji never cared much for Christmas himself. He knew I liked it and was always happy to eat a Christmas turkey"—Etsuko laughed—"but that was about it. He wasn't a devout Buddhist either, but I do know he didn't believe in God, much less a Son of."

Etsuko nodded. "Buddha teaches us that nothing in the universe is permanent, so there can be no immortal soul and no everlasting God."

"But Kenji did believe in an afterlife."

"The Pure Land, yes. Amida Buddha opens the path to that realm. But that is only a way station to one's next rebirth."

Ruth entered, a bit dismayed at the morbid turn in the conversation.

"Only *karma* survives death," Etsuko explained. "If the *karma* has been one of good actions, as set out in the Eightfold Path, it will result in a better rebirth; if the *karma* has been one of bad actions, a lesser rebirth. What survives is not a soul or personality but *karma*. Think of it as a candle flame, which, in dying, lights the flame of another candle. Its light is reborn.

"This cycle of death and rebirth is called *samsara*. But the ultimate goal is enlightenment, or *nirvana*, which means 'extinction.' When you achieve *nirvana*, your *karma* has no further need for existence."

Ruth said dryly, "There's a cheery thought for a Christmas morning."

Etsuko shrugged. "It is not meant to cheer, butterfly; it is what it is. But I am not so prideful to think I have led a perfect life and will achieve *nirvana* after I die. I will continue on the great wheel of *samsara*."

At that, Ruth suggested they see what was on the great wheel of the television dial, and they watched TV until Etsuko eventually dozed off.

Rachel, gazing at her with a sorrow that Ruth shared, said quietly, "She tires so easily. She was always so full of life and energy."

Ruth nodded. "I'm so glad she got to see Honolulu again, while she had the strength. And Chinatown, and our old home."

"She's a remarkable woman," Rachel said. "Kenji and I couldn't have wished for a better mother to love our *akachan*."

As winter gave way to spring, Etsuko's stamina diminished and she became so short of breath that Dr. Higuchi prescribed the use of an oxygen tank, kept beside her bed. Ruth took to sleeping on a *futon* next to her in case she needed help. Once Etsuko woke in the middle of the night, gasping for breath; Ruth jumped up and put her oxygen mask on. Gratefully Etsuko took in the air, but it was terrifying for Ruth to see her mother struggling to breathe.

In midsummer, Ruth wrote to Rachel:

Christmas seems so long ago. When you were here she was lively, still eating at the dining table. All that winter she asked whether the bird of paradise had bloomed yet, but it never did. I think she's hoping that if the crane flower blooms, she might reap some of its legendary longevity. Even I'm praying for it to bloom, hoping it might inspire her to keep fighting.

Oh Rachel, this is so hard. When Papa died it was sudden and distant, like a bolt of lightning. This is slow and invisible, like gravity dragging her down each day. It breaks my heart to watch.

By October Etsuko was almost totally bedridden. She could barely consume more than a few bites before feeling full. Her feet became swollen with edema and her once-fine features became puffy as her face took on more fluid. Ruth became adept at turning her over in bed to prevent bedsores, and perhaps once a week Etsuko would allow her or Frank to put her in a wheelchair and take her into the backyard for some fresh air. The bird of paradise was lush with leathery, bluish-green leaves, but the only other growth was a purplish basal sheath that stubbornly declined to bloom.

Etsuko was mortified when Ruth would give her a sponge bath, but she was also grateful for her tender ministrations. And she felt the need, on a morning when she was having less trouble breathing than usual, to tell her that.

"Dai," she said softly, faintly.

"Yes, *Okāsan*?"

"You have been a gift to me," she said, smiling, "and a joy I never dared dream of after the doctors told me I could never have another child."

"No, Mama. You were the one who gave *me* the gift. The gift of a home, a family, and love." Tears welled in her eyes. "I love you so much."

"I love you, butterfly. I have since the moment I saw you. And I am so proud of the woman you have become."

When Frank came home he looked in on Etsuko, who was asleep, then joined his wife in the kitchen. "You look exhausted," he told her.

"I'm fine," she said. "She's not going to die in a hospital. Not like Papa."

Frank thought that might not be up to her. But he just nodded.

The next morning, Ruth rose early. Her mother was still sleeping with no apparent discomfort, so Ruth slipped quietly out of the bedroom and into the kitchen. She stood by the sink washing off fresh oranges to squeeze for juice, when she happened to look up and out the kitchen window.

In the garden a fire-red flower was opening in the dawning light.

Ruth raced into the backyard. The bird of paradise was magnificent. From the boat-shaped sheath a long-stemmed flower had emerged, flame-red with a blue arrowlike tongue. It did, in fact, look like a crane.

Frank saw her in the yard and joined her. "I'll be damned," he said. "Sure took its own sweet time."

Ruth grinned and hurried into the house to announce, breathlessly, to her mother: "It's bloomed!"

"What?" Etsuko said in disbelief.

"The bird of paradise—it's beautiful!"

Etsuko's face lit up with an excitement Ruth hadn't seen in months. "I want to see," she said, sitting up. "Take me out to see it!"

Ruth and Frank got Etsuko into a bathrobe and then her wheelchair. Ruth wheeled her out of the house and down a wooden ramp Frank had built over the back steps, then to the garden. Etsuko was thrilled by what she saw.

"Ohhh," she said softly, "it *is* beautiful. Like the ones in Hawai'i."

Ruth pushed her wheelchair close enough so that Etsuko could reach out her hand and just lightly graze the delicate, bright orange blossom.

Etsuko's smile was nearly as bright.

Ruth and Frank were willing to stand there as long as Etsuko wanted to, as long as her strength held out. Finally she said, "I'm ready to go in now."

"We can come out again later," Ruth said.

Etsuko nodded, still smiling.

She ate a little more than usual at breakfast, slept through lunch, but woke in midafternoon and was surprisingly chatty, telling Ruth stories she had never heard before—of childhood neighbors in Hōfuna, of her voyage to Honolulu to join Taizo. She was livelier than Ruth had seen her in months. After dinner she tired and was asleep by seven, though not before she told Ruth, "Tomorrow morning I would like to go out and see the flower again."

"That can be arranged," Ruth agreed with a smile.

"Good night, butterfly. I love you."

Ruth kissed her on the cheek. "I love you, *Okāsan*."

Etsuko was asleep within minutes.

The next morning Ruth woke around dawn, and as a red-gold light filtered through the bedroom blinds, she immediately sensed a stillness to the room.

Her mother was no longer breathing.

She went to her, touched her hand. It was cold as a night at Manzanar.

Ruth looked at her mother through a veil of tears, but she knew what had to be done next. She went into the bathroom, ran some water into a cup, and returned to her mother's bedside. Ruth dipped two fingers into the water, then touched them to Etsuko's lips, moistening them one last time in a ceremony called *matsugo-no-mizu*, "water of the last moment"—done in hopes of reviving the deceased.

If only it could.

Ruth bent down, tenderly kissed her *okāsan*'s forehead, then went to Frank and the two of them cried together. When she was ready, she picked up the phone and called Horace.

According to tradition, funeral arrangements were to be made by the eldest son—and since Horace was Buddhist and Ruth was not, it was he who scheduled the funeral with Reverend Hojo and arranged for Etsuko's body to be laid out, in a simple white kimono, for the *tsuya*, "the passing of the night." Stanley's family flew in from Portland, and Don and Peggy arrived that evening. The all-night vigil was long and arduous for Ruth, but even more painful was what followed the next day. Tradition decreed that at the crematorium the family witnessed the sliding of the deceased's body into the cremation chamber, ate a meal while the ashes cooled, and then used chopsticks to pick the bones of the deceased out of the ashes and place them in an urn. Ruth could barely keep her lunch down during this ceremony, but steadied herself with the knowledge that this was what her mother would have wanted.

Later, after the ashes were interred, everyone went to the Harada home to eat, drink, and remember Etsuko. But after the hours spent at the crematorium, Ruth desperately needed fresh air; she went into the backyard, followed shortly after by Ralph, who was carrying two glasses of *sake*. He handed her one. "You looked like you needed this."

Then his attention was caught by the bird of paradise.

"So that's what that looks like?" he asked. "Like one of the paper cranes we had to burn after Pearl Harbor." He took a step closer. "That fiery orange blossom—damned if it doesn't look like a phoenix rising from the ashes."

Ruth understood, at last, what the crane flower had represented to her mother. It wasn't Hawai'i, as much as she had loved Hawai'i. It wasn't good fortune; and it wasn't longevity. No, not even that.

It was rebirth.

Chapter 20

1965

uth took a breath of the moist tropic air, fragrant with plumeria and jasmine; it was like breathing in tranquility itself. She loved making this drive. The Haradas had been to Maui once before, two years ago, to visit Rachel and Sarah, but already the island felt like a second home. She drove south down the Honoapi'ilani Highway; the windward face of the West Maui Mountains, misted blue in the morning light, wore a turban of white clouds. They passed fields of waist-high sugarcane bowing in the wind; brown columns of burning cane smoke, sweetly pungent, flavored the air. At the island's isthmus they turned up what was once called the Pali Road. The coastal drive presented one awe-inspiring view after another: the lighthouse at McGregor Point, steadfast as crashing waves battered the headlands below it; Pāpalaua Beach, where tangled *kiawe* trees hunched over a narrow strip of pristine white sand; Olowalu Tunnel, which looked as if it had been punched out of the mountainside by the demigod Māui himself; and acres of green, terraced farm fields draping the leeward slopes of the mountains.

When they reached the sugarcane fields above Lahaina, Ruth turned left on Prison Street, then right on Waine'e Street. A block down she could see the familiar white bungalow beneath the green umbrella of a banyan tree, its garden ablaze with orange helliconia, anthuriums, and birds of paradise. Ruth felt a sting of remembered pain but reminded herself that Etsuko would have wanted her to feel happy upon seeing these beautiful flowers.

Rachel and her sister, Sarah, emerged from the little house. Rachel, now seventy-nine, still had a youthful air of enthusiasm; Sarah, only two years her senior, somehow looked much older. Both were smiling at their guests.

"Aloha," Rachel greeted Ruth, then gave her a hug. Ruth hugged Sarah as Frank embraced Rachel. But when Don, now twenty-eight, approached Sarah, she just looked at him blankly: "I'm sorry, do I know you?"

"Sarah, for heaven's sake, it's *Don*," Rachel said, "my grandson."

"Oh! Yes, of course, Donnie. I'm sorry, what was I thinking?"

The worry that flickered across Rachel's face did not escape Ruth.

The house was decorated with rattan chairs and burnished wooden tables hand-carved by Sarah's late husband. The Haradas took their bags into the bedrooms once occupied by Sarah's four children, now grown.

At lunch—including a delicious salad of Kula lettuce and fresh tomatoes from Sarah's garden—Rachel wanted to know all about Peggy's new job at a veterinary clinic in Modesto as well as Don's work as a staff oceanographer at Scripps. They were both happy in their work and their parents were obviously very proud of them.

Later, when they were alone, Ruth asked Rachel, "Is there something wrong with Sarah?"

"She's getting a little senile," Rachel admitted. "Forgetful, has trouble staying focused . . . and she gets flustered while driving. Luckily I can walk to Nagasako's Supermarket to do our grocery shopping. But when either of us needs to see a doctor in Kahului, I grit my teeth and pray when she gets behind the wheel."

"Do her children know about this?"

Rachel nodded. "Ellie is the only one who still lives on Maui, upcountry in Makawao. So far I can take care of Sarah on my own, but if there comes a point when I can't, I'm not sure what we're going to do."

"I'm sorry."

"With my brother Ben gone"—Rachel's eyes clouded over—"Sarah is the last of my family. She still recognizes me, but I dread the day she doesn't."

That evening the whole family had dinner at the Lahaina Broiler, through whose windows they could see the islands of Moloka'i and Lāna'i, swaddled in clouds on the horizon. "When are we going to take a trip to Moloka'i," Ruth asked Rachel, "so I can see where I was born?"

Rachel seemed uneasy. "There *are* more pleasant places we can visit."

"But you speak with such love of the people there—your 'Kalaupapa family.' I'd like to meet them."

"I do love them," Rachel said. "But look at this way: How enthusiastic would you be about taking us on a sightseeing trip to Manzanar?"

Ruth saw her point. "Not very, I suppose."

"Don't worry," Rachel said, "you'll get to see Moloka'i—eventually."

Ruth chose not to ask her mother what she meant by this.

The next morning Frank, Don, and Peggy were out the door by seven for a diving trip to Olowalu. After breakfast Ruth told Rachel and Sarah that she would like to pay her respects to their mother, as she had on her previous trip to Maui. They seemed quite moved by this, and soon Ruth was driving them to the little red-clay cemetery at the southern tip of Kā'anapali. Ruth gazed down at the simple stone marker that read DORO-THY KALAMA 1861–1933 and thought about the grandparents she had never known, the loving stories Rachel told of Dorothy's courage and Henry's devotion.

Rachel was gazing up the coastline at the adjacent Kā'anapali Beach Resort: a thousand acres of green rolling golf course, man-made lagoons, and a three-mile strip of lovely white sand. So far the only hotels on the beach were the Kā'anapali Hotel, the Royal Lahaina, and the Sheraton Maui, the latter's buildings perched almost impudently atop the high lava outcropping now called Black Rock but once known as Pu'u Keka'a—a *leina a ka 'uhane*, where the spirits of the dead were said to have made the leap into the next world.

Ruth noticed her distraction. "Rachel? Something wrong?"

"Oh, I was just thinking about the history of this place. Centuries ago the *ali'i*—Hawaiian royalty—would come to Kā'anapali for recreation. Sugarcane and taro was grown here. Then, after the missionaries arrived, they planted prickly *kiawe* trees to keep the *kanaka* from holding their so-called 'pagan' rituals on the beach." Sarah, a devout Christian, rolled her eyes. "Up until six years ago, there was a lush *kiawe* forest here," Rachel said. "Today it's a golf course."

"*Kiawe* trees are ugly and thorny," Sarah said. "Things change, Rachel."

"I suppose so. But Mama wanted to be buried here so she'd always be in sight of Moloka'i. Now she also has a fine view of the eighteenth hole."

Sarah took Rachel's clawed hand and cupped it tenderly.

"She can still see Moloka'i," Sarah said. "But she doesn't need to, because you're here to visit her every Sunday."

Ruth smiled at them, at the obvious love between the sisters despite their differences.

"Mama managed to hide my leprosy from the authorities for months after she discovered it," Rachel told Ruth. "I last saw Mama as I was taken aboard the boat to Moloka'i—I saw the love and heartbreak in her face. That's why, when my brother Kimo came down with it, she hid him up-country in Kula. To Hawaiians there's nothing worse than breaking up the *'ohana*. If a family member becomes sick, you care for them, you don't abandon them. That's why Hawaiians called leprosy the *ma'i ho'oka'awale*—'the separating sickness.'"

Moved by this, Ruth said, "Rachel—Mother—there's something I've been wanting to ask you. I know what it means to be Japanese because my parents taught me about honor, courtesy, filial piety, hard work. But—what does it mean to be Hawaiian? What should it mean to *me*, being Hawaiian?"

Rachel considered that. "It's more than just bloodlines, though that's part of it. It's a way of life, a way of looking at life."

Surprisingly, it was Sarah who turned to her sister and suggested, "Kahakuloa?"

"What's that?" Ruth asked.

"A small village on the windward side of the north shore," Rachel explained. "A few dozen families live there, all Hawaiian. They live according to the old ways—doing their own farming, fishing, getting all they need to live from the *'āina*. It's probably the closest thing to Old Hawai'i that's left on Maui."

"Can we go?"

"I have a friend there, and I'm sure he'd welcome us, but it's a bit of a rugged trip. The highway narrows to one lane along the cliffside and turns into a bumpy dirt road for long stretches."

"Sounds like an adventure," Ruth said with enthusiasm.

"Well," Rachel said, smiling, "that's one word for it."

There was no shortage of scenic views on the way to Kahakuloa, so Rachel and the Haradas packed a picnic lunch and got an early start. Frank drove past Kā'anapali and, farther north, through the pineapple fields of Kapalua. The highway narrowed to two lanes and began a slow ascent into the mountains, winding along sea cliffs overlooking Mokulē'ia Bay and its neighbor, Honolua Bay. They stopped to watch the surfers riding Honolua's wavebreaks and to take in the beauty of its turquoise waters. Later they did the same at Honokōhau, where surfers climbed like billy goats over the boulder-strewn beach to get at the big waves rolling in.

A few miles past Honokōhau, the highway abruptly ended, turning into a rough, unpaved road—County Route 340, also called the Kahekili Highway, after the last king of Maui. The road shrank to a single lane clinging to the side of a cliff, with no guard rail on the driver's side, just blue sky and a sheer hundred-foot drop. Frank took it slow and in stride—until a big Ford pickup truck suddenly appeared from around a blind curve.

"Jesus Christ!" Frank blurted as he slammed on the brakes.

Ruth's breath caught in her chest.

The truck came to a stop just a few feet away in front of them; then it just sat there and idled, waiting. Ruth began breathing again.

Frank turned to Rachel in the back. "What does he expect me to do?"

"On these roads, the bigger vehicle has the right of way," she said calmly. "He wants you to back up."

"Back *up*? We're on the edge of a goddamn cliff!"

"There was a turnout about three hundred feet back," Rachel advised. "Just back up very slowly until you reach it. Drivers here do it all the time."

Seeing his family's terrified faces actually bolstered Frank's nerve. "Okay, boys and girls," he said, turning back, "here goes nothing."

Frank backed up a foot at a time, white-knuckling the wheel. The truck squeezed past them with only inches to spare. As he passed, the truck driver smiled and waved, as if this happened every day, which apparently it did.

Driving no more than fifteen miles an hour, Frank negotiated one hairpin turn after another. The scenery, he was told, was spectacular—deep valleys, breathtaking waterfalls, the thunderous waterspout of the Nākālele Blowhole—but Frank kept his eyes fixed on the zigzagging road ahead.

He was relieved when the road descended to sea level again and they saw a sign: KAHAKULOA. The car bumped along a dirt road leading to an idyllic little village on the pebbled shores of a horseshoe bay. Amid groves of coconut palms and monkeypod trees were a scattering of modest, tin-roofed homes. Neatly trimmed lawns carpeted the town from road to sea. There was a New England-style church painted a Hawaiian green with red roof and white trim, a schoolhouse, grazing cows, and an occasional horse crossing the road.

Majestic green hills sheltered the bay, in particular the six-hundred-foot Pu'u Koa'e—Kahakuloa Head—standing like the tip of a spear on the south side of the bay. "King Kahekili lived here," Rachel said, "and legends say he dove from the top of Pu'u Koa'e just to prove his courage. He was also said to have built houses out of the skulls of his enemies."

"Tell me your friend does not live in one of those," Ruth said.

Rachel laughed. "No. And if it makes you feel better, this also used to be a sacred place—a *pu'uhonua*, or 'place of refuge,' where those who violated a *kapu* could find sanctuary and be absolved by the gods of their crime."

Frank parked near a fruit stand tended by a young girl, no more than ten. *"Aloha,"* she greeted them, "you like buy papaya? Mango? *Liliko'i?"*

Rachel got out of the car, opened her purse, and said, "We get all t'ree, okay? Keep da change." She handed the girl a five-dollar bill, and the eyes nearly came out of the girl's head.

"Honest kine?" When Rachel nodded, the girl ran behind her stand and scooped up three, then four, then five pieces of fruit as she saw how many visitors were emerging from the car. She politely handed one to each of the Haradas, who thanked her.

"'Ey, *keiki*, you know Old George?" Rachel asked.

"Yeah, sure."

"You go get him for us?"

"Sure!" She was off like a shot.

Minutes later, a tall Hawaiian man in his sixties, with chestnut-brown skin and a white fringe of hair, came down out of the valley. The little fruit girl straggled behind, still eagerly clutching her five-dollar bill. The man embraced Rachel in a big bear hug. "Rachel! Been too long!"

"I've missed you too, George," Rachel said warmly. "I've brought my family from California to meet you—my daughter, Ruth, her husband, Frank, and my *mo'opuna*, Don and Peggy.

"This is George Nua. He's the grandson of my Auntie Haleola."

They were all dumbstruck as George pumped their hands and told them how pleased he was to meet Rachel's *'ohana*. Ruth finally found her voice: "The feeling is mutual, George. We've heard so much about your grandmother that we think of her as part of our *'ohana* too."

"*Mahalo.* Come on up to the house, anybody want something to drink?"

"Do you have a—*drink* drink, George?" Frank asked.

"Got some home-brewed sweet potato beer. It's warm, though—we got no electricity in the valley."

"Warm beer is still beer," Frank said with a smile.

George laughed. "Funny how the Kahekili Highway makes everybody who drives it thirsty."

He led them up a dirt path and into the valley, which felt even more like stepping back in time. Serpentine paths wound their way through lush foliage—coconut palms, tree ferns, tall ti leaf plants, explosions of red torch ginger, thick groves of banana, mango, plum, and papaya trees. The air was sweet and fruity. Behind a stand of trees, a stream babbled to itself in the language of water spoken since before life began. Irrigation channels diverted water to terraced taro patches. There were homes up here too, even a few *pili*-grass houses, possibly abandoned. George led them toward his own one-story house, painted sky blue, its tin roof gleaming in the afternoon sun.

Inside it was comfortable and homey, with hand-crafted furniture made from local woods, and a small kitchen. George opened a cabinet and took out a bottle of unlabeled beer, popped the cap, and handed it to Frank, who promptly knocked back half the bottle.

"Delicious," he said. "*Mahalo.*"

"If you think the trip from Lahaina's bad," George said, "try coming from Wailuku—that one's a three-beer drive." Frank laughed as George provided drinks to all of his guests.

"Didn't your family—Haleola's—come from Lahaina?" Ruth asked.

"Oh, yeah, long time ago," George said, sitting down with a beer. "Grandpa Keo owned a general store on Front Street. They had three sons—Lono, Kana, and Liko—all almost grown when Keo and Haleola got sent to Moloka'i. My dad, Liko, was the youngest. Lono and Kana liked running the store, but Pop, eh, he had no head for business. And he hated the drunken *haole* sailors who tore up Lahaina Town when they made port. Back then there was plenty of sugarcane and cattle raised here at Kahakuloa. Pop sold out his share of the store, bought a homestead, moved his *'ohana* here. We've been here ever since; my sons live in the village. Most everybody here—like the Kauha'aha'a, Kekona, Keawe families—have been in Kahakuloa for generations."

"Did you ever meet your grandmother, George?" Peggy asked.

"No, but my dad told me about her—family stories, how she was a *kahuna lapa'au*, a healer, at Lahaina—and when Rachel found us, she opened up the rest of my *tūtū*'s life to us."

George hesitated a moment.

"I never met Haleola," he said slowly, "but I did feel her presence once. When I was sixteen. My dad was teaching me carpentry, my hold on the saw slipped, I cut my left arm." He held up his arm to show a nasty scar snaking from wrist to elbow. "It was a deep cut—I lost a lot of blood. My mom stitched me up with needle and thread—true story. But for a couple of days I was tired and weak.

"I slept a lot. First time I woke up, I saw this bird sitting in the window of my room. Small bird, bright red feathers, dark wings, like nothing I ever saw before. It just sat there, till I fell asleep again—but every time I woke up, there it was again! Then, once I was better, it never came back.

"When I told Mama, she asked me to describe it. I told her it was about five inches long, small beak, and made a funny chipping sound, like chopping wood. Mama was surprised. She told me, 'That's a *kākāwahie*. Their feathers were used to make cloaks for the *ali'i*, so they became very rare. They don't live on Maui. There's only one island where you find them: Moloka'i.'"

Ruth got "chicken skin," the Hawaiian term for goosebumps floating up out of a dim corner of her forgotten childhood.

"My mother believed—like I do—that the bird was an 'aumakua. The spirit of my tūtū, Haleola, watching over me when I needed her."

Don and Peggy looked dubious; the doubt was written even more plainly on Frank's face. Rachel saw this and said, "Haleola once told me that Hawaiians live in two worlds. Life and death are not so neatly defined for us."

"Especially in this valley," George said. "Because this was a place of refuge, the huaka'i pō—night marchers—dwell here. Spirits of ancient warriors who walk the trails, sworn to protect the ali'i in this life or after."

"Warriors?" Frank repeated skeptically. "Have you ever . . . seen them?"

"I've seen their torches in the distance, heard the sound of their drums, the blowing of a conch shell. It's said they float a few inches above the ground, but I wouldn't know. To get closer is to risk death—if any of the marchers see you, you're make, dead, and you walk with them for all time."

"I know how these stories sound to anyone who hasn't grown up in the islands," Rachel said. "But this is far from the only place in Hawai'i where the marchers of the night have been seen or heard."

"Every once in a while some fool builds a house on a night marcher trail," George said. "Last one woke up in the middle of the night, his house shaking like an earthquake. Wood and stone won't stop the huaka'i pō, it just pisses them off. His crops died, his wife left him . . . he got the hint and moved."

Frank remained unpersuaded.

"Whether you believe or not," Rachel said, "this is part of who we are as Hawaiians." She told George, "Ruth wants to know what it means to be Hawaiian. I couldn't think of a better place to show her than Kahakuloa."

"And now they think you've brought 'em to the home of a crazy man! Lolo George!" He laughed good-naturedly. "Ruth, the most important thing I can tell you is what my parents taught me: Aloha means to see the 'uhane— the living spirit, immortal soul, whatever you call it—in everyone you meet. I've done my best to live up to that."

He stood. "C'mon. Let me show you how we live here."

* * *

eorge guided them up the slopes past flourishing vegetable gardens and taro patches. "This is what our people have done for two thousand years," he told Ruth. "Our ancestors came in canoes across thousands of miles of ocean to these beautiful islands, our Hawai'i Nei. They grew taro and pounded it into the *poi* that sustains us. Rachel, you okay with a little more walking?"

"It'll take more than this to put me in the ground, George."

"That's my auntie! Everybody follow me."

Rachel marveled at the thought: Haleola was my auntie, and now I'm her grandson's auntie. It felt right, it felt *pono*. George continued:

"There's an old saying: *Make no ke kalo a ola i ka palili.* 'The old taro stalks are dead but survive in the offspring.' Meaning we have a *kuleana*, a responsibility, to keep the taro alive as our ancestors did for us.

"Kahakuloa gets its name from a taro patch that grew here centuries ago. That's how important taro is to us."

George pointed into the interior of the valley, six miles deep, where a procession of green hills receded into the misty distance.

"Way up there's a waterfall that feeds this stream," he told them. "See how far back the valley goes? Now turn around and look out to sea."

His guests did as they were told. Ruth was struck by the peace and tranquility of this little time-lost valley; all she heard was the sound of water flowing over stones, the trilling of birds, and the distant lapping of waves on the beach, as she might have heard a hundred years ago.

"In the old days," George said, "this was called an *ahupua'a*: a pie-slice of land stretching from the mountains to the sea. That pie-slice provided a family with everything they needed to live: water; earth to grow taro and other food; and the ocean, to fish from. We repaid that debt with *aloha. Aloha 'āina*—that means to be devoted to the land, to nurture it."

Don quoted, "'The land is the chief, man is its servant.'"

George smiled. "That's right. Nurture the land and the land nurtures you. Your *tūtū* tell you that?"

Don nodded. "It's why I do what I do today. I'm an oceanographer. I study—learn from—try to preserve—the oceans."

"And that's one big part of what being Hawaiian means," George said.

"'*Ohana* is another part," Rachel said, "and Ruth, you have the strongest sense of '*ohana* of anyone I know. Maybe because you so longed for one when you were little. I wish that could have been otherwise. But it's shaped you into a loving daughter, a loyal sister, and a wonderful mother.

"And in your love for animals, you see the living spirit in *all* the creatures of the *'āina*. It's what I most love about you."

Ruth was touched beyond words.

"And Peggy," Rachel said, turning to her granddaughter, "*your* love for animals has led you to become a healer, like Haleola. I know that somewhere she's as proud of you as I am."

There were tears in Peggy's eyes.

Don went to Rachel, wrapped his arms around her, and said, "I love you, *tūtū*. We all do. *Mahalo* for everything you've given us."

"It's just a fraction of what you've given me, *mo'opuna*."

"I like your *'ohana*, Rachel," George said, smiling. He turned to Frank. "Frank—it gets dark way early here, and trust me, you don't want to drive that road to Wailuku at night. Stay for supper—I'll have my sons and their *'ohana* come up from the village, we'll talk story about Haleola, you can stay the night and get a fresh start tomorrow morning."

Frank didn't hesitate in speaking for his family. "We'd be honored."

It was a glorious night: George's sons and their wives put together a feast of grilled *ono*, vegetables, *poi*, fish *poke*, and more. One son brought a guitar and strummed beautiful Hawaiian *mele*s. Rachel spoke devotedly of Haleola and the love she had lavished on a little girl cast up on the lonely shores of Kalaupapa. George spoke to Ruth about their people's history, loss of sovereignty, and traditions sacred to Hawaiians, as Don and Peggy raptly listened along with her. When the Haradas at last retired to their bedrooms it began to rain outside, and Ruth drifted asleep to the comforting staccato of raindrops on the tin roof.

Sometime during the night, a sound awoke her. At first she thought it was raining harder, because the *plink-plink-plink* on the tin roof was now sounding more like the beating of a kettle drum. She sat up—Frank was fast asleep after a long day—and glanced out the window.

With a shiver Ruth realized that the drumming was not coming from the roof but from farther away. The percussion was distant but distinct, with an irregular rhythm she intuitively knew was made by human hands.

Or perhaps . . . not quite human?

"Mom?"

Peggy, lying on thick quilting on the floor, spoke but made no move to get up. "I hear it too," she whispered. "Should we go to the window?"

Ruth listened to the distant beating of drums but did not move. "You first," she whispered back.

"Hell no. You know how much I hated being in a marching band."

They lay there, suspended in the magic and mystery of the moment, until the drumbeats faded at last into the deep recesses of the valley.

Ruth was beginning to suspect that there might be more to the universe than any one religion could explain.

"*Never* tell your father about this," she whispered. "He'd think we're *lolo*."

Peggy smiled and closed her eyes.

Ruth lay back, listening to a silence more eloquent than words, feeling connected to the *'āina* of her birth in a way she could never have imagined.

Chapter 21

1969–1970

At eighty-three, Rachel had expected to live with some aches and pains. But she had not anticipated the constant discomfort—muscle cramps, aching joints—that kept slumber at bay despite the sleeping pills her doctor had prescribed. She woke today before dawn after only a few hours of sleep, feeling like a bell that had been rung all night long. These were the kind of pains she had experienced twenty-three years before, when she had lain abed at Kalaupapa, dying of Hansen's disease—until miraculously she was granted a reprieve by the sulfa drugs that reversed her condition and reduced the bacilli to noncontagious levels. But it was not Hansen's that was inflicting these pains on her now; it was the very thing that had saved her life and granted her freedom.

As it turned out, there was a high price to be paid for that freedom.

She lay in bed a moment, dreading what would be required of her today. She glanced over at Sarah's bed, where her sister still slept soundly.

Quietly Rachel got up and padded into the kitchen. She put on a pot of coffee—her only defense against the fatigue that ruthlessly stalked her each day. Everything she ate had a metallic taste to it now, and her stomach was easily upset. She set about making Sarah's breakfast: bacon, eggs, and toast. Cooking it was torture, especially the smell of bacon sizzling in the pan, but she had to restrict her protein consumption as well.

She slid the bacon and eggs onto a plate beside the toast and took it into the bedroom.

"Sarah? Time to wake up. Breakfast."

Sarah's eyes opened. "Oh." She pulled herself up to a sitting position as Rachel placed a tray in her lap. "But I'm not hungry."

"You need to eat. You're going on a trip today. To see Ellie."

"I am?"

"I'll be back in a few minutes to get you washed and dressed."

Sarah thought a moment and asked, "Why?"

"Because you're going on a trip."

"No—why do you *do* all this for me?" Sarah asked, a fog in her eyes. "I don't even know you. Who are you?"

The question wounded Rachel as deeply as ever. But she answered it the same way she had for the past year: "Someone who loves you very much."

That made Sarah smile, as it always did.

For Rachel, getting dressed had never been easy with only one functional hand, but now the fingers of her left hand, her good hand, were plagued with a tingly numbness not unlike the neuritis of Hansen's itself. This, too, was part of the price she had to pay. An hour later, Ellie—Sarah's oldest daughter, who was sixty-two—arrived. Rachel met her at the curb. Her pretty, scarcely lined face broke into a smile. "Hi, Auntie." She greeted Rachel with a hug. "Is Mom ready?"

"Yes, though I'm not sure she understands what's happening."

"It doesn't matter. She loves Makawao, she'll be happy there. I'll do my best to take as good care of her as you have."

"I know you will." Rachel's voice grew soft. "But I'll miss her."

"Auntie, the offer is still good for you too. With the *keiki* gone, we have two extra bedrooms. You're welcome to join us."

"Thank you," Rachel said, touched. "But I'll get by. I appreciate your letting me stay here in the house as long as I need to."

"That's no problem at all. How are you feeling?"

"Like I've gone four rounds with Muhammad Ali," Rachel quipped. "But that's better than yesterday, when I felt like I'd gone five rounds."

Ellie laughed.

Ellie packed her mother's bags and placed them in the car. Before Sarah herself got in, Rachel hugged her sister, kissed her on the cheek, and said, "I'll see you soon, Sarah. I'll come upcountry for a visit when I get back from Christmas in California. I love you very much."

Sarah smiled, her eyes showing not a glimmer of recognition. But she said, "I love you too," as if she remembered the shape of love, if not its face.

As soon as they were out of sight, Rachel finally allowed herself to weep.

uth sensed from the moment that Rachel walked through Gate 7 at San Francisco International Airport that something was—off— with her *makuahine*. She had never seen Rachel looking so weary after a flight to California; usually she couldn't contain her excitement. But she was, Ruth reminded herself, eighty-three years old, and more than entitled to feel exhausted after six hours of flying.

As soon as Rachel caught sight of Ruth, her face brightened.

"Welcome back, Mother," Ruth said, embracing her. She said the word easily now; after twenty-one years, she was able to accept the fact that she had two mothers and that loving one was not a betrayal of the other.

Ruth noted a slight puffiness in Rachel's cheeks. "Long flight?"

Rachel gladly let her take her carry-on. "Yes, very. But how is Frank?"

The week before, Frank had been in a traffic accident coming home from work. His car was T-boned on the passenger side with enough force that it slammed the side of his head into the driver's-side window. The glass didn't shatter, but the impact perforated his left eardrum.

"He's recovering, thanks," Ruth said as they headed for baggage claim. "The doctor thinks the eardrum might heal on its own in a few weeks, so he's keeping an eye on it for now. If not Frank might need surgery to repair it."

"But he wasn't otherwise hurt?"

"A few bruises on his face. He tells people I beat him." Rachel laughed at that. "The new Pontiac fared worse, it's in the shop." More soberly she said, "How are you coping on your own? Without Sarah?"

"I miss her. But I'll—what's that word Etsuko told me?—*gaman*."

At home Frank greeted her warmly, the side of his face swollen and purpled, his ear bandaged to prevent infection. "The doctors say I need to take things easy," he said, "so it's going to be a quiet Christmas."

That was fine with Rachel, who was more fatigued than she tried to let on. At dinner she ate sparingly and took only a few bites of the *ono*, delicious, roast beef Ruth had cooked for everyone but herself. "I'm a little nauseous from the flight," Rachel explained, though the flight had nothing to do with it.

Ruth didn't give this another thought, but the next morning, when her *makuahine* awoke looking just as tired as the day before, she began to worry. "Did you not get a good night's sleep?" Ruth asked.

"Oh, I find the older I get, the less I sleep."

Despite her fatigue, Rachel found the holiday delightful. She spent time with Ralph and his family, with Horace and Stanley and their large broods, and most important with Don and Peggy. Peggy was now married to a fellow vet, David Tanaka, though both were too busy with their veterinary practices to start a family yet. Don—who was quick to tell his *tūtū* about an upcoming trip to study coral reefs in the Maldives—had married Trish, and Rachel was introduced to their seven-month-old son, Charles Kenji Harada. Rachel was immensely moved by their gesture and held the infant tenderly in her arms, tears in her eyes, thankful and amazed that she had lived long enough to be holding her *great*-grandson.

With Frank under orders to rest, Ruth was kept busy handling the cooking, but even in the midst of the holiday chaos she began to notice things that rekindled her concern for Rachel:

Her mother seemed never to eat very much, and had a different excuse for it each time. The puffiness in her face did not go away after the airplane flight, nor did the exhaustion Ruth glimpsed every day in her eyes. Several times Ruth caught her rubbing her back as if it pained her, but her mother had never exhibited any back problems before.

On Monday morning, as Rachel sat in the living room with Frank, watching television, Ruth went into Rachel's bathroom with a scrub brush, sponge, and a can of Comet, intending to scrub the sink and counter—but quickly forgot both when she looked into the toilet bowl.

The toilet had been flushed but, to Ruth's horror, she saw a spattering of blood-red droplets freckling the face of the water.

*F*rank went to take a nap, and once Ruth was alone with Rachel, she sat down next to her on the living room couch and said, her tone solemn as a prayer: "Mother, please be honest with me. What's *wrong* with you?"

"What do you mean?"

"There's blood in your toilet bowl."

Rachel winced. How had she missed that? She didn't want to admit the truth, but the fear in her daughter's eyes shamed her into confessing.

"My . . . kidneys are failing. It's a side effect of the sulfa drugs they give us to treat Hansen's disease. I'm sorry I kept it from you, but . . . it didn't seem an appropriate subject for the holidays."

Ruth was shocked, but not yet alarmed.

"So if you stop taking the drugs," she asked hopefully, "will it get better?"

"I'm . . . afraid not," Rachel said, and saw the fear this sparked in her daughter's eyes. "My doctor says my kidney function is down to eighteen percent. One kidney has stopped working altogether. At fifteen percent you enter what they call end-stage renal failure."

"But—they can *do* something, can't they?" Ruth asked, desperation creeping into her voice. "What about this new treatment—dialysis?"

Rachel sighed. This was just as hard as she thought it would be.

"The doctors say it's not practical yet for end-stage kidney failure," she told Ruth. "And frankly that's just as well. I wouldn't want to spend eight to ten hours a day, every other day, lying in bed, having my blood filtered through a machine."

Ruth hadn't felt this kind of fear and helplessness since the day her *okāsan* had had her heart attack. "There must be *something* they can do!"

Rachel shook her head. "All they can do is treat the symptoms. I take a diuretic for high blood pressure, an iron supplement for anemia. And I have

to watch my diet. Even so, I . . . probably have only about two months before I reach the last stage."

Ruth could barely get out the words: "And . . . and how long before . . ."

"Anywhere between two months to a year," Rachel said stoically.

Ruth's mind was a welter of shock, grief, denial, anger.

"How the hell can you be so *calm* about it?" she demanded. "You sound
like you've given up, like you won't even put up a fight!"

"I won't win this fight, Ruth. I can put it off, but in the end I'll lose."

"No!" Ruth cried, as if through sheer force of will she could command
fate, reverse time. "You've *got* to fight it!"

Rachel heard the anguish in her daughter's voice and put a reassuring
hand on her arm.

"Ruth—don't you see?" she said softly. "The last twenty-three years
have been . . . a miracle. In 1946 I was dying, literally dying. I'd made my
peace with God. Then, suddenly, I wasn't dying anymore. I was cured; free.
The sulfa drugs gave me new life, another *chance* at life.

"I left Kalaupapa. I found my sister and my brother on Maui. I found
you. I couldn't be there to play with you as a child, but you allowed me to
play with my grandchildren and to watch them grow up into such fine people,
so *pono*. And on this trip I was blessed to be able to hold my *great*-grandson
in my arms. Can't you see how miraculous that is?"

Tears were streaming down Ruth's cheeks.

"Yes, the sulfa drugs are killing me," Rachel said, "but without them, I
would never have known the love of my only child."

She embraced Ruth and they sat holding each other until Ruth pulled
back, wiped away her tears, and said, "All right—however long you have,
we can spend it together. Ellie can pack up your things, ship them here to—"

Oh God, Rachel thought. This *is* hard.

"Ruth," she said sadly, "I can't stay here."

"What?" Ruth was incredulous. "Of course you can. We have some of
the finest doctors in California in San Jose, you'll receive the best of care—"

Rachel just shook her head again.

"You watched one mother die a slow, terrible death," she said gently. "I
won't let you watch another one die the same way."

Ruth protested, "But it's not about *me*, I—I want to take care of you!"

"It *is* about you. For me it is."

Ruth's anger was spent, but her need was still great.

"Mother, let me do *something* for you," Ruth implored. "Please."

Rachel understood. She had felt the same way after Haleola's death. She had anticipated that her daughter, so much like her in many ways, might feel the same need. "There *is* something you can do for me, Ruth."

"What is it? Anything."

In her bedroom, Rachel opened her purse, took out an envelope, and handed it to Ruth.

"If you feel comfortable doing it," Rachel said, "I would be honored to have you speak the same words for me that I said for Haleola at her funeral."

Ruth tried not to start crying again. "The—honor would be mine."

"Thank you. And I'm sorry I didn't tell you the truth sooner."

When Frank awoke from his nap, Rachel also told him; she was moved by the tears it brought to his eyes.

Now that there was no longer any need for Rachel to hide her condition, Ruth saw its effects up close. She had never seen her *makuahine* looking so frail, so vulnerable, but as she had been for her *okāsan*, Ruth was there for Rachel: she kept her company through sleepless nights, massaged the cramps in her legs, and helped her to the bathroom when she got nauseous. There was a tenderness of spirit between them now, a new appreciation of the quickening moments they shared, that drew them closer than ever before. Ruth would cherish that closeness for the rest of her life.

Frank called Don and Peggy, suggesting they come say goodbye to their *tūtū* for the last time. Don, who had flown back to San Diego after Christmas, flew right back to San Jose. Peggy drove down from Modesto. Rachel was happy to spend just a little more time with them.

And while they were visiting with their Grandma Rachel—reminiscing about the games she had played with them when they were little, their trips to Hawai'i, Christmases past—Ruth slipped quietly out of the house to make a special request at Onishi's Florist Shop.

In the airport, on the day of Rachel's return flight to Hawai'i, the whole family was at the gate to see her off. After Don, Peggy, and Frank had each embraced Rachel in turn, Ruth surprised her mother by reaching into her tote bag and pulling out a pink carnation *lei* that she now draped around her mother's neck.

"These last twenty-three years have been a miracle for me too," she told her. *"Ā hui hou aku, Makuahine."*

Until we meet again.

Rachel's eyes filled with tears. *"Ā hui hou aku—akachan."*

The mix of Hawaiian and Japanese pleased Ruth, made her smile. She gave her mother one last hug—and then she had to let her go.

R achel returned to Maui and to the house without Sarah, not having told the full truth to her daughter. She had not told her that her doctor had advised her against making this trip, fearing it might be too much of a strain on her already weakened immune system. Nor had she told Ruth that her doctor had also advised, six months ago, that Rachel stop taking the sulfa drugs to reduce the damage they were doing to her kidneys—but Rachel had refused, not willing to take the slightest risk of infecting her family, most especially the great-grandson she was determined to see.

Now Rachel was ready to pay her debt. Her body was leaden with fatigue and she spent many of her days too weak to get out of bed. Ellie stocked her refrigerator with prepared meals, but it was a struggle just to get up and eat them. Her face and legs grew more swollen with edema; a bloated imposter seemed to be staring at her out of her mirror. One day she began to have difficulty breathing and had to call for an ambulance to take her to Maui Memorial Hospital in Kahului, where they drained the fluid that had also been building up in her lungs.

On that day she knew she could no longer care for herself. So as she had always planned, she called Kalaupapa and told them she was coming home.

Ellie came over to pack up Rachel's belongings for her, arranging to send them on to Moloka'i by freight, then drove her auntie to the airport. "Tell your mother," Rachel said to Ellie, "that someone will always love her."

"I will, Auntie," she said. "I love you. Godspeed."

A charter flight took Rachel to Kalaupapa, where she was promptly admitted to the hospital. The resident physician, Dr. Sylvia Haven, prescribed her a sedative that gave Rachel her first good night's sleep in months.

Her old friend Hokea came by the next day to visit and reminisce; it was good to see him again, he always made her laugh. She barely noticed the ravages that Hansen's had wrought on his face. "Rachel, you remember what I used to say about Father Damien's church at Kalawao?"

"I remember you did about a million paintings of it, all beautiful."

Hokea chuckled. "Maybe million and a half. But you remember what I used to say about it? How it had strength and *maluhia*?"

Serenity. Rachel nodded.

"Well, so do you."

Their hands were similarly deformed, but Rachel now rested hers atop his, like two gnarled branches entwined by time and fate.

"Thank you, old friend," she said. "I do feel at peace here."

"No more *kapu* here either. Everybody's free to come and go as they please." He grinned. "So, you like go Vegas and try our luck at keno?"

He always made her laugh.

Rachel spoke by phone with Ruth often in subsequent weeks, but the calendar soon became a jumble of meaningless numbers; the morphine Rachel was prescribed for her worsening pain made the days pass in a painless dream, hazy as a morning mist.

Early on, Hokea had brought over some belongings that Rachel wanted by her bedside, and he agreed to keep the rest in his house. On a shelf above her nightstand—like the old orange-crate shelf in her bedroom as a child—was part of her doll collection, which had mushroomed over the years. From her bed she could see the little cloth *wahine* in her *kapa* skirt that her father had made for her when she was first sent to Kalaupapa, the cherry doll he had brought her from Japan, and the rag baby from San Francisco. Joining these were some from Rachel's own travels: a stuffed koala bear from Australia; a Brazilian *bahia* doll; and a little dancing boy in a *kiri'au* skirt, from Rarotonga.

She smiled. They reminded her that she had, after all, visited those places she had dreamed of seeing as a child, the far-flung ports of her father's sea tales. And more: She had known the love of the best man she had ever met, and would soon return to him. She had been sent to Kalaupapa by people who had expected her to die, and die quickly. But she had lived a long, rich life . . . and would leave it with nothing left unsaid, nothing left undone.

A breeze toyed with the curtains of an open window. She smelled the sweet fragrance of the red *lehua* flowers that grew on the nearby *pali*. She closed her eyes. Soon she would embark on her greatest journey, across an ocean of night to another far port, where her father had already dropped anchor—and where Kenji was waiting for her.

henever the phone rang that day, Ruth had answered it with dread calm, knowing of her mother's worsening condition. When it rang late that evening, as Ruth and Frank were drifting off to sleep, Ruth knew: she just knew. It was, as expected, Dr. Haven at Kalaupapa, gently informing her that Rachel had just passed away, peacefully, in her sleep. Ruth told her, with as much composure as she could summon, that she would be on Moloka'i as soon as she could book a flight. She hung up the phone, her hands trembling.

Frank said, "I really wish I could go with you."

"I know. But you can't risk flying so soon after your ear surgery. And Don is in the Maldives, he'll be sick that he couldn't go."

"Call Peggy."

She did, and Peggy immediately agreed to accompany her mother to Kalaupapa.

"Thank you," Ruth said. "It means a lot to me."

"I loved her too," Peggy said.

Ruth hung up and took a long, shaky breath. Frank came up behind her, put his hands on her shoulders. "You okay?"

She nodded, taking strength from his touch. Then she went to the dresser, opened a drawer, and took out the envelope Rachel had given her. Inside was a piece of brittle old writing paper filled with careful penmanship—written when Rachel was still a young woman, before the disease robbed her of her right hand—and Ruth read aloud the first line in halting Hawaiian:

"Lawa, Pualani, 'eia mai kou kaikamahine, Haleola . . ."

Ruth continued, paraphrasing:

"Henry, Dorothy, 'eia mai kou kaikamahine, Rachel . . ."

Tears fell from her eyes, but she continued to read. She would get through this. She owed that much—and so much more—to her mother.

Epilogue

There were 155 residents living, by their own choice, at Kalaupapa, and nearly all of them were now gathered around an open grave in the Japanese cemetery along the coast. It was a bright, clear day, the tradewinds brisk, the surf lapping up nearby Papaloa Beach, where, Ruth knew, her mother had spent many happy hours riding the waves. It truly was beautiful here, and yet the green *pali* was just as forbidding as the Sierra Nevada, and this necklace of cemeteries along the coastline—like a *lei* strung not with flowers but with gravestones—was an abiding reminder of Kalaupapa's tragic past. She stood beside Peggy as they listened to a Buddhist priest chant a *sūtra* and, toward the end of the ceremony, when the time came for eulogies, of which there were many, Ruth chose to speak last. She was more nervous than she let on as she stepped forward to address the crowd.

"My mother Rachel was a remarkable woman," she told them, her voice quaking a bit, "but you've all known that even longer than I. I've been privileged, these past twenty years, to discover just how remarkable. I'm lucky, you see: I had two mothers. One gave life to me; one raised me. But they both loved me. You know, some people don't even get that once."

She smiled as she recalled, "It took me a while to say the words 'I love you' to my *makuahine*. It was a different kind of love than I felt for my *okāsan*, but founded on the same things. I cherished my adoptive parents for the home, the love, and the past we shared. I cherished Rachel for the love she showed me, the past she opened up to me, and the home I never knew: this place. The people she cared for. All of you.

"There's only one disadvantage, really, to having two mothers. You know twice the love . . . but you grieve twice as much."

She took out the old slip of writing paper and glanced down into her mother's casket. Death had mercifully drained the fluids from Rachel's face and, though scored by time, it appeared as beautiful as ever to Ruth. She began to read:

"Pono, Haleola, 'eia mai kou keiki hanauna, Rachel!"

Some of the mourners were puzzled, but one old-timer recognized the words and repeated the call to ancestors: *"Pono, Haleola,"* he said, his aged treble sounding quite clear and strong, *"'eia mai kou keiki hanauna, Rachel!"*

Now Peggy spoke, her voice as resonant and proud as her mother's: *"Henry, Dorothy, 'eia mai kou kaikamahine, Rachel!* Henry, Dorothy, here is your daughter, Rachel!"

A few more mourners picked up the chant, some in Hawaiian and some in English.

"Kenji-san, 'eia mai kou wahine male, Rachel," Ruth said. "Kenji, here is your wife, Rachel." She struggled with the next words: "O Rachel, here you are departing! *Aloha wale, e Rachel, kaua, auwē!* Boundless love, O Rachel, between us, alas!"

As the mourners repeated that last word, Ruth heard for the first time the resonant Hawaiian wail of *"Auwē! Auwē!"*—"Alas, alas!"—which sprang from every heart at once.

Peggy handed Ruth a small dish of *poi*, the dress Rachel had worn on the day they met at the Hotel Saint Claire, and the cloth doll in its *kapa* skirt that Henry Kalama had made for his little girl seventy-six years ago. Ruth tucked them all in the casket beside her mother.

"Here is food, clothing, and something you loved," she said. "Go; but if you have a mind to return, come back."

She leaned over her mother, tenderly kissed her forehead as she had Etsuko's, and told her again that she loved her. Peggy did the same, bidding *aloha* to her Grandma Rachel before she was overcome by tears. The casket was closed and lowered; within twenty minutes an earthen blanket had covered it, and Rachel Aouli Kalama Utagawa slept again beside her beloved Kenji.

After thanking each guest individually for coming and listening to their fond memories of both Rachel and Kenji, Ruth and Peggy spent a few private minutes at their graves and then on the beach, sitting and gazing out to sea. Earlier that day, their escort, Hokea, had given them a tour of the settlement, but now Ruth realized that there was still one place at Kalaupapa she wanted to see.

Hokea led them to an empty, closed-up cottage, its chipped paint bleached by the sun, on Goodhue Street. "Your mama shared this with her friend Leilani at first," he said, taking them up the steps to the front porch. "After Leilani died, Rachel lived here alone until she met your papa, and after they married they lived here together."

They entered a large front room with three windows. It was musty and layered in dust, but Ruth could imagine it once being charming and cozy.

"This was originally a two-bedroom cottage," Hokea explained, "but Rachel and Kenji made the second bedroom into their living room. It was remodeled in 1930 after Lawrence Judd became governor and poured a lotta money into modernizing and renovating the settlement. He really cared about us."

Ruth glanced into the kitchen, which led into the bedroom, which also had three windows. She tried to imagine the bed that had once been there, the curtains on the windows, the dresser where Rachel said she had placed Ruth's annual birthday gifts—and what happened here on a day a little more than fifty-four years ago.

"This is where I was born," Ruth said in wonderment. "Right here. In the middle of the night. Mother told me how the midwife delivered me and how they had only a few precious hours alone with me before they had to hand me over to the settlement nursery."

Ruth stood there, trying to absorb all the detail she could, filling a hole in her life with images of Rachel and Kenji on that night, holding and loving their only child in these brief, stolen moments. She could almost see their faces looking down at her, smiling, as dawn's light sifted between drawn curtains, heralding the end of their time with her.

Finally she said, "This is all I wanted to see. *Mahalo*, Hokea."

Back at the visitors' quarters, Ruth and Peggy went through a pile of documents, photographs, and letters that Rachel had kept over the decades. On top was a letter in familiar handwriting: the one Etsuko had written to Sister Mary Louisa, assuring her that Ruth and her new family were all comfortably settled in Florin. She smiled to see her *okāsan*'s careful signature and, below that, their old address in Florin. But there was another address, at the head of the letter, which piqued Ruth's interest even more:

> *Sister Mary Louisa Hughes*
> *The Kapiolani Home for Girls*
> *1650 Meyers Street*
> *Honolulu, T.H.*

Ruth put the letter in her purse and asked Peggy, "Do you mind flying back to San Francisco on your own? I just realized I have some business to attend to in Honolulu. I'll catch a later flight back."

"Well . . . sure," Peggy said. "What kind of business?"

"Unfinished."

Honolulu had grown considerably since Ruth's first visit here in 1954, but the traffic was still a breeze compared to driving into San Francisco at rush hour. She drove her rental car east on Nimitz Highway to H-1, getting off at Middle Street. She pulled over, studied her AAA map, then continued on Middle Street, passing through quiet residential neighborhoods as she turned left onto Rose Street and then right onto Meyers Street.

Meyers Street ascended a steep hill and ended in a loop; on the outside of that loop was a ring of modest single-family homes and, on the inside, an "island" of more homes and a few apartment houses. All were lushly landscaped with green hedges, fan palms, banana plants, and purple bougainvillea.

Ruth parked along the curb. On the *mauka* side of the street were actual mountains, the leeward slopes of the Ko'olau Range. The Kalihi Valley was a wedge of green above a circle of mostly concrete and asphalt. She walked the circumference of the loop, searching for some vestiges of an orphanage, but saw nothing but residences. She stopped beside a parking lot and looked out at the city sprawling west to Diamond Head.

"Can I help you, ma'am?"

She turned to see a Hawaiian man looking curiously at her.

"Aloha." She smiled and extended a hand as she approached him. "My name is Ruth Harada. When I was a little girl, I lived in an orphanage that used to be here—the Kapi'olani Home for Girls. Have you heard of it?"

"Oh yeah," the man said, shaking her hand, "but didn't it close down a long time ago?"

"Yes, in 1938; all the girls were placed in foster homes. I haven't been here since I was five years old. I'm just looking to see if there's anything left of it. The address was 1650 Meyers Street. Do you know where that is?"

The man glanced up the street. "I think that's up around the bend. C'mon." As they followed the curve of the road, he added, "This whole subdivision was built around 1950. Underneath is all coral stone." They came to one of the apartment buildings on the inner "island." "Okay, that's 1644 . . . 1646 right next to it . . . it's probably on the other side of this building."

When they found it, 1650 was just a number on one of the apartments. Ruth searched for anything that might seem familiar, but . . .

"Doesn't look like there's anything left of it," the man said. "Sorry."

"Well, *mahalo* for helping," Ruth said, disappointed.

"No worries." The man returned to his house as Ruth stood dejectedly on the street. This had been a total waste of time. She headed for her car.

Somewhere a dog barked.

Instinctively, Ruth turned around.

A small black-and-white dog—looked like some kind of terrier mix—stood in the center of the road, barking.

"Hey, little guy," Ruth said. "You live around here?"

She saw no collar on him, but then Ruth was routinely irked by the number of people who didn't tag their dogs.

As she approached the terrier, his barking became more insistent. But as soon as Ruth came within a few feet, the dog suddenly turned tail and ran.

Ruth's heart started racing, she didn't know why.

Nor did she know why she felt the need to run after him—but she did.

"Hey! Stop!" she called. But the terrier just kept galloping down Meyers Street.

Ruth knew she could never catch him, but nevertheless she continued to run. She had no idea why she felt such a sense of urgency, but at this moment catching this dog seemed like the most important thing in the world.

"C'mon, boy! Stop!" She was getting short of breath. "Stop! Stop, buddy! C'mon!"

The distance between them opened up as the dog raced downhill even faster.

"C'mon, boy! Stop! Stop! Only, stop! *Only!*"

The name came out of her in a scream that shocked her so much she lost her footing—and fell.

She sprawled, face forward, breaking her fall with her hands. The scrape of the asphalt as it skinned her hands made her cry out.

tumbling down the hill, rocks and pebbles raking her skin

She lay in the road, her hands bleeding, but all she could think of was

his light brown fur painted black by the night, the amber circles in his eyes flashing briefly as he turned his head. Ruth listened helplessly to his cries, feeling a grief and sorrow and anger unlike anything she had ever known

Anger. Buried deep. This deep.

Ruth rested her hand on the dog's front legs and closed her eyes, enjoying the softness of his fur, their shared contentment. She wanted to stay like this, warm and loved, forever.

It hadn't been forever. But miraculously, she had him back now—how their chests had touched, the warmth of his body, his heart beating against her, feeling as though their heartbeats were one and the same.

She held that moment in her arms and swore never to let it go again.

"Only," she said softly, like a long-forgotten prayer. *"Only . . ."*

She pushed herself up into a sitting position. She heard someone running toward her, but her attention was fixed on the little black-and-white terrier. He had stopped running, had even come a little closer, and was gazing at her with a dog-smile and what seemed an almost human comprehension.

"Are you all right?"

Ruth turned her head to see a young Chinese American woman standing above her. "Do you need help getting up?"

Ruth turned back to the dog, who was running away again, downhill.

The woman helped Ruth get to her feet. Ruth thanked her.

She looked at Ruth's bruised, bleeding palms, said, "Let me get some Bactine and Band-Aids for those cuts," and hurried back to her house.

Ruth looked down the street. The dog was nowhere to be seen. But that was all right. She smiled because she knew, now, who it was.

The practical, Japanese part of her said it was just a stray dog, or a lost pet. But her Hawaiian half chose to believe it had been her *'aumakua*, Rachel, taking a familiar form to point Ruth where she needed to go—toward the past, and a friend, she had lost.

She tore off a chunk of sandwich and offered it on the palm of her hand. His tongue ladled it up and into his mouth, and Ruth giggled at the pleasant tickle of it on her skin.

She remembers the pain of losing him, but she smiles at the happiness he brought her, cherishing the joy she felt at his side. She even begins to recall the love in the eyes of a woman wearing a nun's white cowl.

She feels a peace that has eluded her all her life. She is Japanese, she is Hawaiian; she is *hapa*, and she is whole.

Author's Note

he Japanese American exclusion and internment—from the declaration of Executive Order No. 9066 on February 19, 1942, to the closure of the last of the main camps on March 20, 1946—spanned barely more than four years. And yet it looms large in America's collective conscience as it does in the memories of those who lived through it and the future generations who were impacted by it. But unlike other cases of injustice—slavery, or our nation's mistreatment of Native Americans—this occurred not centuries in the past but in 1942, by which time we should have known better. President Franklin Roosevelt should have known better. But the same man who gave hope to millions during the Depression and guided the nation through a harrowing world war also enacted one of the greatest civil rights violations in U.S. history—ordering American citizens into concentration camps for no reason other than the color of their skin and the shape of their eyes.

Sadly, it seems, we are never as enlightened, as inoculated from fear and racism, as we might wish we were.

In 1980, the National Coalition for Redress/Reparations (NCRR) was founded by Japanese American citizens from across the country. Among its founding principles were to petition the United States government for monetary and other redress for "each individual who suffered deprivation of liberty" during World War II and to "educate the general public about this tragedy so as to prevent such events from happening again." The NCRR was joined in this fight by the Japanese American Citizens League, the National Council for Japanese American Redress, and members of Congress—white, black, and some, like Senators Daniel Inouye and Spark Matsunaga of Hawai'i, who were themselves of Japanese descent.

Eight years of ultimately successful lobbying led to the passage by Congress of the Civil Liberties Act of 1988, which was signed into law by President Ronald Reagan. The legislation formally apologized on behalf of the people of the United States for the internment, stating that it was based not on legitimate security concerns but on "race prejudice, war hysteria, and a failure of political leadership." A total of 82,264 surviving internees were each paid twenty thousand dollars in compensation, and the Civil Liberties Public Education Fund was established to inform the public about the internment. Five thousand dollars apiece was paid to 645 people of Japanese ancestry who had been living in Latin America when war broke out and whom the United States had forcibly deported from these countries and sent to internment camps in the United States. These Latin Japanese were not released from U.S. custody until February 1948, almost two years after Japanese Americans.

One of those determined NCRR members was Guy Aoki, who would later cofound Media Action Network for Asian Americans (MANAA), which holds Hollywood to account for its casting and portrayal of Asian Americans. Guy, who is a friend of mine, graciously agreed to read my manuscript and vet it for inaccuracies. I am indebted to him for his wide knowledge of Japanese American history and culture, his persistence in confirming every fact, and his keen eye for detail. My thanks, too, to Tomoko Nagata and Marisa Hamamoto, who helped Guy with some of the Japanese-language phrases in this book.

I am equally grateful to National Park Service Rangers Rosemary Masters and Patricia Biggs at the Manzanar National Historic Site. Upon my visit to Manzanar, Rosemary recommended pertinent books, and later she sent me links to rare color photographs of wartime Manzanar and updated texts from the park's exhibits. She also replied to my email follow-up questions, and her colleague Patricia Biggs, who wrote her Ph.D. dissertation on the Manzanar riot, generously answered my questions on the subject.

Any study of Manzanar must begin with the foundational classic *Farewell to Manzanar* by Jeanne Wakatsuki Houston and James D. Houston, but also instructive were *The Evacuation and Relocation of Persons of Japanese Ancestry During World War II: A Historical Study of the Manzanar War Relocation Center* by Harlan D. Unrau; *Photographs of Manzanar* by Ansel Adams; *The Unquiet Nisei: An Oral History of the Life of Sue Kunitomi Embrey* by Diana Meyers Bahr; *Manzanar Martyr: An Interview With Harry Y. Ueno* by Sue Kunitomi Embrey, Arthur A. Hansen, and Betty Kulberg Mitson; *Ganbatte: Sixty-Year Struggle of a Kibei Worker* by Karl G. Yoneda; *Children of Manzanar* by Heather C. Lindquist; *Images of America: Manzanar* by Jane Wehrey; *Desert Exile: The Uprooting of a Japanese American Family* by Yoshiko Uchida; *Nurse of Manzanar* by Samuel Nakamura derived from *My Memories of World War II* by Toshiko Eto Nakamura; "The Manzanar Riot: An Ethnic Perspective" by Arthur A. Hansen and David A. Hacker (*Amerasia Journal*, Vol. 2, No. 2, Fall 1974); "The Problem People" by Jim Marshall (*Collier's*, August 15, 1942); "Resistance, Collaboration, and Manzanar Protest" by Lon Kurashige (*Pacific Historical Review*, Vol. 70, No. 3, August 2001); "A Report on the Manzanar Riot of Sunday, December 6, 1942" by Togo Tanaka (War Relocation Authority document); *Remembering Manzanar: A Documentary* (National Park Service); and the archives of the *Manzanar Free Press* on Calisphere.org.

Details of life at Tanforan Assembly Center were drawn from *The Kikuchi Diary* by Charles Kikuchi, edited by John Modell; *Citizen 13660* by Miné Okubo; *I Call to Remembrance* by Toyo Suyemoto and Susan B. Richardson; *Betrayed Trust* by Motomu Akashi; *The Invisible Thread* by Yoshiko Uchida; and the archives of *The Tanforan Totalizer* at Calisphere.org.

For the history of Tule Lake Relocation/Segregation Center, I looked to *Tule Lake Revisited* by Barbara Takei and Judy Tachibana; *Tule Lake: An Issei Memoir* by Noboru Shirai; *Encyclopedia of Japanese American Internment* edited by Gary Y. Okihiro; and the WRA documents "Tule Lake Incident" by John Bigelow, *Japanese American Evacuation and Resettlement Study, Part II: Period of Army Rule* by Rosalie Hankey, "Tule Lake Incident: Sequence of Events: Sept. 30–Nov. 5, 1943" by Anonymous, and *Semi-Annual Report, July 1 to December 31, 1943* by John D. Cook.

Anti-Japanese prejudice in California is examined in Chris Sager's thesis "American Nativists and Their Confrontation with Japanese Labor and Education in California 1900–1930" (University of North Carolina Wilmington) as well as in *Oriental Exclusion* by R. D. McKenzie; *The Japanese American Problem* and *Japanese in California* by Sidney L. Gulick; and *Prejudice: Japanese Americans: Symbol of Racial Intolerance* by Carey McWilliams. General reference about the internment includes *Born Free and Equal* by Wynne Benti; *Impounded: Dorothea Lange and the Censored Images of Japanese American Internment* edited by Linda Gordon and Gary Y. Okihiro; *America Inquisition: The Hunt for Japanese American Disloyalty in World War II* by Eric L. Muller; *Years of Infamy: The Untold Story of America's Concentration Camps* by Michi Weglyn; *And Justice for All: An Oral History of the Japanese American Detention Camps* by John Tateishi; *Keeper of Concentration Camps* by Richard Drinnon; *Personal Justice Denied, Report of the Commission on Wartime Relocation and Internment of Civilians*; and *Unlikely Liberators: The Men of the 100th and 442nd* by Masayo Umezawa Duus.

Densho.org was an invaluable resource, particularly its interviews with those who experienced the internment firsthand, and I feel it's important to acknowledge their voices: Tokio Yamane (who suffered a brutal beating at the hands of security guards at Tule Lake in Chapter 12), Tamiko Honda, Norman I. Hirose, Grace F. Oshita, Fred Korematsu, Carol Hironaka, Mas Akiyama, Misako Shigekawa, Akiko Kurose, Bob Utsumi, Toru Saito, Jun Dairiki, Taneyuki Dan Harada, Doris Nitta, Hank Shozo Umemoto, and Kaz T. Tanemura.

My thanks to Julie Thomas, Special Collections and Manuscripts Librarian at California State University Sacramento, who provided maps of prewar Florin and helped me navigate the Florin Japanese American Citizens League's Oral History Project, which provided rich detail on the lives of the people of Florin prewar, during internment, and postwar. These voices included Margaret Hatsuko Ogata; Alfred and Mary Tsukamoto; Jerry and Dorothy Enomoto; Myrna, Myrtle, and Teri Tanaka; Masatoshi Abe; Chizu and Ernest Satoshi Iiyama; Hideo Kadokawa; William Matsumoto; George

Miyao; Fudeyo Sekikawa; Onatsu Akiyama; Aya Motoike; Florence Taeko Shiromizu; Eiko Sakamoto; Isao Fujimoto; Toshio Hamataka; Robert and Teresa Fletcher; Donald Larson; and Vivian Kara.

Mary Tsukamoto, mentioned above, has played an even larger role in documenting the history of Florin's Japanese. She is the coauthor with Elizabeth Pinkerton of *We the People: A Story of Internment in America* and author of an autobiographical narrative in *Dignity: Lower Income Women Tell of Their Lives and Struggles* compiled by Fran Leeper Buss. Together they provide a vivid portrait of growing up on a strawberry farm in Florin, evacuation, internment, and return to Florin. I highly recommend both to any interested readers, and to the late Mrs. Tsukamoto I offer my *kansha*—my gratitude and appreciation—for her work.

Other useful sources were *Japanese Legacy* by Timothy J. Lukes and Gary Y. Okihiro; *Changing Dreams and Treasured Memories: A Story of Japanese Americans in the Sacramento Region* by Wayne Maeda; "Florin Is Naturally Adapted to Strawberry Culture" (*Sacramento Union*, January 9, 1909); "Japan in California" by Peter Clark Macfarlane (*Collier's*, June 6, 1913); *New World-Sun Year Book* 1939; "The Strawberry Fields of Florin . . . Remember?" by Elizabeth Pinkerton (*Sacramento Union*, May 28, 1978); "A Brief History of the Florin Area" by Dave Reingold (*Focus Florin*, October 1997); "New Vision for Florin" by Bill Lindelof (*Sacramento Bee*, February 13, 2002); and "Florin Links to Farms Lingers" by Art German (*Sacramento Bee*, July 18, 2002).

My thanks to Amanda G. DeWilde of the Sacramento Room at the Sacramento Public Library and to Barbara Reiswig at the Elk Grove High School Library for allowing me access to the 1933 school yearbook, *The Elk*. Erin Herzog of the San Jose Public Library located Sanborn Insurance Maps of the city for 1948 and recommended books, including *San Jose Japantown: A Journey* by Curt Fukuda and Ralph M. Pearce, which informed my walking tour of the city's *nihonmachi*, one of only a handful still extant.

For details of life at Kapi'olani Home and other Catholic institutions: Janine M. Richardson's "'None of Them Came for Me': The Kapi'olani Home for Girls, 1885–1938" (*Hawaiian Journal of History*, Vol. 42, 2008) and her dissertation, "*Keiki o Ka 'Aina:* Institutional Care for Hawai'i's Dependent Children, 1865–1938" (University of Hawai'i); Hazel Myoko Ikenega's thesis, "A Study of the Care of Children Under the Jurisdiction of the Territorial Board of Hospitals and Settlement" (University of Hawai'i); "Corridors: Memories of a Catholic Convent" by Madrienne C. McDonough (*Historical New Hampshire*, Fall 1978); and *Mercy With Love* by Francis X. Markley.

Melissa Shimonishi at the Hawai'i State Archives assisted me with maps of the Kalihi Valley in the 1900s and Territorial Board of Health correspondence pertaining to Kapi'olani Home.

Viola Yee of the Maui Historical Society gave me access to maps and photographs of Lahaina and Kā'anapali in the 1950s and 1960s.

Particularly valuable for the Hawai'i-set chapters were "Rick Carroll Travels to the Remote Maui Village of Kahakuloa" by Rick Carroll (mauitime.com, July 4, 2013), *The Japanese in Hawai'i* by Okage Sama De, *The Heart of Being Hawaiian* by Sally-Jo Keala-o-Ānuenue Bowman, and *On Being Hawaiian* by John Dominis Holt.

Details about the lives of real people used in this story were confirmed through Ancestry.com, surely the greatest boon to historical novelists ever.

For other research assistance I am grateful to Jack Pearce, Carol Comparsi, Nora Steinbergs, and my wife, Paulette Claus, as always my "in-house editor." Special thanks to my indefatigable agent, Molly Friedrich, who suggested that I tell Ruth's story and who held fast to her faith in that story; and to my wonderful editors, Hope Dellon and Elisabeth Dyssegaard, for the insight, diligence, and editorial acumen that has made this a better book.

I encourage readers interested in Manzanar or Moloka'i to take the time to visit. The Manzanar National Historic Site, nestled at the foot of the Sierra Nevada, is a place of beauty and heartbreak as well as a living museum in which much more can be learned about the internment and the people who lived through it; see the website at https://www.nps.gov/manz/index.htm. The island of Moloka'i is a lovely, often-overlooked corner of Hawai'i, especially for travelers who appreciate a more natural and less touristy environment. Kalaupapa is also a place of both beauty and heartbreak, accessible only via guided tours, but I highly recommend the experience. Visit Damien Tours online at http://www.damientoursllc.com/tour-info.html.

Author's photo by David Wells taken, with kind permission, at the Earl Burns Miller Japanese Garden at California State University, Long Beach.

David Wells

ALAN BRENNERT is the author of *Honolulu*, *Palisades Park*, and *Moloka'i*, which was a 2006–2007 Book Sense Reading Group Pick; won the 2006 Bookies Award, sponsored by the Contra Costa County Library, for the Book Club Book of the Year; and was a 2012 One Book, One San Diego selection. He won an Emmy Award for his work as a writer-producer on the television series *L.A. Law*.

Reading
Group
Gold

DAUGHTER OF
MOLOKA'I
by Alan Brennert

About the Author

- A Conversation with Alan Brennert

Behind the Novel

- Daily Life at Manzanar
- Play Ball! A Conversation with Rosie M. Kakuuchi

Learn More

- Recommended Viewing
- Reading Group Questions

Also available as an audiobook

For more reading group suggestions,
visit www.readinggroupgold.com.

ST. MARTIN'S GRIFFIN

*A
Reading
Group Gold
Selection*

A Conversation with Alan Brennert

What inspired you to write a sequel to Moloka'i?

Not long after *Moloka'i* was published, I was speaking to a book club when one of its members asked me, "Have you ever considered telling Ruth's story?" I had not, and though I found the idea intriguing, so soon after *Moloka'i* I was ready to move on to other subjects. Two books and a decade later, I was talking to my brilliant agent, Molly Friedrich, about an idea I had for another novel when she said, "You know what you should write? You should tell Ruth's story," and argued that there was potentially a powerful story there to be told. Well, I don't need to be hit on the head with an idea a third time! After some initial thought I began to see a perfect three-act structure to Ruth's life: her childhood in Honolulu and California; her internment during World War II; and the final third of the novel, Ruth's meeting with Rachel and her 22-year relationship with her birth mother, which had only been alluded to in *Moloka'i*. Two and a half years later, with substantial help in shaping the story from Molly and my editors, Hope Dellon and Elisabeth Dyssegaard, the structure I first envisioned remains.

Was it difficult revisiting characters you'd written over a decade ago?

Quite the opposite; I think they'd been inside my head all along, waiting for the opportunity to tell the rest of their story. When I wrote the first line for Sister Catherine in the prologue, I slipped back into her voice as if no time at all had passed. I did reread *Moloka'i*—for the first time since I'd corrected proofs back in 2002—to reacquaint

myself with key parts of Rachel's life and to listen again to her voice and to that of the adult Ruth. The first dialogue I wrote for Rachel was an extension of a scene in *Moloka'i*, and she just popped out onto the page, casually continuing a conversation begun years earlier.

For Ruth I had to engage in a bit of reverse-engineering, figuring out from her adult self what kind of child she had been, the childhood and life experiences that had shaped her into the person we met in the first book. It was actually quite a satisfying process, filling in those blank spaces of Ruth's past with people, places, and animals. I began to see this not as a sequel per se, but as a companion or parallel tale that serves as a complement to *Moloka'i*: together they form one large, overarching, interconnected story.

How was writing Daughter of Moloka'i *different from writing the first book?*

In *Moloka'i*—as in *Honolulu* and *Palisades Park*—I was writing not merely the life story of a person, but the history of a place as well. *Moloka'i* had a large cast of characters dating back to the 1870s in Kalaupapa, long before my protagonist, Rachel, was even born. But since Ruth lives in a variety of locales, *Daughter* is more narrowly focused on her life and the point of view of her and her family. As with *Moloka'i*, there was an intimidating amount of research to be done—into daily life at the Kapi'olani Home for Girls; Florin, California, in the 1920s; and the Manzanar and Tanforan relocation centers. At times I felt constrained, not being able to add some interesting historical sidebars because they fell outside the boundaries of Ruth's experience. But what makes Ruth's story so different from Rachel's is the way her life repeatedly turns on a dime: the day Taizo and Etsuko adopt her; their sudden move to California; the jolting loss of her home and freedom; and Rachel's unexpected appearance in her life. It's that ability to cope with the hairpin turns in life, her resiliency, that made her such an interesting character to write, and, I hope, to read about.

What surprised you most about your research into the lives of Japanese immigrants in the early twentieth century?

What struck me most was how similar—depressingly similar—the arguments against Asian immigrants to the U.S. were to those being made against immigrants today. Organizations like the Anti-Japanese League and the Native Sons and Daughters of the Golden West claimed that Japanese farmers were taking land away from white farmers; in reality the Japanese were leasing or buying poor-quality land that white farmers wouldn't touch and using their intensive farming techniques to make the land productive. Today you hear similar complaints that Latino and other immigrants are taking jobs away from American workers. But many of these jobs don't pay enough for American workers and/or are the kind of backbreaking labor, like picking crops, that most Americans don't want to do.

Back in the 1900s, anti-Asian organizations also claimed that Asian culture and religious beliefs were too "alien" and that Asian immigrants were incapable of being assimilated into American culture. But the second generation of Japanese

immigrants, the Nisei, fully embraced American culture and thought of themselves as Americans.

This only made their internment after Pearl Harbor all the more shocking to them: they were hardworking, law-abiding citizens, yet the government viewed them all as potential spies, security risks. The truth is that during World War II not a single Japanese American in the United States was ever convicted of espionage or sabotage.

Do you see parallels between Japanese Americans in World War II and Muslim Americans today?

Yes, though not exact parallels. No one can deny that there have been a handful of Muslim Americans who have committed terrorist acts against the United States. But the majority of law-abiding Muslim Americans are tarred by the actions of a few and so face prejudice due to their ethnicity and religion. We also hear the old canard that they're not capable of assimilating into American society. I think it's useful to remember that virtually all new immigrant groups—Irish, Italians, Jews, Poles, Germans—faced similar skepticism and prejudice when they first came to this country. And over time those prejudices faded (mostly) and the groups came to be accepted as part of the patchwork quilt we call American culture. There's a bit of hope to be had when you look at it that way.

In all my books I've sought to portray other ethnic groups—Native Hawaiians (as well as Hansen's disease patients) in *Moloka'i*, Koreans in *Honolulu*, African Americans in *Palisades Park*, and the Japanese in this book—in terms that anyone from another culture can relate to and identify with, while treating their cultures with the same respect Americans would want shown to theirs. If a reader comes away from my books with a deeper understanding of our common humanity, then I've accomplished what I set out to do.

ALAN BRENNERT is a novelist, screenwriter, and playwright. He was born in 1954 in Englewood, New Jersey, to Herbert E. Brennert, an aviation writer, and Almyra E. Brennert, an apartment rentals manager. He has lived since 1973 in Southern California, where he received a B.A. in English from California State University at Long Beach and did graduate work at the UCLA film school.

His novel *Moloka'i* was a national bestseller and a One Book, One San Diego selection for 2012. It also received the Bookies Award, sponsored by the Contra Costa County Library, for the 2006 Book Club Book of the Year. His next novel, *Honolulu*, won first prize in *Elle* magazine's Literary Grand Prix for Fiction and was named one of the best books of 2009 by *The Washington Post*. Of his novel *Palisades Park*, *People* magazine said, "Brennert writes his valentine to the New Jersey playground of his youth in *Ragtime* style, mixing fact and fiction. It's a memorable ride."

His work as a writer-producer for the television series *L.A. Law* earned him an Emmy Award and a People's Choice Award in 1991. He has been nominated for an Emmy on two other occasions, once for a Golden Globe Award, and three times for the Writers Guild Award for Outstanding Teleplay of the Year. His short story "Ma Qui" was honored with a Nebula Award in 1992, and that same year he co-wrote the libretto for the Alan Menken/David Spencer musical *Weird Romance*, produced by the WPA Theatre in New York and since performed in dozens of regional, high school, and college productions throughout the country. Columbia Records released a soundtrack album in 1993, which is currently available on iTunes.

*About the
Author*

Manzanar Relocation Center, as seen from a guard tower. Photograph by Ansel Adams.

Manzanar internee Tōyō Miyatake and family in their barracks room. Photograph by Ansel Adams.

Agricultural workers in fields outside the camp.
Photograph by Ansel Adams.

Winter at Manzanar. Photograph by Ansel Adams.

Post office. Photograph by Clem Albers.

The Dusty Chicks softball team choosing sides for a practice game. Rosie M. Kakuuchi is fourth from left, wearing a white kerchief. Photograph by Francis Stewart.

Reading
Group
Gold

Kind permission was granted to reprint these photographs by the Library of Congress (Ansel Adams) as well as the Manzanar National Historic Site and the National Archives and Records Administration (Clem Albers, Francis Stewart).

Behind the Novel

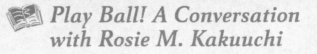

Play Ball! A Conversation with Rosie M. Kakuuchi

Rosie played with the Dusty Chicks, mentioned in chapter 12, one of Manzanar's many women's softball teams.

Were you on any of the baseball teams?

I don't know if you heard of the Dusty Chicks? That was the first softball team that was formed, to my knowledge . . . Yoshio Kusonoki, when she was in elementary school, she was small. Today, she is not too small, but anyway she got the nickname PeeWee, and everyone knows her as PeeWee . . . Chiyo Tashima was known for her bowling. She was a 300 game bowler . . . She was a man's woman, because she played cards with them, but anyway, she was a pitcher and the only open position was catcher. So they said, "You want to be a catcher?" "Sure! All I have to do is catch it, right?" So here I am, and here comes Chiyo pitching. Whoom! it comes. I nearly fell on my butt because she pitches so hard. And I said, "Gee, I don't know if I want to do this."

Our team had Jack Kunitomi's wife, Masa, she was second baseman, a Nisei Week princess, and Mae Noma, who was also a Nisei Week princess, she played third base. So these were kind of glamour people—older age, but they were glamorous. And here PeeWee and I were the two young ones on the team. But we just had a real great time with them.

Did you stay as catcher?

I remained as a catcher.

What else do you remember of who was on the baseball team?

Well, Chiyo's older sister, Misa, was on first base. PeeWee was center field. Alice Yamamoto played left field, and Fuji Kuwahara played right field.

Oh, and then the [camp's] administrative staff, the men, wanted to challenge our team. So we played against them and naturally they hit hard, so the ball went way out in center field. PeeWee caught it and the guy said, "Relocate that gal!" (*laughter*) 'Cause at that time people were starting to relocate and they were trying to get people out of the camp.

So you were playing the staff hakujins?

Hakujins. We played against them.

And they were all guys?

They were all guys.

And who won?

I think we won. Maybe by one point, or barely. But anyway, all I remember is that guy saying, "Relocate that gal!" (*laughter*) And I can never forget that. We were so proud of PeeWee because it was way out in center field.

What did baseball mean to you?

Baseball, to me and to the camp people, is an American pastime. The final game that they had in Manzanar had the whole camp out there to watch. I think a newspaper from Philadelphia came to publicize our team. And it's in one of the books that's put out on Manzanar.

Rosie M. Kakuuchi, interviewed by Alisa Lynch, 2006, Manzanar Oral History Project Interview #MANZ 1083 (transcript). Reprinted by kind permission of Manzanar National Historic Site, National Park Service. Special thanks to Rosemary Masters.

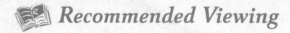 *Recommended Viewing*

There is a wealth of nonfiction books available
about the Japanese internment, many of which
are cited in the Author's Note. But here are some
works in other media that can be viewed with your
entire family and that present vivid and moving
stories of Japanese Americans' experiences in
World War II relocation centers.

Farewell to Manzanar was one of the first films
about the Japanese internment. A powerful
television movie based on the memoir by Jeanne
Wakatsuki Houston and James D. Houston, it
has rarely been seen since its first airing in 1976.
Happily it has recently been released on DVD
by the Japanese American National Museum. To
order a copy, go to https://janmstore.com/products/
farewell-to-manzanar-dvd.

*Learn
More*

Allegiance is a stirring stage musical inspired by
the true life experiences of its star, George Takei.
It fictionalizes and conflates the draft resistance
at Heart Mountain camp with the violence that
took place at Tule Lake to create a poignant
musical drama about conflict, estrangement, and
reconciliation. For information on both stage and
film productions, go to
https://allegiancemusical.com.

Rabbit in the Moon, an award-winning
documentary by Emiko Omori, explores not only
her family's years at Poston War Relocation Center
in Arizona, but takes a wider look at the tensions,
divisions, and resistance in the internment camps

in general. One of the people interviewed is Harry Ueno, whose arrest sparked the Manzanar riot. It too is available through the Japanese American National Museum at https://janmstore.com/products/rabbit-in-the-moon-a-documentary-memoir-about-the-world-war-ii-japanese-american-internment.

The Untold Story: Internment of Japanese Americans in Hawai'i is a documentary by Ryan Kayamoto focusing on the little-known internment camps in Hawai'i, where the majority of Japanese Americans were not interned. The story of those who were—leaders in the Japanese community, Buddhist priests, schoolteachers, often subjected to degrading treatment—has long needed telling. The DVD can be ordered from the Japanese Cultural Center of Hawai'i at https://www.jcch.com/gift-shop. (The Hawaiian internment camps were also the subject of a memorable episode of the rebooted *Hawaii Five-O* titled "Ho'onani Makuakane," which aired in 2013 and is available on Netflix.)

1. If you've read *Moloka'i*, you already knew that the U.S. government used to take away the newborn children of Hansen's disease patients out of fear their parents would infect them. If you weren't aware of this, does it shock you to learn of it—and the fact that this practice continued even into the 1950s? What must Ruth's parents have gone through to give up their child?

2. What do animals represent to Ruth?

3. If you were Taizo, would you have accepted Jiro's offer and moved to California? If you were Etsuko, what would your response have been?

4. What is your opinion of Jiro, and did it change in any way over the course of the story?

5. Would it shock you to learn that Joseph Dreesen was based on a real-life person—his name was John Reese—who made public statements about the Japanese similar to those Dreesen makes in this novel? Were you aware of the widespread prejudice that Japanese immigrants faced in the early twentieth century?

6. Were you aware of the way many Japanese Americans lost their homes and jobs when they were "relocated" and interned? Do you believe Executive Order No. 9066 was justified or unjustified?

7. Can you imagine yourself living under the conditions Ruth's family finds themselves living in at Tanforan and Manzanar?

8. Who, in your judgment, was at fault in the Manzanar riot—the protesters, the military police, or both?

Learn More

9. If you were a Japanese American being interned during World War II, what would your response have been to the government's "loyalty oath"—Questions 27 and 28—referred to on page 157 of the novel?

10. Did you find Taizo's sense of honor baffling or frustrating? Did you come to understand it better by the end of the story?

11. What would you have done in Ruth's place, suddenly confronted with the news that her birth mother was alive—and that she had Hansen's disease? Would you have agreed to see her, as Ruth does, or not?

12. Compare and contrast the kinds of exile that Rachel and Ruth each experienced. Which would you have found more oppressive?

13. Do you believe Sister Catherine ultimately found peace and was forgiven by her God?

14. How is the Hawaiian phrase "The land is the chief, man is its servant" relevant to us today?

15. How would you have dealt with the secret that Jiro and Nishi tell Ruth? Would you have been as angry as she was, and how difficult would it have been for you to keep the secret?

16. Do you believe Ruth and Peggy actually heard the *huaka'i pō* at Kahakuloa?

17. Would you have done what Rachel does in order to see her great-grandchild?

18. Discuss Ruth's changing views on what it means to be *hapa*. Do you think the peace she finds in it has been well earned?